IN DISTANCE

CHARLENE CHALLENGER

The Myth
IN DISTANCE

TIGHTROPE BOOKS

Tightrope Books
#207-2 College Street,
Toronto Ontario, Canada M5G 1K3
tightropebooks.com
bookinfo@tightropebooks.com

EDITOR: Jessie Hale
COPYEDITOR: Heather Wood
COVER ART: Russell Challenger
LAYOUT DESIGN: David Jang

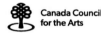 

Produced with the assistance of the Canada Council for the Arts and the Ontario Arts Council.

Library and Archives Canada Cataloguing in Publication

Challenger, Charlene, 1978-, author
    The myth in distance / Charlene Challenger.

Sequel to: The voices in between.
ISBN 978-1-988040-13-4 (paperback)

    I. Title.

PS8605.H3367M98 2016   jC813'.6   C2016-905092-0

For my little one

Chapter 1

"My name's Adoni."

"Hi Adoni! We love you! Let's all count the ways!"

"One!" Clap. "Two!" Clap. "Three and four and five!" Clap. "Six!" Clap. "Seven!" Clap. "Eight... nine... ten!" Round of applause.

Adoni shrivelled behind the podium. No matter how many times she'd heard it, she still couldn't get used to the support group's cheerful greeting. "Yeah, hi." She slipped a fingernail under a sliver of dried skin on her thumb and absently flicked at it.

The pale light of that January afternoon spilled in through the windows and fell across the conference room, over the refreshment table, the coffee urns and store-bought cookies, the stackable plastic chairs and parquet flooring. Adoni's face flushed. A few notes scrawled on a piece of paper would have been a good idea, or cue cards, but she couldn't bring herself to prepare anything as formal as that. Instead, she waited until the last minute to collect her thoughts and then told the group what she thought they wanted to hear.

"Okay, so, my mom's an alcoholic. She's been sort of sober for almost four years now. I say 'sort of' because sometimes I still catch her with drinks. Like, sometimes I come home from school, and I find a couple of cans of beer on the counter. She tells me they're not hers but, like, I know they're hers. Who else's would they be? I don't even mind that she lies about it. She hasn't been super drunk in a long time, so that's good."

Hunched over the microphone, she looked out at the audience, her shoulders creeping up to her ears. *You lie too,* she thought. *You lied just now. You do mind.*

"She's always been an alcoholic. Right from when I was a kid. Well, a younger kid. She told me once that's why my dad left. I've never met my dad, but I bet it's true. And her mom was an alcoholic too. So I grew up with it. Sometimes, I think I might be one too. And now that I'm at U of T, I get weirded out when my classmates ask me to go drinking with them after class. They can pass for nineteen, but I don't know; I don't think I can. And I don't have the money to, anyway. My student loan just barely covers tuition." She chuckled. "I'm rambling. Okay. When I was fourteen, mom was out of a job. Didn't help that she gets really depressed around November, when all the Christmas stuff starts going up. I think it reminds her of when she was a kid, and of her mom, and how her mom committed suicide." She pinched the dried skin between the nails of her thumb and forefinger, and with one swift tug, ripped it off. "So she started drinking again, and she started hitting me again. And I was, like, I'm not sticking around for this. So I took off."

A spot of blood pooled in the new, raw cleft of skin left behind. She looked up and found them all staring at her.

"Then I came back, eventually."

She caught her reflection in the large mirror on the opposite wall. Her eyes were puffy from her rubbing them. Her bottom lip was slack. She looked as though she couldn't remember what she was going to say. In truth, she remembered every last detail. She remembered how many days she was gone. She remembered the agate rippling with blue and orange fire; the forest, and the snowy clearing cradled in its trunks and branches; the cabins, white-capped from months of winter weather, lined up in rows; the chalet, with the tawny glow of firelight in its windows; the water well; the river; the cold.

The In-Between world, in all its sparkling finery.

Not the sort of thing to be brought up in everyday conversation, let alone in front of a support group for teenagers with alcoholic parents.

CHARLENE CHALLENGER

"When I came back, mom promised me she wouldn't drink anymore. She didn't flat out say it, but… Maybe I should have made her flat out say it. I don't know. I see stuff like that all the time in movies. Where the kid has a heart to heart with her parents, and they all of a sudden understand her and agree to get along and shit." She raised her hand. "Sorry! I'm not supposed to swear, right? Sorry." Someone in the audience coughed. She looked down at the podium, and for a moment, lost her chain of thought as her eyes followed a long crack in the wood. "Sometimes I think that's what it's supposed to be like, to really mean anything. Like it's a blueprint for what's normal. Then I'm like, what do the movies know about normal? A movie's, like, the most abnormal thing there is. A promise is whatever it means to you. You know? And my mom…"

The same audience member coughed a second time. Adoni wrapped her fingers around the edges of the podium and squeezed. *They don't want to hear this. Hurry up.*

"My mom meant it. So I believe her. Even when she messes up." She nodded and then said, "Thanks."

The audience clapped politely as she reclaimed her seat in the front row. The group facilitator took the stage and introduced the next speaker. Adoni sank in her chair and slowly let out the breath she'd been holding.

The meeting ended a short time later. By that time, Adoni had had enough of stale cookies and rancid coffee. She slipped her jacket on and tried to sneak out of the room unnoticed when she felt a gentle tug on her sleeve. One of the group members, a teenager about her age, stood next to her. The girl broke into a pleasant smile. Brown and black cookie crumbs furred her crooked teeth. "Thanks for sharing that," she said.

"Yeah." Adoni tugged her zipper up to her throat and stuffed her hands into her pockets.

"You held back a bit," the girl continued, nodding as she spoke. "I can tell you're still a little shy. I was shy too, my first couple of times. But once you get over that and really open up, it's a whole new experience."

"I know, I'm just… I'm not at that point yet."

"Keep coming back," the girl said. "It works. Just take it one day at a time." She pressed her lips together and stuck out her chin. "Okay?"

"Yeah, okay. Thanks." Adoni kept her eyes down as she manoeuvred between several group members who were still lingering around the exit. She managed to leave the room without further interruption.

It was mild out, just a week after the first big storm of the year. The snow had been shovelled into heaps on either side of the walkway. Adoni left the community centre and headed toward Nathan Phillips Square, Toronto's city hall. She unzipped her jacket and welcomed a breeze on her clammy skin. The weather had been fluctuating wildly since the end of December—a few warm days here, a few frigid days there—and it was nearly impossible to dress appropriately. Adoni had once again selected a jacket that was too heavy. By the time she reached the sidewalk, she was sweating.

She went south, past the Art Gallery of Ontario, and then south again to Queen Street. Even on a Sunday afternoon, the streets were full of people. Students packed every café she passed, filled every window seat with their backpacks and laptops. Shoppers wove in and out of clothing and shoe boutiques with paper bags full of expensive designer swag. Crowds of rowdy folks headed toward the movie theatre and bars on Richmond Street, laughing and hollering as they jaywalked through the intersection. Simple melodies, drum-machined and synthesized, made up most of the soundtrack of that afternoon. And then: a single guitar string ringing through the noise like an alarm call, soaring above Adoni's head. She stopped and looked up at where the sound was coming from— an open apartment window above a shoe store. How was it that such a simple, elegant note could be played with such fury, such intensity? How could it cut through the Sunday afternoon drone and refract every other sound until they were all so meaningless? Just as that single note was about to give up the ghost a drum kicked in, rescuing it from a lifetime of solitude with a passionate march, a military march only understood by those who have walked in love. Together, they paved the way for a

CHARLENE CHALLENGER

woman's voice to take command of the song. She sang with a voice that was trying hard to be kind, when it was usually cruel, that was trying to be honest after a thousand years of lies. She let the ends of her notes crumple like dead leaves and summoned the wind to whisk them away. A second guitar tore through the air like a chainsaw, inciting the drums to riot, ignoring the lead singer as she pleaded for understanding. When she sang the song's final line, the guitar and drums rushed in like champions to carry her, triumphant, on their shoulders. That last note lingered, and Adoni continued on her way.

As the light faded from a pastel grey to the emerald wash of a winter's evening, she spotted Theresa's truck, parked on the street in front of the fountain.

"Hey!" Adoni called. She reached up and slapped her hand on the truck's serving ledge. "I'm a Buddhist! Make me one with everything!"

Theresa stuck her head out of the service window, saw the source of the racket, and grinned. "Shut up!" she said before retreating into the kitchen. The back door opened and Adoni climbed inside.

Known fondly to them both as the *Reesemobile*, Theresa's food truck was a travelling spice house, a haven where all sorts of delicious smells mingled together: cumin and cloves, pepper and savoury, mint, rosemary, nutmeg. The narrow kitchen was always warm enough to curl up and fall asleep in, especially in the summertime, when the grill fired away from mid-morning to late at night. The Reesemobile had become one of the most popular places for an afternoon nosh at the Square, which meant Theresa spent more time preparing meat and vegetables and less time with Adoni. She welcomed Adoni with a bear hug. Her tiny transistor radio, propped up on a shelf, played Janis Joplin's "Piece of My Heart."

"What've you done to your hair?" Adoni asked.

Theresa twirled on the spot so Adoni could admire her new hairstyle. "Do you like it? I got it cut yesterday. Want some chili?"

"You don't even have to ask, you know I do."

"Do what? The hair or the chili?"

"Both. Your hair looks nice. Why'd you cut it?"

"So I can fit it all into a net while I'm working. Comfort food isn't as comforting when there's a long black hair in it, you know?" She ladled a heaped serving of chili into a paper bowl and handed it over. Adoni put her face in the steam and inhaled. Coriander, cayenne, and a hint of something sweet—brown sugar or maple syrup—running through a sticky-ribbed broth.

"You're not wearing a net now."

"I'm on my break."

"I'm gonna miss braiding it. But it looks really good on you." Adoni shovelled a spoonful of chili into her mouth and closed her eyes. "So good," she mumbled around carrots and beans. "Thanks."

"How's school?" Theresa asked.

"Different from high school. The profs don't have to pretend they care if you pass or not."

"Nice." Theresa smiled as Adoni's spoon barrelled through the chili. "Where are you coming from?"

"I had group tonight."

"Did you say anything this time?"

"A little bit."

Theresa sat down on an overturned milk crate and propped her chin up with her fist. "How much is a little bit?"

"I never know what to say. Every time I decide to say something, right before I go someone else gets up and tells their story and… I don't know; it makes my story sound stupid. Like this one time this guy got up and told everyone about him and his dad, and everybody started crying, and then I was supposed to go and I was like, I don't wanna go, everyone's crying, I'm gonna look like an asshole."

"It's not a pissing contest."

"I know, but when I go up it's like… I just feel like I can't tell the truth. Sometimes I want to clean it up because I don't want to get into it, and then sometimes I think, everybody else had it so much worse, and it's almost like maybe I should make it sound worse, so they don't think I'm wasting their time. So they think I'm supposed to be there."

"Do you feel like you're supposed to be there?"

Adoni shrugged. "I haven't gotten anything out of it yet."

"It's good to know you're not alone though, isn't it?"

"I don't feel alone. I've got you. You get it." She smiled. "Is that garlic bread?"

Theresa followed Adoni's gaze to the loaf of bread on the counter. "Yeah, want a hunk?"

"Please. It looks tasty."

Theresa stood and ripped off a piece. "I'm not the only person who gets it," she said as she handed Adoni the bread. "I'm sure a lot of those kids would understand."

"Not the important parts. It's not like I can tell them about what happened in the In-Between, right?"

Theresa crouched to pick a bit of squashed potato off the floor. She flung it into the compost bin in the corner of the kitchen. "No, I guess not."

Three young men appeared at the service window. Theresa's dark expression brightened as she went to serve them.

Adoni watched her move about the tiny kitchen with the elegance of a fan dancer, crouching low for extra napkins under the counter, reaching high for paper bowls from the shelves above the stove. Adoni's thoughts drifted back to her first night in the In-Between, the night she met Theresa in The Welcome's homely kitchen. She moved with the same grace then as she did now—a mistress, finally, of her own domain.

Theresa had lived at the northern colony of the In-Between for twenty years; the kitchen, with its enchanted pots and pans, its cupboards overflowing with whatever she could conjure, a sanctuary from the failed hopes and dreams of The Welcome's residents. But it was never her home in the real sense of the word. Everything had been given to her by someone else: the food she ate, the clothes she wore, even the bed she slept in at night. Upon returning to the city she'd left behind all those years ago, Theresa said she wanted to start her own business, and after spending time working as a short-order cook in a greasy diner on Bathurst Street and saving every extra penny she could, she finally had the know-how and the means to make her dream a reality.

Theresa handed her customers their orders and took their cash. "If you're not getting anything out of it, maybe it's just as well you stop," she said when they had gone.

"I'm gonna go a couple more times to see if anything changes," Adoni said. "Then maybe I'll reconsider."

"How's your mom, anyway? Better?"

Adoni nodded as she chewed. "I mean she's been pretty okay ever since I got back, but it's not like she stopped drinking completely. She's been drunk a couple of times. Only now when she's drunk, instead of smacking me out, she just sits in her room and cries. So, like, is that any better? I don't even know."

"Maybe your mom should go to a group."

"She does go, that's why I go too. I went with her once. She totally bullshits in front of everyone. She just made it all sound so..."

"Dramatic?" Theresa returned to the milk crate and took a seat.

Adoni flipped a constellation of crumbs off her lap. "Maybe I'm being unfair because I live with her, eh?"

"Who knows? I'm not one to talk."

"You know what? I don't think I've ever seen you eat anything. You always just sit there and watch me." She pointed at the pot on the stove. "Get in there, man. It's tasty."

Theresa smiled and fixed herself a helping of macaroni and cheese from a casserole she had baked earlier that day. The radio played another grinding rock anthem as both women worked their way to the bottoms of their bowls. Theresa switched on the overhead light when it was finally too dark to see. The fluorescent glow cast heavy shadows under her eyes. She smiled and held her hand out for Adoni's empty dish.

Adoni handed it to her and asked, "Do you miss it?"

Theresa threw both containers into the compost bin. She stood over it and stared at the pile of vegetable peelings and paper towels. "The other day I burned a pan of onions and started to cry. I'm not sure if that means I miss it or I'm happy I'm gone."

"Maybe both."

"Maybe. Do you?"

"*Miss* isn't the right word. It's more like *obsessed*."

Theresa frowned as she fished her hair net out of her apron pocket. "Looks like a slow period right now, so I'd better get some food prep over with. You going home now?"

Adoni shook her head. "There's a band I like playing at Lee's tonight. I'm gonna go see them. Lee's hardly ever has all-ages shows, so I don't want to miss it."

"What band?"

"Slamdango."

Theresa chuckled. "What a dumb name."

"I know, but they're really good. They're like what Captain Picard would listen to on the Enterprise if he was into funk."

"That paints a picture. You're going alone?"

"Yeah. I actually like going to gigs alone. That way I can really listen to the music. Plus if I see someone I want to talk to, she won't confuse one of my friends for my bae."

"Makes sense." Theresa put her hands on her hips. "How are you guys doing for food? Do you want to take some of this home with you tonight?"

"Mom went shopping on Friday, so we're good." She got to her feet. "What time are you closing shop?"

"Tonight's going to be slow so not too late. What time does your show let out?"

"Depends on if they're on time. I probably won't see you tonight." She opened her arms.

Theresa took the cue and gave Adoni a goodbye hug. "Enjoy your show."

"I will. I'll come by next group night, okay? Next Sunday."

"I'll be here." She blew Adoni a kiss.

Adoni bundled up and started the trek to Lee's Palace.

Theresa often asked Adoni if she and her mother, Ida, could do with some leftovers. Theresa had met Ida several times, outside of the apartment she shared with Adoni. Ida was pleasant enough on those occasions—she smiled politely, even engaged in small talk about the weather or Theresa's business—but Adoni could tell her mother's misgivings about strangers still held fast. It didn't help that Theresa was significantly older than Adoni and affectionate with her.

Adoni hadn't told Ida anything about the In-Between, or that Theresa was one of the people she met while she was gone. Ida avoided the topic of Adoni's disappearance, as though mentioning it would inspire her daughter to take off again. Of Theresa herself, when Adoni asked Ida what she thought of her friend, Ida said, "She's nice. But, you know, you've already got a mother."

Adoni turned up Bay Street and headed toward Bloor. The taste of Theresa's chili and garlic bread lingered on her tongue. If she hadn't been on her way to the venue, Theresa could have easily talked her into taking another portion. She appreciated when Theresa offered to pack her some takeaway, though she couldn't help but feel a little embarrassed. It was too close to a handout, not that Theresa meant it as such, and it reminded her that she still didn't have the part-time job she had promised herself she would get to help Ida with the bills. She had spent two summers working at the Exhibition, handing over the majority of her earnings, but trying to secure a job the rest of the year proved to be more challenging. Ida told her not to worry about it—"I want you to concentrate on school anyway," she'd said—but Adoni still felt she wasn't pulling her weight. And it made the twelve dollars she'd shelled out to see Slamdango play the Palace seem a fortune, the event itself an absolute luxury.

CHARLENE CHALLENGER

She wanted to get there on time and not miss a single minute of music, not even the opening act, which was usually a limp version of the headliner. She kept her head down and her hands in her pockets as she hoofed it all the way to the Annex.

Chapter
2

Adoni arrived at the Palace early enough that the doors hadn't opened yet. The line to get in was short—just a few hardcore indie concertgoers smoking and shivering in their shoes. Adoni took a spot at the end of the queue.

Bloor Street came alive at night, when the sun had set and the sidewalks were crammed with revellers. Swatches of white and yellow light spilled out from shawarma shops and sushi bars, from boutiques selling comic books and graphic novels, records and DVDs. There was the flickering of the incandescent bulbs from dollar store signs. A busker played his guitar, badly, on the corner outside a popular pizza joint. The air smelled of charcoal bricks and cigarettes.

After more than thirty years, the Palace was still a sight to be seen, a brick behemoth painted up to look like Mardi Gras had exploded all over it—a mural covered its façade, colours dancing together in the forms of alien creatures, monsters with mouths full of jagged teeth, multi-levelled, octagonal spaceships, staircases to nowhere, gushing fountains. The Palace was well past its prime by the time Adoni saw her first gig there—she'd been to see Tectonics, an electro-pop duo, that spring—but it retained the mythic rock n' roll qualities Ida had told her about on its grungy walls, on its sticky floors.

Adoni was still last in line when the doors opened. Most of the people who bought tickets were fine with missing the opening act, so there was plenty of room for Adoni to scope out a place to stand and watch the night unfold. She chose a spot in the middle of the floor where she could catch the best acoustics of both overhead speakers and hopefully see the entire band.

Members of the opening act took to the stage to set up their equipment: synths and pedals, a single snare drum embossed with a plastic mother-of-pearl motif, a set of bell chimes, three microphones, and miles of electrical cables. The three long-haired musicians had to hop and skip over the cords to get from one side of the stage to the other. They checked their mics with grunts and plosions, their t-shirts and jeans too tight for them to bend at the waist. When it came time to play their set, they felt no need to introduce themselves, or to thank the audience for coming out. They stayed glued to the spot in their respective corners, their eyes on their instruments, and let loose an angry snarl of heavy electronica.

Adoni wouldn't have chosen this particular act to open for a band as bouncy and fun as Slamdango. *Who knows who puts these things together*, she thought. She stuffed her earplugs in, tilted her head, and crossed her arms. The other audience members did the same.

The band—Infinity Splitter, Adoni read on her ticket stub—was tighter than she thought they'd be when they started playing. Before long they settled into a groove, synths thrumming, swelling and receding, snips of melody stealing in and pulsing like fireworks. Their closing number was a ten-minute din of drum loops walled in by the masonry of their synthesizers. The song ended by dropping into silence. One of the musicians muttered, "Thanks a lot" into her mic. The tiny audience clapped, Adoni included, without much interest or zeal. The house music came on as the band members set about disassembling their gear.

Adoni asked the bartender for a glass of water and downed it while surveying the thickening crowd. Most of the audience was made up of people around her age; the rest were adults, with a few conspicuous older folks standing in the back and off to the sides. She put her empty cup on the end of the counter and nudged her way back to her spot in the middle of the floor. Slamdango's roadies swarmed the stage. They plugged in cables, checked the mics, tuned guitars, asked for lights to be brought up, or toned down. Tattooed arms and hands, black jeans, and old-school high-tops; Adoni smirked as they checked their sound levels. She'd seen pictures on the Internet of classic rock acts setting up—Joplin, Hendrix, Zeppelin, Sabbath; the roadie aesthetic hadn't changed in more than forty years of rock and roll. These were the kinds of technicians Ida saw set up her favourite acts in the 1990s.

That Ritter saw, no doubt, in the '70s. In the '60s.

After years of searching, Adoni had given up any hope of being reunited with the piper whose enchanted voice first led her to the In-Between. Ritter wasn't the type to stay put for long if he could help it. He'd probably gotten bored of Toronto and left a long time ago. She'd held out hope that his last words to her would eventually ring true, and they'd see each other again. But the weeks turned to months, and the months to years. Once he'd secured his freedom from Ansgar, Ritter had no reason to stick around. Adoni couldn't blame him for abandoning their friendship to rediscover himself somewhere else.

There were nights when she dreamed of breaking through the agate by sheer will and storming Ansgar's fortress in the north. Adoni didn't know what the creature looked like, but in her dreams Ansgar took on the form of the little girl who used to bully her in first grade—a stuck-up, moon-faced child who made fun of Adoni for being poor—and Adoni gleefully throttled her until she turned to dust in her fists. In other dreams the agate opened right before her, but her legs felt as though they were stuck in molasses and she couldn't move into the light. Every time she dreamed of the In-Between, she woke up shaking and feeling more helpless than ever, and her entire body stayed tense for the rest of the day. Certain smells reminded her of the In-Between—fresh linen, lemon oil, mothballs. She'd be walking down the street, or browsing in a store, and the odour would catch her by surprise and take her right back to her first night at The Welcome. She'd squint and stare into thin air, hoping to catch a glimpse of the world beyond her own, knowing it was impossible from her side of the divide.

Ritter's absence meant Adoni had no way of returning to avenge the unfortunate souls still trapped in the In-Between. Only a piper's enchanted voice could summon the portal, and since the pipers of The Welcome had abandoned Ansgar's code, they no longer roamed the city at night looking for children to sing away.

She reached back and put her hand over her left shoulder, dug her fingers into the hardened muscle. Whenever the weather changed, the scar on her shoulder throbbed. Some days she could still feel the white-hot seal bearing Ansgar's name pressing into her skin and burning her into silence. If Theresa hadn't sliced the name away—all of it, that is, except for the letter A—its enchantment would have driven Adoni insane, just as it had the changelings, the ill-fated beings pipers left behind when a real child was brought to the In-Between.

The A on Adoni's shoulder gave her voice the dreadful violence she had used to throw the leader of the changelings, Sylvester, to the ground, to knock the very wind out of him, to force him to cower and run. He swore revenge before he slunk away into the night. Adoni knew he would one day make good on his threat, and she desperately wished to return to the In-Between, so that she could make him pay for his trespasses. She hadn't had the chance to discover the full extent of her might before she left. She knew that she could do more with her voice than shout people off their feet. Just as Sylvester had wrapped his hands around her neck and tried to choke the life out of her, she had driven her voice like a knife and obliterated one of his empty blue eyes. She daydreamed about ripping off his limbs and shattering his bones. She wished her voice could seek him out and drag him back to The Welcome. She wondered if her voice could freeze, if it could burn, if it could destroy him. Not just a part of him; if it could destroy him completely. But while Ansgar's initial granted Adoni supremacy in the In-Between, it was useless in the everyday world—just a tattoo, really, next to a length of puckered skin—so there was no way of knowing just how devastating her power could be. Adoni's only hope of finishing the revolution she had helped to start was to find Ritter and have him sing the agate open for her.

The house music faded from the speakers. The crowd welcomed the sextet of hairy miscreants from Brooklyn with whoops and cheers. The band, dressed in white suits and ties, waved back. The lead singer grabbed hold of the microphone and snarled, "What's up Toronto?" which seemed to garner even more of a reaction, with people clapping over their heads and someone throwing them a pair of horns before they played their first note. The singer responded with an amped-up rock scowl and pointed at them. "Thanks a lot for being here. This first song is about PILLS." He raised a sweaty fist and swung it down by his side, and the band started to play.

A guitar chord swung between the speakers, finally settling in the middle of the room as the drums stepped in and the bass started throbbing. They stayed tight, swaying together and pinwheeling apart with an arrogance that brought smiles to even the most reserved audience members. Then came the trumpet, shooting skeet over their heads, and finally the saxophone, oozing corruption in every pull and wail. Red, yellow, green, and blue lights flashed and swirled, splashing the band members' white suits with colour.

Adoni shouted as enthusiastically as she could without drawing too much attention to herself. She stole quick glances to her right and left; couples with their arms around each other, groups of boys, groups of girls. Everyone there seemed to have a date, an ear to shout in, someone to gush to when the music was just right, to laugh with when it was trying too hard. Even if she did scream like a rabid fangirl, there was no chance of it turning anyone off, since there was no one available for her to turn on.

She noticed a girl standing off to the side, refracted stage light falling across her face like gold dust. Adoni wished she could catch her eye from across the crowded room. She'd sidle up to say hello, pay the band a few backhanded compliments, and then ask her out somewhere, maybe for a coffee after class at one of the cafés on campus. They'd talk music and movies, favourite places and pastimes. There would be the awkward conversation about Ida eventually, but whoever the mystery girl was wouldn't see it as a big ugly secret worthy of pity. She'd see it as no big deal at all. She'd be funny and caring, a good listener, and she'd find Adoni smart and bewitching. They'd share a kiss while their tongues still tasted of coffee and promise to see each other again.

She would want to meet Ida. And Adoni would finally have the courage to bring somebody special home with her.

A boy with a bad haircut appeared beside the girl and handed her a beer. She let him put his arm around her waist and kiss her cheek. Adoni kissed her teeth and returned her attention to the band.

Slamdango gave it their all for the next few numbers. Adoni closed her eyes and nodded to the beat. Halfway through the set she peered through her lashes at the spectacle playing out all around her. The singer pranced from one end of the stage to the other, pointing at the audience, leaning over and squealing into his microphone with gritty gusto, letting the beads of sweat on his face roll off his chin and the end of his nose. Most of the crowd let itself go and rollicked along with him, bouncing on the balls of their feet in time with the drums. Some even had their hands in the air. The lights, the colours, pulsated throughout the club, pasting the crowd's silhouette onto the walls. Adoni turned her head as a beam of light swept the stage. She looked at the wall, trying to discern her crown of curly black hair from the other shadows.

Adoni rooted herself to the floor and rolled her fingers against her palms. She stayed that way until the band played the last note of its set. "Okay Toronto!" the singer bellowed. "No encores! Good night!" He turned and threw the microphone over the drummer's head. It hit the back wall of the stage and sent a loud crack through the speakers. The crowd sent them away with a final round of applause.

A thin layer of snow kissed the sidewalk outside the Palace. Adoni's heavy footsteps swept them aside as she headed toward the subway. She pulled her hood over her head and bent forward as she wove between the pedestrians headed in the opposite direction. The traffic lights were in her favour when she reached the corner; the beacon turned green and she started to cross.

Halfway across the road, she recognized a girl standing on the other side.

It was *her*. A little older, a little thicker, black hair instead of purple. Still, it was definitely *her*.

"Natalie!"

The girl looked up. Her expression ripped Adoni's memory wide open. Adoni hurried toward her. The opposite light turned green, and Natalie turned and crossed the street.

Adoni called after her as she jogged to the corner. *Maybe she doesn't recognize me. Maybe...* "Natalie!"

Natalie kept on walking.

Adoni watched her go.

Chapter
3

If it had been just an ordinary gig, an ordinary night, Adoni's mind would have been swimming with the band's best numbers. As it turned out, all she could recall on the ride home was Natalie walking away.

When Adoni first returned to the city after her time in the In-Between, Natalie was almost constantly on her mind; Natalie, the girl with the purple hair and glossy lips that Adoni had spent the night with, the girl who'd given Adoni her first kiss, the first to make her feel special. Natalie had been on the colony before Adoni showed up; she'd been sung away from the fractured home she shared with her parents by a piper named Paj. She had a mean streak that she let fly whenever someone hurt her, but her tenderness had touched Adoni in a way she'd never known before.

After the battle with Sylvester, before leaving the In-Between, Adoni asked Natalie to come back with her. But Natalie refused.

She could still see Natalie shaking her head over and over. *No, no, I'm not going back.* The sadness of that moment found its way through to Adoni's every whim. She was used to it lurking under every failure, every joy. The roots of that memory ran so deep in Adoni's mind that, on some days, she felt as though they held her together.

And now Natalie was back.

She was shorter than Adoni remembered.

Why hadn't she answered when Adoni called? Was she deliberately ignoring her? Or had she simply not heard?

She stepped off the bus and headed toward her apartment. At first she didn't pay any mind to the sound of footsteps behind her—a lot of people in her part of town worked the night shift and headed home at that hour—until she paused in front of the house with the broken fountain to tighten her bootlace. The moment she crouched down, the footsteps ceased. Adoni peered over her shoulder. The street behind her was empty, apart from a stray cat that darted across the road and disappeared behind a collection of garbage bins lined up against a neighbour's fence. She finished retying her lace and started back on her way.

There they were again: footsteps, loud enough that she could hear them, but soft enough to disguise just how far away the person was. Adoni turned around and walked backwards a few paces, her gaze moving back and forth, searching for the source of the noise. She stood still and listened. Nothing; the street was silent. She took one last glance around.

A man's face, pale against the darkness, there in an alley between two houses, staring at her.

Adoni turned and ran all the way to her apartment, her heart pounding in her throat.

She tripped up the broken concrete path to her building's front door and tore her keys out of her pocket. The street at her back was silent; still, she shoved the key into the lock and yanked the bolt back before dashing over the threshold and pulling the door shut.

The lobby smelled of wet canvas and winter boots. Flyers for discount department stores stuck out of the neighbours' mailboxes. A single thumbtack pinned a stack of two-for-one meal deals to the new bulletin board. Three of the four light bulbs above were burned out and still hadn't been replaced. A wilted fern decorated one particularly drafty corner. Someone had hung a red Christmas ornament on one of its browning leaves as a joke. Adoni stumbled past it and bounded up the short flight of stairs to her apartment.

She approached the door and put her ear to the wood. Silence. She opened the door and stepped inside.

Ida was seated on the couch. She turned her head and put her finger to her lips. Adoni eased the door shut and slipped off her boots. She tiptoed over to her mother and gave her a peck on the cheek. Tyler, the little boy who lived with his mother in the apartment across the hall, was lying next to Ida, asleep, his head on a flattened pillow. Ida nodded at him. "Olivia hasn't come back yet."

"I think someone's following me," Adoni said, quickly, quietly.

Ida scowled and stood up. "Who is?"

"Some white guy. I saw him up the street standing next to one of the houses. He was staring at me."

Ida jammed on a pair of winter boots and marched out of the apartment. Adoni followed and poked her head over the threshold as her mother opened the lobby door and walked halfway down the front path. She stood there a full minute, staring ahead at the darkened street, before coming back inside. "Did you see what he looked like?"

"Not really. He was thin. I didn't get a good look at his face."

Ida flipped the bolt on the apartment door. "He was staring at you? Was he jerking off?"

Adoni wrinkled her nose. "I don't think so."

Ida nodded, though her scowl didn't fade. "If you see him again, we'll call the cops."

"I didn't know you were babysitting tonight." She pointed at Tyler.

"She asked me to watch him for a few hours this afternoon, about two o'clock. I thought she'd be back by now."

"Where'd she go?"

"She said she was running a few errands. No concept of time, that woman. Drives me nuts. Want some toast?"

"No thanks, I went by Reese's truck and she gave me some chili."

A frown briefly flashed across Ida's face. She went to the kitchen and slipped two slices of bread into the toaster.

Adoni leaned over Tyler. Expressionless, he looked like the perfect statue of a sleeping boy—lips loose, not a single crease in his brow. He was small for a six year old, the efforts of a long torso cancelled out by a pair of short legs. His arms were folded in front of him, fingers curled gently over his empty palms. She watched his chest rise and fall as he breathed.

The toaster popped. Adoni glanced up. Ida was holding a fist of white knuckles against the counter and watching her. She caught Adoni's eye and turned sharply, retrieved the toasted bread from the machine, and scraped both slices with a knife and a slathering of butter.

This was another thing left unspoken between the two of them: Adoni had a connection with the boy across the hall. Adoni knew her mother wasn't stupid; Ida had noticed that Tyler went missing the same night Adoni ran away from home. Ever since then, she kept a wary eye on her daughter whenever he was around.

Afraid I'll take off with him, Adoni thought. There was no chance of that happening twice. Ritter wasn't around to sing him away again. None of the pipers were.

Ida never talked to Adoni about the time she disappeared, but she did come close. "You should have seen her eyes when she found out he was gone," Ida told Adoni a month after she returned, when Tyler's brutish father had finally walked out on the family for good and things had settled down. "Huge. That's her kid, right? When it's your kid, you just…" She nodded gravely. "I heard her crying for days. From the day he disappeared to the day he came back."

She left it at that, but Adoni wondered if Olivia, too, had heard Ida through the thin apartment walls. She wondered if that was the basis of their newfound, tenuous friendship.

"School tomorrow, eh?" Ida said.

"Yeah. Two electives, then philosophy."

"Look at you! Philosophy, eh?"

"She went out to run errands?" Adoni asked. "Who's got errands to do at night?"

"It's not the first time she's left him here longer than she said she would."

"She didn't go to work or something?"

"Maybe she did, I don't know."

"Can you call her?"

Ida put her toast on a plate and returned to the living room. "I could call her, sure, but I've got a feeling she just needs a break and didn't want to ask."

"So what, she's just gonna come back whenever, and you're okay with that?"

Ida took a bite and chewed for a moment before answering. "She wants to go out for a while and leave him here, it's fine with me. He's asleep, it's not like he's gonna miss her."

"What if she doesn't come back for a while? Like, a *long* while?"

Ida took another bite of toast, chewed slowly, and swallowed. "If I don't hear from her in an hour, I'll give her a call."

Adoni gave Tyler one last look before going into the kitchen and retrieving a mug from the cupboard. She poured herself a drink from the water pitcher in the fridge. There on the bottom shelf, pushed all the way to the back, was a six-pack of Ida's favourite beer.

Adoni frowned. She replaced the water pitcher and flung the refrigerator door shut.

Ida glared at her. "You're gonna wake him up."

"Why've you got beer in the fridge?"

Ida rolled her eyes. "Because I'm having a friend over tomorrow, *mom*, all right? Maybe he'll want a drink. Like a hostess, you know?"

"You told your group you weren't drinking anymore."

"You see me drinking?" Ida looked around. "I don't see anything around here except the living room."

"You're supposed to tell your friends, so they know they can't drink when they come here."

"Says who? And they *can* drink while they're here, because they're my guests."

Adoni crossed her arms. "He?"

Ida smirked. "Yeah, *he*."

"Who's he?"

"An old friend of mine."

They stared each other until Adoni broke into a smile. "Yeah? How old?"

"Old. If you're around tomorrow afternoon you'll meet him."

"Uh huh. What's his name?"

"Kofi. By the way, I love how you work for CSIS."

"How come I've never heard of him?"

"Because sometimes you don't know me like that."

Adoni heard a sigh come from the couch. Tyler sat up and rubbed at his cheek with the back of his hand. "Hi sleepyhead," Ida said. "Looks like we're gonna have a sleepover, okay?" Tyler nodded and looked around. His face lit up when he caught sight of Adoni standing in the kitchen.

"Hey bud," Adoni said. "Comfy?"

He slid off the couch and shuffled over to her. She grinned as he wrapped his arms around her waist and buried his face against her stomach. Ida stood and faced the two of them, her gaze as sharp as a tack. Adoni blushed and eased out of his embrace. "I'm gonna set up the couch for you to sleep on, okay?"

"Okay," he said, his voice cracking.

"Want some milk?" Ida asked him. He nodded again.

Adoni exchanged a brief, strained look with her mother before heading to her bedroom to retrieve a clean blanket from her closet. She put the blanket to her face and took a whiff to check for mustiness before returning to the living room. Tyler was lying on his back, his glass of milk, half full, on the coffee table in front him. He grinned at Adoni as she spread the blanket between her hands, ready to tuck him in.

Ida stepped in front of her, took the blanket, and finished the job herself.

"See you in the morning bud," Adoni said. She looked at Ida. "In an hour, right?"

"She'll be here soon."

Adoni went back to her bedroom and closed the door. She turned on the lamp that sat on her nightstand and changed into her pyjamas. A pile of clean clothes sat atop her dresser. She hadn't gotten around to folding and hanging them yet. Her schoolbooks and binders were still spread across her desk, the pages marked up with different coloured pens and sticky tabs. She took one look at the clutter and sighed. Ignoring the mess, she went straight to the window to peer out at the night.

An ochre light swaddled the alleyway below. Adoni pushed the glass up and leaned on the sill. This was where she'd first heard Ritter singing, his enchanted voice splitting into other voices, other sounds, other timbres. On winter nights like this she stuck her head out the window and listened carefully, hoping to hear that familiar resonance drifting through the air. She closed her eyes and let the swish of city nightlife soothe her. She stayed at the window for a few moments while she let the cold air rush through her nightshirt, through her hair. When she'd had enough, she ducked back inside, turned off the lamp, and went to bed.

The knocking started as a gentle thumping in the middle of Adoni's dream, barely audible as the pictures in her mind swirled together. It grew loud enough to finally wrench her awake. She opened her eyes and glanced at the clock on her nightstand. Four in the morning. Next door, Ida shuffled into the living room. Adoni heard her murmuring to Tyler, easing him out of his sleep. She got out of bed and opened her door. Ida welcomed Olivia into the apartment.

The familiar circles under Olivia's eyes seemed darker at this time of day. She wore a dishevelled sweater under her winter coat and a pair of skinny blue jeans. Adoni stayed close to the wall and listened as Olivia stuck her hands in her pockets and muttered her excuses. Ida's head bobbed up and down as she went about folding the blanket and tossing it over the back of the couch. "Sure, sure," she said. "Just give me a call, okay? Just so I know." Olivia put her hand on Tyler's shoulder and ushered him into the hallway. She asked Ida a question, something Adoni couldn't quite hear. Ida responded, "I don't know, he only ever talks to her. Right honey? Just shy is all." She wished them both a good night and closed the door behind them.

Adoni smiled as Ida, seeing her standing outside her bedroom, went to her and gave her a kiss on the cheek. "Go to sleep, baby," she said. "Everything's all right."

Adoni returned to her room, to her still-warm bed. She wanted everything to be all right, despite the way Tyler had looked at her from across the room before Olivia shuffled him back to their apartment—glazed eyes, sagging shoulders. Adoni remembered the first time she learned what four in the morning looked like.

He'll get used to it, she thought. *He'll have to, anyway.*

Chapter 4

Adoni's favourite class was Philosophies of Love and Sex. For a two-hour course it was relatively easy. The professor, a sophisticated woman with a sleek grey bob who had a fondness for silk scarves, didn't believe in tests or exams and only assigned two term papers to determine whether a student passed or failed. Participation also contributed to the final mark, and Adoni was never too shy to take part in the lectures.

That afternoon the professor asked her students to list all the slang terms they knew for "penis" and "vagina." After half an hour of giggling and blurting out terms that both amused and horrified, the brainstorming shifted into a serious conversation about the different types of imagery associated with genitalia. "When it's guys, the slang's all powerful," Adoni said. "And there's less of it. Like, most of that slang is about vaginas. When it's vaginas, all the slang's violent, or gross."

"Thoughts?" the professor asked. "What does it say about our society, that we ascribe these terms to our sexual organs?"

"Something's wrong with us," Adoni said.

"But they're just words," one of the male students called out. "You can't give them too much power, or they'll end·up defining you."

Adoni turned around. "Okay then, why don't we call my junk a 'love muscle' and call your junk a 'gash?'"

"The term 'junk' seems to be interchangeable," the professor noted.

"I understand it's supposed to be funny," Adoni said. She pointed at the whiteboard. "But when you think about it, that's just messed up right there."

"So, you're always going to call it what it is?" the student asked. "You're never going to use a slang term for it?"

"You can't even say it," Adoni said. "Say 'vagina.'"

"I can say it, I'm just saying..."

"Say 'vagina.'"

"*Vagina*. I can say vagina, I'm just saying, you can't say vagina all the time. What if you're, like, getting it on with someone?" Their classmates sniggered. "Are you going to keep calling it a vagina?"

"I'm not gonna call it a *gash*," Adoni said. "And none of that up there is romantic."

"Well, you're not going to call it a 'love muscle' right in the middle either. Would you really say 'love muscle' right in the middle of sex?"

"Listen man, I don't know about you, but when I'm in the middle of it, I'm too busy to say *shit*." She waved her hand at the whiteboard. "So, none of that applies."

"Let's move on," the professor said with a smirk.

Adoni listened to the rest of the lecture intently, jotting her notes down on the ruled sheets in her binder and tagging pages in her textbook. Not long ago, she wouldn't have participated in a class discussion like that. Before her spell in the In-Between, she'd been introverted to the point where she wouldn't even answer a simple question. She hated the regimented schedule, the itchy uniform, the stuffy rooms and stuffy teachers, the gossipy students and lonely lunch hours, the filthy hallways, and the never-ending feeling that she was wasting her time—that there was more, that there was better, somewhere else.

That all changed once she returned. Since she realized her first goal—to return to the In-Between and bring Ansgar down—was unattainable without a piper's help, she went back to school with a different purpose: to knuckle down and get through it, without beating herself up for not loving it the way the other students seemed to love it. She spoke up in class, even won the respect of a few teachers who usually treated her with indifference. She graduated on time and with fairly decent grades. For the first time in her life, going to university was an achievable option.

When the time came to start sending out applications, Adoni still hadn't decided what to major in. She thought she might take a year off to figure it out, to get that part-time job, to make those considerations. And a part of her thought a year's leave might afford her the chance to find Ritter wandering the world somewhere, if she could rustle up enough money to go travelling. Then one night, while leaning into the frosty air and listening for that plaintive voice in the distance, her thoughts took her back to The Welcome, and the fragile society she was a part of, briefly, before it crumbled. She wondered why it had worked for so long, and why it failed so suddenly and completely by the time she left.

And then it hit her: sociology, the study of how societies were developed and structured, and how they functioned. Societies like The Welcome, and the other colonies of the In-Between. She told Ida her decision in the morning. "Right on," Ida said. "What kind of job can you get with that?"

"They can call me when they want to set up a city or something," Adoni replied. "And I can tell them how to keep it going and how to make it fair."

"Like a consultant."

"Yeah."

"Can you make a lot of money doing that?"

Adoni pressed her lips together tightly as she fixed herself a bowl of cereal. "I don't know," she said after a time. "Probably. It depends on the city, I guess."

"Maybe they'll give you a free house in the city you help set up," Ida laughed. "Make sure it's someplace warm, eh? I'm sick of this polar vortex crap."

At the end of the lecture, the professor thanked the students for their contributions as they gathered up their belongings. Adoni stuffed her books into her backpack and got to her feet. It was nice to be thanked for her time, as it was nice to be allowed to leave without having to wait for an electric bell to sound over the PA system. She shuffled out the door and down the hall to her assigned locker, to replace her books and backpack with her swimming gear. Once equipped, she headed to the pool.

Adoni's preferred time to swim was early in the afternoon; the lanes weren't too crowded, the change rooms relatively clean, and there were still plenty of fresh towels for students who needed them. The humid hallway leading to the pool smelled so strongly of chlorine it obliterated any other lingering odours. Adoni couldn't stand it and held her breath until she passed through.

The lane swim was in full swing by the time she arrived. Adoni welcomed the privacy the empty change room provided. She wasn't shy about changing into her swimsuit in front of others, but solitude allowed her to be more fluid with her movements. For one thing, she didn't have to change while facing the wall to avoid offending more modest swimmers, and she could bend right over without worrying about bumping someone with her rear end. She raised her arms right over her head when pulling her sweater off, instead of curling forward and peeling it over her back. And when it came time to put her swimsuit on, she took a moment to run her hands over her belly and down each of her thighs. She tied her hair back, slipped on her flip-flops, and went into the natatorium.

She made her way to the end of the pool, to the first of the three slow lanes. She slipped out of her flip-flops to the gentle sound of pool water licking the tiled walls. Her first plunge—headlong, with her arms forward, hand over hand—sent a delicious shiver right through her. She gasped as she broke the surface and then started down the lane.

When she first learned the university had an Olympic-sized swimming pool, Adoni convinced herself she didn't want to be anywhere near it. She and Ritter had nearly drowned in a raging river during their escape from Sylvester and the changeling compound. She still felt the ache in her lungs on nights she couldn't sleep, and in unexpected moments of silence. Fellow students, however, raved about being able to go for a swim before or after class, and eventually Adoni decided to try it out. Her first, timid free swim became a regular jaunt, until she developed the discipline to show up to the lane swim three times a week. The suspicion faded; she trusted herself to know what to do if she ever faced drowning again.

On any other day the swim would have helped her to relax. That day, as she swam up and down the lane at her own leisurely pace, all she could think about was Natalie. *She must have heard me*, was her initial thought. *I was loud enough.* But when she remembered what she'd meant to Natalie in the In-Between, and what Natalie meant to her, she wasn't so sure. If only she could have gotten back to the In-Between while Natalie was still there—if she could have broken the barrier and returned to The Welcome in a blaze of glory—if only she could have shown Natalie she was capable of defeating Sylvester and Ansgar for good…

Things weren't great when I left, but they weren't bad. Why would Natalie want to ignore her? Had time given Natalie some reason or other to be upset? *She wanted to come with me, she just couldn't.* What if, the moment she left, Natalie began harbouring a resentment for Adoni's freedom?

Just stop it, she thought at last. *That's the kind of shit Shabnam would have pulled, not Natalie. She just didn't hear you; that's all.*

The cold of that first plunge gave way to an amniotic warmth as her muscles worked and the water resisted. She looked up at the window that spread across the natatorium, parallel to the street, and saw the black whisper of snowflake shadows falling against the white and cloudy sky. The weather forecast that morning called for another storm, and this was the beginning of a reported fifteen-centimetre dump. Swimmers weren't supposed to rest in the middle of the pool during the lane swim, but Adoni couldn't help herself. She paused, treading water, gazing at the snowflakes as they tumbled, and pictured the mess the streets would eventually be in. It would take a while for folks to dig themselves out, but until the shovels cut through to the asphalt the city would be steeped in silence, the streets empty as citizens waited out the storm, the tires of passing cars and trucks muffled by the spill.

She left the pool when the lane swim ended and shivered on her way back to the change room. Of course the other swimmers, mostly students, were there, as well as a group of senior citizens preparing for an aqua-aerobics class. Adoni showered under a pelting stream of warm water, dried herself off, slathered her skin with cocoa butter, and ran her oily palms through her hair before putting her clothes on again. She paused, savouring the buzz in her limbs and the smell of cocoa on her body, then left the change room before the aerosol perfumes and deodorants overwhelmed her. After one quick stop at her locker, she was suited up against the storm and on her way outside.

Adoni usually went straight home after class. That afternoon she was tempted to stick around so she wouldn't disturb Ida and her guest, but it wasn't a good idea to stay out with a storm on its way. She pulled the hood of her coat as far forward as it would go to keep the snow out of her eyes.

Adoni didn't trust that the beer in the fridge was meant for Ida's guest. Worse than finding her mother alone and drunk was finding her in the company of someone else who was equally as drunk. Ida fed off the energy of other people; it was one of the traits that made her so compelling a speaker in her recovery group. She came into the middle of conversations with a seasoned flare, as if she'd instigated the topic herself. But it meant she could also keep up with drunken friends; if they were obnoxious, she was obnoxious; if they were violent, she was violent too. Ida had mentioned her guest was an "old friend." Adoni hoped it wasn't one of the friends she swore to abandon years ago, when her drinking was more than an occasional overindulgence.

Spadina Avenue winked behind the curtain of snowflakes—old houses with pointed roofs, a stone church with high, arched windows, the bank and the barbeque house, the side-by-side rival pizzerias, and the student residence: a gloriously ugly building that stood on the corner. Adoni turned up the street and headed toward the subway station. There wasn't enough snow on the sidewalk for her boots to make the delightful squish she was so fond of, but it was well on its way. She reached the station just as the storm picked up momentum and the snow started falling sideways.

Adoni took the stairs down to the second level and walked past the streetcars toward the extended walkway that bridged the east-west platforms with the north-south platforms. Dense crowds of pedestrians made their way from one end of the walkway to the other. Adoni fell into determined step with those headed for the southbound trains. Her pace slowed, however, when the first notes of a wistful tune sounded from the other end of the walkway. The jolt of a memory pierced her stomach.

Someone was playing a saxophone. Playing it the way no one else could. As if life itself depended on it.

She picked his profile out between the pedestrians as the crowd ebbed and flowed—black pants, black jacket, pale skin and golden hair, the tarnished instrument hanging from his neck, held between his slender hands and singing as his skilful fingers whizzed up and down, driving patterns through ears, through chests, through legs. The length of the hallway, the low ceiling, channelled the music—a force of nature—through the station. It advanced slowly, a team of red-eyed horses over a battlefield, coiled and waiting for the whip to spring.

She stopped in the middle of the walkway, felt her hands go numb. She heard his lust and his pain, the pounding of his heart. The music cupped her face, kissed her, and welcomed her home. She couldn't take a step. She could barely breathe.

Hardly anyone minded the young man with the saxophone at the mouth of the walkway. Most commuters barely glanced at him as they passed by, paid no attention to the way he poured himself into the song, couldn't hear that every note was both fractured and complete. It was as though he existed on a different plane, one that transcended the mediocrity of their own. Two younger men stood next to each other, listening to his performance and nodding appreciatively. He played on, eyes closed, bent at the waist, his saxophone humming with melody and harmony, until the final note sounded, until the city's routine noises swallowed it up.

An older woman had the generosity of spirit to toss a coin into the open case at his feet. He smiled and nodded at her, then crouched and counted up his earnings.

Adoni got a hold of herself and walked toward him. She stared at him, her lips moving but no sound escaping them. *Say something*, she thought; and then in an instant: *No, don't.* She stopped a few feet away from him and stuffed her hands into her pockets.

He stood and straightened his back, and as he moved to put the mouthpiece to his lips again he saw her standing in front of him, and his smile melted.

It was only gone for a moment, until the past caught up with them and their gazes bridged the chasm of the last few years. He unclipped the saxophone from the strap around his neck and laid it in its case before stepping forward and gathering Adoni in his arms. They held each other tightly, muscles shaking, for a time.

Ritter put his lips to her ear and whispered, "Told you so, darling."

Chapter

5

"The streets are meaner now," Ritter said at last.

They sat in a coffee shop around the corner from the station, a tacky little place painted in bold, bright colours, golden sun motifs silkscreened on the backs of uneven wooden chairs. The warm air kissed the windows, fogging them up, so that the city beyond looked like a daydream. There were two young people behind the counter, packing espressos and frothing milk. Adoni and Ritter sat hunched over a tiny table in the corner, against a filthy strip of glass that was supposed to be a window. Students claimed every other table in the place, oblivious to the beautiful creature in their midst—the only changeling ever gifted with a piper's voice. Under the tapestry of pop music on the speakers: the sound of fingers typing away on laptop keyboards.

Ritter put the white ceramic mug to his lips and closed his eyes as he sipped his hot chocolate. Adoni grinned. She'd missed the way he savoured the things he loved, be they sweet, steamy drinks, or music, or an embrace. He pressed his lips together and bowed his head, a tiny purr vibrating in the back of his throat. He ran his lissom fingers over the mug's curves and lightly traced the handle. He puckered up as he swallowed the drink, and when he looked at her again his green eyes twinkled with recognition, even though Adoni could see, deep within them, an enduring sadness.

"What do you mean?" she asked.

"It's hard to describe. There used to be magic in these streets. A kind of camaraderie. You couldn't walk thirty feet without exchanging words with someone. Most of the time the words were encouraging. People had a certain look on their faces. A kind of charm. This city was disco when the rest of the country was still in a tiki craze. It was punk before punk mattered to anyone other than the louts and the liars. People didn't mind stumbling into an adventure." His smile was forlorn. "I don't recognize it anymore. If it's there, it's hidden from me." He winked. "I shouldn't have expected it to stay."

"I love how you still talk bullshit."

He lifted the mug, held it mid-air as though about to toast. "University!" he said. "I'm proud of you, Donny girl, applying yourself and all. University is an admirable venture."

"I'm gonna be in so much debt when I'm finished," she said, covering her face with her hand. "I'm never gonna be able to pay it back."

"Don't worry darling, you're safe. Newgate Prison's more than a hundred years in the past."

She felt the prickle of tears in her eyes, tucked in her chin, and stared at the table. Ritter reached out and put his hand on hers. "I've missed you," he said softly.

"Where've you been?" she croaked. "I looked everywhere for you."

"Here and there. Did some travelling, played some music. Looked for clues. What one usually does when one has nothing but time on one's hands." She chuckled with more than a little spite. "If I'd known, Donny," he said. "If I'd known you were looking for me…"

"You would've gone anyway," she said. "I wouldn't even expect you to stick around after being trapped at The Welcome for all those years. But I would've appreciated, like, an email address or something, so I could at least know what you were doing. Lucky for me Reese is around. But sometimes I needed you, too."

He gave her hand a squeeze. "Nonsense. No one needs me. You only think you need me. Like a drink, or a cigarette. You don't still smoke, do you?"

"Sometimes, when I get stressed out."

He stuck his tongue out and grimaced. "Filthy habit."

"Reese and I still talk about it sometimes."

"My dear, sweet Theresa," he cooed. "How is she? I'll bet she's found an empire of her own by now."

"Yeah, she's got her own food truck."

He ran his fingers through his thick blonde hair. "A chance to celebrate food *and* develop a taste for wanderlust. Sounds marvellous. You'll have to show me where she operates."

"You've never bumped into her? Haven't you been by City Hall yet? She's there every day."

"Not since I got back from abroad."

Adoni smirked. "Oh, you went *abroad*? What's *abroad*?"

"Adventure, darling, since this city seems to be lacking it so."

"How'd you pay for it?"

He put the cup to his mouth and took a long swig. "Donny, didn't anyone ever tell you it's déclassé to discuss money with friends?"

"You spend forty years on a colony in another dimension and you come back and you have enough money to fly around the world. Maybe you can give me some pointers for when I have to pay off my student loan."

He smiled. "When you've been around as long as I have, you learn where to stash your cash. You forget I've got several hundred years of amassing wealth on you."

"So where'd you go?" she asked.

"Hungary."

"What's in Hungary?"

"An old friend's stomping grounds."

"What old friend?"

He took another sip, turned his head, and picked at a clump of dried mud on his pants. She didn't look away until his eyes met hers again. He didn't even have to say the name.

Istvan—known by his nickname, Steppe—was Theresa's former

boyfriend, Ritter's former best friend, and the former leader of The Welcome. He stayed behind when the colony abandoned Ansgar's decree. Ever loyal to those who depended on him, he swore he'd protect everyone who chose to stay. Ever loyal—even to those who'd broken his heart—he watched two of the most important people in his life walk out of it, without uttering a single word. Adoni wondered if he still carried his anger around with him, the twisted rage she knew he was terrified would break loose. She remembered the way he stood so stoically and watched Ritter disappear through the agate, the haunted look on his face, the urgency in his last kiss with Theresa. Steppe was unforgettable, enduring just below the surface of their thoughts, relentless even in his silence. No matter that no one had seen him in years; he lived with them all, as much a part of them as their own hearts and lungs.

"Have you heard from him?" she asked.

He shook his head. "Not a word. But then I haven't been around much."

"Reese never talks about him, eh? She hasn't mentioned him once since we got back. I don't know what she'll do if I bring him up."

"I assume she'll avoid the subject for as long as she can."

"I don't understand that. Not even mentioning someone's name when you were together for so long is, like, weird to me."

"When she has something to say about him, she'll say it." He swirled the hot chocolate against the sides of the mug. "That woman's not averse to talking. Give her time."

Adoni looked past him, more at the window than through it. "What do you have to say about him?"

Ritter smirked. "Damn it. You're still as fierce as ever." He crossed his arms behind his head and leaned back. "I miss him. And I hate him. And I love him, more than ever. And even I find it hard to call him by name, even in my own head."

"I didn't know he's Hungarian," she said. "He doesn't have an accent."

"He doesn't have a *Hungarian* accent. That's not unheard of, given how young he was when he left. I've had my share of accents. I'm sure you will too, once you drop that horrible vernacular you young people are so fond of."

"So, what? You saw where he grew up?"

"I did. It's an empty lot now. Weeds coming up through the concrete and broken trees surrounding the place. It's... unpleasant."

Adoni sank in her chair and gripped her mug with both hands. "They say you can tell when you're standing in an important place. Like when you go to visit an old prison or an asylum. They say you can feel it in the air that something happened there before."

Ritter lowered his chin and looked at her.

"Could you still feel him?" she asked.

"Always," he said.

They stared at each other.

"I saw Natalie," she said.

His brow lifted. "Really."

"Outside of Lee's, yesterday."

He grinned. "Ah yes, the Palace. Greasy dump that it is."

Adoni frowned. "Did you hear what I said?"

"Of course. But I thought we could use some levity before diving right into it. Did you speak to her?"

Adoni sipped her tea. "I tried to, but she crossed the street."

"It doesn't surprise me," he said. "A girl like Natalie wouldn't stay in the In-Between forever. She'd get bored. The hope chests can only conjure up what their owners dream of. A few more years of life at The Welcome, and she wouldn't be able to dream up a glass of water. You know that as well as I do." Adoni didn't speak. "You didn't expect her to stay, did you?"

"This whole time you've been gone I've been looking for you. Ansgar's seal won't let me open the agate. I need a piper's voice. I want to get back to the In-Between."

"What for?"

"To get back at Ansgar," she said.

He shook his head.

She let out a huff and shifted in her chair. "I only left the night before a big fat war erupted with the pipers and the changelings, on a colony where a bunch of kids who have nothing to do with anything are still living. Yeah, I want to go back and finish the job. What's wrong with that?"

"Nothing at all. I'd be surprised if you didn't."

"So what do you say?"

"About what, darling?"

"Opening the agate for me."

"Not a chance."

Her stomach reeled. "Why not?"

"Because there's nothing there for you."

"What about the—"

"War? Precisely my point. You're not good for war, Donny. I've seen you in action."

"What do you mean? I'm plenty good for war."

"You'll go in dick swinging and get yourself killed, simple as that."

"No I won't!"

"Donny," he said, leaning onto the table and folding his hands. "You may have torn Sylvester's eye out with that voice of yours, but a legion of changelings with Ansgar at the helm is frankly more than you can handle."

"I can't even believe this!" She seized his gaze with her black eyes. "How do you know what I can handle? You've been gone for years. You don't know me anymore."

"I'm sorry I've upset you."

"I've been waiting forever for this and you're just gonna tell me no?"

"That's right."

"This is such garbage!" She pushed away from the table, scraping the legs of her chair on the floor, and reached for her backpack.

"That's it then? You're just going to leave?"

"What else should I do? Besides, I have to get home and make sure Mom's not off her face."

"You still don't know where I live."

"Whatever."

"Donny."

"What?"

"Don't you trust me?"

She glared at him. "Trust you about what?"

"Trust that I care deeply about you. That I don't want to see you hurt."

She grabbed hold of the zipper on her backpack and pulled it back and forth; it sounded like the revving of a distant car's engine. "If I don't go back, none of the last few years was worth it. I dreamed about taking Ansgar down, like, every day. I'm itching for it. I thought when we met up again you'd understand and let me back into the In-Between. For years. It was *years*."

"I understand. But I won't change my mind." He put his hands on the table, palms up, and wiggled his fingers. Adoni put her hands in his. "Am I some glorious prince in your head?" he asked. "Dazzling, charming, willing to give you everything you want?"

"No," she muttered. "You're just some dude I was counting on."

"Funny how that happens when we spend some time apart." He kissed the backs of her hands. "But don't worry. I promise I won't lose you again. This is forever."

She rolled her eyes. "'*This is forever.*' You need a boyfriend."

"All right missus, get a pen and paper. You young folk still use paper and ink, yes?" She took a notebook from her backpack and readied a pen. "My address," he said as he jotted it down.

"Put your number too."

"No phone number. No phone either."

"No phone?"

"I've never had a phone."

"How do you survive?"

"Quite well, actually."

"What if I need to talk to you?"

"Knock loud." He slid the notebook across the table. "I'll be home."

They left the coffee shop as the storm hit its stride, with sticky snow whirling through the air, heaps of it piling up in doorjambs and on windowsills. Ritter turned to Adoni and pulled her into an unyielding embrace. "You're taller," he said. He turned his face into her hair and took a deep breath. "And you smell like a vacation."

"Don't disappear," she said. "Okay? I need you. You have to meet up with Theresa too, okay? You have to try her food truck."

"I'll have to, yes. Actually, I have something for her. A souvenir from Hungary."

"Come out with me tomorrow. We'll go visit her truck and you can give it to her."

"All right. My place at seven o'clock. And don't be late, darling. You know how I worry."

"Yeah, you worry." She held him close for another moment and then pulled away. "I'm the one who should worry."

"Don't. I'll be a good boy, I promise." He kissed her cheek. "Tomorrow. Bring that gorgeous pounding heart of yours. I'll have it mended in no time." With that, he turned on his heel, waved over his shoulder, and disappeared through the brilliant curtain of snow. Adoni watched until the black of his clothing had dulled to grey, and then to white, before tearing her eyes away and heading home.

Chapter
6

Adoni thought about her conversation with Ritter all the way home. She wanted desperately to believe he'd change his mind, that he'd see how ready she was to confront Ansgar's cruelty head on, and open the agate for her with his blessing. She was face to face with the one being who could give her the chance for vengeance. And he wouldn't budge. In just a few words, years of longing came crashing down on her.

Worse, she had no idea what Ritter was to her anymore. She'd pictured their reunion in minute detail, right down to the time of night. She'd pictured it as something greater, not the quiet moment it turned out to be, not an ordinary conversation in an ordinary place, surrounded by ordinary people who knew nothing of the In-Between. *What did you expect?* she thought. *That he'd just do it right there?* But it was true; it's what she expected: Ritter, throwing his arms around her, welcoming her as though she were a saviour, listening to her emphatic plea to be let back into the In-Between so she could right its wrongs and triumph, ripping the fabric of the air apart for her, quickly, easily. It all seemed ridiculous now. Her face flushed. She pulled her hood over her eyes.

The driver pulled the bus tight against the curb and came to an abrupt stop. She disembarked and made her way down the street with her keys in her fist. Sure enough, the neighbours were waiting out the storm before taking a shovel to their sidewalks. Adoni slipped in the snow several times but managed to avoid a nasty spill before reaching her building. She climbed the lobby stairs and put her ear against her front door.

She heard Ida talking enthusiastically to her guest. And music.
Led Zeppelin.

She drove her key into the lock and shoved the door open.

Ida, mid-laugh and standing at the kitchen counter, stopped abruptly as Adoni entered. A man sat on the couch, a bottle of beer in his hand. As he turned his head, Ida left the kitchen and stood in the middle of the front hall, blocking Adoni's view of him. "Hi baby," she said, her smile, her eyes, a little too wide, her voice a little too loud. Adoni put her toes to the backs of her boots to pull them off and jerked her zipper open. She craned her neck to get a better look at Ida's hands. Ida scowled and held them up, empty. She shot Adoni a look of warning and stepped aside. Ida's guest was on his feet.

Handsome and stocky-framed, Adoni could see, with wide, dark eyes, a broad nose, smooth dark skin. The living room smelled of his cologne, a rich bay rum with a whisper of something clean and citrusy underneath. His smile was friendly enough, if a little guarded. He lifted a hand in greeting.

"This is Kofi," Ida said.

"Hello," Kofi said.

Adoni nodded at him. "Hi."

"How was class?"

"It was all right."

"There's leftovers on the counter," Ida said.

Adoni shuffled into the kitchen as Ida rejoined her guest on the couch. Their conversation continued in a more subdued tone than earlier. Adoni fixed herself a plate of chicken and fries and tried to distinguish what they were saying from the melodic purr of voices and guitars on the stereo. *They don't want me to hear them*, she thought as she dipped her chicken in gravy and stuffed it into her mouth. She watched them from her perch at the counter. They went on, their drone interrupted by occasional peals of Ida's laughter. True to her word the night before, she wasn't drinking. Neither was her guest; Kofi's bottle remained in his hand, half full, and there were no empty bottles on the coffee table or stashed next to the microwave.

Their thighs are touching, Adoni thought.

She finished off her dinner and rinsed her plate in the sink. "Can you get me some water?" Ida called out. The domestic lilt in her voice made Adoni blush. She poured her mother a glass, brought it out to her, and tried to steal a discrete glance at Kofi, only to find him looking at her with the same pleasant smile he'd greeted her with.

"Sociology," he said. "You like it?"

"It's good so far."

"Late class tonight."

Adoni's back went rigid. "Yeah? What's late to you?"

Ida coughed and took a sip of water.

"When I picked my classes I took them all in the morning so I could have my days free," he said, agreeably, unfazed. "Morning person, you know."

"I met up with a friend after class."

"Good, good."

She stared at him. The moment felt eighteen years long.

Adoni turned to Ida. "I'm gonna be in my room."

"Okay."

Adoni went to her bedroom and shut the door. She dropped her backpack on her desk, sat on her bed, and stared at the flurry of snowflakes falling past her window. The blue beacons of city snowplows flashed up and down the street.

Ritter relished the obscurity of life beyond the In-Between. Here, there was no reputation to precede him, no wild stories or colour of infamy. Ritter loved the regular, mundane interactions he had—the cashier muttering the price of his groceries, the nod of thanks he received when he held the door open for someone, even the rare smiles he encountered while busking in the subway. There were no ghosts here, nothing to disturb him. Not one of these people knew his secret: that he wasn't made of the same stuff they were made of; that he wasn't human.

He stopped by the green grocer's on the corner to pick up a few things before reaching his apartment—a bachelor pad above a hardware shop. It was well after dark when he opened the door to the narrow staircase leading up to his room. The naked bulb hanging over the cramped foyer gave off a pathetic halo of light just bright enough to outline the first few steps. Ritter took off his coat and hung it on a hook behind the door, removed his wet boots, and climbed the squeaky, carpeted staircase.

He opened the door at the top of the stairs, stepped into the room, and flipped the switch on the wall. The apartment, small and sparsely furnished, was nonetheless comfortable and inviting. The previous tenant had painted the walls bright red, and though the colour had faded somewhat by the time Ritter moved in, it still radiated joy. Mismatched sets of curtains hung over the miniscule windows, giving the room the feel of a summer cottage. The ancient refrigerator and stove, both enamelled in a hideous shade of mustard yellow, stood in a tiny kitchen with an uneven linoleum floor. A futon crouched in the corner of the room, next to a threadbare rug. The room smelled of fresh laundry, and a hint of cigarette smoke. Nicotine tar left a permanent stickiness on the floors.

Ritter put his groceries on the counter and went into the bathroom, where an exposed radiator warmed the broken tiles and the towels hanging over a plastic rail. He took a long, languorous shower, washing away the day's grime before drying off and slipping on a clean pair of jeans. He walked, shirtless and barefoot, into the kitchen and drew a knife from the drawer, then set to work dicing his vegetables.

He smiled as the smell of the vegetables wafted up to his nostrils. At The Welcome, Theresa had cooked all the pipers' meals, and though she was no doubt an excellent chef—aided, in small part, by Ansgar's enchanted pots and pans—he still took humble pleasure in his own cooking. The dishes were never more glamorous than stews or stir-fries or pasta, and they left him feeling wonderfully heavy and sated. The pipers at Seventeen Bay, the eastern colony, were notoriously gluttonous; Ritter swept the vegetables into a heated skillet and wondered if things would have turned out differently if he'd been imprisoned there instead of at The Welcome.

Of all the colonies in the In-Between—Ocean's Wake in the west, Long-and-Gold and Accueil-Silencieux, and Seventeen Bay in the east—The Welcome, in the darkest north, was the most unyielding, its pipers the most feared. When Ansgar sent a slave to bring Ritter back to her, she naturally chose Steppe, the most terrifying of them all, to do her bidding. Ritter was kept prisoner not just by Ansgar, but by the unforgiving cold, the almost perpetual darkness, and, strangely, by the colony's melancholic beauty. He may have learned to love the In-Between, he thought, if he'd been surrounded by pipers who loved it too, instead of by pipers whose every action and every song were dense with resentment. But he quickly pushed the notion aside. Nothing came close to the simple pleasure of living by his own code, his own creed: *life has to be lived according to one's own desire, astride the world's beauty and ugliness.*

He poured himself a glass of wine and turned.

And there he was, seated on a chair next to the window, gazing silently at Ritter as he put the glass to his lips: Sylvester.

Crisp white shirt, a snug grey vest and trousers, the tarnished chain of a watch dangling from his pocket, and a black cravat; every piece of clothing painted the portrait of a gentleman in graceful recline. The illusion would have worked, had it not been for the doll-like face, the one blue, lifeless eye, and the angry lump of scar tissue where the other should have been.

"Your door was open," Sylvester said, his voice as silky and malevolent as ever.

Ritter reached back and wrapped his fingers around the knife's handle. "I'll remember to lock it next time."

"You won't need that." Sylvester tilted his head, indicating the knife. "Do you think I'd give you any warning if I'd wanted you dead?"

Ritter stiffened. "Ansgar's finally granted you passage through the agate?"

Sylvester ran the tip of his tongue over his bottom lip until a smile bloomed, wide and sharp, a shark's smile.

"What do you want?" Ritter asked.

Sylvester's eye scanned the width of the room. "It's nice. A little on the dilapidated side. But we cling to places like these, don't we? Places with history."

"I don't know why you're trying," Ritter said. "We'll never be able to talk like old friends. Have you forgotten? We were never friends to begin with."

"You're right, we weren't. We were brothers. You told me that."

Ritter sat on the futon, the knife on his lap. He stared at Sylvester as though, at any moment, the changeling would spring from his chair and attack. Sylvester remained perfectly still, his eye running up and down the length of Ritter's body, his top lip twitching as though he were stifling a sneer. Ritter sipped his wine. "You haven't answered my question," he said.

"I want you to open the agate."

Though tempted to frown, Ritter clung to his poker face. "Popular request tonight. You can't open it yourself?"

"I wouldn't be here if I could."

"It must have been spectacular, whatever it was you did to get kicked out."

"You don't know the half of it."

"What do you want with the In-Between?"

"Steppe."

Ritter smirked. "I didn't expect you to say that. How is Steppe, anyway? Still clinging to his virtue?"

"I'm going to kill him."

He laughed. "You can't kill Steppe. If you even try, he'll destroy you." He leaned back against the wall and crossed his ankles. "I'm a little insulted. I thought you were going to kill me first."

"It wouldn't be prudent to kill you now. Not when I need the agate opened. I'll get to you eventually."

"All those years negotiating with Steppe," Ritter said, shaking his head. "You'd think you'd have learned a thing or two about diplomacy."

"There's nothing Steppe can teach me that I don't already know." He curled a finger, tucked it beneath his bottom lip, and stroked his skin. "I miss those days sometimes. I miss watching him squirm."

"You're a charmer, Sylvester, truly."

"Come now, Ritter," Sylvester said. "You mentioned Steppe's virtue. Are you telling me you wouldn't appreciate seeing him lose it before you? All his benevolent posturing, crumbling at your feet? I won't deny the pleasure I took from watching him beg for his pipers' lives. Or for yours."

Ritter glared at him. "You take pleasure in suffering."

"I'm my mother's son. As you are."

"I'm happy to play the black sheep."

"I know. So does she."

"Does she know you killed one of her pipers?" Ritter asked. "Does she remember Aniuk? Or is she so lost in her own madness she can't tell one piper from another?"

Sylvester lowered his hand and laid it in his lap. "What's the loss of one piper to her? Aniuk defied Ansgar by leaving Ocean's Wake to meet her twin at The Welcome. Her days were always numbered."

"Interesting. Ansgar told you this? Or do you assume it because it's been a long enough while to build the myth up in your head?"

"Who can say? I have no interest in such things." Sylvester smiled again, and this time Ritter noticed the way his lips turned up at their corners. They were no longer the clipped, puppet-like movements from his last encounter with the changeling, that night in the woods that bordered The Welcome, when he tried to strangle Adoni; the night he would have had his revenge against Ritter, if Adoni hadn't screamed his eye out. There was still a calculated aspect to the way he sat, the way he spoke, a carefully constructed façade; but a smoothness had settled in now, and it gave Sylvester a sophistication that was inexplicably becoming, if still menacing.

"You and I aren't so very different," Sylvester said.

"How so?"

"Simple. Determined. Stubborn to a fault."

"You're a cold-blooded killer."

"And you're a wretched narcissist. Nobody's perfect."

Ritter sipped his wine. "What makes you think I'd open the agate for you?"

"I thought your cowardice would inspire you to rid yourself of me. For a time, at least."

"I wouldn't piss on you if you were on fire," Ritter said. "So you've come to the wrong place, *brother.*"

Sylvester sniffed the air and looked toward the stove, where a cloud of smoke rose from the skillet. "Your dinner is burning."

"Let it burn."

"You're not much of a cook. Not that you had to be, with Theresa catering to you."

"You're free to leave now, Sylvester."

"You could always visit her food truck if you're hungry," Sylvester said. "Nathan Phillips Square, every day except Tuesdays. From noon until ten."

Ritter's face turned pale.

Sylvester stood. "I'd rather not cause her any trouble. But I will, if it's the only choice I have."

"Duly noted," Ritter said through gritted teeth. "Now fuck off, before I stick this knife in your chest. It might even pierce your heart. If you have one."

"Do you? That's the real question, isn't it?" He took his leave, gliding down the staircase without provoking a single creak underfoot.

Ritter gave it a moment before springing up and swooping down the stairs. He threw the bolt and chain on the front door, then bounded back up to his apartment, where he flipped another two deadbolts into place. He leaned his forehead against the cold wood, took a deep breath, and inhaled the acrid scent of vegetables burning. He pulled the skillet off the stove as the sharp pulse of the fire alarm stabbed his ears.

Chapter

7

Adoni lay on her back and stared at her bedroom ceiling. Pellets of ice flung themselves at her window, tapping at the glass with a dedicated rhythm, like a thousand fingers at once. The storm was still hours away from tapering off. She pictured the disorder she'd have to walk through to get to class the next day. There would be slipping, sliding, deep drifts one had no choice but to slog through, wet socks and boots and coats, salt stains on pant legs. She wondered how Kofi got home that night. She didn't peg him as the type to own a vehicle, and if he did, he'd be crazy to drive it in such unremitting weather.

She had left the pile of homework in her backpack untouched and spent the rest of the evening in her bedroom trying to eavesdrop on Ida and Kofi as they chatted in the living room. Ida had had plenty of visitors during her saturated years, but recently, apart from Olivia and Tyler, she'd kept mostly to herself. Adoni had all but forgotten the appearances Ida tried to keep up whenever one of her friends came calling. Here they were again, in full swing: the Zeppelin album she used to listen to while getting loaded, its lush melodies calming the atmosphere; giggling every few minutes, particularly when the visitor was a man; the polite way she asked Adoni to fetch her something—her way of demonstrating how close they were, how stable their relationship was.

She rolled onto her side and tucked her legs up against her chest.

A snowball splattered her window.

She sat up and watched the icy remnants drip down the glass. When a second snowball hit, she threw her legs over the side of her bed and hurried over to the sill. She peered down into the alleyway and saw Ritter packing together another two fistfuls of snow. Adoni flipped the window latch and slid the pane open. "I'm awake! What?"

"I need to see you," he called in an ardent whisper. "Get dressed and meet me downstairs."

"What do you need? It's past midnight."

"We need to call Reese. Do you have her number?"

"I bet she's asleep."

"We have to call her now. It's important."

"What's going on?"

"I'm not going to shout it for the masses! Come down here!"

She ducked back inside and shut the window with her heart on the edge of racing. She pulled on a pair of jeans and a sweater, stuffed her cell phone into her pocket, then, as quietly as she could, slunk out of her bedroom and tiptoed to the front door. On went her winter gear—boots, scarf, coat, hat, and mitts. She gently pulled the door closed behind her before locking it and heading outside.

Ritter stood waiting for her at the mouth of the alley. "What's wrong?" she asked.

"I had a visitor earlier this evening. Sylvester's escaped the In-Between. He's somewhere in the city."

Adoni gawked at him. "You saw Sylvester?"

"He came into my apartment. I hadn't locked the door behind me. I won't make that mistake again, I can promise you."

"Jeez, first Natalie, then you, then Sylvester. I haven't seen you guys in years and then… What the hell's going on? What did he say to you?"

"He wants passage to the In-Between so he can kill Steppe."

She held up her hands. "He just said it, just like that?"

"I've got to hand it to him, he certainly has a way with words. I'm starting to envy Steppe all the hours spent lending him his ear."

"What about Reese?"

"Simple, darling. Either I open the agate for him or he'll pay her a visit. Something tells me if that happens he'll skip the verbosity. We have to warn her."

Adoni found Reese's number in her list of contacts and dialled. The phone rang four, five, six times, until an automated voice asked her to try her call again later. "She's not picking up."

"We have to see her. Where does she live?"

"In St. James Town."

"Let's go."

Adoni looked up at her window. "I can't go all the way out there now! If my mom wakes up and I'm not there, she'll freak."

"We have to tell her right away, Donny. Sylvester's known to strike without much more warning than he's already given."

Adoni kicked at the snow. "Does he know where she lives?"

Ritter rolled his eyes. "I didn't ask. I was too busy being terrified. I'm sure you understand."

"What if he's followed you here?" She felt a sudden stitch of panic. "Someone was following me the other day," she said. "When I was on my way back from the concert. He was standing on the street and watching me. I didn't get a good look at his face. It must have been him!"

"You couldn't have mentioned that earlier?" Ritter huffed.

Adoni glared at him. "I'm sorry, I got distracted by the love and the friendship and whatever."

Ritter shook his head. "All right, we're both ridiculous, now let's go."

"Wait!"

"Donny," he said. "What's worse to you? Getting yelled at by your mother, or knowing Sylvester's about to go toe to toe with someone you love?" His wide eyes searched her face. "He set Aniuk on *fire*."

Adoni pressed her lips together. "We'll have to take a cab. Do you have any money on you?"

He leaned forward and kissed her cheek. "Language, Donny."

They left the alley and trudged up the street toward the main road, where it would be easier to flag a cab down. Their breathing grew hoarse as they fought through the snowdrifts; they needed a moment, at the top of the street, to swallow and let the burn in their legs dissipate. Adoni stuck out her hand and waved at a cabdriver who was slowly inching along the road. He pulled up to the curb and waited for Ritter and Adoni to climb over a heap of solid snow and pile into the back seat. Adoni gave him Theresa's address, and they were off.

The back of the passenger seat housed a touch screen that flashed a series of obnoxious advertisements in Ritter's face. He snorted and snapped it off. "Damn things," he grumbled.

"What else did he say?" Adoni asked him.

Ritter looked out the window. "A lot of rot. A lot of blustering nonsense."

"Like?"

"Threats, Donny, do I really have to go into them?"

"You got me out of bed in the middle of the night, so…"

"Fair enough, but now's not the time." He nodded at the driver. "You'll have to wait until we get to Reese's place."

She folded her arms over her chest and shivered. She'd always felt safe with the knowledge that Sylvester was trapped in the In-Between. Now that he'd breached the portal and was somewhere in the city walking among them, she felt the hairs on the back of her neck stand up and her palms grow sweaty inside her mitts. She kissed her teeth as the cab juddered along. "I'm gonna try her again," she said, pulling her phone out of her pocket and hitting the redial function. The same professional voice came over the receiver, asking the caller to try again later. Adoni jammed the phone back into her pocket. Her left leg bounced, until Ritter reached over and put a firm hand on her knee.

"We're on our way, darling," he said. "It's all right."

"What does he look like now?"

Ritter turned his head. "You're written all over his face," he said. "Satisfied?"

"You bet I am," she said with a nasty grin.

At long last, the cab pulled up in front of Theresa's high-rise. Adoni saw three people standing in the glass atrium, pulling on their gloves and winding scarves around their necks, preparing to face the cold night air. She left Ritter in the back seat and stumbled through the snow toward the entrance, shuffling into the lobby as the neighbours shuffled out. She remained shivering at the door until Ritter joined her. Together, they took the elevator up to Theresa's floor.

They marched up the brightly lit hallway to Theresa's front door, the musty carpeting dulling the sound of their boots. Adoni yanked her mitten off and knocked as hard as she could. Silence at first, she scowled at Ritter and put her ear against the door. "Try it again," he said. She stepped out of the way and pulled her phone from her pocket. Ritter hammered on the wood as Adoni redialled Theresa's number. They heard her ring tone—an electronic calypso tune that punctured the silence and drove their anxiety home—beyond the frame. Just as Adoni considered throwing her weight against the door, the sound of resolute steps came across the floorboards.

"Who the hell is it?"

"It's me! Open the door!"

An unlatched chain, a deadbolt flung back—Theresa yanked the door open and stood in the frame in her silky purple nightdress. She blinked hard and held a hand up to shade her puffy eyes from the overhead lights. Mussed hair, a film of night cream on her face; she'd been asleep all this time. "What's wrong?" she asked. "It's late."

Adoni threw her arms around her. "We tried to call you. Sorry we're waking you up." She felt Theresa's body tense up and pulled away.

Theresa was gaping at Ritter.

He smiled. "Hello, darling."

She slipped out of Adoni's embrace and stepped aside. They took their cue and entered, and she shut the door behind them.

Theresa's tiny apartment still smelled of that night's dinner, a rich aroma of garlic and onions and spices. The oven's overhead light shone down on splatter marks and a sink full of dirty dishes. Theresa brushed past them and turned on a lamp in the living room. Adoni could just make out the rest of her abode in the dim glow. Framed black and white photos covered the walls. Several pieces of clothing hung from every hook and handle in the place. The floorboards couldn't be seen past Theresa's shoe racks—four of them, each one sagging under the weight of runners, summer sandals, muddy boots. A tube television sat on a stand in the corner, in front of a sagging loveseat and armchair. Beyond the tarn of light, past an Asian-inspired room divider, was Theresa's unmade bed.

Adoni knocked the snow from her boots before pulling them off and joining Theresa in the living room. She sat on the loveseat and leaned her elbows against her knees. "I'm so sorry," she said. "But this is really important."

Theresa's eyes followed Ritter as he joined Adoni on the loveseat. She sat down in the armchair and leaned her head against her hand, her eyelids sagging. "I can't believe you're here," she said to him.

"I wish the circumstances were better," he replied.

"Sylvester's somewhere in town," Adoni blurted out. "He wants Ritter to send him back to the In-Between."

"So send him back," Theresa muttered. "What does that have to do with me?"

"I'm inclined to deny requests made by villains of Sylvester's ilk," he said. "What with their penchant for destruction and the like."

"He said he wants to go back to kill…" Adoni stopped herself short.

Theresa grinned. "Steppe?"

"Yeah."

Theresa tucked her legs up and pulled her nightdress over her knees. "He can't kill Steppe," she said. She looked at Ritter. "How is he?"

"I don't know," he replied. "I haven't been back."

She held her hand up and examined her chipped fingernails.

The impatient bounce in Adoni's leg returned. "Sylvester said he's gonna come after you if Ritter doesn't open the agate," she said. "We have to do something!"

"Donny, it's almost one thirty in the morning, and you come knocking on my door, and there you are with…" she held her hand out, indicating Ritter, "… and tell me that Sylvester wants to go back to the In-Between, but you don't want to let him, but unless you let him he's going to come after me…" She closed her eyes. "What's he going to do, come after me right now? This whole neighbourhood's swarming with cops."

"We didn't even have to buzz in to get to your apartment. What good'll the cops do if Sylvester breaks in here?"

"They can handle it."

"I wouldn't be too sure about that," Ritter said.

Theresa rose and went into her kitchen to put a kettle of water on the stove. Ritter got to his feet and joined her. "He told me when and where you park your food truck. He's been watching you, Reese."

"I can't *not* run my truck. I don't run the truck, I can't pay my rent."

"At the very least, change your schedule and park it somewhere else. There are plenty of high-traffic areas in the city."

"At this time of year, with the tourists and the ice-skaters? No way. I can't afford it."

"If it's just about money—"

"*Just* about money?" Her eyes, two black orbs encircled by dark rings, burned brightly. "I'm already short for next month with all the crappy weather. The landlords in this neighbourhood don't mess around with folks who don't pay their rent. They don't care about sob stories and excuses. They toss people out on their asses. I'm a month's wages away from being homeless." She turned away, opened a cupboard, and retrieved a mug. "Sorry, Ritter. I fear poverty more than I fear Sylvester. Right now I've got a roof over my head and four walls to protect me. If I hide, I'll have nothing at all." She tossed a teabag into the mug and waited for the whistle on the kettle to blow.

"Reese, listen to me," he said gently.

Theresa whirled around and lobbed her arms about his neck. Adoni watched as she shook against Ritter's chest, her fingers seizing his hair, her shoulders heaving. "My vegetables!" she sobbed. "They won't be in until Thursday because of the storm! I have just enough for tomorrow's run, and then I'm out for two days! I have to make close to a thousand before the first or the landlord's going to change the locks! *Where in the hell have you been?*"

Adoni slid off the couch as Ritter put his arms around Theresa's waist. "I'm a sorry sight, I know," he murmured as she bawled against his neck. "Especially now. What can I say? I've had terrible timing these last few years."

"I don't know what to do," she whimpered. "I know Sylvester's dangerous. But I'm so tired..."

"Sorry Reese," Adoni said. "We didn't mean to upset you."

Theresa turned her head, still clutching Ritter close. "No, I'm sorry. I should calm down. This is serious." She pulled away from him and took the kettle off the stove before the water reached a boil. They returned to the living room. "I never thought I'd have to worry about him on this side," she said.

Ritter settled back against the loveseat. "Sylvester's eager to face Steppe again, and confident that he'll succeed in destroying him. Either he's completely off his nut, which I wouldn't rule out..." He paused. "Or he's right. Either way he's planning to wreak havoc on The Welcome the moment he returns."

"So you keep him here," Theresa said.

"Which means we'll have to take precautions."

"How can he be right?" Adoni asked. "Steppe's voice can tear people apart. If he sees Sylvester coming all he has to do is let it rip, and Sylvester's screwed."

"He's traded Ansgar for something that will do the deed," Ritter said. "I'm sure of it. Probably payback for his lost eye."

"Traded for what, though?" Adoni said.

"I don't know," he said. "Something horrendous. Does it matter? The

Welcome is safe, so long as he remains outside its borders. Of course this means he's our problem, not theirs. We'll have to hold him off."

"Maybe we can get him arrested before he attacks us."

Ritter rolled his eyes. "For what, Donny?"

"For threatening us."

"Yes, I can picture it now. 'Hello officer. Threatening them? No, not *them*. All I asked was that they open the portal to another dimension. It's a piper in the In-Between I want to kill first.'"

"So maybe they'll throw him in a psych ward, and we'll get rid of him that way."

"Don't be absurd. And anyway, I doubt any institution would be able to hold him. He's inventive and vindictive. We'll have to set up a schedule to keep Reese safe." He looked at Theresa. "I can stay with you during the ending hours of your shift and escort you—"

"Maybe you need to go back to the In-Between," Theresa said. "Maybe you need to talk to Steppe about this."

He uncrossed his legs. "I'm not going back there," he said. "I had enough of the In-Between a long time ago."

"Not even to warn Steppe that Sylvester's out to get him?"

"That's not news, Reese. I'm certain Steppe's been anticipating this. The fact remains, Sylvester's in the city. And apparently he's been stalking our girl too," he said, nodding at Adoni.

"You've seen him?"

"I didn't get a good look at him," Adoni said. "It happened the other night when I came home from the concert. He was standing a little ways off and watching me. It was dark. It couldn't have been anyone else."

Theresa shrugged. "I'm stumped, guys. You can't be with me twenty-four seven. We can't call the cops. I can't pack it in. And you're right," she said to Ritter, "knowing why he's here doesn't change the fact that he is."

They stared at the floor.

"I don't want to be a jerk," Adoni said, "but can I go home now? If my mom wakes up…"

"Of course," Ritter said. "Call a cab. I'll give you the money to get home."

"What are you gonna do?" she asked.

"If it's all right with Reese, I'd like to stay here. Just to be sure." He smiled. "I think I can fit on this couch if I bend my knees."

"I'll sleep on the couch," Theresa said with a snort. "I'm shorter than you are."

"I wouldn't dream of it."

"I'm calling a cab," Adoni said. She took her cell phone from her pocket and dialled.

"I've already invited myself over," Ritter continued to Theresa. "I'm not going to oust you from your bed. It wouldn't be gentlemanly."

"You're not a gentleman," Theresa muttered with a grin. "So you don't have to worry about it."

"A lot of thanks I get for coming over and warning you of potential doom," he grumbled. "It may have been unceremonious of me, but if it doesn't make me a gentleman, I don't know what does."

"Dispatcher says ten minutes," Adoni said. She went to the door and slipped her boots on. Ritter rose from the couch and stood in the foyer with her. He fished his wallet out of his back pocket and opened it up.

Adoni's lips parted. Ritter's wallet was two inches thick with brown, one hundred dollar bills. He fished one out and handed it to her, then put a finger to his lips. She took the money and shoved it into her back pocket.

Theresa gave Adoni a hug before opening the door. "Text me when you get home," she said. "I can't take this calypso shit in the middle of the night."

"You can put it on silent, you know. Or change your ringtone."

Theresa waved the suggestion away. "Text me, don't forget."

"I won't forget."

She held Theresa a moment longer before stepping into the hallway. Theresa closed the door behind her.

She took a deep breath, mind speeding in all directions, and then pressed the button to call the elevator. She felt a little better knowing Ritter was there. But then his words came back to her—"He set Aniuk on *fire*..."—and all at once, her calm disintegrated.

The bell sounded. She stepped into the elevator.

Chapter
8

Theresa locked the front door and sighed. "Maybe one day everything'll be normal," she said. "Especially when you come around."

"I'm sorry, really. If it's any consolation, our reunion was less than twelve hours short of joyous. Donny and I were going to visit your truck tomorrow."

"That would've been nice." She put the kettle back on the stove.

"Contrary to popular belief, I actually prefer the absence of drama when I visit friends. It makes things so much easier."

"Want some tea?"

"I'm not expecting you to play hostess."

"I'm making some anyway. You don't want in on this?"

Ritter went into the kitchen and leaned against the counter. "It *is* cold out."

Theresa reached into her cupboard and retrieved a second, chipped mug. She placed it on the counter and dropped a teabag in. Next, she opened a tin of plain, sweet cookies and laid a few out on a plate. A carton of milk soon followed, placed next to the mugs as the kettle reached its boil and released a high-pitched squeal throughout the apartment. Theresa poured the water into the mugs. She picked up the plate of cookies and held it out to Ritter. "*Plus ça change*," he said with a grin. He took a cookie and bit into it.

Theresa had missed Ritter's rakish smile and effortless allure. His voice and his posture brought back a boatload of memories of The Welcome; the kitchen she spent most of her time in, the dried bouquets of witch hazel she hung around the room, the morning and evening songs that were sung according to piper ritual and Ansgar's decree, the smell of pine wafting in through the open windows. For a moment she lost herself in Ritter's green eyes, which were fixed on her and sparkled with impishness, and in the way his body seemed so relaxed, so utterly at ease with his surroundings.

"My mom used to keep a box of these in the cupboard at all times," she said, indicating the cookies. "You never know when someone's going to drop in, she'd say. They're good for hosting." She pulled a chip of green paint off the cupboard and crumbled it in her palm. "Boxes of cookies and tea and nice napkins. Little things that make people feel comfortable, you know? Special knives for spreading jam. Ceramic spoon rests. And candles, boy did she love candles. Potpourri. I used to hate that stuff. But this place didn't feel like my place until..." She held up the cookie tin. "And now it feels like home. Isn't that strange?" She fished the teabags out with a spoon.

"You won't lose your home, Reese. I can help you. You need a thousand, yes?"

"You really think I worked this hard for a handout? I went to night school, apprenticed for a year. I'm not okay with taking your money just because I've had a bad few weeks."

"You'll never be okay with it," he said. "All I care about is your safety."

"I'll get comfortable with it," she said. "Just taking your money whenever I'm short." She nodded at his prepared mug of tea, inviting him to pick it up and follow her into the living room. "It's an easy habit to fall into and a hard one to break." She put her mug on the coffee table and disappeared behind the room divider.

"Take it for this month then," he called to her. "Just to make up the shortfall."

"And what about the next time I've got a shortfall?" She reappeared wearing a purple terrycloth robe. "And I call you up with the same story?"

"You can't call me. I don't have a phone."

"You don't have a phone?"

"You and Donny both," he said. "Two peas in a pod."

"Get a phone, hippy."

"Don't change the subject."

"What'll you do?"

"I'll look after you. How can I not?"

She sat in the chair and lifted her mug to her lips. There was the quarrelsome Ritter she knew from the In-Between. True to form, he'd included a kernel of sense in his argument. Taking his money would be better than being turned out by the landlord or risking Sylvester's violence. But, as always, he'd failed to understand what it would mean for them both further down the line. She sipped her tea, lowered her arms, and levelled her gaze at him. "All right. A thousand. But I don't want you hanging around. No chaperoning at the start and end of my shifts, no following behind me at a distance, none of that stuff."

He let out a snort. "I'll not have you running around the city alone."

"Really? What makes you think you can tell me what to do?"

He was about to say something, but caught himself and shook his head instead. "I see what you're getting at, but—"

"You'll get to make the rules," she said. "And I'll feel guilty for not following them, even though I shouldn't. That's the way it is. It's part of the reason why I stayed at The Welcome as long as I did." She shrugged. "Well, that and—"

"And Steppe," he finished.

She shrunk in her robe and pinched the collar closed at her throat, feeling all at once as though he was about to rip off a bandage and expose an old scab. "You haven't heard from him at all?" she asked.

"Not a peep."

"Neither have I. Not that I expected him to stay in touch." She propped her elbow against the chair and pressed her knuckles to her lips. "He hates me," she murmured.

"How could he hate you? You're adorable."

"I didn't want to hurt him. But I've just got this feeling, like—"

"Stop it. You're spinning a nasty tale in your head, that's all. Going over every detail, trying to remember every word said, every move made, thinking you'll find something there that you missed, a meaning hidden in another meaning. It's nothing but distance and boredom."

"I can't help it." She took a cookie from the plate. "I'm glad to be alone. I just wish... sometimes I want to see him again, to talk to him again. When I think back to that night, every time, I think maybe it looked like it was too easy for me to leave."

"I didn't see you leave," he said. "So I don't know how you came across. But if you're anything like Steppe, and I suspect you are, which is why I love you, and why he does, too, you're beating yourself up for no reason. You were most likely an exemplar of grace and charm, as always. Well, when you're not screaming at me and trying to break my door down." He winked at her. "And you probably said goodbye in a way that made it clear how much you still adore him."

She grinned and took a bite of the cookie, chewed it, and then asked, "Why do we do this to ourselves?"

"I told you darling, boredom. Human, piper, or changeling—" he said, lowering his gaze, "—we all have fantastic imaginations. Nothing passes the time better than reinvention."

She rubbed at her eyelids, trying to ease the prickle of fatigue. "Maybe there'll be a lot of skaters tomorrow," she said. "I can make chili. Not as thick as I usually do, but they'll be too cold to notice anyway. I'll put in a lot of beans. Beans are cheap."

"My offer still stands."

"I know."

Ritter reached into his coat pocket. "Now that we're thinking clearly," he said, "and since we're on the subject, I have something for you. A bit of Steppe's past." He retrieved a folded piece of paper and held it up. "In my travels over the last few years, I finally had an opportunity to visit Hungary again. Gorgeous country, Hungary. Particularly Budapest. Magnificent architecture, for one. The spires all lit up at night. History in the air. It's breathtaking. And one of my very favourite places to go in Budapest, aside from the spas, of course, is the public library. It's one of the very few places on earth where one still has access to archival materials on microfilm. And during my last visit, between all the thermal baths and the bitters, I stopped into the library and did some research on our dear friend's hometown. Unfortunately it no longer exists; it was wiped out during the Second World War. I did, however, find this."

He handed her the paper. She unfolded it.

It was a printout of an old newspaper clipping, written in Hungarian, from 1940. The colour copier had captured the yellow of the newsprint, the blotches of ink where the press misprinted. The bottom half of the article had been torn away prior to being archived; just above that rip, there appeared three images, three people involved in the story.

Theresa recognized one of them: Steppe, aged fourteen.

She looked at Ritter. "What does it say?"

"It's an article about Steppe's father murdering his brother," he replied.

She stared at the paper. "His father killed his brother?"

"*Twin* brother," Ritter said. "Just like Sylvester."

"He never told me that."

"No, I didn't think so."

"He told you."

He grinned. "We were close once, he and I. Very close. In one of his weaker moments, he told me what happened."

Very close. What did it mean, that Ritter knew and she didn't? She bowed her head, her cheeks suddenly red and burning. "What happened?" she asked, holding the paper up.

"One night his father, in a drunken stupor, strangled one of his sons out of terror of poverty and starvation. Unable to live with what he'd done, he borrowed a neighbour's pistol and shortly thereafter put a bullet in his temple. The second son was never found. They dredged every river within a twenty-five mile radius for seven days but couldn't find a trace of him."

"Did Steppe know what his father did to his brother?"

"He watched it happen."

Theresa cringed.

"He was hiding under the bed when his brother was attacked," Ritter said. "His brother held him back, to keep him safe. And before he died, as is *tradition*—" he said, with bite, "—he passed a piper's voice on to the one he loved most in the world. Steppe has no clue how his brother found the voice. But he admitted to me, the first sound he sucked up and took away with him was the sound his brother made while he was dying. It's the source of all Steppe's power, and all his pain."

Theresa held the paper under the lamp to get a better look. Steppe's father was a plain man, with a marked, brawny aspect to his brows and chin that was almost incompatible with such a tapered face. The photo the editors selected was a three-quarter profile portrait of the man sitting in a chair in a nondescript room, his left arm leaning against a table. His expression was mostly blank, save for a hint of passion in his dark eyes and a slightly brutish twist to his lips.

An image of each of his boys flanked his portrait. Their pale eyes and subtle features were in contrast to their father's; it was clear they owed their handsomeness to their mother's side of the family.

She ran her finger over the images, feeling the paper's glossy finish; stared at them, trying to connect with this part of Steppe's past. Here he was, not only a teenager but cleft in two, his second soul almost an absolute duplicate of the first. Her eyes flicked from left to right, from brother to brother. The tingling in her hands dispersed, and two deep groves formed between her brows. "They switched the names," she said.

"What?"

She held the paper out to him. "Look." She pointed to the image on the left, underneath it, the name *Istvan*. "That's not Steppe," she said. She pointed to the image on the right. "*That's* Steppe." Ritter took the paper from her. "Look carefully," she said. "Look at his eyes. I'd know them anywhere."

He studied the picture. "You're right," he said warily. "Dead ringers, though. The paper must have mixed them up."

"The article's ripped there," she said. The name beneath the second picture was missing. "Did he ever tell you what his brother's name was?" she asked.

He glanced up at her quickly, held her gaze for an instant. "No," was his flat reply. "He didn't."

"Damn it," she muttered. "You think you know someone." She leaned forward to hand the paper back to him.

"Keep it," he said, looking away. "I brought it for you."

She watched him for a while as he picked at his jeans. He looked older, and utterly spent. He stifled a yawn with the back of his hand. "All right, time for bed," she said. "Get up."

"I'm not sleeping in your bed," he said. "The couch will do just fine. I could use a blanket though. I feel naked without one."

Too tired to argue, Theresa pulled a handmade quilt from her linen closet and brought it to him. He stood and unfolded it, emancipating a smell of plywood and mothballs from its knitted fibres, and then laid it, with a dancer's poise, across the loveseat cushions. Another smell mingled with the first when he finally removed his coat and draped it over the armrest: Ritter's own faint, sweet musk.

Theresa gazed at the supple play of muscles beneath his shirt as he bent over and fussed with one of her throw pillows. He hammered at the thing, fluffing it with both hands before tossing it down again.

She reached out for him and wrapped both her arms around his torso, pressed her face against his chest.

He chuckled and returned the gesture, holding her close and swaying back and forth. "It's good to see you too." They stood in each other's arms, their hands clasped behind the other's back. Theresa swallowed and leaned into him, her hips pressing against his thighs. She heard his heart beating, a gentle, steadfast rhythm that reminded her of the grandfather clock in The Welcome's music room. She'd spent many an afternoon in that great, dusty hall, listening to Steppe play his piano for her, watching his fingers deftly sweep over the keys, letting the melodies take her away.

Ritter rested his cheek against the top of her head.

She tilted her face toward his, and kissed him.

He uttered a slight, surprised cry, and his body stiffened as her lips parted. His hands unlocked and moved over her back, over her hips. Her hands climbed up his back, urged him forward, closer to her. He turned her around, eased her onto the couch, and knelt in front of her, his hands on her cheeks, his lips moving against hers, coaxing for more.

He reached for the belt of her robe, held it tightly in his fists, sucked a sharp breath in through his teeth.

They stopped as abruptly as they'd started. She opened her eyes. They gazed at one another, their heavy breathing slowly returning to normal, and everything, all of a sudden, was clear.

"I miss him," she whispered.

He nodded, and drew back. "Good night."

She leapt up from the couch and pulled her robe tighter around herself. Head lowered, she shuffled behind the room divider and threw back the blankets on her bed. She lay down, facing away from the living room, and pulled them up around her ears.

She heard the weight of Ritter's body sink into the loveseat. A moment later he switched the lamp off, and the entire apartment went dark.

Chapter
9

Adoni woke up exhausted. The storm was over and the temperature had dropped. Her temples throbbed with the change in air pressure. By noon she'd taken four painkillers and made her way around campus in a daze. Barely able to concentrate in class, she took frequent breaks from note-taking, rubbed at her eyes, and raked her fingers over her scalp.

Her headache finally cleared up by the time class ended. She decided to go for a swim before heading over to Nathan Phillips Square to check on Theresa. She left the building and headed toward the pool. As she rounded the corner she noticed a young woman walking down Harbord Street toward Spadina Avenue.

Adoni froze. If Natalie hadn't been dressed in a bright purple vintage-style winter coat, Adoni might not have recognized her as she passed.

"Natalie!"

Natalie didn't stop walking, didn't respond. Adoni gritted her teeth and dashed after her. "Wait!" She managed to match Natalie's step, and then all but jumped in front of her. "Hey, wait!"

Natalie finally stopped walking. Their eyes met. Her lips twisted into an awkward smile. "Hi."

"Oh my god, let me hug you!" Adoni threw her arms around her without waiting for permission. "You came back!"

"Yeah..."

"I can't believe you're here! It's been so long! How are you?"

"Oh. Good, I'm good."

"Do you live around here? You didn't go back to your parents' place, did you?" She pulled away.

"I live near Parkdale," Natalie replied.

"That's great!"

"Well…" She chuckled. "I don't live in the great part."

"Whatever, you've got your own place, that's nice! Are you going to school or do you work?"

"I work. Actually I'm going to work right now."

"Really? Where do you work?"

"Down in Kensington Market."

"That's great! I always pictured you working down there. I should visit you! What store do you work at?"

Natalie paused a moment before answering. "Um… at The Spill. It's a café. Do you know it?"

"I've seen it but I've never been inside. Wow, that's great! Do you like it?"

"Yeah, yeah. Yeah, I like it a lot."

Adoni cocked an eyebrow at her. "Are you okay? I didn't freak you out by stopping you just now, did I?"

"No, no. Of course not."

"I saw you the other night outside Lee's Palace. I tried to get your attention but you didn't hear me."

"Oh yeah? Sorry, I just…" Natalie looked past Adoni's shoulder, her eyes fixed on the horizon.

Adoni's heart started to sink. "Hey… you remember me, right?"

Natalie's grin didn't waver. "Um… Sorry…"

"Adoni."

"Oh, yeah…"

"It's Adoni. Remember? I met you in the In-Between when we were kids."

"Yeah, sorry, I just…" She chuckled and pointed at her temple. "Space cadet."

Adoni frowned. "You don't remember me at all? I spent the night in your cabin that one time. The changelings attacked, and you made me an axe to use against them. We tried to get to Ansgar's fortress, but we had a fight and you didn't come with me."

Natalie nodded. "Right."

"What do you mean, 'right?' Don't you remember?"

She shrugged. "To be honest, the last few years are... like, a blur."

"A *blur*? You have to remember the In-Between. Steppe and Ritter and Reese? Do you remember Paj? She sang you away in the first place."

Natalie shook her head. "Listen, I can't... I can't really explain it, okay? Some things are just... they're gone."

Adoni felt her face grow hot. "You're messing with me."

Natalie winced as though she'd been slapped in the face. Her eyes, a startling shade of grey against her black hair, gazed down at the snowy sidewalk. "I'm not. I'm not. You sound like you know me, and I believe you, I just don't..."

"You don't know me." They stared at each other until Natalie shook her head. A winter breeze brought the smell of Natalie's perfume to Adoni's nose. Her shoulders sagged. "You have to remember something about the In-Between. You were there for years. We can't have all just dropped out of your head."

"I remember going to sleep one night a few years ago," Natalie said. "And then... I'm just walking up the street one afternoon a few years later. I don't even remember waking up. It feels like I just appeared."

"You don't remember the pipers? The changelings? The *agate*?"

Natalie laughed. "Give me the name of your dealer. I want the same stuff you smoke."

"I'm serious! You don't remember the cabins or the hope chests or the other kids? You don't remember the fires or the singing or *anything*?"

Natalie's smile grew wider. "That sounds nice."

"*Nice*?"

"Well, yeah. Cabins, hope chests..."

"The In-Between's not *nice*, it's a *prison*! The kids can't leave unless they're kicked out, and the whole thing's run by—"

"I'm sorry, I don't even… Well, I mean, if that's a prison, it sounds pretty sweet to me."

"No, no, no, you're bullshitting me. You *have* to be. You can stop smiling now. This isn't funny."

"Look, I should really get to work."

Adoni shook her head.

"I don't want to be late," Natalie said. "Listen, if you want to talk some more about… things, you can always visit the café. I usually work afternoons. You can stop in if you want. I can take care of your drink too." She shrugged her purse higher on her shoulder. "I'm really sorry. Maybe I'll see you there, okay? It's Adoni, right?"

"Right."

"See you around, okay?" With a small smile and a half-hearted wave, she continued on her way. Adoni bit her lip to keep it from trembling.

She reached the Square and saw the Reesemobile parked in its usual spot. A short line-up of patrons stood in front of her serving window. Adoni hoped the crowd meant it would be a successful day. She strolled up alongside the truck and kept out of view until the last customer left with his late lunch, then approached the window.

Theresa noticed her arrival and smirked. "Forget something last night?"

Adoni put her hand to her forehead. "Shit, I was supposed to text you! I totally forgot! I'm so sorry! Were you worried?"

Theresa opened the back door, and Adoni climbed inside. "I basically went to bed after you left," she said. "I'm lucky Ritter doesn't snore."

"He fit on your couch?"

"Barely. I bet he's all cramped up now. It's his own fault, I offered him the bed."

Adoni sat on the milk crate in the corner. "How's today been?"

"Pretty good sales, actually," Theresa said. "The chili's popular because it's so damn cold. It's really beany." She stepped up to her stove and ladled a portion into a bowl, then handed it to Adoni.

"No, no," Adoni said with a shake of her head. "Sell that. I'm not even hungry."

"You're always hungry," Theresa said. "Come on, a bowl isn't going to break the bank for me." She held it out with a firm and steady hand.

"I can't, really. I'm not hungry." Adoni folded her arms and curled over her lap. Her gaze dropped to the dusty floor.

"What's wrong?" Theresa asked. She put the bowl on the counter and crouched in front of Adoni.

"I saw Natalie on my way to the pool."

Theresa shook her head. "Jeez, when it rains it pours. Are you okay?"

"No," she said. Theresa handed her a pile of napkins. Adoni clutched them in her fist. "She didn't remember me."

"Oh, come on!"

"I mean it. She had no idea who I was."

"You're kidding."

Adoni shook her head.

"How can she not remember you? That's ridiculous."

"It's not just me. She doesn't remember anything about the In-Between. I asked her about it, and she looked at me like I was nuts."

"I don't believe it."

"I'm serious. I mentioned your name, Steppe's, Ritter's, the night we... When we spent the night together. She said the last few years were a *blur*."

"A *blur*?"

"She doesn't remember any of it."

"That's crazy. Are you sure it was Natalie and not just someone who looked a lot like her?"

"She didn't say I had the wrong person."

Theresa sighed. "This might sound harsh, but do you think she's pretending not to know so she can... I don't know, get on with her life here?"

"But why would she even do that? Maybe she'd lie to her other friends, but why would she lie to me like that? There's no point if she knows I won't believe her."

Theresa frowned. "That's very strange."

Adoni kissed her teeth. "She was probably high or something. She just had this goofy grin on her face the whole time. You know the face you make when someone you don't like starts talking to you, and you're just waiting for them to go away? That's how she looked." She smoothed the napkins out on her thigh.

Theresa started to speak when a new customer approached her serving window. Adoni stared at her lap as Theresa took and prepared the guest's order. The moment he was gone, she turned back to her. "I don't know what to say, honey, except I think she's lying, and I don't know why she would. She's got nothing to gain by it."

"Do you think she's ashamed of me?"

"Come on! No way, why would she be ashamed of you?"

Adoni crumpled the napkins. "I don't know."

"If she's ashamed of you, then to hell with her."

Adoni shot a quick glance at the bowl of chili, still on the counter and slowly losing its steam. Theresa smiled and handed it to her. She dug in. "Holy beans. Don't stand downwind of me after I eat this, eh?"

"Is it too much? I had a ton of them, and I cut the vegetables up really small."

"Still tasty." Adoni finished her mouthful. "So Ritter left this morning?"

Theresa nodded. "Made him some toast, and then he headed out. He said he'd be here later."

"And he doesn't snore?" She looked up from her bowl. Theresa was leaning against the back counter and staring out the serving window, the corners of her lips drawn down in a pensive grimace. "What?"

"If I tell you something, will you promise to keep it a secret?"

"Yeah."

"I kissed Ritter last night."

Adoni beamed at her. "Really? Like a sexy kiss?"

"It was pretty sexy."

"No way! Is he a good kisser?"

"*Amazing* kisser."

"That's because he's got *experience*. Are you guys getting together?"

"No, no. I was just... I was missing Steppe, and Ritter was there, and he just reminded me of..." She ran her fingers through her hair before reaching down and grasping the hem of her apron. "Steppe would freak out if he knew I kissed another guy."

"Why? You're not his girlfriend anymore."

"He'd be hurt all the same. Especially if he knew it was Ritter. That would end their friendship, for sure. What friendship they have, anyway. I don't really know what's up."

Adoni sneered. "Guys still get upset about stuff like that?"

"Are you kidding?"

"Well, Steppe's different. You know any other guys dumb enough to stop being friends because of a woman?"

"I know four. John, Paul, George, and Ringo."

Adoni polished off the chili while Theresa served another two customers. Theresa leaned out the serving window and looked up into the overcast sky. "I think we're good for storms for a few days," she said. "It's going to get dark soon."

"Have you been keeping an eye out while you've been here?"

"Yeah, but I know Sylvester wouldn't try anything in daylight. He'd wait until after sunset." She stepped up to her counter and fished a bag of carrots out of the refrigerator. "I've got so much prep to do."

Adoni stood and tossed her empty bowl in the compost bin. She caught sight of a black smudge of clothing on her periphery. Ritter was making his way across the street. He held his saxophone case in his hand. "Ritter's coming."

"Don't tell him what I told you, okay?"

Adoni nodded as Ritter, sporting a toothy grin, sidled up to the truck. "I'm a Buddhist..." he began.

"That's *my* joke!" Adoni said. "You have to change yours."

"Change comes from within."

"You both suck," Theresa called out.

Adoni opened the truck's back door. Ritter peered around the frame and eyed Theresa's spread before hoisting himself up. He stooped to keep from banging his head against the ceiling. "These are cramped quarters," he said as he looked about. "It smells nice in here."

"Are you hungry?"

"Not in the slightest. I've had my fill of dumplings from a charming little place in China Town." He backed into a corner, turned over an empty pail, and sat on it. "How goes the day?"

"Good," Theresa said with an enthusiastic nod. "Some good sales."

"And you, Donny?"

Adoni rolled the napkins into a ball. "You know how I told you I saw Natalie on Sunday? I saw her again when I was at school."

"Indeed. What did our Natty have to say for herself? Did she tell you her impetus for finally leaving the In-Between?"

"No. She said she doesn't remember it."

Ritter's brow wrinkled. He glanced at Theresa, who looked back at him and shrugged. "What do you mean?" he asked.

"I mean she doesn't remember the In-Between. She doesn't remember you or the other pipers. She doesn't remember me either. At least, that's what she said." Adoni crossed her arms over her broad chest.

He shook his head. "Tell me exactly what she said."

Adoni went through the entire conversation, trying her best to match Natalie's inflections. Ritter listened intently, interrupting her only once to ask for clarification. All the while Adoni spoke, Theresa chopped her remaining vegetables, dumped them into stainless steel trays, covered them in foil, and put them back in the refrigerator.

By the time Adoni finished telling him everything, Ritter was frowning. She waited for him to break the silence, to say something, anything, to make the conversation seem less fraught. Theresa, too, stopped what she was doing and stared at him, until his body finally shifted and he put a sentence together. "That's not right," he muttered softly. "That's not right at all." He looked from Theresa to Adoni. "That sounds like Ansgar's work."

The women stared at him.

"Does Tyler remember the In-Between?" he asked.

"I think so," Adoni replied. "We don't talk about it."

"Ever?"

"We can't. My mom won't leave me alone with him. But he still only ever talks to me. I don't think he would if he didn't remember anything. He knows we're buds."

"What are you thinking?" Theresa asked him.

Another stretch of silence. He tented his fingers under his chin. "Are you sure it was Natalie you were speaking to?"

"She may have dyed her hair, but I know what she looks like. She even answered me when I called her."

"Did she seem to know where she was? Was she lucid?"

"She knows her name, she lives in Parkdale, and she works at The Spill in Kensington."

"Could she tell she was speaking with a human being?"

"What? Yeah, I guess so."

"What did she smell like?"

"What did she *smell* like?" Theresa huffed. "What kind of question is that?"

"Did she smell sort of... plastic?" Ritter asked.

Adoni shook her head. "She smelled like... I don't know, like perfume I guess. She smelled nice."

"Was she wearing a lot of it?"

Adoni snorted. "Why are you asking me all this?"

Ritter tilted his head. "I don't think you were talking to Natalie."

"Okay, so who was I talking to, the pope?"

"I think you were talking to a changeling spy."

She stared at him. "Why do you think that?"

"We left on the eve of an uprising," he said. "A night when the pipers' power outweighed the changelings'. I know Sylvester would have paid her a visit, if only to get her to even the score. He must have told her about you, about what you did to him. Ansgar's given Sylvester an advantage. I can feel it. And if she's gone back on her word to never breed another changeling... for any purpose..." He cracked three of his knuckles. "Did Natalie give you a way of contacting her?"

"She told me she'd buy me a drink if I visit her at The Spill."

"And you think you can tell the real Natalie from a changeling?"

"Yeah, I mean... I know what she smells like."

"She's at work now, is she?"

"That's where she said she was going."

"All right. I'll be right back."

He slipped out of the truck. Adoni stuck her head out the back door. "Are you going to her work?"

"Stay with Reese," he called. She watched him flag down a taxicab and climb into the back seat.

"See, if he had a *phone* he could just call the place and ask to talk to her," Adoni said to Theresa.

"I don't think you can tell if someone's a changeling by just talking over the phone," she replied.

"But she didn't *act* like a changeling. I mean, she was spacey and weird, but she still seemed... I don't know, isn't it supposed to be really obvious when you're talking to a changeling? Ritter told me that once, that you can always tell when you're talking to one. You can tell Sylvester's one just by the way he moves. She moved the way she always did. The way I remember she moved, anyway. You even said it once too; you said they're like dolls because they don't have souls."

"Right."

"She seemed like she had a soul. And why would Ansgar want to spy on me anyway, when I'm stuck here?"

"I can only think of one reason: because if anyone's going to lead her to Ritter, it's you."

Adoni gritted her teeth. "I hate that little monster."

Theresa served the occasional guest while they waited for Ritter to return. He pulled up in the same cab less than an hour later. Adoni watched him march up to the Reesemobile. "You look pissed off," she said as he climbed into the back of the truck. "Did you talk to her?"

"No. She wasn't there." He sat down on the milk crate.

Adoni frowned. "What does that mean? Do you think she was lying to me about where she works?"

"She works there all right. Her co-worker told me she didn't show up."

"Where the hell did she go? She told me she was going to work. Do you think she didn't show up because she was afraid I'd drop by?"

"Maybe she called in sick," Theresa said.

"Maybe she's not Natalie at all," Ritter said. "Maybe Ansgar's given Sylvester a changeling slave to do his dirty work on this side. Maybe she'll breed herself an army and destroy everyone still living at The Welcome. Damn her."

And then he said, "I have to go back."

Adoni shook her head. "Wait a minute. Before you said you couldn't go back. Now you *have to*?"

"If Ansgar's breeding changelings again it's because she thinks they're expendable. Have you ever looked into the face of a creature who doesn't know his life is worthless?"

"But you're not even sure if she's a changeling!"

"I'm as sure as I need to be. Damn her. She can't *do this*."

"How would she even know who Natalie is or what she looks like? Sylvester couldn't have told her. He doesn't know her."

"I'm not sure what he knows, Donny."

Adoni folded her arms across her chest. "Then I'm going with you."

"No you're not."

She glared at him. "If you're going, I'm going too, that's it."

"Not a chance. Your impatience alone is a liability."

"You knew me when I was fourteen," she snapped. "And you haven't seen me in years. You don't know who I am anymore. You wanna find out? Then let me come with you."

"I told you before, you're no good for war."

"Oh, and you're good for war?" She leaned forward, her chin thrust out, her eyes burning. "That's funny, coming from someone who spent his whole life hiding from it." Adoni dropped the napkins, now a damp and shredded mess, into the garbage bin.

"Yes," he said quietly. "Right again."

Her heart sank. "Don't be like that, man. I want to go back too. Not just for Natalie. If I don't I'll just feel… like everything's unfinished."

"I understand," he said. "All right."

"I'm sorry, I just—"

He held his hand up. "Donny. Enough."

Theresa's brow puckered. "You're going tonight?"

"Damn it," he murmured. "You must think I'm a cad, running off after that histrionic display last night."

"I told you you're no hero," she replied.

He stood quickly, knocking the milk crate aside. His body unfurled to its full height. The top of his head grazed the ceiling. "Yes, you did say that, didn't you?" he hissed.

Adoni caught sight of the flush of anxiety in Theresa's cheeks, a scarlet plume that also found its way onto Ritter's face. They stood silently for a time, until Ritter took a deep breath and squared his stance. "We'll go when you're safe at home," he said to Theresa. "At the end of your shift, when it's dark."

"Are we gonna go talk to Ansgar?" Adoni asked.

"The Welcome pipers should be able to shed some light on all of this. We'll pay them a visit and ask them what they know. They may be able to clear things up without our having to face Ansgar at all."

Adoni frowned. Her whole reason for returning was to confront Ansgar, to make her pay for what she'd done. But she knew Ritter wouldn't bring her with him if she insisted on travelling to the fortress. "We can go after my mom falls asleep," she said instead. "I'll tell her I have an early class tomorrow, so if she wakes up in the morning and I'm not there, she'll think I'm at school." She addressed Ritter again. "Meet me in the alleyway at… like…"

"Midnight, I assume."

"Mom goes to sleep before then, so I can sneak out."

Ritter gave her a single nod and yanked down the hem of his coat, snapping out the wrinkles. "I'll be back at ten," he told Theresa.

"If it makes you feel better," she replied.

Adoni followed Theresa's gaze; she was looking at Ritter oddly, coolly, and rolling her fingers against her empty palms. Adoni stood between them. "We're coming back though, okay?" she said. "We'll tell you what we find out, first thing." She turned back to Ritter.

"If you see Steppe…" Theresa began.

"Only if he says hello first," Ritter finished. The look he gave her was equally detached. "Of course. We'd never give you away." He looked at Adoni. "Midnight sharp," he said, before ducking out of the truck. She heard the heels of his boots grinding chunks of winter salt into powder as he walked away.

Chapter
10

Adoni nibbled a fingernail on the ride home from the Square. She knew Ritter could be temperamental; she'd gotten a taste of his mood swings at The Welcome. He could be sharp with his words, and he could fix such an unforgiving scowl on his face that others would shrink with embarrassment. His outburst that evening, however, was more than just Ritter being his old capricious self. He had run away from duty on more than one occasion in order to survive. The rest of the pipers called him a coward for it ever since. Theresa had come close enough to calling him a coward to bring out the worst in him.

Adoni couldn't stop herself from picturing them in the throes of a passionate embrace, lips locked and arms entwined, and wondering if Ritter's stab of temper at being chided had something to do with what took place between them the night before.

Adoni chewed her nail down to the quick as the bus reached her stop. She disembarked and trudged up the street, through the aftermath of last night's storm, and arrived at her front door with soaking wet boots and sore thighs. She put her ear to the wood and listened carefully; silence.

Ida strolled out from her bedroom as Adoni stepped into the front hall. "Hi baby," she chirped as she went into the kitchen. "I bought some cold cuts if you want to make a sub for dinner." She turned her back and opened the refrigerator.

"Maybe later. I went by Reese's, and she gave me some chili."

Ida withdrew from the refrigerator holding the plastic jug full of apple drink. She put the jug down on the counter with a hard knock. "Really? Do you like her chili?"

"Too beany today," Adoni replied as she hung up her coat and slipped out of her boots. "It's usually got more meat and vegetables in it."

"Beans are good for you. Didn't Reese teach you that?" She pulled a clean glass off of the dish rack and poured herself a drink. The juice splashed up from the bottom, sprinkling the counter with yellow drops.

Adoni dropped her backpack on the couch and ambled into the kitchen. Ida chugged the entire glass of apple drink and immediately poured herself another. Adoni sighed and retrieved the fixings for a sandwich. "It was basically beans with some chili around it," she said as she hunched over and pulled a head of lettuce out of the vegetable crisper. "Yours is better." She spread the ingredients out on the counter and glanced at Ida, whose fitted frown became a tiny, grateful smile. Ida pulled up a stool, sat down, and opened one of the magazines she'd brought home from the supermarket.

Adoni kept an eye on her mother as she put her sandwich together. Ida's smile stayed where it was as she turned down each glossy page. The sordid lives of reality TV stars filled every inch of space. The headlines screamed at their readers in blocky, hot pink letters. Ida lifted an arm and leaned her head against it, gazing at the magazine as though she were sifting through one of her treasured photo albums. Adoni spread a thin layer of mayonnaise on a slice of bread while hiding a grin of her own. Her mother must have already devoured every glimpse of cellulite and rumour of divorce in that rag. It hit Adoni right then, square in the stomach: she was making a sandwich on the eve of her return to the In-Between. That night, when Ida—who loved gossip magazines and smoked more than ever—Ida, who'd held on to the same job for more than a year now, and called her daughter "baby"—was asleep, Adoni would sneak out and join Ritter in the alleyway, and finally go back to the vast, frozen expanse of land she'd been dreaming of.

The first time she stepped foot in the In-Between she didn't want to come back. She was angry and hurt, and it was easy to jump through the agate, close at Ritter's heels. She'd been running from something then. Tonight, though, she was running toward something; answers, a key to the histories of people she cared about—Steppe, and Natalie.

And she wanted nothing more than a chance to take Ansgar down.

But leaving with everything around her, Ida included, just like this, was infinitely harder than dashing out the door in a fit of anger. She had just gotten used to seeing her mother smile again. It didn't seem right, or fair, to lie to her, especially when Adoni knew how much her first disappearance had terrified her, and how difficult it was for her mother to trust her again. If something prevented Adoni from coming back home on time, or at all, Ida would be devastated.

I'll be careful, she thought. *So that takes care of that. But…*

"You didn't introduce me to your friend yesterday."

Ida looked up from the magazine. "Sure I did."

Adoni shook her head and took a bite of her sandwich. "No you didn't."

"Try not talking with your mouth full."

Adoni swallowed. "You told me what his name was, but you didn't tell him mine."

"He knows who you are."

"What do you mean, he knows who I am?"

Ida closed the magazine and pushed it to the end of the counter. "I only have one kid."

"So he's met me before?"

Ida frowned. "What are you getting at?" Adoni shrugged. "I told him about you," Ida said.

"Okay." A pause. "How much?"

Ida slid off the stool. "As much as he *should* know," she replied. "I haven't seen him in a long time. I told him all about you before you got home. Anyway, we had a lot of catching up to do. We talked about a lot of things." She left the kitchen and sat down on the living room couch.

"He seemed like he knew me already."

"He's like that. He's really friendly. You know when you meet someone, and they're friendly? They make you feel like they've known you forever. It's his smile. He's got a great smile."

Adoni put her sandwich down. "I've got a really early class tomorrow," she said. "Just so you know."

"Okay." Ida retrieved another magazine from the coffee table and flipped to the table of contents.

"Mom?"

"Yeah?"

"Did you know Kofi before I was born or after?"

"Before," Ida replied, without looking up.

Okay.

Adoni wrapped the sandwich in wax paper and put it in the fridge. "I'm gonna take the rest for lunch tomorrow," she said.

"Sure."

She skirted around the kitchen counter and crossed the room to the CD player. She ran her finger over the jewel cases, her thumbnail down their plastic spines, until she found the album she was looking for. She put the disc in the player, skipped ahead to the song she wanted to hear, turned the volume up loud enough to discourage conversation. Then she sat down on the couch and curled up against her mother's side.

The song began to play: Led Zeppelin's "Stairway to Heaven."

First, a single guitar echoing in an empty room, the strings plucked expertly, lovingly. Next, a chorus of flutes woven together, playing in solidarity. Finally, a voice, raspy and thin, singing about a woman, about the stairs and the signs, about gold, about greed, and desire; one voice, swelling and fading as the melodies joined each other. There was always something sad about the way the song began, an impenetrable loneliness about the tune in those early bars. But then, a change: the flutes receded, the voice gained strength, the guitar was joined by another, and all the while the tune remained the same; a strange and splendid alchemy. Adoni leaned her head against her mother's shoulder. And then the drums kicked in.

Ida wrapped her arm around her and squeezed.

They listened as rock replaced the melancholy, as the instruments, having found the guts to brag about how unstoppable they were, signed a pact and banded together. Guitar and bass and drums and vocals erased those downhearted opening moments, picked up the tempo, vibrated with colour. Every solo stood perfect among its peers, bits of melody and harmony breaking the surface and soaring for a few precious seconds. All of it throbbing, all together, until a heart could break, until everything stopped, and that single note sang the rest of them away.

"I'm gonna go to bed," Ida said. She leaned over and kissed the top of Adoni's head before heading to her bedroom.

Just in case...

"Love you," Adoni said before Ida was out of earshot.

"Love you too, baby." Her bedroom door latch slid softly into the jamb.

Adoni turned the CD player off and waited, in silence, until she heard Ida snoring in her sleep.

Chapter
11

At ten minutes to ten, Ritter made his way to Nathan Phillips Square. He carried himself through the streets on measured steps, looking left and right and taking note of every pedestrian who seemed to be going his way. The temperature had dipped to well below freezing. He crossed his arms for warmth and leaned into the wind. He wiped his face with the back of his hand; this weather was nothing, he knew. Compared to the plunging temperatures and the blizzards that hammered away at The Welcome's doors and windows, it was positively balmy.

He reached the corner of Queen Street and squeezed his wind-chapped hands into fists. The clock in the tower at Old City Hall struck ten. The bell sounded off with a heavy gong, and Ritter craned his neck to see where Theresa had parked. Other food trucks lined the street, each selling its own version of hot dogs and greasy chips. Theresa's purple truck would distinguish itself between the beams of pale white light coming from the other serving windows.

Ritter stopped in the middle of the sidewalk. The truck was there, though the serving window was shut for the night. He could hear Cuban Son Montuno music being loudly played over her shoddy radio's speakers. He scowled and approached the truck. "You know," he said, peering through the open doors, "loud music isn't going to scare him off. Especially when it's so infectiously upbeat."

Theresa glanced at him before returning to wiping down the counters.

Stubborn woman, he thought. He climbed up into the truck. "These doors should be locked."

"I dropped some grease on the burner," she said. "I had to air the place out."

"The air seems pretty clear to me."

"You think so?"

He sighed. He should have known better than to snarl at her the way he did. Theresa was sensitive, despite all her blustering, and it would be a long time before he forgot the uneasy look on her face when he snapped at her. It was more than just shock at being told off by a friend.

Afraid I'd hit her, he realized, and his stomach sank. *I'd never... not ever, not in a million years.* But she couldn't have been sure; not when he'd risen up so quickly. Not when there had been such fire behind his eyes.

"Let's play a game. It's called 'be angry at Ritter forever.' Do you know it?"

"Know it? I'm a pro."

"All right missus, I'm sorry for my outburst this afternoon. I behaved badly. Mind you," he said, crossing his arms and leaning against the wall, "it would be nice if you acknowledged your part in the matter."

"What?" She stood up and tossed her dishcloth aside.

"You heard me. I'm referring to the snarky little remark you made at my expense."

"I was teasing you. It's not my fault you don't have a sense of humour."

"Well, darling, some people can tell a joke, and some people can't. You fall in the latter group. Your timing alone. *Phew!* Atrocious."

"Oh, and *you're* a funny guy, eh?"

"I'm waiting for an apology."

"You're right," she said. "I should've locked the doors." She went back to tidying up her kitchen.

"It occurs to me," he said, "that I don't know much about your past." She thrust her hand into a drawer and pulled out several bungee cords. "Steppe sang you away to the In-Between when you were, what, fourteen? You must have been running from something. Violence, or the drink, or a combination of the two. Or something worse."

"I'm not up for a therapy session. I've been working all day."

"I should have been kinder to you."

"Great, that's just great. I told you before, I don't need your pity."

"I'm not here out of pity."

"And by the way, you've got a lot of nerve pulling this psychobabble shit on me and then asking for an apology."

"Actually, I asked for the apology first and then got into the psychobabble shit, but who's keeping track?"

She tossed the bungee cords onto the counter. "I don't like to be yelled at."

"I've already apologized for it. Twice, in fact."

"You can be so smug sometimes."

"Indeed. Why don't we cut to the chase, eh? You and I have had our disagreements in the past. I'm positive I've raised my voice to you before. Since when are you so sensitive about that?"

"Since you came back after being MIA for a few years and then expected to get away with talking to me like that."

He laughed. "You would have preferred if our relationship had regressed to something more formal in the meantime? I don't believe it. You admitted it all last night. You're exhausted from running this place by yourself. You're stressed about making ends meet. I think seeing me out of the blue reminds you that we left so much unfinished in the In-Between, and that makes you angry. And then there's..." He winked at her.

She rolled her eyes. "Are you actually saying that because we kissed I'm just acting extra butthurt?"

"Reese, I'm teasing you." He wagged his finger at her. "Now who's the one without a sense of humour?"

She turned to her cash register and stabbed her finger down on the "no sale" button. The drawer spat open. She dug into the pile of nickels and counted out a dollar's worth from her palm. "All right, so you've come to check on me and here I am, safe and sound. Satisfied? Why don't you go meet up with Adoni now and get on with it?" She flung the nickels back into the register and began counting out another dollar's worth.

Ah, he thought. *There it is.*

"I'd prefer to see you all the way home, if it's all right with you," he said.

"I don't need you to take me home. I've got my truck and a full tank of gas. And you're getting on my nerves."

He gritted his teeth. "You're absolutely right. You're a grown woman, you don't need an escort." He leaned out the back of the truck. "I'll meet you at your apartment. Promise you'll keep the doors closed and locked." He glanced over his shoulder. Theresa quickly looked away. "Goodnight, Reese."

"See you," she muttered.

He closed the doors behind him and immediately hailed a cab. In a minute, he was on his way.

The driver quickly picked up speed and whizzed by the department stores that made Queen Street famous. Ritter smirked at a display of a mannequin family preparing to venture down a virtual ski slope. Two adult and two child-sized dummies standing straight, staring ahead, with poles taped to the palms of their hands: captives in time with vapid expressions on their synthetic faces. How long did Theresa have to play at happy family, before she found herself on The Welcome's doorstep? He'd never asked, so he didn't know.

I'll make it up to her.

The ride afforded him one last look at the city he loved. He took in all the sights he'd grown fond of: the sweaty windows of coffee shops and restaurants, the queues of concert goers lining up behind velvet ropes, spires of churches reaching into the blackened sky. He cracked the window and smelled logs and newspaper burning away in fireplaces, tasted the smoky air on his tongue. He couldn't deny the In-Between's gloomy magnificence, but nothing could excite his senses quite like a night out on the town.

As the cab approached Victoria Street he heard the primal thumping

CHARLENE CHALLENGER

of a bass guitar and drums. Massey Hall's neon sign cast a vivid red glow over the sidewalk. The doors were shut, the show inside just beginning. The band, whoever it was, thundered through the stone façade: guitars, drums, loops, synths. The musicians played with ferocious precision, effortlessly switching back and forth between time signatures as though they commanded time itself. Ritter hadn't heard this syncopated pop before, with every layer playing on top of the next and soaring with joy. This is what first drew him to the city; there was so much music to be heard. And it was everywhere, playing live, every evening, into the wee morning hours. It had been a long time since music had stirred him so. He wanted to remember this loaded evening. He parted his lips and opened his throat, and as the driver passed the venue, Ritter closed his eyes and drew the music's veiny reverberation into his lungs, knotting it into his voice, making it a part of himself. He sighed gently. The newly acquired rumble tickled his chest. The song was his forever.

The moment he arrived at Theresa's apartment, a dreadful feeling settled in his chest. He waited in the cold until two young men approached the building and managed to slip into the lobby behind them. *Look at that. They're not paying the slightest attention. If Sylvester finds out where Theresa lives, he can easily...*

Damn it. Me and my pride. I shouldn't have left her alone.

He jabbed at the elevator button until the car arrived, then dashed inside and selected Theresa's floor.

He waited outside her apartment for what felt like an age. *How long does it take to pack that buggy up?* he wondered. *Unless she's already here.* He knocked on her door. No answer. He knocked again, harder and faster. Again, no response. He put his ear to the wood, hoping to catch the sound of her heels on the floor, or the kettle boiling on the stove. Perhaps she was ignoring him on purpose. He knocked again—softer this time, an attempt to sound contrite. Silence.

Damn it. This is what Adoni meant by needing a phone.

It was too late to retrace the ride to the Square; Adoni was expecting him for midnight, and there was no way to contact her to let her know Theresa hadn't shown up at her apartment, and he would be late. He rummaged through his pockets until he found a scrap of paper and a pencil, and scrawled a note.

Reese,

Forgive me for being an ass this afternoon. If you get this note before midnight, send a message to Adoni to let us know you're safe. I hear telephones can do that now.

Love, always—you know that,

Ritter

He folded the paper up and shoved it under the door.

He reached Adoni's apartment just before midnight and stepped into the alley to wait. Piles of snow crowded the space between the buildings. The neighbours, not bothering to brush off the lids on the dustbins, had heaped their trash bags in the centre of the shovelled path, a few feet from the mouth of the alley. Ritter rolled his eyes and pressed himself against the wall, where he hoped to be out of sight from the street. The cold air kept the trash from stinking, but the thought of standing so close to refuse made him queasy. He had only a sideline view of Adoni's bedroom window and couldn't see her shadow moving behind the pane. He decided to wait in the alley on the opposite side of the building, away from the filth, until the stroke of midnight.

The opposite alley was wider and brighter, which increased the risk of being spotted, but cleaner. Ritter leaned against the wall and stared at the bricks, until his eyes unfocused and the individual squares blurred together. His mind wandered through the events of the last few days. It was easier for him to dwell on the past rather than to consider the future and what he and Adoni were about to do. He took a breath and let it leave his lips on a single, low note.

It was loud enough.

A light went on in the window above his head. A shadow approached the glass. Ritter caught the movement too late and had no time to step out of sight. The curtains parted, and two bright black eyes peered out over the ledge.

Ritter froze.

Tyler.

The boy stared down at him. Neither one of them moved. Recognition flooded Tyler's face. A moment later, he was gone.

Ritter's heart started racing. He scurried out of the alley and across the lawn. Adoni had just stepped from the building's foyer, her backpack slung over her shoulder, looking very much like a student on her way to class. "Hey," she said. "Are you just getting here?"

"We have to go now," he blurted out, grabbing her arm and pulling her toward the piles of trash. Adoni slipped and nearly toppled over.

"Wait a sec! You want me to fall and break my neck?"

"We have to—"

The front door swung open. Tyler bounded down the steps toward them. He wore a thin jacket over two sweaters and a pair of vinyl boots. He'd pulled his woollen cap down low, to the point where it almost covered his eyes. Instead of pushing it off his brow he lifted his chin and looked up into Ritter's face. Ritter shot Adoni a look. She held his gaze for a moment, then turned to Tyler. "What's up bud? It's late, eh?"

"Donny," Ritter murmured.

"You remember Ritter?" she asked Tyler. "You remember what happened?"

Tyler reached out, took her hand, and nodded. "I'm coming too."

Ritter's legs started to shake. He took Adoni's other hand and urged the two of them into the narrow alleyway.

"You better stay here," Adoni gently told the boy when the three of them were out of sight. "We don't even know what we're gonna be dealing with."

"I'm coming too," he repeated.

She shook her head and let go of his hand. "No way, you have to go home."

He stood next to Ritter and grabbed onto his sleeve.

"Come on, Tyler, you just can't," she said. "It's not safe. You remember last time? The changelings?"

"Make her let me come too," he said to Ritter, pointing at Adoni.

She folded her arms. "We can't take you, okay? Go back upstairs."

"I'm coming too!"

Adoni's lip quivered. "Why? So you can have your little cabin and play with your hope chest again? All that stuff's gone, understand? I messed the whole thing up before I left. It's not a pretty place anymore. It's gonna be dangerous."

"No it's not," he said. "You can sing."

Adoni gripped the straps on her backpack and glared at Tyler. "Your mom'll wake up and find out you're gone, and she'll go over to my place and wake my mom up, and she'll find out I'm gone, and we'll both get in shit..."

"Mom's not home."

"Where'd she go?"

Tyler shook his head.

"When did she leave?" Adoni pressed. Another shake. "Why didn't you come over when she didn't show up?"

Tyler brushed his hand across his forehead, finally pushing his hat above his eyebrows. He sucked in his bottom lip and glared at her.

Ritter pinched the bridge of his nose. He felt as though something inside him had cracked open and now lay bare and bleeding in his chest. He looked at Adoni. "We can't leave him here."

Adoni stared at him. "He'll get hurt," she said at last.

"We'll look out for him."

"He can just use the spare key and go into my place!" she said. "Him and his mom both know where it is. He can camp out on the couch until morning. Mom'll even make you breakfast," she said, turning back to Tyler.

"Toast and eggs and everything. You'll be safe. Go back inside."

"We can't leave him behind."

Ritter's face grew hot under her gaze. "We're not *leaving him behind*," she said. "He belongs here."

"Donny."

She rolled her eyes. "First nobody can go but you, and now everybody can. Want me to go get my mom too?"

"I was wrong. I can be wrong sometimes, can't I?"

"It takes you five seconds to say yes to him, and I had to practically beg!"

"Another time, Donny, please."

She stepped up close to him. "What's the matter with you?" she asked. "First you snap at Reese, now you're all flustered..."

Cheeks burning, he took a sharp step backwards. "Because I'm fucking terrified, all right?" He clasped his hands together and squeezed. "I thought I could go alone but I can't. I need you with me. I need an *army* with me. I need as many people as can wrap their arms around me, to keep me from shaking out of my skin. All right?"

He heard footsteps approaching. A young couple, holding hands, traipsed over the stretch of sidewalk in front of the building. Ritter listened to their giggles and chatter recede as they passed, then turned to face Adoni's relentless glare.

"You'd risk his life just so you can feel *safe*?"

I've left children behind before, he wanted to say. *You don't know what happens to you, when you leave a child who needs you behind. Everything changes. Everything.*

He whispered a single word, as sour as bile at the back of his throat. "Yes."

Adoni said nothing.

Ritter put a finger against his lip and hummed softly. There was a swish, like the sound of a sword slicing through the air, and there it was, rippling before them like so many tongues of blue and orange flame.

The agate. The way back.

Ritter stared at the portal. He held out his hand. No one moved.

Please take it, he thought. *Someone.*

Adoni stuck out her chin. He let his arm drop down to his side.

Each one of them took a breath and one last look at the snow and the trash and the brick walls around them. Ritter took the first step through.

Chapter
12

With one great swoosh, it all came rushing back to her: the dizziness, the pounding in her ears as the air around her bent and stretched, the buzzing in her arms and legs, hands and feet, the pounding of her heart and the gasping for breath. She closed her eyes as a great white light flooded her pupils, shrinking them to the size of pinheads. Her stomach flipped over and over again.

Eventually the vertigo subsided, and Adoni opened her eyes. She was on her hands and knees, though she couldn't recall hitting the ground. Beneath her palms, instead of the clean white snow she'd been anticipating, was a craggy sheet of ice. The moon's glare bounced off its surface in one unbroken, luminescent path ahead. Ritter was already on his feet and staring into the distance. Tyler stood next to him, the hem of Ritter's coat balled up in his hand. Slack-jawed, the boy caught Adoni's gaze. She pushed herself up from her crouch and nearly slipped on the ice, which, she could now see, spread across the clearing and extended into the forest.

Or what was left of the forest.

The horizon, once lush with pine and spruce and maple trees, revealed an expanse of trunks, frozen solid, slick, and glittering in the moonlight. Broken branches lay in heaps over exposed roots. The branches that hadn't snapped hung low to the ground, sheathed in a thick, glistening rime. A breeze glided between them, jostling them, knocking them against each other so that they clacked like so many beaded curtains. The clearing, which used to be lit by four magnificent burning pillars, was now sharply edged in winter darkness.

The tiny cabins where the children used to live were sombre and obscure. The grand chalet, where the pipers slept and ate and sang their morning and evening songs, was silent.

Adoni whispered, "What happened?"

"A storm..." Ritter murmured.

"It's empty. It's empty. Everyone's gone." She walked up to the closest cabin and pressed her face against the window. There was nothing beyond the pane but shadow and dust. Her skin prickled. She backed away from the blackness, turned on her heels, and faced Ritter and Tyler and the now unfamiliar colony.

Both her hands flew to her mouth, concealing the wide, nervous grin that snuck its way onto her lips. Adrenaline rushed through her and set her ribs shuddering. A sharp laugh escaped her throat. She squeezed her eyes shut.

She'd waited years for this.

Drawing a deep breath into her aching lungs, Adoni raised her head, let her arms drop to her sides, and howled loudly, joyously, at the pale full moon.

The trees endured the brunt of her impressive shriek. Along with her enchanted voice, the air filled with a sound akin to a thousand cracks of lightning. The ice on the trees burst like silvery fireworks, releasing the branches and sending them snapping back against the sky. Glittering shards of winter flew through the night, blotting out moon and stars, and then rained down on them, on their shoulders and backs, on their jackets and boots. Adoni expelled every ounce of air in her lungs. Her voice was replaced by the crackle of icy shrapnel showering the frozen ground. Beaming, invigorated, she turned to face Ritter and Tyler, who had crouched down behind her when she let her voice rip.

"So loud!" Tyler grumbled. Ritter pulled his fists away from his ears and started to laugh.

Adoni stretched out her arms. "Yes!" she cried. "Yeah!" Ritter went to her, stood in the circle of elation she had cast around herself. She hugged him close.

They heard a soft click and the chalet door opened. All three souls held their breath as an orb of candlelight materialized in the doorway. The flame was held aloft by a hand that trembled, either from the cold, or else out of trepidation for unwanted, possibly dangerous visitors. The toe of a shoe, stepping out from beneath the hem of a long black robe, crossed the threshold and planted itself on the porch. A patch of ice cracked under the stepper's weight. Adoni reached for Tyler and settled her hand on his shoulder, though he didn't appear to be afraid.

She squinted as the stepper inched to the edge of the battered porch and the moon dusted her face with light. There came a simple, "Who's out there?" Nestled in the many folds of sound: laughter, in all its incarnations, undulating as the breeze carried it to their ears. Adoni recognized it the second it left her lips.

"Paj?"

The woman set the candle on the newel and shuffled down the steps. They could see all of her clearly, now that she was no longer shielded by the chalet's sloping roof. She wore a simple robe and left her hair unbound, so that it fell in a silky black river to the top of her hip. She hadn't taken the time to throw a cloak over her shoulders, or to put on a hat or scarf. On each cheek, she wore a wide, flat stone. One was onyx, the other a vibrant turquoise.

She moved toward them, sliding her boots as though she were skiing over the pocked and icy ground. She stopped in front of Ritter and cupped his chin with a trembling hand. "Paj," he said tenderly. Wide-eyed, Paj turned her head and stared at Adoni as though the girl had just come back from the dead. Unable to speak, she divided her wonder between them, stroking and patting Ritter's cheek and then gazing at Adoni. "Are you alone?" Ritter asked. "Where is everyone? Finnur? Roxanne?"

"Gone," Paj said at last. "All gone."

"And Steppe?"

"Gone too. Gone a long, long time." She put a hand against her throat. "Come inside. It's warmer inside."

They followed her back to the chalet. Adoni was the last one up the stairs. The others had failed to pick the candle up from the newel to bring it back inside. Ansgar's name was on the brass handle, the letters worn almost smooth with age. Though there was hardly wind enough to do it, the flame had been extinguished.

The chalet was indeed warmer, though not by much, and dark save for an orange radiance on the floorboards toward the kitchen. Gone were the fragrances of Theresa's more exotic meals, the scent of pine and cedar, the smell of other bodies. All had been replaced by the sweet pungency of rotting wood. Adoni put her hand on Paj's shoulder and nudged her arm with the candlestick. She thought Ansgar's enchanted name would be enough to ignite the flame once Paj took the candlestick from her, but the wick remained unlit when Paj looped her finger through the handle.

A fire dwindled in the kitchen's pot-bellied stove. Paj threw a log on top of the embers and tore a page out of a thick book that sat nearby. She put the paper into the fire, setting it alight, then touched it to the candle to bring it back to life. "Are you hungry? I could fix you something." She nodded at the kitchen counter, where two heels of bread and a dish of boiled potatoes lay together in a plate. Neither looked appetizing, and combined they weren't enough to feed one person, let alone three.

"Paj," Ritter said. "What happened here?"

Paj pursed her lips and took a seat at the table. "Ansgar removed her blessing," she said. "From the chalet and from the residents' hope chests and cabins. There was no negotiating, none. Steppe didn't even try. Well, he knew what her answer would be." She paused, staring at the bread and potatoes. "Do you remember the night you left us? The storm had subsided. Steppe told us The Welcome had abandoned the code. You all went outside and said your goodbyes, and I sat on the stairs and waited for him to come back inside. He did. Oh… he was a changed man, Ritter.

"He went to the kitchen and started to pull whatever he could think of out of the cupboards. Canisters of fuel, candles, medical supplies, food and water, as much as we could stuff into the cellar. Before Ansgar found out about the betrayal. We spent the night going up and down the stairs, packing the shelves until they sagged under the weight. He worked until dawn broke and he was too exhausted to move. He fell asleep right there." She pointed to a dusty corner of the kitchen. "He's handsome, when he's asleep. Handsome and sad. I came down to wake him and bring him upstairs to bed. He wasn't here. I looked down in the cellar: not there either. I looked in the music room: no. Then I went up to the attic. I found him sitting on Theresa's bed, staring and staring into an empty wooden jewellery box. Just staring. He looked… shell-shocked. It was so quiet, I remember, all through the chalet. He said, 'Ansgar knows.' He could just tell, I suppose. And then I knew it too. No more enchantments, no more supplies, no more hiding behind her name for protection. We were on our own.

"But we could speak to the residents now. Some of them refused to speak back, at first. The older ones. They'd had more time to cultivate wariness and fear. They came around eventually. For the first time we pipers learned who they really were, all those souls. We even learned some of their names. Carrie. LaShane. Michael. Khadija. Ben…" She held a hand up and breathed deeply. "Others never came around. But they were happy for a while, even without the hope chests. I think they were, at least. For a little while.

"It's so difficult… so difficult… providing food and shelter and care for fifty souls. The supplies wouldn't last for long. We thought there'd be enough until the spring, when the snow melted, and we could start planting. Plant what? Potatoes, maybe. They multiply so easily; all you need is dirt and luck. The snow hadn't begun to melt before the residents started to get restless. They fought more often. They formed groups and stuck to them. We started rationing. Divide and conquer. We started to divide, and the residents… they expected us…" Her hand went up again, and she touched her knuckles to her trembling lips.

"Couldn't you have brought back food from the other side?" Adoni asked.

Paj shook her head. "We tried. We found that food can't travel through the agate. Bags of fruits and vegetables, and all of it turned to dust the moment we returned."

Adoni leaned over and opened her backpack. The sandwich she'd packed was gone, replaced by scraps of foil and a pile of ash. *Damn it*, she thought. "Why not just let the kids go for food and then come back?"

"We did. We gave them time to go off, and then crossed to the other side to wait for them to return. Some never did. We looked for the lost ones everywhere. We don't know what happened to them."

"You could've gone with them."

"We would have risked detection if we accompanied them. Imagine being caught with a child who's been missing for years."

"Well you could always just open the agate and go back really quick, before anyone saw you…"

Ritter snorted. "And have an already terrified society on extreme alert? You know better than that."

"Well, if they went back and didn't return they're not your responsibility anymore, right?" Adoni said.

Paj sighed. "We thought they wanted to stay, and now we don't know if they're safe. We'll never know.

"When he knew we were in trouble, Steppe went to the other colony leaders. He thought they would help us. After all he'd done for them, negotiating with the changelings and keeping them here instead of allowing them to wreak havoc on the other colonies. But the leaders wouldn't help us. Why would they, when they knew what Ansgar would do to them if they did?"

"Didn't he tell them the changelings attacked?" Ritter asked. "Didn't he tell them Ansgar's game is to watch her subjects suffer?"

"I wasn't there. But he must have…"

"And they still didn't help?"

"Not a one. They were afraid."

"Didn't he persist? If he'd caught them on a better day, when they were feeling more generous…"

"He was gone for weeks," Paj said. "Finnur and Roxanne and I did everything we could to keep the residents calm. We tried playing games the way they do at Long-and-Gold, and holding bonfires, and singing to them the way they sing at Accueil-Silencieux. We tried extra rations one day a week, thinking maybe it was hunger that was driving their anger, let them eat the way they do at Seventeen Bay, and then we tried intimidating them like the pipers of Ocean's Wake. All of these worked, but for too short a time. They knew what we were really doing.

"Some of the residents asked to leave. So we opened the agate for them. We asked if they wanted us to accompany them on their way back, to make sure they were safe. Some of them did. Those were the sweetest goodbyes. And some of them even thanked us for letting them stay so long. The others… they were too afraid to return. We promised we'd protect them. We promised."

Ritter shook his head. "I can't believe it. Why didn't the other leaders at least take The Welcome's residents on as boarders? Ansgar couldn't begrudge them sheltering the children, even if she'd cut their pipers off."

"No one knows. And no one will ever know."

"Why not?" asked Adoni.

"Because they're dead."

Silence.

"Dead?" Ritter whispered.

"The first was Winnifred, the lead piper of Ocean's Wake. Torn apart. Obliterated. We know Steppe's rage, don't we? Who else in the In-Between can do that?"

"It can't be—"

"Finnur, Roxanne, and I… we didn't want to believe it. But then news came that the leader of Long-and-Gold had been killed, the very same way, and then the leader of Accueil-Silencieux… so, by someone who was making his way across the In-Between…"

"Who told you this?"

"A piper named Shekou at Ocean's Wake. He announced Steppe to Winnie in her quarters. She'd been to Ansgar and knew The Welcome was no longer an honoured space."

Ritter sniggered. "*Honoured space.* Ghastly choice of words there."

Paj continued as though she hadn't heard. "Ocean's Wake couldn't risk the same fate. Winnifred told Shekou to come back in a little while and escort Steppe to the edge of the colony. When he returned he heard arguing through the walls. Loud and heated, more him than her. Shekou said he felt it through the floorboards. He felt it shaking the air. When he interrupted them there were new cracks in the walls. Pictures hanging askew. One of the lenses in Winnifred's glasses had shattered. He said it was plain to see Steppe was livid."

"Arguing for the wellbeing of fifty children," Ritter said. "Fifty children their leader didn't see fit to defend. That would raise the ire of any decent soul, don't you think?"

"But there's no justification for violence," Paj said.

"Allowing children to starve is violence."

"Winnifred was afraid of him. Shekou said he saw it on her face. When he came back after the room had gone quiet… And you know what Steppe can do to flesh and bone."

"Steppe is not a killer!" Ritter barked. "He's made mistakes in the past, yes, and he's caused some damage, some of it irreparable, but he's not a murderer. If I saw him throttle someone with my own eyes, I'd rest assured it was a trick of the light!"

Adoni glanced at him. It was nice to hear him take Steppe's side.

"Finnur and Roxanne left us before Steppe returned," Paj said. "They were afraid too. And they couldn't bear it anymore. All the staring. That's all we could do toward the end, just stare at them helplessly and hope they understood. Children don't understand." She rubbed her eyes. "They don't have to."

"What did you say to Steppe when he came back?" Adoni asked. "Did he explain anything to you?"

"There wasn't time to speak," she said. "He came back the night of the shooting."

She burst into tears and bent forward, her black hair curtaining her face, then leaned her elbows on the table as a sob wracked her chest. Dumbfounded, Adoni glanced at Tyler. The boy's attention was on Ritter, whose face had gone white.

"Of course," Ritter murmured. "Anything they want, so long as it can fit in a hope chest. Drugs. Liquor." He paused, then added, with bitterness, "If I told you I was surprised it took this long..."

Paj nodded. "I wouldn't hold it against you."

Ritter sniffed sharply and sat up straight in the chair. "How many were here?"

"Twelve. Including the shooter."

"How old?"

"Thirteen. A boy. Just a boy." She parted her hair and smoothed it back with shaky palms.

"And he...?"

"... was the last to go."

Ritter took a deep, steadying breath. "They're buried with the others?"

"Yes."

Adoni hadn't come across the gravesite where fallen residents were buried. At least she didn't think so; Ritter once told her they were buried without a marker somewhere in the forest. She may very well have trod over the final resting place of the children who'd taken their own lives. Or had had their lives taken from them.

She looked at Tyler, who was sitting as quietly as ever on the broken kitchen chair. Adoni reached over and urged him into her lap. She wrapped her arms around him. He let himself be held without a fuss.

"And Steppe?" Ritter asked.

"He arrived an hour later."

"He said nothing?"

"It was so quiet, Ritter," Paj said. "It was so awfully quiet, like the world had stopped turning and all the things in it had stopped vibrating and there was this... stillness. He just stared at the aftermath. Then he turned around and left. Not a sound. Not a sound." She shuddered and put her head in her hands.

Adoni adopted that same silence, retreated into herself to make sense of Paj's words. She looked at her hands, clasped around the forearms she'd locked about Tyler's waist. One of the residents had finally resorted to violence, and a shameful heat broke out across her chest. She could still remember some of the kids she'd encountered and morbidly wondered if they'd been among the residents who'd been cut down. They were all too far away for her to feel any real sadness. Last time, she sat on the steps of a cabin with a candle between her hands, to honour the dead, for what it was worth. Things were different now.

But Natalie's okay, she thought. *Natalie's safe.*

"Why did you stay?" she asked Paj.

Paj put her hand over her heart. "My sister walks in this place. We walk together, always. We need each other."

"Funny," Ritter said. "The souls on this colony needed someone too. And no single piper moved a finger to help them. Do the other colonies know about the shooting?"

"They must."

"I wonder if they blame themselves for those children's deaths. It astounds me that not a single one of them did anything to prevent it."

"Their leaders were destroyed."

"Of course," Ritter sneered. "They needed to be told to care. The Welcome is remote, but not so remote that they didn't know Ansgar had cut the colony off. What did they expect a group of starving children would do? No, they waited until Steppe came begging to even consider it. And even then they turned him away. This isn't about his visit, or the crimes you think he committed. You don't wait for a fire to rage before you douse the flame. You lick your fingers and snap it out. Do you think Steppe is guilty?"

"I don't know," she said quietly.

"Oh, *you know*. You know goddamn well. You're afraid to admit it. What makes you think Steppe is anyone other than the man you know him to be?"

"Maybe we don't know him," she whispered.

Ritter didn't move. The hard glare in his eye didn't soften.

Adoni broke the heavy silence. "Sylvester's trapped on the other side," she said. "He came to Ritter's apartment the other night and told him he wants to be sent back to the In-Between. And my friend Natalie doesn't remember me, and she can't remember anything about the In-Between."

"Natalie," Paj murmured, turning the name delicately over her tongue.

"She used to have purple hair. You're the one who sang her away." Paj squinted down at the table and clasped her hands together. "Like this," Adoni said, and she took a breath and started to sing the tune Paj had composed for the girl.

Of course she still knew it. Ever since she'd heard it that long-ago wintery morning, hanging in the air half woven like a swatch of silk on a loom, ever since she'd heard it full and furious that long-ago wintery night, Natalie's song had hidden in her blood, in her synapses, waiting to escape. She sang it in the shower sometimes, when Ida was out. It went through her head, over and over, when she had to get somewhere in a hurry, its pulse urging her to pick her feet up and move. If it got into her head at night, she could kiss eight hours of sleep goodbye. Some days it was an unwanted friend, a toxic friend, leaning over her shoulder and telling her everything she did was wrong. It could be so easy to hate. It could be desperate. Its fury, its power, was undeniable.

Paj closed her eyes, her shoulders slumping, her head hanging low. Adoni stopped singing. "Remember now?" she asked.

Paj nodded. "I sang her away. She was sitting on the steps of an apartment building. Lonely, angry, frightened. I brought her here and showed her to her cabin. She had grey eyes, such clear grey eyes, bright as a winter sky. She carried every pain she'd ever known on her shoulders, and they were stiff, those shoulders. When we started to bury the children, she was gone."

"You didn't open the agate for her?"

"No."

"Then how…"

She held up her hand. "Stop. Listen."

Behind the sudden silence, a distance away and getting closer, the air hissed through a hundred sets of teeth.

Adoni held her breath. She'd heard that terrible sound before.

Chapter

13

"Changelings! They're coming again! They're coming!" Paj pushed away from the table and leapt to her feet. "The cellar," she said, pointing to a braided rug skirted by boxes in the corner of the room. She hurried toward it, lifted an edge and tossed it back to reveal a door in the floorboards. She grabbed two thick straps that snaked out from either side of the opening and pulled them up, lifting the door with them. A set of narrow steps disappeared into a roiling darkness beneath the chalet. Paj turned around and scuttled down into the black.

"But I can fight them off!" Adoni said. "I've got Ansgar's voice!" She put Tyler on the floor and started to move toward the kitchen's back door.

Ritter hooked his fingers around her forearm and pulled her back. "Damn you if you try that stupid trick now!"

"Let go of me, jackass!" She jerked her arm out of his grip. "We don't have to sit here and let them tear the place apart! We can finally fight back!"

Ritter pointed at the door in the floor. "Get into the cellar." Adoni ignored him and skirted around the table. "You think pushing them back is enough to stop them? You'll push them into a corner and they'll come out fighting!"

"Then I'll fight back!"

"Donny, please," Ritter begged.

Adoni turned back to Ritter and growled, "I can hurt them if I want to!"

Ritter stared her down. "Don't you *dare*."

Tyler grabbed her coat with one tiny fist. She gnashed her teeth behind tight lips and urged him over to the top of the steps. The smell of the cellar hit her nostrils, the odour of freshly turned earth and wet stone. "Come after me, so I can catch you if you fall." She shot Ritter a spiteful look before heading down.

The cellar air was damp. Tyler let out a squeak and stamped his foot. "I'm right here, don't worry," she said. He turned around, put his hands on the floor, and reached for the first step with the toe of his boot. Adoni kept her eyes on him as she eased her way down, until her boots found the ground and she stood up in the gloom. When Tyler was still a foot above her she reached out and pulled him off the steps and into her arms. Behind her, Paj struck a match and lit two candles that stood on top of a short table in the middle of the room. Adoni took one from her as Ritter scrambled down the stairs. Paj reached back and pulled the braided rug over the door as she closed it. She secured the door's iron latch by wedging a thick metal spike through the loop.

Adoni turned around once to take in her new, dank surroundings. The ceiling loomed just a few feet above their heads. The walls were covered with broken shelves, empty except for a layer of grey silt that cloaked their cracks and splinters. One corner had accumulated a pile of old furniture that included several damaged chairs, a loveseat with torn upholstery and rusted springs, a credenza covered with chipped and sticky polish. Next to the pile of furniture was a wheelchair with flat tires, several empty picture frames, and a crate of candles. The earthen floor was mostly bare, apart from two torn rugs that lay beneath the table from which Paj had retrieved the candles. The only bit of decoration, if it could be called that, was a bundle of dried witch hazel that lay on top of the table as a centrepiece.

They converged in the centre of the room and stood on the rugs, staring up at the ceiling as though they could look past the beams, through the earth, to where their attackers were rushing toward them. They waited.

Adoni heard a pane of glass shatter, and then the battering of footsteps as the changelings broke through the doors and stormed the chalet.

She heard them charge through the front hall and into the sitting room, slamming their hands against the walls, scratching the wood with their fingernails. Furniture was thrown aside or thrust across the floor. The mob separated and changelings surged toward the back of the chalet, into the kitchen. The pounding of their feet on the floorboards shook the dust free from the cellar shelves and sent it fluttering to the ground. Banging, thrashing, hammering between the walls, more glass smashing, the *whiz* of knives soaring through the air, the *thunk* of their points hitting soft wood. Paj put a finger to her lips and gazed around the circle at each of their anxious faces.

The changelings left the kitchen and battered their way up the staircase. And though an entire floor now separated them from the cellar, Adoni still heard them tearing through the instruments in the music room—the awful thud of brass hitting the floor, the snap of bows across the backs of chairs, the sickening boom of something exceptionally heavy hitting what could only be Steppe's treasured piano. They trounced from the music room to the bedrooms—more noise as they pulled drawers out of their chests, as they shattered picture frames and trinket boxes, as they tore through curtains and hurled bed stones and firewood at the walls, the floors, the ceiling.

And all the while, that awful hissing—the wheeze of arrested voices in vengeful throats.

Adoni sat down on the cellar floor. She felt the entire chalet vibrate with hatred, felt it creep into the scowl on her face. All she had to do was release the full extent of her voice to send them scurrying back to their compound in the forest. *Just a few good screams*, she thought. *That's all it would take. Why do we have to sit here hiding like a bunch of assholes?*

Little fingers clutched at her hair. She looked up. Tyler stood next to her, one hand tucked in her curls, the other behind his back. Paj stood close by, staring at her candle's tiny flame. Ritter leaned back against a wall of shelves, his arms folded, staring at his boots, his mouth stiff with a frown.

He lifted his eyes and peered at Adoni for a moment before looking away. *He looks like how I feel: useless.*

She instantly regretted the thought. *Okay, so that's unfair. Maybe he's freaked out. And maybe I don't know what the hell I'm doing. But it beats sitting in the basement like chickenshits.*

The noise above their heads crescendoed to one last blow that shook the chalet, and then the changelings quickly fled, their feet pommelling down the stairs, across the front hall, over the steps, into the night.

Paj spoke softly. "Let's stay here until we're sure they're gone."

"No plaque, no protection," Ritter said. "How many times has this happened?"

"Three, not including tonight. They get worse every time."

"Let me guess. They started when Steppe disappeared."

Paj nodded. "They broke the windows this time. We can't get new glass."

"What about Natalie?" Adoni asked, still angry that they hadn't let her fight. "How did she get back to Toronto?"

Paj gave Adoni a long look, shook her head, and spoke to Ritter in piper language. Ritter answered her in kind. It was a rich tongue, Germanic in nature, which she'd only ever heard sung, not spoken, and he articulated it in his velvety tenor with a gentleness she found difficult to interrupt. "No no no no no!" she said at last. "Don't even start that! It's rude and I'm not stupid!"

"Of course you're not stupid," Ritter said. He put his hand over his face and rubbed his eyes. "This is a nightmare. An absolute nightmare."

Paj picked up the witch hazel and ran her hands over the dead leaves. "I don't know what to say."

Adoni put her hands on the table and dropped her head, stretching her neck. She knew what they had to do, now that their questions couldn't be answered by the pipers alone. She straightened her back and looked Paj in the eye. "We came back to figure out what's going on. You don't know, but Ansgar does."

CHARLENE CHALLENGER

"You'll go to her?" she asked.

"There's no alternative now," Ritter replied. "Sylvester's been expelled from the In-Between, Steppe has disappeared, the piper leaders have been murdered, there's nothing here to protect you from starvation or another changeling attack... And I suspect Adoni's friend isn't who she says she is."

"What do you mean?"

"She might be a changeling."

Paj gawked at him. "But Ansgar wouldn't make another changeling. She hasn't bred them for decades. Surely she wouldn't—"

"What's stopping her?" He drew in a deep breath. "I'd recognize it anywhere. This is her game. And this time she's *cheating*."

"When do we go?" Adoni asked him.

"When it's light out."

"I'll come with you," Paj said. "It'll be safer if we all travel together."

"Normally I'd try to talk you out of that," Ritter said. "But I don't like the thought of you staying alone in this dump."

"Are you gonna talk *piper* the whole way there?" Adoni asked him. "I don't want to have to hear you keep saying *leezen* and *shreekoo* and whatever else you guys were talking about."

"*Lebshen*," Ritter said. "And *shrictus*."

"What does that mean? *Lebshen*?"

"*Alive*." He came away from the shelves.

Her rancour softened. She could never stay mad at him. She crossed her arms, closed her eyes, and half-murmured the word, *lebshen*, to feel it on her tongue.

She ignored the pain that briefly stabbed her shoulder.

"If anybody..."

Paj let out a squeal and dropped the bundle of witch hazel onto the table. She raised both her hands, her fingers spread wide, and stared at the bouquet. The parched and wrinkled branches plumped and smoothed themselves out. The brown, shrivelled petals softened as a golden hue spread through them. They curled and uncurled like so many fingers on so many hands.

Adoni's stomach jumped as the bouquet, of its own accord, turned itself over and began crawling toward her.

They leapt back from the table and watched the bouquet inch forward like some underwater creature climbing ashore. It picked up speed, tentacle-like branches scurrying forward, yellow petals reaching for the ceiling, pulsating as though they could detach themselves and scamper in any direction they chose. It fell over the edge of the table and landed with a click, those branches, those limbs, hysterically circling in the air until the bouquet righted itself and continued its trajectory. Ritter grabbed it and held it up. It kept moving as though it were still striding across a flat surface.

"What the hell is that?" Adoni cried. "Kill it!"

He pointed at Adoni. "You sang something just now. Under your breath. What was it?"

"Lebshen," she replied.

"Which means..."

"Alive," Paj said. They stared at the creature. "Ansgar's initial on your shoulder!"

"No way," Adoni said. "I can bring things to life!" She looked at Ritter, her smile first growing wide when she caught his eye, and then shrinking to nothing when she saw the look on his face.

Fear.

"What if she sings the piper word for 'death?'" Paj wondered aloud.

"What's the word for 'death?'"

Ritter blurted out, too late, a sharp "NO!"

"Shrictus," Paj said.

Adoni turned to the wriggling bouquet and half-murmured, in the back of her throat as she did before, *shrictus.*

The bouquet palsied in Ritter's hand. Adoni heard a dry twist as the branches and petals shrank to their former state. Ritter put it back on the table and let his hand linger over it as though paying his last respects. "Damn it, Paj," he growled.

Adoni turned on him. "You want the thing running around the basement while we're down here?"

He glared at her. "You're quick to kill," he said. "Not a moment's hesitation."

Adoni ignored him. "What do you mean, 'no?'" She crossed the cellar floor. He pressed his back against the shelves as she approached. "You think I'm gonna go on some rampage?"

"Calm down," he said.

"Is that what you think?"

"When you raise your voice at me like that? *Yes.*"

She stomped back to the bouquet and brought the word to her lips again: *lebshen.*

Nothing.

She tried again: nothing. Not a twist. Not a flinch. An awful loneliness settled in her chest as she eyed the dead petals and wood. "I can only do it once," she muttered.

"Once is enough," Ritter said.

"Must make you happy anyway."

"This is bad." He leaned his head against the shelves and closed his eyes. "This is very bad."

"What's so bad about it?"

"You can't be as powerful as Ansgar... can you?" Paj said.

"Why not?"

"There's no chance of that," Ritter said.

Adoni snarled, "Answer me!" One of the empty picture frames clattered down to the floor. She turned back to Ritter. "I'm not gonna go on a killing spree; I'm not some psychopath!"

"I guess this is why we're supposed to keep the In-Between hidden from those who aren't pipers or residents," Paj said to him, baldly, without malice or sympathy.

"She followed me through the agate when my back was turned," Ritter said.

"NO I DIDN'T!" One of the shelves behind Ritter exploded in a dense cloud of slivers and dust. "You always say that. Always! It's not true! And I'm sick of it! We were standing outside my building. You yelled at me like an asshole; you opened the agate *right there* in front of me, looked me right in the eye, then you turned around and left! You make it sound like you don't understand how I knew what to do, or why I did what I did, or why I followed you the next time I saw you. *You* let me in on the secret! *You let me in*." She couldn't hold them back any longer; her chest heaved, and she started to wail. "Why wouldn't I want to come with you? Why wouldn't I? You act like it was just some fluke, like I was just in the right place at the right time, like you don't understand but, oh well, here she is, guess I have to deal with her now..."

Her sobs seized her throat, her lungs. She cried out all of the anguish she hadn't realized she'd been harbouring, a deluge of hurt and resentment and something else: confusion. Why had she let him rewrite this aspect of their past as though it were the be-all and end-all of the story? When she opened her eyes and looked at him—at his expression, an expanse of remorse laid bare—she cried even harder, because it was clear, so crystal clear, that he'd done it on purpose.

Eventually the tears stopped, and she hiccupped until her breath returned to normal.

Paj approached and put her hands on their shoulders. "You're tired. Both of you. You should sleep." She squinted. "I can... make a bed for you... somewhere upstairs."

Adoni sniffled. "You think we're gonna be able to sleep after this?"

"My old room," Ritter said. He chuckled. "Does it still look the same?"

"With that last attack," Paj said, "the changelings..."

"Of course. Good thing I'm not sentimental." Ritter got to his feet and looked into Adoni's scorching black eyes. "Stay with me tonight. I need your protection."

She looked down at her boots.

"Donny?" he said softly.

She sniffled and nodded, but couldn't meet his gaze.

Chapter
14

Paj pulled the spike out of the latch and lifted the cellar door a few inches. She stood on the steps and held her hand out behind her as she surveyed the kitchen floor. After a moment she said, "It's safe," and lifted the door all the way up and back. One by one, they ascended the stairs and took in the damage the changelings had wrought.

The wind howled through two smashed windowpanes. Two chairs lay overturned against the back door; three others had their legs snapped in half. Knives had been thrust into the table, the walls, the cupboard doors. The cracked ruins of bowls and plates lay over the countertops. The only thing left undisturbed was the dish of boiled potatoes and heels of bread, though slivers of glass had found their way into the flesh and crusts.

The pot-bellied stove's door was open; a log lay in the dwindling embers, half-charred grey and in need of a thorough stoking. The changelings hadn't thought to set fire to the chalet. *Maybe that's next time,* Adoni thought. *Maybe they left it open as a warning. Can they even think like that? Can they think that far ahead?*

She peered at Paj, who set to work righting the remaining functional chairs and nudging the larger pieces of glass out of the way with the toes of her shoes. Solemnity had settled in her eyes and in the corners of her tightly drawn lips. Despite her sombre aspect she didn't appear to be angry; she seemed more resigned to dealing with the mess. "The windows," she said. "We'll have to fix them fast to keep them out. We'll use wood, I guess.

It will block out the light but it will have to do. I should take care of this before morning. I'm sorry, I'll be hammering for a while."

"I won't be able to sleep anyway," Adoni said.

"We'll leave tomorrow after sunrise. The sun rises late this time of year, so we should have plenty of time to rest." She crossed her hands over her heart. "The beds... I hope they've left the beds..." She moved across the floor carefully, bits of ceramic crunching under her shoes, into the hallway. Adoni took hold of Tyler's hand and followed her. She heard Ritter's footsteps behind her.

They climbed the stairs to the second floor. Adoni glanced into the music room. Violins were nothing more than piles of shattered wood and snapped strings lying on the floor. Trumpets and trombones were bent and warped and would never sound rich or beautiful again. The most grotesque display of all: the grand piano, legs kicked out from under it, its middle buckled against the floor, lying in almost perfect halves like a pair of fallen angel wings. Paj peered around the doorjamb. "The brutes," she murmured.

Adoni glanced over her shoulder. Ritter walked toward the room at the end of the hallway. The door was slightly ajar. Ritter's name was still engraved there; no attempt had been made to strike it from the wood. He pushed it open and reeled back on his heels. One hand went up to the side of his head. Adoni stepped over an oil lamp that had been smashed off the wall and approached him. She saw the shattered windowpane, and that the bed was gone, and that the rug had been kicked into a corner lined with shelves she couldn't remember being there before. There were no CDs, no records, no photographs or works of art. The beanbag chair had been shoved into the empty fireplace. Blankets were strewn everywhere. Adoni followed his stare to the bedroom floor.

In blood—black blood—across the floor, one word: *brother*.

Ritter crossed the threshold and stood in the middle of the room, the toes of his boots touching the oily letters.

Paj followed him and put a hand on his shoulder. "Paint," she said. "It must be paint. Changelings can't bleed for long in the In-Between. Their skin heals too quickly."

Adoni shuddered. Sylvester's skin sewed itself back together the night she sliced it open, with the sickly slurp of flesh meeting flesh and clotting closed. It remained the single most unsettling thing she'd ever witnessed.

"Only one way to get that much blood from a changeling," Ritter said, his voice trembling. "Beheading."

"They wouldn't."

"I've seen beheadings," he said. "There's something... about the eyes..."

Paj pointed at the floor. "They'd have to kill one of their own." Ritter shook his head and turned away. "They *wouldn't*," she continued. "They wouldn't just—"

"They would."

"There are other rooms," she said. "Finnur's. Roxanne's. The windows are broken but..."

"No," Ritter said. "I'll stay here."

Paj's brow crumpled into distressed lines. "There's no need to do this," she said. "It's no way to atone."

"Atone?" He laughed. "I'm beyond atonement." He crossed the floor, pulled the beanbag chair out of the fireplace, and brushed away the soot with the sleeve of his jacket. "The changelings are my brothers in arms, as much as I've tried to deny it. They're my family. They've sacrificed one of their number to remind me of this. The least I can do is bear witness."

Paj sighed and nodded at the fireplace. "I'll bring up some wood."

"Not with a broken window. The wind could fan a spark out of place and set the room on fire. Blankets will do." He looked at Adoni. "We'll have to stay close together."

She shrugged and glanced at Tyler. The boy looked back at her as he ruthlessly gnawed on one of his fingernails. "Do you even want to be in this room?" she asked him, her voice still raw from her earlier meltdown.

He shook his head. "Let's go in the other room."

Ritter turned his back and knelt down in front of the beanbag chair to spread it out alongside the changelings' message. Adoni watched him reach for one of the discarded blankets before replying. "You go with Paj, okay? I'm gonna stay here."

"No!" he whined. "It's cold and scary!"

"Go with Paj," she said firmly.

He grabbed hold of her sleeves and leaned back, weighing her down. "No! I don't like this room!"

"What did I say before we left?" she asked. "I told you what it would be like when we got back." Tyler started to cry. "Go with Paj, she'll make a room up all nice for you," she said, trying as best she could to bring that same music, that same magic, into her voice as she had in the cellar. "Maybe you can make a blanket fort with her. Wouldn't that be fun?" She glanced at Paj and nodded, hoping to coax her into following her lead.

"You can stay with me," Paj said to him. "I've got lots of blankets. And pillows too, lots of pillows."

"See Tyler? Even pillows! You can have a pillow fight!" He continued to cry.

"Go with him," Ritter said without turning. "I'll be fine." He reached for another blanket and dusted it off with an open hand.

Adoni's jaw went tight. "Go with Paj *now!*" she said to Tyler.

"No!" he cried.

Her throat tightened up. She didn't want to be charged with protecting him, especially since she hadn't wanted him along in the first place. She didn't want to curl up next to a child for the night; not one whose helplessness reminded her so much of herself, of nights spent alone in rooms almost as cold as this one, ignored, or worse: taunted by Ida for not being able to face the darkness alone.

Shut up in there! She remembered it clearly, in her stomach, in her bones. *Or I'll really give you something to cry about!*

"I'm not your mommy!" she yelled, matching the volume, the timbre, the pitch that still lived in the back of her mind. "Go with Paj NOW!"

She heard the snap of a second pane of glass cracking. The break spread across the window, a jagged web of white against a black sky.

Tyler let go of her sleeves and leaned forward, hands as fists, mouth open, soundless, his airless lungs paralysed before a gasp could overtake him. Paj took the boy's hand; he didn't resist as she led him away. "It's all right," she cooed as he wept. "It's all right. I can tell you stories. Would you like me to tell you a story? I'm an old woman, you know. I've got lots of stories." She pulled the door closed behind her, taking her candle's flame away with her, leaving Adoni and Ritter in the moonlight.

He turned.

"I'm not his mother," Adoni muttered when she saw the look on his face.

He draped the blankets over one end of the beanbag chair and lay down, then shifted his arms and legs until every limb was propped up. She stood still, waiting for the sound of crying to fade completely before approaching. She knelt and crawled on top of him, settled her head against his chest. He reached down and pulled the blankets over her shoulder.

The black letters lay beneath the shadow cast from the broken windowpane, still wet and glistening. A gentle wind whistled through the shattered glass. It swept across the roof and blew a veil of snow into the room; the tiny flakes melted as they touched her cheek. She pulled the blanket up higher and snuggled closer to Ritter. He put an arm around her and gave her shoulder a squeeze.

The wind soon gave way to stillness. Adoni was about to fall asleep when a thought occurred to her. "Why'd you open the agate in front of me?" she asked. "It would've saved you so much trouble if you didn't."

He paused, and then leaned his cheek against her head. "Because I saw your angry little face and thought, *here's my chance*," he murmured. "Because I went with my heart too quickly, the way I always do, without thinking about the damage or the wonder I'd cause you. Because I was too selfish to keep my prison to myself and jumped at the prospect of sharing it with someone else, someone who could look at it with fresh eyes and tell me I was crazy. Or tell me I was right. Because I wanted you to save me. Because I wanted you to save us all. And it's unfair, I know, to have someone make that choice for you. And I can only hope one day you'll forgive me for that."

She tucked her arms in close to her chest. "If it was anyone else I wouldn't," she said. "Just so you know. But it's you."

He hugged her. "I'm honoured to know you, Donny," he said. "Honoured beyond space and time."

Chapter
15

Theresa covered the last of her gastronome containers with plastic wrap and put them in the refrigerator. Feet sore, back aching, she sat down on the milk crate and pressed the heel of her hand against her brow. Hours of dealing with ravenous customers who were ill-tempered from the weather and eager to take it out on her; and then Ritter showing up to keep an eye on her. She couldn't wait to get home and crack open the beer she'd been saving, even if it meant having another awkward conversation with him. The alcohol would warm her stomach while she fixed herself a nighttime snack.

She stretched her legs out and let her eyes glaze over. It hadn't been as bad a day as she'd anticipated. She hadn't made as much as she normally did when the weather was good, but the haul had still been decent, and she'd used the lulls in traffic to prep as much as she could for the next day. It wasn't going to be glamorous—more chili and casseroles since they were so easy to make and she had all the ingredients—but most of her clientele came to her truck specifically for comfort food. The real question was what she wanted to eat, now that she'd ended her shift. She thought about swinging the truck down Spadina and getting Chinese take-out, having someone else cook for her for a change, but couldn't justify the expense when she remembered the loaf of bread and sandwich meats next to the beer in her fridge.

The load off her feet was so welcome she lost the will to lock up the kitchen and drag herself around the truck to the driver's seat. She wanted

CHARLENE CHALLENGER

to leave but didn't have the energy to stand.

Every time a young man came to her window to place an order, she remembered what Ritter had said to her. Who was he to snap at her like that anyway? He'd kept Ansgar's secrets for years, and so Steppe had danced around in vain trying to satisfy the whims of a psychopathic changeling and a maniacal child-god. But Theresa couldn't deny that she'd spoken carelessly and hurt him, and it was written all over his face.

It tainted the feel of his lips against her mouth, the memory of his kiss, of his arms around her, his chest against hers. The smell of him. The sound he made when he first gave in to her.

You're just lonely, she thought.

There had been no other man since Steppe. She'd spent time getting her driver's license, taking night courses, reacquainting herself with a city she barely recognized. There wasn't time left over to even think about that kind of companionship. Ritter was familiar, handsome, confident, and there in her living room when she finally had needed someone else's body pressed against her own. At the same time, he was an undiscovered country, underneath an exciting skin. She was curious too; he wasn't human. How would he hold her? How would he taste?

Like Steppe, she discovered. Like a man.

She stood up and hobbled out the back of the truck. She finished locking up and got into the driver's seat, wincing as her fingers wrapped around the cold plastic steering wheel. *Worst part about working in winter*, she thought as she dug through the glove compartment. Grocery receipts and dried-out pens, a pair of sunglasses, an old pack of gum that still smelled minty fresh. *Figures there wouldn't actually be any gloves in it.* She put her keys in the ignition and started the engine; let it run for a minute before blasting the heater. The clock on the dashboard was still an hour ahead from the last time the clocks changed. She could easily have changed it while the engine warmed up; instead she turned on the cabin light and used the mirror she'd pinned to the visor to examine the circles under her bloodshot eyes. "Jeez, you need a nap," she muttered. She pulled away from the curb and steered the truck toward the garage.

First things first: she turned the radio on and up. An old tune she couldn't place came over the speakers, a bluesy, cobwebbed guitar two-stepping with an uninspired piano and exhausted drums. The kind of song one would hear in some dive bar in the middle of nowhere, just background noise for beer-swigging, middle-aged hockey fans. The worst kind of music for the end of a long day. She stuck out her tongue and switched stations.

It was when she leaned closer to the dash that she noticed a rattle coming from the engine. The last thing she needed was an expensive visit to the mechanic. *It's just cold*, she told herself. *No need to panic. It'll stop when the engine warms up.* She busied herself with flipping through the stations. *Commercial. Commercial. Man I hate that track. Commercial.*

She drove over a pothole that knocked something loose. The rattle doubled in sound and fury. *Shit shit shit! Not tonight!* She kept her eyes open for an alley she could pull into. Every one she spotted was blocked by a bright orange construction barrier or cordoned off with pylons or reflective tape. *When are they going to finish building this damn city?* she thought as she gripped the steering wheel.

She drove into the narrow street where the garage was located. The ticket booth was vacant at that time of night. Rather than risk driving down the ramp with brakes that may or may not hold, she drove up onto the curb and turned off the engine. Her limited knowledge of trucks would have to do until she had the money to bring it to a professional. She giggled in spite of herself. *What are you going to do besides check the oil on the dipstick and kick the thing a few times, dingaling?* Still, she waited a few minutes for the engine to cool before sliding out of the driver's seat and popping the hood.

The fluorescent lights from the garage made it easy for her to see. She peered down at the engine and squinted at it, as though it were some ancient scroll she couldn't possibly decipher. Her breath escaped her lips in puffs of moist white cloud. She'd known it since her first day in business: if she wanted to run a restaurant on wheels, she'd better understand how to keep those wheels in tip-top shape. She'd put it off, trusting the relatively new machine would hold for at least a few years until she had the resources and time to learn how to keep the engine purring. She checked the oil level and flicked the spark plugs with her finger before admitting she had no idea what she was doing. *Next continuing education course I take: Car Repair 101.* She let the hood slam closed and looked over her shoulder.

There he was, looking dapper and as sinister as ever. A fine suit under a long winter coat lent a smart aspect to his silhouette. No empty smile pasted on his face this time, no joker's grin or affected, genteel posture. He walked ramrod straight against the cold, his hands thrust in his pockets, his chin low, and that pale blue eye, that violent scar, pointed directly at her.

Ritter was right. He hadn't wasted any time.

She made a break for the truck, dove for the door handle. Sylvester grabbed her collar and ferociously yanked her back. She stumbled and fell, her gloveless hands scraping against the ice-pocked pavement, sending the shock through both her wrists. She turned over and tried to scramble to her feet, the toes of her shoes slipping as she fought to stand and run. Sylvester drew back his leg and viciously kicked her stomach, knocking the wind out of her.

Theresa gulped and gasped. She felt him straddle her back. Three young men passed by the end of the road. She squawked with all the air she had left in her lungs. The sound was thin but loud enough to get their attention.

They turned their heads and glanced her way. What they saw wasn't enough to stop them. They continued along as though they'd seen nothing at all.

Sylvester chuckled. "How do you like that?" he asked. "They probably think you fell over, and I'm helping you up. Everyone's afraid of confrontation in this city. Everyone's so docile and discreet. No eye contact. No casual hellos. The perfect place to disappear."

Keys are still in the ignition, she thought. *Can't jab him in the eye. Make a break for the truck and drive.* She put her palms against the street and heaved back, attempting to throw him off. He clapped a gloved hand over her mouth and dug his fingers into her cheek. She bucked and struggled, her screeches muffled by his palm, not caring if he struck her again. She heard something small and plastic hit the pavement, felt some sort of liquid douse her hair, drip down her face and into her eyes, stinging them so badly she squeezed them shut. She reached back and grabbed a handful of his hair.

The smell of the liquid hit her nose; she heard the unmistakable strike of a spark wheel next to her ear, and froze.

Butane. Lighter.

"You always hated when I came to The Welcome to negotiate," he jeered. "I told Steppe a long time ago I was through negotiating. You were there the night I told them what I did to Aniuk." Theresa sucked down a sob. "Don't worry. It's just your face. I'll put it out before it gets too carried away. I want you alive, so you can tell Ritter what I did to you." She heard the spark wheel strike again, twisted and screamed against his palm, tore at the back of his head with her fingernails.

Behind them, the truck roared to life.

She felt Sylvester scramble off of her and dragged her sleeve across her face and over her wet hair, pasting it back. She opened her eyes and they instantly flooded with tears to wash away the sting.

The truck's high beams switched on. The engine revved. Someone slammed down on the accelerator. The tires squealed as they spun over patches of ice. The truck rushed forward.

Sylvester ran past it, toward the other end of the street. Theresa's every limb locked up as the truck sped up and swerved around her. She watched it chase Sylvester down and skid to a halt when the changeling ducked into the narrow space between two buildings and disappeared.

Theresa got to her feet, head rushing, stomach still throbbing where Sylvester had kicked her. She opened her jacket, wiped her face with her shirt and looked up. Two cameras flanked the garage's gaping entrance and pointed in toward the ticket booth. Had she been attacked close enough for the whole thing to be caught on video? Had the cameras filmed the person who'd climbed into her truck and stolen it? She stepped onto the sidewalk, leaned against the garage's brick wall, pressed her hands against her cheeks. She smelled the lighter fluid in her hair and another wave of burning tears flooded her eyes.

The truck turned around and rumbled back toward the garage. Theresa stayed flat against the building, convinced the back tires would be the last she'd see of the vehicle as it continued down the street and disappeared around the corner. Instead it came to a stop in front of the garage. The driver slipped out of the cab and stood in the glare of the high beams.

Theresa collapsed against the wall in a fit of giggles and sobs.

Of course it was him. *Of course.*

"Are you all right?" Steppe asked.

She wiped the spittle on her lips with the back of her hand. *Of course.* She didn't answer him, didn't know what to say. She buckled over, put her hands on her knees, and stared at the toes of her shoes.

He was there, not ten feet in front of her, and she had no idea what to do.

"Theresa?"

She straightened up and looked him in the eye.

Other than the white hair curling at his temples, he looked exactly the same: wolfish, cagey, steely, and concerned all at once. He wore black jeans, a blue sweater, a green leather jacket; quite the change from the piper clothes he wore during his days at The Welcome. "You still remember how to drive?" she asked.

He let a faint smile play across his lips. "It's sort of like riding a bicycle, really." He looked over his shoulder at the truck. "Handles well. You really have to ease up on the gas when you're making a turn, though."

And because she didn't know what else to say, she asked, "Can you fix it?"

"That rattle in the engine? I bet it's the timing belt. I can try to fix it, but you should really have a good mechanic look at it."

"Can we make it down to my spot at least?"

"I think so. It's definitely not your brakes."

They stared at each other.

"Definitely," he said.

She walked back to the truck and got into the driver's seat, leaned over and unlocked the passenger door. Steppe climbed in and buckled his seat belt. Theresa leaned toward the radio to turn it on but stopped. *There's no reception underground, you're not going to hear anything.* She sat back, checked her rear view and side mirrors, swiped her parking pass on the access panel at the ticket booth, and eased the truck down the ramp.

She needed every movement, every thought, to be mundane. The first man—the only man—she'd ever fallen in love with, the man she parted ways with in order to start her life anew, was sitting in her truck. She didn't know where to begin.

Timing belt. What does that even do?

Shit.

She steered the truck around two bends and parked in the spot she rented. She turned off the engine, and the cab filled with an electric silence. Steppe took off his seat belt and opened the door, strolled around to the front of the truck and propped the hood open. Theresa joined him and peered over his shoulder. "Do you have a tool kit of some sort? Ratchets, wrenches, a pair of gloves?" he asked.

"I have a cell phone and a tow company on speed dial."

"You should really keep a tool kit in the cab. The timing belt connects the bottom of the engine with the top of the engine to run the valves. If it breaks, you can get into trouble on the road. It's even worse if you've got an interference engine. The pistons could hit the valves..."

Theresa ran her hands through her wet hair. "This is lighter fluid," she said, pointing at her head.

Steppe's eyes searched her face, briefly, before he closed the hood. "Get a mechanic to look at it."

"I can't afford a mechanic right now."

"You should get it taken care of as soon as you can."

"As soon as I've got the money."

"It sounds pretty bad..."

"Well, you need money when you're on this side. I can't just pull a new piston belt out of a cupboard."

"Timing belt." He took a step backwards and nodded at the back of the truck. "I'd love to see the kitchen. And maybe you can... maybe there's... do you have a towel?"

"I'll have to clean up at home," she muttered. "But if you want to see it..."

"I'd *love* to see it," he said softly.

Theresa unlocked the back door. The light from the garage barely illuminated the kitchen. Still, they climbed in and she pointed at the cupboards, the shelves, the supplies as though Steppe could see them all clearly. "So, I stand here, and like, people come up to the window over here, and I take their order and just get it for them, because everything's right behind me, and then... when it's not busy I just do my prep work. And... umm... usually I just put everything back at the end of the night, and like, bungee cord things down because when you're driving with all this equipment it's hard to keep it from sliding all over the place. I lost a couple of casseroles that way. Umm. They were good casseroles."

"Tight fit."

"Huh? Yeah. Well it's just me. It's enough. It's enough space for just me."

"Alone."

"Yeah. I work alone." She nodded. "He was going to burn my face." She wrapped her arms around herself.

Steppe shoved his hands in his pockets. "I'm sorry. It's my fault. I should have known... I mean, I shouldn't have..."

"He was going to burn my face. He would've done it too, if you hadn't..." She glared at him. "Do you follow me? Do you watch me?"

"No. I watch him." He ran a finger over his jawline. "I like your hair. The length suits you."

"You watch him."

"Yes."

"And? Do you—"

"And Adoni."

"The other night, right?" Theresa sniffled. "She thought it was Sylvester following her."

"She saw me."

"You scared the crap out of her."

"That wasn't my intention."

"Well, that's what happens on this side when guys follow women around at night."

"You keep referring to *this side*, as if I've never lived in this world myself. As if I don't have any memory of this city."

"I'm sorry," she mumbled, pressing her palm to her forehead. "I'm..."

"Angry. Upset."

"I told you Sylvester wasn't messing around anymore."

"I've known that for a long time."

"He wants to go back to the In-Between. To kill you, he said. Not to me, he didn't say it to me. He said it to Ritter. They're going back tonight."

Steppe glowered. "What do you mean, tonight? *When* tonight?"

"At midnight."

"To see Ansgar?"

"I don't know."

"I can't let them go back." He moved toward the door.

"Wait!" She put her hand on his shoulder and gasped when he vehemently shook her off. "What's the matter with you?"

"Why would you ask me that?" He turned back to her quickly, a spark igniting his eyes. "Why would you ask me something like that? I have to get to them before they cross through to the In-Between, and it's a bad idea to drive your truck right now. I need to get into a cab."

"I meant—"

"There's *nothing* the matter with me."

"You pulled away from me!" *You've never pulled away from me before.*

"Goddamn it, Reese, not now!"

Tears leapt to her eyes. "I was right. You do hate me."

He took in a long breath. "I don't hate you. I love you enough to know you deserve better."

She found the milk crate with the backs of her legs and sat down. "That's so bullshit."

Steppe moved before her, blocking the garage lights, casting his face in shadow. "But you don't need me to love you," he said.

"You're acting like there was never anything between us."

"Theresa... it was *inappropriate.*"

"Are you kidding me?"

"We've had this conversation before. I took you to the In-Between when you were a girl."

"When you and I were together I was an *adult. I am* an adult."

He shook his head. "I have to go."

"I know what you think," she said. "It wasn't like that for me."

"I'm *eighty-eight* years old. I'm old enough to be your grandfather. One day I might look it, too. What will you think of me then? Still attractive? Still someone you want holding you?"

"It wasn't like that for me. I can't explain why. Or if it's right or not. Right for who, anyway?" She peered at his silhouette, terrified a single blink would snap it out of existence. "You're here... and I don't remember who I was, or what I wanted."

He stood very still, the edges of him catching the greenish fluorescent light. "I'll see you home."

She wove her trembling fingers together and nodded.

They left the garage, Theresa walking slightly ahead, afraid of looking back and seeing that determined scowl on his face; afraid of looking back and finding herself alone. But of course he stayed two paces behind her all the way, as she knew he would, and when they reached street level he walked to the corner and hailed them a cab. They stayed silent the entire ride back to her apartment.

What will he say when he sees Ritter? Maybe I should say something...

Jeez...

She stared at her lap as the car drove on, counting the squares of yellow streetlight as they swept over her folded hands.

Steppe kept his head turned, his gaze on the dark and icy roads. When the driver pulled into Theresa's driveway and stopped the meter she thrust her hand into her purse and tore out her frayed wallet, only to find Steppe already handing him a fifty-dollar bill. "I'll get this," she said, fumbling with the buckle that kept her wallet from falling apart.

"It's the least I can do," Steppe said.

"God, you *and* Ritter," she muttered. "I've got my own money." But she watched him finish the transaction and murmured, "Thanks," before they stepped out of the vehicle.

She noticed him glancing around quickly as he walked her to the front doors. "Do you want to come up?" she asked, instantly regretting the way the words came out. "I mean, in case he's there," she said. "Not for anything else."

He smiled. "Of course."

He escorted her into the elevator. She avoided his gaze in the mirrors, but couldn't help stealing a glance of his profile when he poked his head into the hallway to ensure the coast was clear. *Still handsome. Still worried.*

Where's Ritter?

They walked to her front door. She tried the lock and found it still bolted in place. "Doesn't look like it's been jimmied open," she said, fumbling for her keys. She unlocked the door and flipped on the lights. Her apartment appeared just as she'd left it that morning; blankets tossed over the sofa, a pair of pants slung over her hastily-made bed. She stepped inside and flung open her clothing and linen closets. Nothing. She went to the kitchen and found her breakfast bowl and mug still in the sink where she'd left them that morning. "One sec," she called out before grabbing a large knife from the block and heading to the bathroom. She held it above her head and yanked the shower curtain back. Nothing. She sighed and returned to the front door, gripping the handle tightly in her fist.

Steppe remained where he was: holding the door open, his feet on the other side of her threshold. She couldn't help but chuckle. "You're welcome here," she said. "You should know that."

"I should go," he said. "Put the chain on when I leave. And keep your windows closed. If you have a piece of wood you can lodge in the jamb to keep someone from shoving them back from the outside, that would be—"

"I'm on the sixteenth floor. What is he, Spiderman?" He chuckled. She smiled. "I can still make you laugh."

"Just be careful, Reese," he said. "If anything happened to you, it would... kill me."

She reached for him, put her arms around his neck—her head too slow to stop her heart from acting on its desire—and kissed him. She wanted his arms around her. She wanted to feel his body pressed against hers. She wanted to hear the sound he always made when she kissed him after an argument, that grateful murmur of relief that she'd finally come back to him.

His arms stayed down by his sides, and he didn't kiss her back.

She pulled away.

"We can't do this," he whispered.

"Right." Her chin dipped until she found herself staring at the floor. She reached into her purse and groped through it until she found the piece of paper she'd been searching for. She unfolded it and held it out to him.

"Ritter gave it to me." Steppe took it and studied it for a time. "I didn't know you had a brother," she said. "Or a father, actually. I mean, I knew you had a father, of course, but... you never told me anything about the man you were before..." She waited for some comment from him, some movement, some indication of what he was thinking. "They got your brother's name wrong."

"No they didn't."

"They did. Look at it."

"My brother's name was Istvan." He handed the paper back to her. "It's my name now."

She looked up and stared numbly at him. "Huh?"

"I remember exactly what you said to me, that night you left the In-Between. You said you wanted more. And you deserve it, too. So go ahead, take more. Take whatever you want. Just don't take it from me."

He ducked into the hallway. She listened to the echo of his footsteps thumping on the carpeted floor—left, right, left, right. She could almost hear the sound of war at his heels.

She closed her door, locked it, threw on the chain, and then noticed the corner of a piece of paper sticking out from beneath the welcome mat. "Damn it," she whispered when she finished reading Ritter's note. "When it rains, it pours."

Steppe emerged from Theresa's building and jogged the salted sidewalks to the end of the street. He'd hail a cab from there, out of Theresa's sight, preferably out of her mind too, but that was less likely. Theresa held onto things. It's one of the reasons why he fell in love with her: every step she'd ever taken, every word she'd ever said, every moment she'd ever spent awake, amazed—all of it was written on her face, in the folds of her skin, in her eyes.

CHARLENE CHALLENGER

And she wasn't afraid of all the ugly things he tried so hard to keep hidden. She could suss out his frustration and his joy as though she could feel them herself at the same time. One day he saw her, as he left the colony for Ansgar's fortress, pouring hot maple syrup onto a bed of freshly fallen snow. She fixed those brown eyes on him, and as her new piper robes snapped in the wind around her ankles, he realized she wasn't fooled.

That pitying look on her face: *there goes a man straight to his doom.* She knew him, almost from the very start.

He glanced at his watch. There was still plenty of time to catch a ride to Adoni's apartment. He saw a cab headed down the street toward him. He held up a hand and waved the driver over to the curb.

He would wait outside Adoni's place, at a far enough distance to see what was going on and when he should intervene. He pulled the door shut. The driver sped away.

A small screen mounted on the back of the front passenger's headrest flashed a series of aggressive advertisements at him. He'd ridden in cabs hundreds of times before, but this was the first time he'd ever encountered one of these screens. It took him a moment to figure out how to turn the thing off. When he succeeded he could almost hear Theresa's voice in his ears, clucking at him with mock disdain. *You're going to start telling kids to get off your lawn now*, she'd say, or something to that effect.

Why not? he thought. *I may as well act my age.*

But what age was that, really? Was it the eighty-eight years he'd lived in this world? The age his body physically manifested, having sloughed off fifty years or so by possessing an enchanted piper voice? Or was it the age he felt when the weight of a dense past sat heavy on his shoulders? Occasionally he wondered how Ritter managed to remain so careless, so youthful, given he'd existed for almost a millennium. Then he remembered how easy it was for Ritter to abandon all the things that frightened or upset him.

Steppe kept all of those things with him. Most importantly, they hadn't scared Theresa away.

He settled back and peered out the window, his eyes peeled for a glimpse of Sylvester prowling the streets.

Chapter
16

He arrived at the shoreline after dark, when a shard of moon cast barely enough light for him to find a boat. He had hoped he wouldn't have to walk all the way around the bay. That night, by chance, one of the pipers had rowed to the mainland instead of making the same trip on foot. Steppe took a quick look around to see if the piper was anywhere in sight before climbing aboard and loosening the hitch from the dock cleat. Whoever it was that left the boat unattended would kick herself when she returned and found it gone. He dipped an oar into the black water and began to paddle toward Seventeen Bay.

He'd been travelling across the In-Between for weeks, walking from colony to colony, begging for supplies, for assistance, for reprieve. His words failed and his tenacity threatened to follow suit. Seventeen Bay was the last stop on what had so far been a fruitless journey, and Ichabod, the colony leader, was his last hope for a sympathetic ear.

The wind picked up the further he sailed from shore, a steady gust that slapped the water against the sides of the boat and set the vessel teetering between the waves. He brushed his hair out of his eyes and drew the briny air into his lungs. The calm, the hundreds of stars piercing the mantle of darkness, seemed to be promising signs for the conversation he was about to have. He put his hand in the water until the ocean chill penetrated his palm, then brought it up and pressed it against the side of his neck to refresh his weary skin.

The candlelit windows of ten tiny cabins speckled the cliff side and gave him a sense of where to bring the boat in. He rowed up to a shoal and stashed the oar under his seat before stepping into the shallow water and dragging the boat onto the sand. To his right, a crooked stairway crept up the side of the hill toward the cabins and the three-storey cottage that served as the pipers' living quarters. He put his foot on the bottom step and let it take his weight; it was steadier than it looked, so he started to climb, his fingers gripping the handrail as he ascended.

He'd assembled his thoughts and prepared his words before engaging the other colony leaders. They didn't want to hear about *duty*, he realized, unless it was duty to their own charges and to Ansgar. *Honour* and *mercy* were likewise taboo, as were *war*, *futility*, and *cowardice*.

Please upset them too, but he couldn't think of a more fitting word.

His mind went blank as the light from the first landing of cabins edged the top of the stairs. He kept his eyes on the cottage at the top of the hill as he started up the second set of stairs.

Tell him the truth, plainly, simply; we need his help, or we'll die.

An unnerving silence greeted him as he reached the second landing. The cottage stood to his left, its eggshell-blue siding catching the tiniest glint of moonlight as he turned to face it. There was firelight beyond the windowpanes, but the night was unusually quiet. Steppe stood on the front porch and listened for footsteps behind the door, for a cough or a sneeze or some other sign of life. Met with more stillness, he raised his knuckles and knocked.

The door swung open. Ichabod stood back from the threshold and levelled a shotgun at Steppe's chest. The piper stood six feet tall, black-haired and barrel-chested, an unstable flicker of alarm in his eyes. Steppe leapt away from the door, held up his hands. "Whoa whoa whoa whoa! Don't shoot!"

Ichabod glared at him. "What do you want?"

"Put the gun down."

"What do you want here?"

"To talk. Just to talk."

CHARLENE CHALLENGER

"Start talking."

"The *gun*."

Ichabod held it steady. "You can put your hands down. Lord knows it ain't your hands that'll do me in if I give you the chance."

Steppe lowered his arms. "Where are the others?"

"Sent them to the mainland. I knew you were coming."

"The lights in the windows?"

"Keep the home fires burning."

"You're afraid."

"You're damn right."

"The Welcome needs your help."

"The Welcome ain't my problem."

"You're afraid of *me*."

Ichabod held the shotgun higher. "You've got two minutes."

"The Welcome's home to fifty souls. We abandoned Ansgar's code, and she cut us off. All I ask is for Seventeen Bay to keep the children safe. You have ten cabins, and it'll be a tight fit, but it's the only place left for them in the In-Between." No response. "Ichabod, please."

"Only place left, eh? That figures."

"The pipers can take care of themselves; it's the children I'm worried about. They need a safe place to stay. They're not ready to go back."

"They don't need to be ready. Just open the agate and shove them through."

"Listen to yourself. Is that what you would do?"

"I wouldn't take out another colony leader for wanting to protect her own residents over yours."

"*Take out?*"

"It was your choice to abandon Ansgar's code. You knew what would happen. She lifts immortality for disobedience. I'm a hundred and eight years old, and I'll be good for nothing if I follow in your shoes."

"Do you know her own code is meaningless to her? Do you know she changes her rules on a whim?"

"I don't question demigoddesses."

"Do you know she gave Sylvester a seal bearing her name? And that he used it to brand a young girl and condemn her to silence? On a whim, because she wanted to play a different game."

"And? I don't understand it, and it makes no difference to me and mine. Ansgar makes the rules, and I follow them as best I can."

"Until she changes them. What's to keep her from changing them and throwing you out of her favour?"

"That's why I stay under the radar. Keep to myself. Keep the residents and the pipers of Seventeen Bay happy as best I can. Time's up."

"What do you mean, 'take out?'"

Ichabod glared at him. "They had to scrape them off the walls. That's what you did to them."

Steppe shook his head. "What are you saying?"

"You know what I'm saying!" He put his finger on the trigger. Steppe reared back and snarled. His voice knocked the shotgun from Ichabod's hands and sent it spinning off the cliff side.

"They're dead?"

"Winnie... Cassandra..." Tears sprang to Ichabod's eyes. "And Edith! You know she took me around the In-Between when I was first posted here? To introduce me and show me the lay of the land. She was a good woman, a kind soul, and you... you..."

"I didn't kill them."

"Like hell you didn't!"

"They were alive when I left them."

Ichabod lunged at him but stopped short of crossing the threshold. "You didn't have to do it! If you went back to Ansgar now and begged her forgiveness maybe she would..."

"She wouldn't, and you know it. Not for me. The leaders—"

"Get out of here!" Ichabod shouted, pointing at the blackened horizon.

"I didn't kill them, I swear it!" He pursed his lips and drew in a deep breath. "You believe me," he said with a nod. "Otherwise you wouldn't have opened the door."

Ichabod shuddered and leaned against the jamb. "I want to believe no one'd be that cruel. Edith always said you were a good man, just trapped. We all knew The Welcome's lot was unfair, and we knew what you did with that changeling, keeping him distracted so he wouldn't go after the rest of us. That don't mean I believe you."

"You want me to prove it?"

"You'll be hard pressed. No one in the In-Between can do to them what…"

"Ansgar can."

"But there's no reason for her to."

Steppe rubbed his eyes. "No, there isn't." He stopped. "Unless it wasn't her at all. Unless she gave Sylvester…" The realization came crashing in. "He's following me and when I leave…"

Ichabod's face went pale. He brought a heavy hand down on the knob and slammed the door shut before Steppe could grab hold and force it open. Steppe pressed his chest against the wood and hammered with both fists. "Ichabod, please!"

"He's coming, and he'll wait out there for my pipers if he don't get what he wants," came his muffled voice through the door. "It's them or you."

"You wondered how anyone can be that cruel!" Steppe cried. "Please, Ichabod, there are *fifty* of them! Open the door!"

"I'm sorry Istvan."

"Ichabod!" He pounded harder. "At least take the kids, at least until they're ready to go. None of this is their fault; it's mine! Ichabod! Goddamn it, have mercy!"

Steppe pressed his ear to the door and listened hard; nothing but silence. His impulse was to kick the door, to throw his weight against it and force it off its hinges, but what then? All piper homesteads were protected by a plaque bearing Ansgar's name. If he managed to get the door down, he couldn't cross the threshold without Ichabod welcoming him in. He slammed his fist against it one last time and glanced up, expecting to see the plaque hanging there above the frame, proving Seventeen Bay still had the gift of Ansgar's benevolence, unless Ichabod, taking the same precautions as Steppe had years ago, had nailed it beneath the porch steps so it couldn't be found and removed.

Steppe's eyes were met with nothing more than a discoloured imprint and four holes in the wood where nails used to be.

"Ichabod? Tell me you—"

He heard the chant—softly, softly—start up behind the door. For a split second he was back in his father's house, back under his bed, the smell of peppermint candy on his breath, his twin brother gripping his collar, holding him still, keeping him out of sight. Watching the dullness that crept into his brother's eyes, as they looked their last on that ugly little room. The sound his brother made that forced open his throat and sent a piper's voice careening through his blood. That last, terrible gasp: the anguish his brother felt as his soul tore free.

"It's all right," he heard Ichabod say. "I'll—"

One terrible moment later, Ichabod's blood splashed the tawny windows dark.

Steppe stood aghast, unable to comprehend, unable to believe. But there was no mistaking the way the darkness trickled down the glass. He leapt off the porch and ran toward the edge of the cliff.

The front door flew open as he pounded down the stairs to the first landing. There'd be no warning from Sylvester this time; the changeling would stalk him silently for as long as he had to, and when they finally faced each other, one of them would scream that devastating scream. Steppe turned and snarled at the steps, his voice filled with flying daggers and swords, slicing through the wood, pulling the staircase down into a heap next to one of the cabins. He ducked behind the wall and looked up the side of the cliff. Sylvester's shadowy figure sidled up to the edge and leaned over to survey the remains. A moment later he disappeared; Steppe heard his footsteps dashing and then receding through the long grass that grew over the hill.

Steppe's eyes darted over the shrouded cliff side. There was no way to climb back up again; the slope was steep, the rocks flat, nary a footfall in sight. The only way left to go: down to the shoreline.

Certain the changeling planned to overtake him at the rowboat, he scrambled down the second set of stairs and ran along the base of the cliff in search of a stony ledge he could squeeze behind. He listened for Sylvester's boots pursuing him across the sand. Gentle waves licked the shoreline, the wind whistled in his ears; otherwise the beach was silent.

As he drew nearer to the curve in the shore he turned his head to confirm how far behind Sylvester was. The beach was empty; his footprints alone distorted in the immaculate sand.

He felt Sylvester's fist in his gut first, heavy as lead, and then a thick tree limb slamming into him, knocking him onto his back. The impact robbed him of air, his throat of sound. He arched his back, his heels digging into the ground, gawping like a fish out of water.

Sylvester tossed the tree limb aside and strode toward his prey. He raised his boot and stomped on Steppe's stomach, paralyzing his muscles so he couldn't breathe. He pounced on him, wrapped both his hands around his neck, and squeezed hard enough to wrest his gaze.

"Look at me," he said as Steppe clawed at his fingers, frantic for escape. "Look at me. How could you stand it? All that power for all those years? I wouldn't have hesitated. Ever."

Sylvester started to hum, and the voices—those devastating voices—slunk up his throat like thieves. Steppe felt them washing over him, penetrating his skin. He'd had his immortality lifted several times on Ansgar's caprice and knew what it was like when dread came rushing in, but this sensation was nothing like the suffocating panic that came with her malevolence. There was no euphoric tease, no bait and switch. When he seized Sylvester's collar the veins in his hands bulged unnaturally as his blood boiled hot. His bones softened, a muscle ripped, a fingernail came loose from its bed.

Death was coming for him, relentless, indefatigable.

If he'd had the breath to do it he would have begged Sylvester to strangle him, to take his life the way his father had taken his brother's: clumsily, familiarly. Anything but this.

Compared to this, Ansgar's malice was nothing. No: this was torture. This was horror.

But he'd survived countless horrors. He would do so again.

His right hand let go of Sylvester's collar and lashed out in the darkness, slicing it open, summoning the agate from behind its wintry veil. With everything he had, with everything he held dear locked tight in his breast, he rolled sharply over and threw Sylvester off of him and into the light.

Sylvester's eyes were cruel and bright as molten metal as the agate seared itself shut behind him. Steppe saw them glowing with hatred on the other side. Sylvester stood and stared at the space he'd just traversed, his entire body as tight as a bowstring ready to snap, shaking with rage. Steppe watched the changeling until he finally had the strength to turn his back.

He pressed his cheek against the damp sand and breathed in slowly, steadily, watching the moon edge the black waves with silvery light. His heavy limbs kept him anchored to the shoreline, despite the frigid wind coming in from the ocean. He raised his left hand off the ground and held it up. He'd broken three of his fingers in the fight and extended the crooked digits as best he could. The pain speared his arm. He grunted and sagged against the sand. He doubted he'd be able to play piano, even after they healed, not with the skill and precision he was used to. He closed his eyes and listened to the water as it rolled onto the shore.

Belinda loved the sound of water, he remembered.

The water, the wind, loon song and cricket song; he opened his mouth and drew them all in; his blood cooled and his sinews strengthened. He raised himself on his elbow, propped himself up on his hands and knees, carefully got to his feet. His head swam; he took a step and stumbled, almost falling over completely but managing to stay upright long enough to reclaim his senses.

He turned back and peered through the fabric of the In-Between, into the darkness of the world beyond. Sylvester was gone.

But there it was, tiny, insubstantial, glinting under the moonlight, half-buried in the sand: Ansgar's seal.

Steppe stooped and picked it up. Her name, spelled backwards in the brass, ignited the hatred in his guts. *He dropped it.*

Dear god, he dropped *it.*

He stuffed the seal into his pocket and wrapped his fingers tightly around it.

He found the boat and, fighting the terrible pain in his broken fingers as best he could, rowed back to the dock on the other side of the bay. The moon was on its way down. In the east, a reddish glow began to creep across the sky.

He'd make the trip back to The Welcome, now that he knew no one was going to help them, no one was going to save them. Now that he knew all the leaders were dead.

Steppe felt the weight of their souls hanging from his neck as he climbed up the hill toward a beaten path heading west. Four lives villainously, deliberately, snuffed out. Sylvester must have demanded Ansgar level the playing field, Steppe thought, and she'd obliged him with the one thing that gave Steppe dominion over him: a voice that could tear the universe asunder, with the sound of death vibrating between the notes. The most terrible gift there was. And she'd given it to him without a second thought to the destruction he'd cause. *I should have known*, Steppe thought. *With Ritter on the other side whom else would Sylvester punish? And with what weapon?*

He stopped his ascent and gazed at Seventeen Bay in the distance. It looked peaceful; its adorable cabins were nestled in the rocky ledges, candlelight still flickering in their windows. If he hadn't let Ritter leave the colony, if he hadn't forsaken Ansgar's code, if he hadn't convinced the pipers who'd trusted him with their lives to follow suit—*they'd be alive*, he thought.

And Sylvester would still fear me.

He followed the curve of the bay until the land stretched north before him, and then he set out toward The Welcome.

❖

His heels were blistered and bleeding by the time he reached the outskirts of the colony. He looked forward to melting a pan of snow and heating the water warm enough to soak his aching feet, but couldn't guarantee there'd be time for such luxury if word of the piper leaders' deaths had reached The Welcome. Ichabod had immediately accused him of their murders the second he found Steppe at his door. Would Steppe's charges do the same?

Not to my face, he thought.

In the weeks leading up to his trip across the In-Between he'd been increasingly temperamental, the fear of failure weighing heavily on his heart as he rationed out supplies and plotted the colony's next move. He was almost impossible to be around, snapping answers to simple questions, grinding his teeth whenever his thoughts were interrupted, and retreating to the solitude of his room immediately after a task was finished to avoid explanations or compliments. One afternoon he stubbed his toe on his way into the kitchen and let out a curse and a snarl of pain forceful enough to crack the wall. The other pipers witnessed what happened. He caught them staring at him later as he drew a clean drink of water from the well.

He set out for Ocean's Wake that very night. He'd hoped removing himself would give them all a chance to breathe more easily, to be free of his oppressive moodiness. As he drew closer to the western colony his optimism grew, so that by the time he reached its threshold he was certain Winnifred would wholeheartedly welcome his request and The Welcome would be saved.

But Winnifred rejected him, souring his hopes in a matter of moments. No matter how angry he became or how fervidly he begged, she would not be moved. Nor would the others, he discovered in his many months away.

His pipers would wonder about his guilt for the rest of their days, but they'd understand what he sacrificed for their sakes, and they'd bring him back into the fold when he returned. They'd lived alongside his darkness for decades. It may have scared them, but they were used to it.

He stepped through the trees and into the clearing, where the first of The Welcome's cabins stood in the early morning glow. The pipers couldn't keep the four pillars burning bright and hot; no longer enchanted by Ansgar's name, fire would annihilate the intricate carvings in the wood and eventually burn them down to the ground. Now they stood solemnly, unlit, around the colony, half their size, their majesty threatened but not quite defeated, on the edge of a new day. Steppe kept a sharp eye out for any sort of movement of child or piper, his toughest answers at the ready.

No, no one is going to help us. No, I won't let us starve. No, there's nothing to be afraid of.

As he walked between the cabins toward the chalet, a smell, like the funk of rusted iron or steel, came into his nostrils. At first he thought Paj had simply burned her potatoes again. He kept his gaze on the chalet's front porch, dimly lit in rose by the rising sun. But the smell grew more pungent the closer he drew to the clearing, until he realized that he did indeed know it, not as The Welcome's fragrance but as a stench that had visited the place before.

Blood. Violence. He stopped walking.

He saw their crumpled, lifeless figures lying in the snow. He wouldn't turn his head.

The chalet door opened. Paj stepped onto the porch. She moved to the top of the stairs and caught sight of him standing there, staring ahead, hopeless, defeated. "Istvan!" she called, her voice cracking open, every hint of laughter gone but still harbouring the faintest expectation that he could set things right again.

His heart broke. He was too late. Nothing he could do would save them now.

He turned around and left them all behind, for their own sakes, for good.

Chapter
17

He walked for an hour, retracing his steps through the woods, his nerves crackling. With no destination in mind he knew exactly what he was doing: running away, from all his promises and all his responsibilities, escaping into a great unknown for a chance to live a stretch of time without hurting anyone. A play to relive the selfish notions of his youth.

How many were dead? Did any survive? He didn't want to know.

Despair came rushing in as he gazed up the great lengths of the evergreen trees, up at the lightening sky. It was all on his watch. The death of his first beloved, the changeling threat, the suicides, the violence, all of it. He had failed every one of The Welcome's remaining souls, had caused their destruction by sheer proximity. His leadership was marked by ineptitude and folly, and he'd turned tail and ran when faced with the repercussions. His desolation only served to fuel his hatred for Ansgar, who'd placed him at the forefront of this unwinnable war and threatened him with devastation if he refused to do battle. Even as he walked—as he ran—he considered his departure long overdue.

The ache in his heels spread throughout his body. Exhausted, he stepped into a smaller clearing and sat down on the nearest heap of snow. His muscles throbbed. He closed his eyes and filled his lungs with crisp, clean air. Stillness gave way to the effervescent chirps of robins and starlings. As dawn broke he looked around the clearing and noticed other mounds of melting snow. Each was a different size and all seemed deliberately placed. The remnants of a snow fort, he reckoned, from a happier time. Stone

Xs marked out the fort's significant spots. He assumed they were there to demonstrate where snowball artillery would be kept at the ready. Or perhaps they were symbols representing the areas out of bounds. But one of the patterns stood out to him. He squinted at it until its empty shape filled with the shadow of a guitar, lying on a bedroom floor on the other side of the In-Between.

He saw a flash of movement near the largest heap of snow and heard the scrape of clothing against the ground. He stood up to get a better look. Sylvester's changelings were still around to terrorize the In-Between; though they weren't as great a threat as their leader, they still posed a risk to the safety of those they caught off-guard. Their indiscriminate ferocity made them unpredictable foes, but Steppe had never known them to sneak around or lie in wait for their prey. He marched toward the heap of snow, drew in a breath, and rounded the corner with a petrifying roar at the ready.

The shivering creature crouched in the snow was no changeling; it was Natalie.

Her purple hair and mottled cheeks startled Steppe, who leapt back when she screamed at the sight of him. When she realized who he was, she started to cry.

Steppe knelt in the snow and threw his arms around her. "It's all right, Natalie," he said. "It's all right. You're safe."

Natalie sagged against his chest, sobbing, shaking. "Did you get him?" she asked him weakly. He pursed his lips and held her tighter. "*Did you get him?*"

"I'm sorry."

"He just started shooting!"

"Are you hurt?"

"Tell me you got him!" He could hear Paj's tribute to her in her voice. Her sobs left no space for his reply.

The wet snow seeped into his pants at the knees and his muscles shuddered as he held her. He stared at the trees as fear wracked her body, until her crying subsided. "The last thing I ever said to my mom was *I hate you*," she muttered, her bottom lip trembling.

"Are you hurt?" he asked again.

She shook her head. "I heard a pop—pop, pop, pop, like that—and he was there just walking between the cabins, so I ran for the porch and hid under it... I saw his legs and he passed me... and he said something, I don't know what, I don't know if he was even talking to me... and he'd walk and then he'd shoot someone..." She wiped her cheeks with the backs of her hands. "He'd shoot another kid. He's younger than me. He's a kid *too*."

"When did it happen?"

"Just a few hours ago." Her mouth twisted and soon another bout of crying seized her chest. "Why'd he have to *shoot us*?"

He reached into his coat pocket and retrieved the clean handkerchief he kept there. "Wipe your face."

"Did you get him?"

"No."

"*Why not?*" He put his hands on her shoulders and urged her to her feet. "You could get him!" she said. "You could go back and get him and make sure he's stopped!"

He wouldn't meet her gaze. "Get up now, there you go, that's it."

Natalie pressed the handkerchief to her face. "I saw all this blood on the snow. When I thought he was gone and I ran out from the porch and went into the trees... they fell with their arms and legs all backwards..." She bent her arm and twisted her wrist. "If you fall like that you never get back up..."

"It's going to be all right."

"Why don't you go back and stop him? You could go back and take him out!"

"*Don't say that.*"

"You've done it before!"

"Don't say that!"

She choked on her sobs and swallowed hard, stifling them completely.

Her expression hardened. She crumpled onto the heap of snow and curled her knees up to her chest. "My mom doesn't even know where I am..."

Beneath her, on the other side, Steppe saw a bed, a simple comforter, two pillows, and mere inches before her, but a dimension away, a brown and tattered teddy bear.

She looked so much like he did the night he cowered under his bed, the night he shrank against the wall, away from his father's touch. It seemed such a waste to him; this would be what she inevitably took away from the In-Between, when she finally decided to go. This last day would wipe out every other day she'd had, any day that was yet to come. Haunted and hunted, with eyes forever edged with panic and anger.

Unless...

He put his hand on her shoulder. "Let's go."

"He's still there," she said. "Maybe he's waiting for other people to show up. Or..." She turned back to him. "Do you think he killed himself too?"

"We're not going back there."

"Where are we going?"

You'll see. Someone should see.

He started to sing. It was a simple, unassuming melody, the kind of tune sung softly under a person's breath while he went about completing mundane tasks. He knew the intricate play of sounds behind the notes would bring her to her feet and move her to follow him. He chose them carefully, based on the tribute Paj had composed for her: water and fire where earth stood unopposed, sweetness to lay alongside sourness, endings for the things left undefined.

Natalie's expression softened. She rose from her bed and watched him brush the snow from his knees. When he met her gaze he could tell his voice had enchanted her, and by the glint in her eye, he knew she was aware of his spell. Their senses never left them completely; the children simply allowed the music to overtake them, because it filled the empty spaces in their hearts. They couldn't get enough of it, because it almost worked.

"Follow me," he said. "I know exactly where we're going."

He started through the trees, humming the tune now that he had her attention and trust, and she followed closely behind him. His body still ached, but eventually his momentum made the pain easier to ignore. The forest floor was uneven, with patches of snow and ice melting in different stages and exposed roots jutting out from the ground. He stepped over them and kept an even pace that Natalie eventually matched. They walked until they arrived at the river that ran through the forest. It was mostly frozen but enough water still trickled over the rocks and sheets of ice to entice them to pause for a drink. Steppe knelt at the river's edge, cupped his hands, and brought a mouthful to his thirsty lips. Natalie did the same. She turned to him. "This is where the changelings got Adoni," she said. "Maybe not exactly here. Along here, though. She was drinking at the river."

"Really."

"Do you think she's okay?"

"I'm sure she's fine."

Natalie sat back on her haunches. "I was so freaked out, I remember. Changelings are scarier when you can see them clearly. They look like old dolls someone left in the rain for a few years. Giant ones. They all kind of look the same, actually. Do you know why?"

"They come from the same era, those ones. There were thousands more, but most of them didn't make it back to the In-Between. The ones that attacked us are from the last days of changeling subjugation, most likely left in the same geographic area, so they're dressed the same and have similar features. They formed a collective when they came back to the In-Between." He looked across the river. "They live in the woods."

"They burned Adoni's shoulder with that seal," Natalie said. "Remember how loud she can scream now? She shook the whole place up. I wonder if she can do that on the other side too."

"She can't."

"She'd be so badass if she could." Natalie grinned at the thought. "She could tell her stupid mom off anyway. Bet the bitch wouldn't ever hit her again. Sometimes I wish they'd gotten me instead. The burning would suck, I know, and it's not like I'd want to feel the pain, but then I'd have this power and I could..." She sighed. "Stop the shooting. Or whatever. Maybe it wouldn't even have happened in the first place. You think maybe if you hadn't left...?" Her cheeks flushed, and the rest of the thought stuck in her throat.

"Yes and no," he finished. "I don't know. I don't understand children."

"It's because you have to do what she says, right?" Natalie said. "That Ansgar person wants you to take children away, right?"

"She does."

"How can you not understand kids?".

He smirked. "I wasn't a kid for very long."

"Is that why you got mad at that one kid and messed his face up?"

"Who told you that?"

Natalie's eyes were bright, her grin more pitying than impertinent. "Ritter did. He was the only one who used to talk to us."

The child she was referring to was a boy Steppe thought he could save without abiding by Ansgar's code, someone he tried to reach by relating every experience the boy had had to his own, by saying things like, "I know how you feel" and "I understand." But he didn't know how the boy felt, and he didn't understand, and when the boy lashed out at him and called him on his hypocrisy, he let his anger get the better of him and snarled so viciously, he tore one of the boy's eyes out of his head. He'd been trying to forget that terrible moment ever since.

"He offered you that information?"

"I asked him. We could all hear you guys singing at night, you know, all the time. One of my first nights there you sang this one song, and it was really intense, like, more intense than any of the other songs I heard you sing before, so I asked him about it, and he told me it was for this kid from a long time ago."

Steppe found a flat rock to sit on. "He should have stopped there."

"I just kept asking him though, and he told me."

"Ritter's a fool."

"But it's true, right?"

"It's true."

"Because you couldn't understand him?" She reached down, picked up a handful of tiny pebbles, and worried them between her fingers as she spoke. "All the people who are supposed to know what's best for us were only kids for a few years too, so how are they supposed to know how we feel?"

"They act on their own fears, the things they feared as children, assuming they'll be yours," he said. "It's all they have to go on."

"What if they remembered it wrong?"

"I don't know." He stood. "Time to go."

"Aren't you ever gonna tell me where we're going?" she asked. "How far is it?"

"Not much farther. There's something I have to do."

"Can't I just stay here?" She looked around. "Well, not here... I can hide while you go do your thing."

"I want someone to witness it." *Someone to tell me if I've gone too far.*

"Is it because you don't want to be alone? I get that, don't worry."

He nodded.

They walked along next to the water until the riverbank grew narrow enough to cross with a single leap. He crossed first and waited for Natalie to follow. She gnawed on her bottom lip while she considered her footing.

He hadn't sung a tribute to the boy he'd maimed in a long time. The melody used to sneak into his throat when he felt exceptionally guilty or powerless and wanted desperately to take back the mistakes of his past, but he rarely gave it voice. Natalie likely heard it that last time he sang it.

Ritter had been insufferable that day, avoiding Steppe in the clearing, pointedly leaving a room if Steppe entered. When it came time to sing evening songs he'd become openly petulant, snorting at the tributes and muttering under his breath when Steppe chose to compliment the pipers who sang them, until at last Steppe invited him to share his real thoughts.

"Well, we're all singing very prettily tonight," Ritter said, "and we're patting ourselves on the back for it, as usual. But it all gets a bit cloying, don't you think? If this ridiculous ritual is supposed to connect us with our glorious piper heritage and pay homage to our creator, surely we can afford an evening of tangible soul-searching."

Steppe was intrigued in spite of himself. "Do you have something particular in mind?"

"We sing about the children we didn't reach or couldn't reach. We sing about our failures." He folded his hands together and set them on his knees.

"What good will that do for anyone?" Paj asked. Her fellow pipers muttered in agreement.

"Being difficult on purpose," Roxanne grumbled.

"Oh, and Ansgar forbid any one of us be *difficult*," he said with a scowl.

"Maybe he is," Steppe said. "But he's right. We do make it too easy on ourselves sometimes."

"He's not just trying to get us out of our comfort zones," she snapped. "He's being a brat, as usual. And what do you know about soul searching anyway?" she asked Ritter. "You barely even sing evening songs anymore. Even the *easy* ones."

Finnur put his hand on her knee. "You're wasting your time," he said gently.

Ritter raised his hands. "You've got me," he said. "Far be it for me to try and contribute something meaningful to this pointless display. Let's all just sit around and sing about our triumphs. It's a much more comfortable way to spend eternity."

Steppe heard a timbre that only rarely crept into Ritter's quips. Maybe his intention was to run his mouth off in the hope of annoying the others, but he'd reconsidered when Roxanne called him out. The last thing Ritter ever wanted was to be accurately pegged by anyone. No matter what the purpose may originally have been, at that moment he spoke in earnest, and it moved Steppe in a way he'd recently thought impossible.

He threw down the gauntlet. "You'll start us off, then?"

Ritter gazed back at him with a frown on his face. *If he's going to back out*, Steppe thought, *this is his moment.* Ritter could easily have played his unwillingness off as hurt feelings for having to defend himself. Steppe was about to speak again when Ritter got to his feet and moved to the middle of the music room. He put on his ceremonial piper mask and turned toward the fireplace, where an inferno had been burning steadily away for most of the evening. Orange flames danced in his green eyes. He started to sing.

He didn't shy away from the challenge, nor did he pick an insubstantial failure that ultimately meant nothing; no ill-timed encounters with children in distress who were then left to fend for themselves, no stories of rebellious youth who left The Welcome more hurt and angry than they were when they first arrived. Ritter went for the weakest link in their chain. He sang a simple, elegant melody for the unnamed children who were buried somewhere deep in the woods; the children who'd taken their own lives.

The other pipers were suddenly alert on their chairs and listening intently. Ritter drew closer to the fire and held his hands out toward the flames, his silhouette a black slash against the brightness. He seemed to conjure each child, one by one, from the shadows, and gave each of them their due, with ribbons of melody and harmony that crowned their heads and invited the pipers' reverence. In a moment, after years of obscurity, the children's faces came so clearly to their minds, it was as if they stood with Ritter in the firelight. He sang with exceptional conviction, without faltering, without losing his nerve or his way. As though he could bring them all back to life.

Steppe was taken aback. He knew Ritter sang beautifully, knew how intricately Ritter could weave melodies together, as though they were plaited strands of brilliant gold in his hands. Ritter's voice was unique from the others in that, aside from a few licks of other instruments and one or two vibrations of the natural world, it was mostly comprised of other voices, other people he'd encountered in his many long years of life within and beyond the In-Between. It occurred to him that Ritter was the only piper among them who sounded like a thousand souls at once.

Among Ritter's many voices, one in particular was capable of breaking Steppe's heart. He prayed that he wouldn't hear it calling out to him from among the others.

The song came to an end. Ritter had left Belinda out of it. He took off his mask and sat down again. The others remained silent, their eyes cast on various spots in the room, each in his or her own world.

Steppe thanked him with a nod.

He put on his mask—three strips of brass that lay flat across his forehead, over his nose, over his chin—took his place before the fire, and started to sing.

His biggest failure felt at first, to him, like drowning, constantly drowning. And so up came the waters: the waters that crashed against rocks, the waters that tore away at cliffs and shores, the waters that dragged freighters to the depths of oceans and seas, the waters that stopped mouths and lungs and hearts. Underneath those waters, the earth's foundations shook and split, chasms formed and swallowed every trickle, every wave. In the desolation that remained, over every parched mile, a searing wind blew across crook and crevice, scouring the barren landscape as smooth as a marble and tossing it through an empty sky. It seemed as though, in every lyric, every line, the boy stood next to him, shadowing his every move, his remaining eye ever watchful, fixed squarely on the man who had violated his trust.

He brought the song to an end, removed his mask, and turned back to his pipers. All gazes remained transfixed on the music room's distant corners, except Ritter's. He alone had the courage to welcome Steppe back from the edge, with a smile and a hand over his heart.

That was the last time Steppe sang the boy's tribute, to anyone.

Natalie leapt over the river and landed safely on the other side. They continued into the forest. The wind picked up; tiny drops of rain stung their cheeks as they walked. The air smelled of soggy earth, and faintly, of smoke and flame. Steppe heard Natalie huffing and puffing behind him but wouldn't slow his pace. At one point she stopped and bent over, trying to catch her breath. "Just a little further," he said. "You'll have plenty of time to rest."

"Okay, seriously, where are we going?"

There was no need to answer her; beyond the now-thinning trees stood a collective of rusted shacks and hovels that were easily visible from where they stood. The huts were built among several thick trunks and shared one great sagging roof. Even at that distance, Steppe could smell the changelings' skins; their synthetic scent permeated the air around their crumbling home.

"Isn't this where…" She looked at him with wide and fearful eyes. "This is where the changelings live!"

"Yes." He marched forward.

"What are we even doing here? What are you gonna do?" Natalie called after him.

He strode into the narrow clearing and stopped at the ramshackle entrance to the compound. No doubt the flimsy door barely protected the changelings from the elements. Electric lights shone through the cracks in the walls. He heard the purr of a generator on the other side of the structure; all else was silent and still.

Were they asleep? He couldn't tell. But they weren't anticipating his visit, and they were about to be terrified.

Good.

He raised his foot and kicked the door in.

A tangle of uneven hallways buttressed with fallen tree limbs, and sheets of aluminum siding, greeted him. The repugnant smell of old plastic instantly filled his nostrils. He marched down the hall leading left, stepping over the steel jambs that occasionally protruded from the earthen floor. He passed several empty rooms, until he reached another corridor that veered off to the right. He took it, and soon noticed another sound accompanying the steady beat of his boots on the ground: a quiet hissing through relaxed lips, akin to gentle dozing. Up ahead, a colourful glow cast down upon the empty space before a crooked doorway. He stepped into it and glared across the threshold.

Several changelings sat together, limbs intertwined, heads on each other's shoulders, their jaws hanging loose, under a giant knot of Christmas lights. Their eyes were open and staring dreamily across the room. Had they just woken up? Or was this how they spent their days when their leader wasn't ordering them to attack?

Steppe sneered. *Mindless animals*, he thought. *Just waiting for the word. Stinking, slobbering creatures. Lying all over each other. Disgusting.*

Guilty.

He drew in a breath and roared.

The resulting shockwave pulled the changelings up to their feet and scattered them. A broken-down table and two chairs careened across the floor and smashed to pieces against the walls. Steppe snarled again; the changelings cowered along the edges of the room. He stood in the doorway, leering at their fright, and not a single one of them dared to try and get past him. Their hissing intensified, as did the fear in their glassy eyes. Some of them turned and started scratching at the beaten floor, trying to dig their way under the walls; others stood paralysed, their chests heaving, their arms up around their heads. Steppe lunged into the room, clearing a path behind him, and bellowed, "WAR!"

The changelings swept past him and dashed through the corridor. He left the room and continued on his way through the compound, screaming and snarling at every changeling who passed him by. He stomped into other rooms, his voice breaking light bulbs and shattering glass, curling up soiled rugs and flinging them into corners, smashing everything made of wood; shelves, crates, tables and chairs, the very tree limbs that held up sections of the roof and walls. Whenever he encountered a changeling, he saw it cringe and cower before it made its escape.

Let them cower, he thought. *Let them run. They attacked The Welcome with a hundred times the verve. They terrified the children without a second* thought. *They nearly killed one of them. With an axe. No pity. No pity for them. Mongrels. Savages.*

He burst into another room and stalked toward two changelings who clung to each other and crouched behind a dusty upholstered chair. "Get out!" he snarled, and they took their cue, scrambling to their feet and out the door, hissing all the while. He craned his head and listened for changelings foolish enough to return and attack. The compound was completely silent.

He turned back to the room and held his tongue as he gazed at its simple furnishings. A small bed stood against the wall, draped with threadbare blankets and flat pillows. A collection of notebooks was propped up on a shelf. Steppe approached and took a notebook down. He found the ruled pages filled with relatively neat handwriting, the entries dated. A journal, he realized, which meant this was the room he had been searching for. The last entry Sylvester had written in this particular volume ended ominously: *We'll have our revenge.*

Steppe whipped the book at the wall and set to work tearing the place apart. He snatched the sheets from the bed and flipped the mattress over, smashed the frame with his boot, pulled the other journals off the shelves and ripped them in half before throwing them aside. Sylvester's dilapidated wardrobe was next on the route of destruction; Steppe hauled it away from the wall and pushed it over so that it crashed against the floor. A hinge snapped in half, a knob broke free and rolled across the room. Steppe pounced on the wardrobe and ripped through the meagre outfits it contained. He wanted the satisfaction of tearing the entire room apart with his hands. Then, he stood up and surveyed the fallout of his rage.

The girl was waiting just outside. He'd seen the fear in her eyes. She'd carry the ugliness around with her, and it would seep into her every filament like a poison. Her body in a constant state of fight, muscles never able to relax completely. He knew too well what it felt like to spend entire days consumed by thoughts of utter helplessness. He hoped he'd be able to fulfill this one last act of generosity.

CHARLENE CHALLENGER

He found the entrance to the compound and leaned against the jamb. "Natalie? Where are you?"

She'd tucked herself away to avoid the changelings' detection and now hauled herself out from behind a hedge of rock and snow. "They all went running..." she muttered, pointing off through the forest.

"It's all right."

"You just went in there and... what? They all came out like they were... and I heard you yelling..."

"Come on." He curled a finger and beckoned her over.

"What are we gonna do now?" She inched closer to him. "Did you wreck the place?"

"You'll be fine, I promise." He started humming the tune from earlier.

The dismay drained from her face. "Are we going back to The Welcome?"

"No."

"Then are we going to one of the other colonies?"

"No." He opened his arms.

She walked into them and rested her head on his shoulder. He fished the seal out of his pocket and brought it up to his lips. He continued the song, delicately, as Natalie spoke. "I guess I should go back," she said, voice quivering. "But I don't want to go back. I don't know... what am I supposed to do when I get back? I can't go home. I don't want to see them, but..." He felt her body trembling in his arms. "I miss my mom. But I still hate her! But I don't know what else I could do, except... I don't want to live on the street. Maybe my friends will let me stay with them. The last time I saw them we were good, things were good, so they should still be good, right? You know when you don't talk to your friends for a while, and they get mad at you even though you didn't do anything? Maybe they're mad at me... Do you think Adoni would let me stay with her?"

Steppe stared through the In-Between to the other side. *A regular street. Doesn't look like there are a lot of people around. Perfect.*

"Maybe not," Natalie continued. "Maybe she's mad too. She probably is." She let out a sob. "She's probably at home even though her mom's a bitch. She's so stupid, going back. But I bet she has everything all figured out, though. I bet she's making plans and going to school and maybe she's even got a job or something. I hope she got rid of that stupid friend of hers. I hope she's okay. Do you think she'd let me stay with her?" She swallowed. "I don't want to go back."

Steppe took the seal away from his lips. Ansgar's name was white hot in the overcast light; he'd whispered enough fire and flame to set the brass glowing.

"I'm sorry," he said.

He gave her a reassuring squeeze, brushed her hair off the nape of her neck, and pressed the seal firmly against her flesh.

He felt her seize up and heard her gasp, and wished, with all his might, that she would forget her time in the In-Between. Then he sliced the agate open, tore the seal away from her skin, and pushed her through. The agate sealed itself up again.

Steppe stared at the now-empty compound. He crossed its threshold and retraced his movements until he found Sylvester's room once more. He picked up one of the discarded journals and put the corner of a page to the seal. Flames crept up the edge of the paper and spread to the rest of the pages. He tossed the burning lot back onto the pile and watched the fire grow. Before the heat could overtake him, he turned to go.

The seal.

He stopped for one brief moment. His fingers closed around it, and he made his decision.

Chapter
18

Adoni opened her eyes and let them settle on the empty fireplace. In the glow of early dawn, she could see the black residue of fires past creeping up the bricks and disappearing into the flue. Each of her senses sharpened as she stirred; she felt a breeze on her exposed cheek, and the blankets tucked up under her chin, and smelled the warm musk of Ritter's skin as he dozed away next to her. She peered at his upturned nose and thought about waking him by mischievously pinching his nostrils closed, but decided against it. Instead she stared at him, listened to his soft breathing, until he finally woke. He gazed up at the ceiling for a moment, then felt her eyes on him. "I know. I look terrible first thing in the morning."

"How'd you sleep?" she asked.

"Fine, as soon as you stopped snoring."

"I don't snore!"

He smirked. "Like a truck stuck in a snow drift."

"You're lying."

"I had half a mind to put a pillow over your face and smother you."

"I don't even know what you're saying, I don't snore." She sat up and rubbed her eyes.

"And you?" He propped his head up with an arm and winked at her. "What's it like sleeping with the hottest guy in town?"

She rolled her eyes. "You can stop right there. Fine. I slept but I don't feel rested."

"A wise man once said the key to happiness is a good night's sleep."

"Yeah, well, he never slept in a beanbag chair."

Her eyes drifted across the floorboards and settled on the black letters. Still shiny, still menacing, they put an end to their lightheartedness. "You really think they'd kill one of their own to send a message?" she asked.

"I do. But I don't think they attacked one of their numbers and made an example of them. I think whoever the unfortunate was, they volunteered for the sacrifice."

"Can they even think like that?"

"Can they? Of course they can."

"But how would they know what the other one's thinking? They can't even talk."

"Language isn't the only way to communicate, darling."

"But they're *crazy*," she said. "Look at them, look at their eyes and the way they breathe and the way they tear things apart—"

He sat up. "Look at the way they *write*. Look at the way they organize themselves. Look at the way they carry out their attacks. They have a community. They understand each other. There's nothing *crazy* about it."

"You think attacking us and smashing things all the time makes sense?"

"It doesn't have to make sense to us. It's up to us to listen and to try to understand." Adoni scratched at a patch of dry skin on her elbow. Ritter smoothed a hand over her back and sighed. "This is going to be a very long day, I can tell."

"When's the last time you saw Ansgar?"

"The day I begged her to let you stay at The Welcome without an invitation. I didn't leave on good terms, exactly, but she let me keep my life. So that's something."

"What does she look like?"

Ritter got to his feet and went to the windowsill. "She takes on any form she likes," he said, scooping up handfuls of snow and rubbing his wet palms over his face. "Which is probably why she's so unpredictable. No one can keep their wits about them when they constantly change into other forms. There are different truths for different beasts. I suspect Ansgar lost the ability to tell the difference between them a long time ago."

"Shape-shifting is enough to make her nuts? I thought she was all-powerful."

"Power corrupts, Donny girl. They haven't taught you that at your fancy university?"

"It just seems like such a dumb reason to drive you crazy. Especially when you're a demigoddess."

"There's no reason for her to remain in a state we puny humanoids consider sane." He turned back to her. "She used to be closer to our version of normal. She's always been headstrong, but in her newer years she was calmer, almost... almost benevolent. Still a child, but an unspoilt one. She could still feel remorse when she hurt something or someone. And I used to be able to reason with her. Those years are long gone now. Even if she wanted to change her ways, I don't think she can. I don't think she remembers the way she used to be.

"The last time I saw her, she appeared as a full-grown woman in a splendid gown. Playing dress-up that time, I suppose. She's appeared to me as a man, a wolf, a rat, a unicorn. One time she appeared as a dragon. Nearly scared my pants off with that one. Sometimes she's only a voice in the dark. That's when you really have to watch out. I learned early: if she doesn't show herself at all, she's angry enough to kill."

Adoni joined him at the window and washed her face with the snow, as he had. "Will she be angry if she sees us?"

"No. I'm sure of that. No, Donny, this is what she loves most of all—listening to others beg for her esteem or her forgiveness. She'll be delighted to see us, I've no doubt." He turned around and leaned against the broken sill while Adoni freshened up. "Do yourself a favour and follow my lead when we're in her presence. If we come on too strong, or too formal—"

"Too much like Steppe?"

Ritter nodded. "—Too much like Steppe, she won't want to tolerate us at all."

Adoni looked out at the pale white sky. "Did you ever tell Steppe that?"

"I did. And he wouldn't listen. He's a bit of a know-it-all, that one."

She heard a knock at the bedroom door. Paj peeked in on them. "I thought I heard you. I made potatoes for breakfast. There are plenty of them. I even used rosemary and a bit of cracked pepper, the way Theresa used to. Oh, those meals…" Her stomach growled. She pressed a hand over her belly. "Sorry. I hope you like them. Potatoes are really easy to grow."

Adoni felt her stomach rumble and came away from the window. "We should bring some with us too, right?"

"Mashed potatoes. With a side of roasted potatoes." She blushed. "They're the only things I've got around to cook."

"I'm sure they're delicious," Ritter said. "Potatoes are perfect for long journeys. Ask any Irishman and he'll tell you the same thing."

Adoni followed Paj and Ritter down the stairs. Tyler stood in the hallway with two stuffed gunny sacks at his feet. "It'll be a tough journey," she said as they reached the bottom step. "We should bring the sled, in case one of us gets tired."

"We'll make our way north to the river, so we can take on extra water and cross at its narrowest point," Ritter said. "Then we'll move east to avoid the thickest part of the forest. Anyway, let's *really* get down to brass tacks. How many potatoes are there, and how many of them can I eat without exploding?" He strolled toward the kitchen.

Adoni followed him and took one of the remaining seats at the table. Several wooden boards covered the broken window. The floors were free of glass and debris. Paj must have worked well into the night to put the room back in order before dawn.

"Ansgar's not one to be toyed with," Paj said as she entered the kitchen.

"Good thing she's not the toy. I am."

"Ritter…"

"There's no sense in working yourself up. Ansgar can't be predicted, so there's no sense in fretting about it."

"That's just what I thought you'd say."

"Meaning?"

CHARLENE CHALLENGER

Paj smiled and didn't answer.

He rubbed his hands together. "Smells delicious."

"I hope you like them," she said. "I try to make them like Theresa did. She's a fantastic cook, Theresa. The things she can do with spices…"

"She has her own food truck," Adoni said.

Paj smiled. "That's so nice. Is she happy?"

"Well," Adoni said, thinking back to Theresa's brief outburst of worry, "she's got good days and bad days, but she's pretty happy for the most part."

"That's so nice to know that a child left The Welcome… happy. For a change." She folded her hands together and held them up under her chin.

Ritter found a bowl that was relatively intact and heaped himself a generous serving of potatoes from a tureen on top of the potbellied stove. "Go on, darling," he said to Adoni. "There's plenty enough for all."

Adoni found two tin plates in one of the cupboards, dusted them off with her sleeve, and approached the tureen. Paj's potatoes were a sorry sight when compared to Theresa's: pale and mushy as opposed to crispy and golden. Adoni's stomach wasn't up for being picky. She fixed a plate for Tyler and held it out to him. He took it and joined Ritter at the table without saying thank you. *Bet he's still mad*, she thought. An icky feeling stole into her gut. *I was right*, she reminded herself. *I told him to stay behind.* She helped herself, leaned against the counter, and started eating the spuds with her fingers. Mealy and bland, she nonetheless enjoyed scarfing them down. The very act of eating warmed her up. She popped the last potato into her mouth and licked the tips of her fingers clean.

"Yeah, I needed that," she said as she looked at the others.

Paj smiled. "Thank you."

Adoni noticed Ritter's wrinkled nose as he ate each mouthful. "So what happens now?" she asked, hoping Paj wouldn't notice.

"I'll prepare the sled," she said. "We'll leave in half an hour. Wrap your feet up well before you put your boots on. It'll keep them warm, and hopefully keep your skin from blistering."

"Who's gonna talk to her?" Adoni asked. "Because I think it should be Ritter and me." Ritter and Paj started speaking at once. She shook her head and waved until they stopped speaking. "You're a piper," she said to Paj. "So if you go in there and piss her off, she'll lift your immortality. And you," she said to Ritter, "you're gonna need someone there to back you up, and it can't be her."

"Someone to 'back me up?' This isn't a buddy cop movie. I'm perfectly capable of carrying on a conversation with the little bissum myself."

"Right, and she's gonna be so happy to see you after you've been avoiding her?"

He smirked. "I didn't say it wouldn't be awkward."

"I'm going in with you." She looked at Paj. "Make sense?"

"It worries me," she replied. "Is she above harming a human?"

"It depends on how old she is," Ritter said. He glanced at her.

"You don't know how old I am?" Adoni huffed. "Jackass."

"Ah, the poetry of adolescence," he said. "How I've missed it. I'm being facetious, of course. It doesn't matter how old she is. Is Ansgar above harming a human? No, I wouldn't put anything past her. But Ansgar doesn't necessarily come out swinging. She likes to bide her time, see where her mood takes her. If she can have more fun with a human in the picture, we better believe she'll keep her in the picture."

"I don't like this," Paj said to Adoni. "I'd rather risk my immortality than your life."

"No way," Adoni said. "You're forgetting what I can do."

"But you don't know what you can do, really. None of us do."

"Well, we've got a few hours to find out."

Paj sighed. "We'll leave soon. I'll get my things. And I'll bring another coat for you," she said to Adoni. "You might need extra padding the further north we get." She turned and left the kitchen.

Adoni watched Paj's back recede into the darkness beyond the kitchen door and heard her footsteps as she climbed the stairs. "You should really—" She stopped. Tyler sat staring at Ritter, who had pushed his bowl away and

CHARLENE CHALLENGER

put his head in his hands. "Are you okay?" He nodded, but didn't look up. "Is it the potatoes?"

He chuckled, sat back, and pinched the bridge of his nose with shaky fingers. "I'm all right. A touch of the nerves, that's all. I thought for a moment…" He took a deep breath. "Even millenniarians get hazy on the finer details of dealing with demigoddesses. If my instincts are wrong… it will get dangerous, very quickly."

"We're gonna be fine," Adoni said. "We're total badasses. Well, I am anyway."

"If she asks about Steppe…" He grimaced. *"No piper shall forsake his brethren, nor give them up for destruction."*

"Then tell her Steppe wouldn't go on a killing spree because a bunch of pipers refused to help him. Right? He'd figure something out himself. Right? We both know that." He avoided her gaze. "No way," she said. "No way. What are you thinking?"

"I'm not thinking," he said. "Not clearly, anyway."

She shook her head. "I don't even want to have this conversation again. You can't go all stupid on us, okay? You better nap in the sled."

He got to his feet. "That's just what I need. A nap, on a bumpy sled, in the middle of winter."

She pointed at him. "Look me in the eye and tell me you don't think Steppe is a murderer."

He straightened up and met her gaze. "I don't think Steppe is a murderer. I think I'm… a bad friend."

Adoni sighed. "You're not a bad friend. You're a jackass." She went to him and wrapped her arms around him. "And I don't snore," she said, her voice muffled against his chest.

"Very well," he said as he hugged her back. "If you prefer to live in a dream world, it's fine by me." He pulled away. "I'll have a quick look around for anything useful we might have missed packing up. I'll be down in a few minutes." He patted Tyler on the head before leaving the room.

Adoni looked at Tyler, who was picking at the last few bits of potato on his plate. "Are you gonna be okay for the trip?" she asked. The boy nodded without raising his eyes. Adoni sighed. "I'm sorry I yelled at you yesterday. I was being a bitch because Ritter wouldn't let me fight back. I shouldn't've taken it out on you, though. Did you have a good sleep with Paj?" He nodded again and licked his fingers before wiping them dry on his pants. "Forgive me for being mean?" she asked.

He slid off the chair and leaned his head against her belly. "We're gonna go on a sleigh ride."

"Yeah, but we're going someplace really far and it's gonna take a while. It's gonna be cold and dangerous. So we're sticking together. You don't mind, eh? You're gonna do whatever we say to make sure we all stay safe, right?"

"Uh-huh."

"Okay." She smoothed her hand over the back of his head. "You're an awesome kid, you know that? If I ever have a brother I want him to be just like you." He peered up at her, a small grin on his face. "Let's get ready to go, okay?" She collected the empty plates and bowl and placed them both in the sink, where they would be ready for washing upon her return.

She took Tyler's hand and led him to the front hall. Paj was sifting through a pile of clothing that had fallen onto the closet floor. She emerged with her arms full of coats and cloaks. "This should fit you," she said to Tyler, handing him a bundle of thick red cloth. Adoni took it instead and shook it open. It was a shorter cloak and hood that would undoubtedly swallow the boy in fabric while keeping him warm. "And here," Paj continued, "take this." She held out another cloak and hood. Adoni caught a heavy scent of cedar and mothballs and could tell it hadn't been worn in a long while. She took it and draped it over her shoulders. "I've already taken the blankets for the sled. Where's Ritter?"

"Right here." Ritter appeared at the top of the stairs with Tyler's winter gear in tow.

Paj flung a blue cloak around her shoulders and stuffed her feet into a pair of mukluks. "We'd better go now." She stepped onto the porch and disappeared around the corner, leaving the door open and allowing a frigid breeze to sweep through the hall.

He joined them in front hall, looking as self-assured and carefree as ever. Tyler took his coat and boots and put them on. Ritter nodded at Adoni's cloak. "That used to be—"

Adoni frowned. "Aniuk's?"

He nodded. Adoni helped Tyler into the cloak as Ritter dressed himself for the journey. "All right. Onward and upward." He stepped onto the porch.

Adoni took Tyler's hand and joined Ritter in surveying the frozen landscape. A sunless sky hung above their heads. Adoni drew the winter air into her lungs. Behind the crisp scent lay the perfume of a thousand forest trees. Paj emerged from the side of the chalet. "The sled's ready," she said as she approached. She fished an iron key from a pocket in her dress and locked the front door. Adoni couldn't help but remember a time when all it took to keep the changelings out was a plaque bearing Ansgar's name. Paj waved at them to follow her to the sled, which was piled high with the blankets and gunnysacks. "Ready to go?"

Ritter picked up the sled's reins and started off toward the trees. "Let's hope it all goes well."

Adoni's feet were already aching by the time they reached the river. Though the river itself wasn't situated too far from The Welcome—a half hour's walk on a good day—the icy ground made the journey especially treacherous, and they arrived much later than they would have liked. The trees along the shore had experienced the worst of the storm; bent branches hung almost to the ground and several trunks had split from the weight. Much of the river had frozen over, but a steady trickle of water lapped the shoreline, where Paj bent and filled several canteens. Adoni took a moment to pee behind a tree, then gathered her cloak around her rump and sat down on a rock that was covered in ice. The cold crept into the backs of her legs. She reached over and pulled one of the blankets off of the sled and onto her lap. Ritter and Paj each found a spot to sit and rest. Adoni tuned them out as they talked.

This was where the changelings plucked her from the river's edge and dragged her to their compound to face Sylvester. She'd let her guard down for only a moment and almost immediately fell under their grips. She stared at the path she'd just walked through the trees and could almost feel their fingers around her arms, in her hair.

The sound of breaking wood caught her attention. Tyler had wandered some fifty feet away from their makeshift camp. He had started a game of seeking out fallen branches and snapping them in half with his boots. He waddled next to the forest edge, where the trees could obscure anyone approaching from the right. Adoni's guts shook. She sprang up from the rock, dashed over to him, and grabbed his hand. "Come sit with me," she said as she hauled him back to the others. "We don't have a lot of time to warm up." She sat down on the rock and pulled the boy onto her lap.

"I'm not tired," he said.

She draped the blanket over the both of them. "Your feet are gonna freeze if you get them wet."

"I wasn't in the water!" He started to squirm.

"What did I say before we left? You promised you'd do whatever I asked, right?"

"But I'm not cold!"

"Of course you're not, you're under a blanket." He let out a dramatic, childish sigh. "Don't give me attitude, okay?"

"I'm *not*," he said.

"Okay, good." She held him close and glanced at Ritter. His eyelids were threatening to close. Adoni leaned over and grabbed a handful of snow. She squeezed it into a ball and tossed it at him. She pointed at the sled. "Take a nap."

CHARLENE CHALLENGER

"Yes ma'am," he said, pulling himself to his feet. "Wake me when it's over, would you?" He climbed into the sled, tucked himself behind the gunnysacks, and pulled a blanket over his head.

An hour passed before they headed out again. Ritter led them to the narrowest bend in the river, where the water was frozen solid enough for them to safely cross to the other side. Tyler began dragging his feet as his face grew wan with exhaustion. Ritter gave him his spot in the sled and walked alongside Adoni. "You look like you've seen a ghost," he said to her.

"I didn't get a good look at this part of the forest the last time I was here," she said. "I don't even know where we are."

"You didn't miss much, in my opinion. If you've seen one pine tree, you've seen them all."

"It was so dark. Are we near the changeling camp?"

"No, thankfully. Though that doesn't mean we shouldn't keep on guard."

"I pulled you in the river with me, remember?"

"How could I forget? I nearly froze to death."

She smirked. "Sorry. I shouldn't find it funny."

"Why not?"

"I could've killed us."

"True, but you didn't."

"But what if I did?"

"Then we wouldn't have the pleasure of laughing at it now, would we?" He flashed a cheeky smile. "Humour's a gift, Donny girl. Never look a gift horse in the mouth."

They made their way east, each of them occasionally slipping on thick patches of ice and tumbling against the tree trunks and each other. Ritter fell more often than any of the others. After one exceptionally comical spill, Adoni called out "Whoopsie daisy!" to the amusement of the rest of the group.

"Yes, yes, go on," he muttered. "Far be it for any one of you to help an old man to his feet." Paj held out her arm, which he used to pull himself up. "You're a good woman, Paj."

"You're heavier than I thought." She straightened her back and peered across the forest.

Adoni watched the corners of Paj's mouth pinch together and pull her lips down. She veered away from them, stumbling over the very patch of ice Ritter had just wiped out on. Adoni followed her between the trees, until the woman abruptly stopped a short distance away from where they had been standing. "Are you all right?"

Paj sank to her knees and pressed her forehead against the frozen ground. Before her: a single, branchless tree, black from a fire that had burned out long ago, nestled among other trees that had escaped the flames. A trace of acrid smoke still clung to the scorched wood. Paj placed her hands on the tree's exposed roots, let out a tiny cry, and started to weep softly. "Hey," Adoni said. "It's okay. It's all right. Are you all right?"

"She walked with me always," Paj whispered, and Adoni finally realized where she stood: in the very spot where Paj's twin sister Aniuk met her horrific end.

It made sense Sylvester would pick so gloomy and solitary a spot. It was far enough away from The Welcome that no one would be able to see the flames. It was well enough out of earshot for rescue to be impossible. The tall trees blocked out much of the afternoon light, so that nothing but a murky shade hung overhead. Adoni stared at the burned tree, felt a sob rise in her throat and, out of respect, swallowed it down.

Ritter made his way to Paj's side. He knelt and put his arm around her. "I never thought we'd see it," he said softly. "Dear Paj…"

I wish I could do something to make it better, Adoni thought as she crouched and sat on the ground. Her heart sank. What could she possibly say to ease Paj's pain? What could she possibly do to take away the burden of Aniuk's death? She could still hear Sylvester's voice echoing in her head, the words he used to taunt them as he broke the news. When Adoni was a prisoner in the changeling camp, he claimed Aniuk's death was necessary to avenge the changelings. But Adoni could tell he'd enjoyed carrying out the deed. *If he hadn't spilled Aniuk's ashes*, she thought, her muscles shuddering, a headache coming on. *If he hadn't torn the piper leaders apart, maybe I could have…*

Could have what?

Lebshen.

She shivered. *That's sick. Sick, sick, sick.*

"I'm sorry," Paj said at last. "I don't mean to slow us down."

"There's no need to apologize," Ritter said.

"I guess it's good, coming across this place. I know where it is now. And new life sometimes grows out of ashes." She looked at him. "It's better to have a marker, isn't it? A marker honours the dead. Don't you think? Don't you think we owed it to them…?" She clasped her hands together and turned away.

Paj's words seared themselves across Adoni's heart. A marker wouldn't bring Aniuk back, wouldn't bring the children back, but it would respect the time they spent in the In-Between, and protect them all from being forgotten.

She got to her feet and approached the burned tree. *I can bring things to life*, she thought. *Of course.*

Think of everyone who came here with the pipers. Think of everyone who never got the chance to leave.

She closed her eyes, thought of them all, and whispered again and again, *lebshen, lebshen, lebshen, lebshen.*

Her shoulder began to throb and ache, her skin to itch. She heard the rustle of roots driving into the earth, the twisting of wood, the whistle of wind interrupted by branches and leaves. She heard Ritter's voice, an astonished "Look!" and opened her eyes once more.

She reached out and put her hand against the tree's trunk—desiccated only a moment before, but now tall, thick, and brown—a steady foundation for the thousands of branches that had sprouted from its once-wasted bark. A new canopy of golden leaves spread across the tiny clearing and seemed to channel warmth into that otherwise dismal place. Adoni stepped back from the tree as the others rushed to meet her. The branches above her were odd, she noticed. Something about the way they wove together was uncanny, unnatural. When their mystery revealed itself, she whispered, "Look up there!"

There in the branches: *Sabrina, Jonathan, Hector, Marianne.*

Higher still: *Carrie, Khadija, Ben, LaShane.*

Aniuk.

Spelled out and immortal.

"They must all be there," Ritter said. "Every last one of them. How did you do it? How did you know their names?"

"I don't know," Adoni said. "I thought about whoever they were, and I just did what I did last night."

"Their faces," Ritter said. "I can see them when I read their names…"

Adoni looked up and found a name among the leaves. She read it—*Jen*—silently to herself, and somewhere in the back of her mind she could see a girl, chubby, like she was, with glasses and long red hair, sitting on the steps of one of The Welcome's cabins, smiling as though she had no concept of what it was like to frown. The name *Martin* conjured a short young man with closely shaved hair, an athlete with a poet's spirit coursing through his veins. *Jacob* was a painter; *Daniela*, an amateur astronomer.

Aniuk was a woman who loved to laugh.

Belinda, a lover; a warrior.

"My god," Paj said. "My god, it's *beautiful*."

A high-pitched scream broke their amazement.

Adoni whipped her head around. The hiss of changeling laughter filled the forest. Adoni caught a flash of movement from the corner of her eye.

"That way!" she yelled, pointing at the crimson blur of Tyler's cloak flitting between the trees.

Chapter
19

Adoni kept her eyes on Tyler's cloak as she and the others raced forward. From what she could discern from the blur of movement, Tyler was being carried by a single changeling—one who dodged as deftly between the trees as any lynx. The icy ground didn't seem to encumber its steps; if anything, it knew exactly where to tread, and used every slip and slide to propel itself onward. Adoni cursed as she and the others slammed into trunks and fell over heaps of solid snow. The changeling would disappear, prisoner in tow, if she didn't do something to clear the path ahead. She drew in as deep a breath as she could and screamed, sending her voice into the ground. Before her, the ice shattered and exploded, foot by foot, into an earthen trail wide enough for she and the pipers to charge single file after their quarry.

The changeling's hoots grew louder as they started gaining on it. Paj's bright eyes scorched the gloom as she leapt ahead of Adoni. She opened her mouth, and Adoni heard her suck in a sharp breath that caused her ears to pop. Paj defiantly sang out in her piper voice: a corolla of laughter, now skewered through with the changeling's own sniggering. It glanced over its shoulder as it ploughed through the snow, its eyes wide, recognizing itself in Paj's throat. The piper's voice clanged again and again, its mirth warping into menacing, psychopathic laughter. The effect stunned the changeling; it lost its footing and violently careened against a tree. Amazement stabbed Adoni's heart. Even Paj—gentle Paj—was capable of intimidation.

The advantage her voice gave them was short lived. The changeling recovered and, with Tyler still screaming in its arms, reached up and used a low-hanging branch to pull itself into the tree. Adoni couldn't believe her eyes; it began climbing from bough to bough, from tree to tree, and very soon regained the speed it had reached on the ground. She remembered the way Sylvester had pursued her through the forest—with the same agility and skill—and thought it must be a changeling trait; the way their limbs were made, the way their black blood coursed through their veins. "Go after it!" she shouted to Ritter.

"I'm not a bloody gymnast!" he yelled back.

"How can it move like that?" Her steps began to slow. She was losing her breath. "It's getting away!"

"Don't slow down," Ritter called to her. "On my back." They stopped long enough for Adoni to throw her arms around Ritter's neck and hitch her legs around him. He looped his arms behind her knees and started to run. To her surprise, her weight had no impact on his speed. The changeling changed its direction, first leaping west and then back toward the river. With every turn, Adoni shouted the path ahead of them clear. Clouds of powdered snow and ice misted their faces and clung to their cloaks. Paj's mocking laughter grew more intense, until it sounded as though her throat were on fire. They pursued the changeling back to the river's edge, where it made a prompt about-face and retreated the way it came.

"Shit!" Adoni snarled as she slipped off of Ritter's back. Tyler wailed as his captor changed course. "It's too fast!" She glared at him. "You seriously can't do that?"

"I'm an older model," he sniped. "Ansgar doesn't make us the way she used to."

"We have to outsmart it," Paj said. They started after it again, keeping it in their sights as best they could.

"All right," Ritter said. "A good old-fashioned sneak attack." His chest puffed up, and he let his voice fly.

No sounds vibrated in his throat, no melodies, no harmonies, no instruments or weather, no other voices weaving in and out. Adoni looked down at her boots and realized she could no longer hear them pounding against the earth.

She shot a look at Ritter. His open mouth made it clear to her he was singing—the tune, absolute silence.

It cushioned their steps, blanketed their breathing, muffled their flapping robes and cloaks. Adoni glanced at Paj, who charged ahead without acknowledging the sudden heavy stillness, and then at Ritter, whose jaw hung open as he fought to maintain his breath. Disoriented by the hush, she stumbled forward a few more paces before lifting her gaze toward the branches overhead.

The changeling appeared to be slowing down; the red cloak was no longer distorted by speed, but a tangible thing within their grasp. Adoni slapped Ritter on the shoulder and, when he turned his head, pointed up to where their foe clung to the branches of an impressive cedar. They stopped well out of sight and listened to Tyler's helpless whimpering. Paj put a finger to her lips, looked at Ritter, and mouthed the words, *Lead it to the edge of the forest.*

Ritter nodded and poked his head forward, craning his neck at an almost unnatural angle. He drew in a breath and shouted, "Bring me the boy!" The words echoed north across the forest and resounded a great distance away, as though he'd shouted it from the other side. Adoni shuddered. The voice that left Ritter's lips was Sylvester's, not his own.

She saw Paj nod and realized the piper must have known about Ritter's way with other voices. *She thinks he's just mimicking,* she thought, but Adoni knew the truth: that Ritter had taken notes of Sylvester's voice away with him the night he left the changeling to his fate on the farmer's doorstep.

The changeling turned its head toward the edge of the forest. It found more solid footing on a sturdy bough and stood up to get a better view of whomever it thought was calling it away. Ritter motioned for the group to crouch out of sight. Adoni sunk to her knees and watched the changeling heft the sobbing Tyler underneath its arm. The boy hung there limply, too terrified to struggle free and risk falling to the ground. "Bring him to me!" Ritter called again. The changeling began making its way through the branches once more.

Ritter waved at them to follow behind. He resumed his silent song, and they inched forward, their eyes fixed on the changeling's back. It leapt across to another cedar, another pine, until the distance between the trees was too great for it to clear. Finally, it slung Tyler over its shoulder, climbed down the trunk of a massive elm, and stood motionless, waiting to be reunited with its master.

Adoni kept her arms down by her side as she and the others crept toward it, determined not to alert it with an inadvertent flap of her cloak or sideways step. As she and the others stepped out from behind the thickest of the trees, Tyler lifted his head and looked over the changeling's shoulder. Adoni caught the glimmer of recognition in his teary eyes and put a finger to her lips. Ritter continued to muffle their advancing steps, timing his calls of "Hurry up!" and "Now, now!" with his muted aria. Adoni's heart pounded harder as she came closer to Tyler and his captor. Though she knew she had to remain cautious until just the right moment, she wanted nothing more than to race forward and snatch the boy from the changeling's grip. They were no more than twenty feet away when Ritter took a breath as Paj's boot broke through a patch of snow that had avoided being iced over. The resulting crunch drew the changeling's attention; it whirled around and caught sight of their advance. Panic tore across its face. It turned and started to run.

Adoni and the others lunged forward, Adoni shouting the ice apart, Paj's relentless cackle-song ringing in their ears. The changeling circled back toward the forest. *Damn it!* Adoni thought. *This is bullshit! We're never gonna catch it like this!* Her foot came down on a thick fallen branch and nearly toppled her. She looked down at the trail she'd just cleared. Behind her, more fallen branches, some as thick as her arm, lay like a carpet over their path. With no other ideas, no other course of action, she drew in a breath and sang out to them: *lebshen, lebshen, lebshen,* over and over.

The branches sprang to life and started racing toward her. Paj and

Ritter turned their heads at the rush of wooden steps scurrying over the ground. "What the hell are you doing?" Ritter shouted. "You're mad!"

"How do you say 'get him' in piper?" she called, her voice dry from running, singing, screaming.

"You're going to send a bunch of rowdy twigs after it?"

"You got a better idea?" she snarled. "Tell me!"

"*Fin aust!*" Paj cried.

Adoni pointed at the changeling, turned her head, and half spoke, half sang *fin aust*. The branch and bough creatures surged ahead of her on their spindly legs. She watched, exhilarated, as they scaled the craggy ground and were soon nipping at the changeling's heels. Tyler saw their spider-like approach and resumed his screaming, shredding his voice with the force of his breath. He clung to the back of the changeling's ragged smock as though he preferred being slung over its shoulder to being rescued by a legion of timber furies. "Tyler, jump!" Adoni shouted at him. Her voice seemed to snap him out of his fit, though his tiny body remained petrified. "Jump! They're not gonna hurt you!"

"You don't know that!" Ritter said to her.

"Yes I *do*!" she snapped. What else would they do besides obey her? Didn't all creatures owe a debt of servitude to their masters?

The thought, combined with the exhaustion of racing after the changeling, slowed her steps, until she abruptly stopped and bent to catch her breath. "*Fin aust!*" she ordered again, pointing at the changeling as it stampeded toward the edge of the forest. A massive belt of mountains rose just beyond the last row of trees; this was the final leg of the trip to Ansgar's fortress.

The changeling swerved west and ran along the face of the rock. It shot a frantic glance over its shoulder at its otherworldly pursuers. Adoni watched in horror as the changeling hefted Tyler up over its head and tossed him at her wooden avengers. Tyler shrieked as he hurtled through the air toward them. "No!" she screamed, and the magnitude shook the air around them, tripping her two companions, sending them faces-first into the ice and snow. The branches and boughs quickly climbed over each other, rising like an ocean wave before a storm. Adoni gasped as the creatures reached out and caught the boy before his body could hit the ground. She started running again, passing the pipers as they regained their footing. "Tyler!" Her soldiers passed him back through their ranks and continued their pursuit. Adoni reached for Tyler, plucked him up, and held him tightly against her chest. The boy threw his arms around her neck, nearly strangling her, and sobbed. "Poor little guy," she said, choking up as he wailed. "Poor little guy. It's okay now."

"Mommy!" he howled. "Mommy!"

The rest of the group caught up with her. Ritter put his hand on Tyler's back and patted him gently.

"Look there," Paj said. They followed her gaze just as Adoni's creatures seized hold of the changeling's feet, anchoring it in place.

Adoni marched forward with the boy in her arms. The changeling twisted and squealed as the branches, hooking onto each other like links in a chain, climbed higher up its body and clamped down. Soon they covered the changeling's legs, torso, and arms; it tried to struggle free but the branches held it fast. Its screeching intensified as they started to wrap themselves around its neck.

"They'll kill him!" Ritter cried. He turned to Adoni. "Do something!"

"How do you say 'stop?'" she asked.

"*Vinat!*"

She repeated the word in a deep, booming voice. The branches stopped their advance up the changeling's body, but didn't let go. She stepped in close and tried to look it in the eye, even as its gaze darted back and forth, frantically looking for a way to escape. For a moment she felt she ought to say something to intimidate it into confessing why it wanted to drag Tyler through the forest, but knew she lacked the words, and the understanding, to urge an explanation. Instead she asked Ritter, "How do you say 'let go?'"

"*Dau bruge*," he said.

With Tyler whimpering in her arms, she finally caught the changeling's eye. "Go away," she muttered, before lending her voice to Ritter's words. The branches fell away from the changeling's body and settled in a pile at its feet. It sprang away from them. Adoni watched it flee to the forest, where it disappeared between the thickest of the trees.

She put her cheek against Tyler's shoulder. "It's okay," she said as she swayed back and forth. "I've got you." He quieted down, though his chest still heaved with sniffles.

They stood still, breathing heavily, staring at the pile of writhing branches. "What will you do?" Paj asked her at last.

Adoni leaned over and whispered, "*Bruge.*" The pile slowly untangled itself. Each branch separated from the rest and started off toward the trees, no longer scurrying but strolling at an almost leisurely pace over the ice-covered ground.

Ritter put his hand on her shoulder. "Thank you."

"They can think," she said softly. "They have feelings. They have souls."

"I can't possibly imagine what they'll do to the ecosystem."

"Who cares about the ecosystem!" she snapped.

Tyler put his head against Adoni's shoulder and stuck his thumb in his mouth. She craned her neck to take in the mountain's height. "How far away are we from the fortress?"

"Just a little further," Ritter said. "We'll have to retrace our steps somewhat, but it shouldn't take too long. We need to find the path between the mountains and work our way up."

"What kind of path is it? Are we gonna need equipment?"

"It's not steep enough for that, but it's narrow and tends to be slippery all year round." He looked at the sled. "I hope that will fit. It's a little wide."

"We can carry what we need and leave the sled behind," Paj said.

"Right then. This way."

They made their way east, where the slope of the mountain grew steep and jutted into their path. Ritter jogged ahead of them and stopped a short distance away. "It's here," he said, waving them over. He nodded at a narrow pass between two cliff sides. "Ansgar's fortress is at the top. It's just as I thought, that sled isn't going to fit."

Tyler began to squirm in Adoni's arms. "What's wrong?" she asked.

"I don't wanna go up there!" he whimpered. "It's scary!"

She looked at Paj. "Actually, it might be better if he stays down here," she said. "What do you think?"

"I agree," she replied. "Can the two of you make it up alone?"

"Well, I'm no expert mountaineer," Ritter said, "but I've scaled this pass just fine by myself. I'll keep an eye on our girl here, make sure she doesn't lose her footing and come tumbling down again."

Adoni gave Tyler a reassuring pat on the back and handed him to Paj. "If anyone's gonna slip, it's you. You're the one who's been taking flips all day."

"Just warming up, darling. I feel I've hit my stride now. And you?" he asked Paj. "Will you two be all right down here?"

"We'll be fine. Be careful," Paj said, leaning over and giving Adoni a hug. "You know that, of course, but… it makes me feel better to say it out loud." She reached out and put her hand on Ritter's cheek. "Take care of each other. I don't trust Ansgar."

"Neither do I," Ritter said. "Which is probably why I've lasted as long as I have."

Adoni eased out of Paj's embrace and gave her a kiss on the cheek. She watched Paj place Tyler back in the sled, watched her tuck a blanket around the boy's shoulders, and felt her heart begin to ache. There was something about the way she looked at the boy, something about the way she protected him against the winter chill, which moved her. When Paj stood up again, she couldn't help it; she sprang forward and hugged her. She felt Paj's arms close around her and smiled.

Ritter offered Adoni his arm. "Shall we, then?"

She gave Paj one final squeeze, then pulled away. "You can put your arm away, I don't want you dragging my ass down with you."

"Classy, darling, very classy." He tipped an invisible hat at Paj.

They edged up the pass, Ritter leading the way, their arms out, their hands pressed against the sides of the cliffs, the pressure reinforcing their steps. "All right missus, it's time to speak plainly."

"Uh huh."

"As I said before, there's no way to predict how the little munchkin's going to react to our arrival. She may be delightful and sweet at first—"

"Yeah, right."

"—Or she might be a holy terror. In any case, the last thing you want to do is let her know her name has given you those powers."

I can't wait to let her know. "Sylvester probably told her already."

"Nonsense. He may have told her about your screaming capabilities, but there's no way he could have told her the rest. You didn't know yourself until last night."

"Couldn't she guess?"

"I suppose, but I don't think she has. I think she was too busy trying to even the score between the changelings and the pipers to give you much notice. Remember, I bargained for you to stay at The Welcome, and she gave Sylvester that seal in exchange. Whatever you do, keep your power under wraps. Another thing: let me do the talking. That means no sass back, no matter how great the urge to give her a piece of your mind may be. This won't be the time or place to lecture her on the plight of pipers or the state of the In-Between. There is no time or place, actually."

Adoni thought of Belinda, how her immortality was taken from her when she tried to get Ansgar to see reason.

"And one last thing," he said, turning to her. "Ansgar is my creator. She's the only mother I've ever known. As much as she terrifies me, I owe her my entire existence. She's cut me infinite slack, much more than I've deserved sometimes. I haven't always been loyal, but I can never turn my back on her completely. Do you understand what I mean?"

"Yes."

He arched an eyebrow. "Really."

"I do."

"Good. Because you may not like me when you finally see me in her presence."

Adoni frowned. "What's that supposed to mean?"

"It means, darling, that when I play her game, I play by her rules. It means snivelling when it's time to snivel, coddling when it's time to coddle, and generally behaving as though she's pulling all my strings." For a moment she thought he was trying to lighten the mood, but his fierce green eyes remained fixed on her. "I won't pretend it's anything other than vulgar," he said. "It's caused me to lose esteem in more than a few pipers' eyes. I need you to understand, before we get there. Just…" He paused, then turned away and started up the pass once more.

The light grew dimmer the further they walked. Rivulets of sweat trickled down her back, soaking her waistline and dampening her jacket. Their slow ascent meant ample opportunity to feel the winter chill, even as she sweated beneath several layers of clothes. A light snow began to fall, further slickening the ground. Adoni thought about using her voice to clear the ice as she had during her flight through the forest, but decided against it. Screaming would have certainly attracted Ansgar's attention; unless she was so deep inside her fortress she couldn't hear what went on beyond its walls. *She's gotta have bionic ears. And a sixth sense or something. Maybe she's spying on us right now.* She looked around her, behind her, and then followed Ritter as closely as she could, at one point almost treading on the backs of his boots.

At last, beyond Ritter's shoulder, Adoni could see the tops of the steel doors that opened in on Ansgar's fortress. Her guts began to churn. She felt as though the cliffs were closing in on her, merging together, blocking off her path. The sound of her boots no longer reassured her, and Ritter hadn't said anything, pointed or jocular, in some time. *Maybe I should say something*, she thought, but nothing appropriate came to mind. *Let him do the talking, don't get freaked out, and when you see your chance, take it.*

Ritter suddenly stopped walking and stood perfectly still in Adoni's path. "What's wrong?" she asked, standing on her tiptoes and peering over his shoulder.

"Steppe," he murmured. "My god. *My god.*"

Chapter
20

"My god, you wouldn't believe the mess we're in," Ritter said.

"I have some idea," Steppe said.

"Then you can help us put this whole thing to rest. The colony leaders have been murdered, do you know that?"

"Yes."

"I told Paj you weren't responsible for it, but she seems not to…"

"I am, in a way."

Ritter's face turned pale. "What do you mean?"

"I failed to protect the In-Between from Sylvester."

"Oh *damn it*! I'm not talking about *metaphysical* guilt!"

"I didn't kill them."

"I know. I know." He shook his head. "My word, Steppe, you look… It's so good to see you. Paj told us what happened. About what happened to the colony and… the shooting…"

"Yes."

"I can't imagine how you must have felt."

"I'm sure you can," Steppe said, curling his fingers into fists.

Ritter glanced at Adoni. "What are you doing here?" he asked Steppe.

"Theresa told me you were coming back."

"You saw Theresa?" Adoni asked. "Is she okay?"

"She's fine."

"Sylvester's threatened to harm her," Ritter said.

"I'm not surprised."

Ritter let out a nervous chuckle. "I know things haven't always been good between us, darling, but I'm starting to get the feeling you're not particularly happy to see me."

"You shouldn't be here," Steppe replied.

"What did Reese say to you?" Adoni asked.

"Ansgar's dangerous," he said to Ritter.

"Sylvester's been banished from the In-Between and that Natalie girl has apparently lost all memory of the In-Between," Ritter said. "You remember her, yes? Purple hair, bad attitude?"

His expression darkened further. "Go back to the other side."

Ritter frowned. "I suspect the girl's a changeling spy. I want Ansgar to answer for it. No bargains, no special favours."

"No special favours?" He laughed bitterly. "But that's her favourite game. She always expects something in return. An eye for an eye. You know that. You *told* me that."

Adoni heard the sound of rushing water in the back of his throat. Something about what he had said, his presence, didn't make sense. Something about the way he looked when Ritter mentioned Natalie—a shiftiness that snuck its way into his eyes—left her feeling cold.

"I'm hoping she'll make an exception," Ritter said.

"Why? Because you're her chosen messenger?"

"Yes, as a matter of fact. Look, Steppe, I know you're still angry. I know I should have told you about her ways instead of keeping it to myself. I was stupid and selfish, and I'm deeply sorry for it."

"You don't know how angry I am," Steppe growled, his voice trembling through the rock. "Neither of you do."

Adoni saw tears spring to Ritter's eyes. She took his hand, held it gently, and set her sights on Steppe. "No? So tell us."

"The way we left it—" Ritter began.

"A lot of time has passed since then," Steppe said. "I've had a lot of time to think. Not quite forty years, but enough. Forty years is a long time, Ritter. Not for you, of course, but that's almost half my lifetime.

Do you know what happens to you when you realize you have forty years' worth of wasted time under your belt? You realize how little a few moments' worth of truth means compared to all those years in the dark." The sound of rocks tumbling down the side of a mountain, of a volcano boiling, ready to erupt; Adoni squeezed Ritter's hand tighter as Steppe's words lingered in the air.

"So you've let it fester," Ritter said, nodding. "I should have expected as much."

"You're not one to talk," Steppe said. "You've never faced a real consequence in your life."

"And I'm ashamed for it! Deeply ashamed! But my word, Steppe, I've tried to make amends. I'm still trying!"

"You're trying. So you brought Adoni with you, instead of facing Ansgar alone."

"I wanted to come!" Adoni snapped.

"And convincing him to let you back into the In-Between didn't take much, did it?" Steppe asked. "You're here because he's afraid of what Ansgar will do to him."

"That's not true! I told him I was coming whether he liked it or not!"

"So he brought you because you demanded it, is that right?"

"Yes!"

"And he brought the boy, too, because... why, exactly?"

Ritter eased his hand out of Adoni's and turned away, hands on his hips, face turned up to the grey and unforgiving sky. Adoni gnashed her teeth. "Tyler's mom skipped out on him," she said. "We couldn't leave him alone in his apartment."

"He didn't have to stay alone. He could have spent the night with your mother."

"What do you know about it?" *How the hell would he...* Finally, it dawned on her. "You watched us cross through the agate!"

"I did."

"So, what, you're a spy now?"

"I'm telling you to go back, Adoni."

"It wasn't Sylvester following me that night!" she said to Ritter. "It must have been *him*!"

Ritter shot Steppe a bitter look. "Charming, sneaking up on a girl at night."

"I kept my eye on Sylvester to see when he'd show his face," Steppe said. "And I don't have to explain myself to you."

"I'll be sure to take a page from your book, then. If your *intentions* are honourable, you don't have to apologize for them."

"And what was your intention, then, bringing that boy back?"

"You were there. You tell me."

"Because you're a coward," Steppe said, throwing the words at his feet. "And your misery *loves* company."

"Say what you want about me," Ritter said. "Call me whatever you want. You might be right, and I might deserve it. I probably *do* deserve it." He shook his head. "What's the point? What are we doing here?"

His wondering knocked something free in Adoni's mind, shed light on the ignorant shadow lurking behind Steppe's presence. "We're here to see Ansgar," she said, digging her heels into the ice. "What's *he* doing here? That's what I want to know."

"I'm not going to tell you again," Steppe said. "Go back."

"How did you know we'd be here?" she asked.

"Theresa told me."

"No, she didn't. She told you we were going back to the In-Between, not that we were going to see Ansgar. She didn't know we were coming to the fortress, because we didn't know until yesterday. You saw us go through the agate and you know my street opens up at The Welcome. You assumed whatever we found out there would make us want to talk to Ansgar." She glared at him. "What don't you want her to know?"

"You're asking me to explain why I wouldn't want you to talk to a being that can harm anyone she chooses at will?" He pointed at Ritter. "She can tear you apart if she wants to. She can break every bone in your body, snap every limb, rend your insides into a thousand little pieces. And she can do it slowly. She can make it feel like a million years."

"If you cared about us being *harmed*, you would've tried to stop us at the colony," Adoni said. "It's not about us being harmed, it's about us finding out something you don't want us to find out."

Steppe smiled at her; a gentle smile, despite her pointed questions. "I should have taken the time to know you better," he said.

"We're *going* to see her."

"No, you're not."

She heard the boom of cannon fire and lost her breath as a gust of wind punched her chest. She tumbled backwards, landing hard on her rump and skidding across the ground. Ritter fell onto his hands and knees and slammed against the side of the cliff. Adoni struggled to get back on her feet, the toes of her boots slipping on the ice, no knotted root or jutting rock to hold on to. Steppe remained motionless, watched her as though she were a bug trapped in a jar. "What are you trying to hide?" she growled. "You know something."

"Donny, be careful," Ritter muttered under his breath.

"I told you to go back," Steppe said through clenched teeth.

"Did you kill them?" she asked.

"No."

"Did Ansgar?"

"You're trying my patience."

She found her footing and helped Ritter to stand. "You *do* know something. And you're *ashamed*. You're ashamed to admit it."

He glared at her. "If I have to hurt you, I will."

"I'm not afraid of you," she said. "You're not gonna bully us off this mountain."

"Lajos," Ritter murmured.

The word snuffed out the cruel glint in Steppe's eyes and drained the colour from his face. "What does that mean?" she asked. "That word, what does it mean?"

"It's not a word," Ritter replied. "It's his name."

"What do you—?"

Steppe sucked in a tremendous breath and roared: the long, low roar of a primitive beast, the relentless grind of a war machine. The ground beneath their feet began to quake and buckle. Steppe's voice sent them hurtling even further back from the great steel doors. His fury leapt back into his eyes. He bared his teeth and sent his voice thundering through the ground. Adoni flipped onto her stomach and screamed as the rock before her split, as the stones broke off and fell away. A torrent of powdered ice and snow fell from the mountain peak. Adoni fought for breath as the spray flew up her nostrils and stuck to her face. She felt Ritter's arms around her waist, felt him haul her away from where she lay sprawled in the middle of the narrow pass. She watched in horror as a chasm opened before them, too wide to circumvent, too wide to cross, too deep to see the bottom from the top. Steppe, and the entrance to Ansgar's fortress, lay on the other side, completely out of her reach.

"Have you completely lost your mind?" Ritter snarled.

"Go away, Ritter," Steppe said, his voice echoing across the chasm, bouncing from cliff to cliff. "The next time my voice flies, I won't be so gentle."

Adoni inched toward the blanket of snow that covered the edge of the chasm and used its roughened surface to regain her footing, her body shaking, her heart pounding hard enough to bruise. She gritted her teeth and forced herself to breathe deeply. *No way*, she thought. *No way. I'm not going anywhere but inside that fortress.* She leaned over, scrutinizing the blackness that swallowed the mountain's foundation. "How do you say 'bridge' in piper?"

"Donny, what are you doing?"

"Just tell me." When the word didn't come, she growled, "*Now.*"

Ritter frowned. "*Jesrut.*"

"*Jesrut,*" she repeated, testing the word in her mouth, without song. "Okay."

She knelt at the chasm's edge and started her chant. "*Lebshen…
lebshen… lebshen…*" The pain in her shoulder grew sharper every time the
word left her lips. "*Lebshen… lebshen… lebshen…*" she crooned, and then,
"*jesrut… jesrut… lebshen… jesrut…*"

It started as a distant rumble from the bottom of the gorge. She felt
the vibrations through her knees. A breeze wafted up from the darkness,
bringing with it the smell of earth and water and something else—a peculiar,
organic scent she couldn't name. The rumble slowly lost its nebulousness,
sharpening into a steady *tok, tok, tok*, that grew louder with each passing
moment. Adoni stopped her chanting and got to her feet. She turned her
back on Steppe and strolled away from the edge. She found Ritter staring
at her. Behind her, the noise bloomed into a percussive symphony of rock
and stone. She waited until the booming reached its peak before turning
around. There before her, climbing up from the depths: the stones, piling
themselves one on top of the other, the rocky silt filling the cracks. Foot
by foot, they formed a sturdy bridge across the chasm for their mistress
to traverse.

As the final stone locked itself in place, Adoni wiped the snow from
her cloak and set her gaze squarely on Steppe's face. She kept her eyes
locked on his as she boldly strode over the bridge toward him.

When she reached the other side and stopped in front of him, she said,
simply, plainly, "Get out of my way."

Steppe stared at the bridge, wide-eyed, bewildered, and then met
Adoni's gaze. For a moment he seemed to be wondering what other
powers she had hidden behind her terrific voice. Then he glared at her, his
shoulders curling forward, and stooped as though he were about to lunge
at her. But he didn't lunge; instead, he drew a sharp breath through his
nose and opened his mouth.

Behind him, the steel doors flung themselves open and slammed back
against the rock. Steppe buckled at Adoni's feet, some great and unseen
force shoving him to his knees. She gasped as his entire body suddenly
flew backwards through the open doors and into the fortress. Past the

threshold, she saw the brilliant orange glow of four towering bonfires standing all around a circular foyer. She watched Steppe sail through the air and disappear into the shadows beyond the flames.

"Adoni!" Ritter screamed. She turned.

The same invisible terror wrapped itself around her waist, yanked her off her feet, and ripped her through the air, past the fires, into the darkness.

Chapter
21

Adoni's eyes had barely enough time to adjust to the dark before her body slammed against the stone floor. She grunted and lay still, allowing the pain to dissipate through her limbs and her head to settle. She eased herself up on her elbow, lifted her hand and wiggled her fingers, hoping the sight of them would calm her nerves. Wherever she was, there were no lanterns lit, no bonfires burning, not a single crack of light to split the murk apart. The darkness swallowed not just sights, but sounds as well; the only things Adoni could hear were her nervous swallows and the pounding of her heart. She couldn't tell where the danger had gone, or when it would come back. She sat up, wrapped her arms around her knees, and tried to settle her breathing. It worked; after a time, though still anxious, she no longer felt as though she'd been buried alive.

Soon, the quiet was too much for her to bear. "Steppe?" she whispered, her voice alien when compared to the silence, coming back to her as though she'd shouted his name instead. "Are you here?" No response. Adoni pressed her cheek against her knees and rocked forward and back.

Then, out of the darkness: "Mommy?"

Ritter!

She couldn't quite tell where his voice had come from—only that it was near, and that it seemed to slice right through the darkness. Ritter called out "Mommy?" again. There was something about the word itself, and the way he said it, that jolted Adoni's heart and left a sickening upset in her stomach.

She heard a spark, like the striking of a match, and squealed as, beside her, a fire sprang up in a shallow pit and started roaring away. She got to her feet and looked around. The light wasn't strong enough to penetrate all the way to the walls, so it was still impossible to tell how large the room was. The only thing she could see, besides the fire pit, was a single wooden chair that faced the flames.

Gentle footsteps soon joined the crackle of burning wood. Ritter's body materialized out of the darkness. He caught sight of her and put a finger to his lips. "Where are you?" he called. "It's me, mommy. I've come back to you."

Someone sighed. Ritter briefly held Adoni's gaze, his eyes absolutely electric. He crossed the room and sat in the chair. "Don't be angry," he said. "I've missed you terribly."

Adoni's eyes darted left and right, scanning the gloom beyond the firelight.

A tiny foot—a child's foot—stepped into the glow. The toes curled, spread, stretched apart. A second foot joined the first, a pair of knees, a pair of childish thighs, a torso without a pubis, without genitals; a belly, pale and slightly swollen, without a navel. Adoni started to shake. A naked chest emerged, the skin smooth and without nipples, followed by two arms, two hands, a chin, a pair of rosy lips, a nose.

Ansgar had two black holes for eyes.

Adoni stared at her.

"There you are, my darling," Ritter murmured.

Ansgar tilted her bald head. Her smile revealed two rows of a hundred miniature teeth. The corners of her mouth almost touched her ears. "Are you shy today?" Ritter cooed. The weird smile grew wider. He held out his hand. "Come here. Let me hold you."

Ansgar put a finger to her lips and pressed her knees together. The holes narrowed to slits. Ansgar's childish voice slithered through the room. "Beg me."

Ritter lowered his chin and pouted. "Please, mommy, don't be angry with me. I'm going to be good from now on. Please?"

Ansgar turned her menacing gaze on Adoni. Her smile shrank to a mere slash across her face. The holes opened up slowly; they seemed to recognize her. Adoni froze.

"Please, please mommy," Ritter said, his tone insistent, almost to the point of panic. "Please forgive me... or I'll start crying."

Ansgar's head snapped back to Ritter.

"You don't want me to cry, do you?"

She nodded eagerly.

Tears sprang to his eyes. His lips quivered, then opened wide. He let out a high-pitched wail and began sobbing. Adoni finally understood what he'd meant by his earlier warning; she winced as his theatrical bawling grew louder. "Mommy hates me!" he yowled. "Mommy wishes she never made me!"

Ansgar started to laugh.

Ritter put his hands to the corners of his eyes and mimed wiping his tears. "Mommy, please! Please, please, please, please!"

Adoni ground her teeth together.

Ansgar came forward, her smile returning to its unnerving width. She climbed onto Ritter's lap and tore his hands away from his face. He shut his tears off almost as quickly as he'd turned them on. Adoni's back went rigid as Ansgar grabbed a handful of Ritter's hair, pulled his head back, and roughly kissed him. He didn't resist, even as she forced his lips apart and snaked her tongue into his mouth. He wrapped his hands around the wooden seat and squeezed until his knuckles turned white. Adoni cringed.

"Thank you, mommy," he said.

"Dolly!" she squealed, fisting his hair in her hands and yanking his head left and right. "Dolly dolly dolly dolly dolly dolly dolly!"

"How are you, my darling?" he said, his voice serene, even as she tore at him.

"Play with me!"

"What shall we play?"

"You were gone *so long*. You're always gone for *so long*."

She turned her head again and locked Adoni in her bottomless sights. Adoni held her breath. "What shall we play, mommy?" Ritter asked again. His voice failed to distract her. He nuzzled his nose against her ear. "Shall we play *House*? Or *Tag*?"

Ansgar slid off his lap and strolled around the fire pit. "*Hide and seek*," she said, her voice no longer that of a child's, but a grown woman. She giggled and slipped into the shadows.

"All right, shall I count to ten?" He stood and shot Adoni a look that seemed to beg her pardon. She very nearly looked away.

Ansgar's mature voice crept into Adoni's ears. "Who are you looking for?" Adoni shrank from the vibrations and shivered.

"You, darling, of course," Ritter answered. "Who else would I be looking for?"

Ansgar didn't reply. Ritter stepped away from the chair and to the very edge of the fire's glow. "Mommy? Are you hiding?" He walked around the puddle of light, his eyes cast upon the darkness. "Shall I count to ten? Or one hundred?" He grinned. "Or *one million*? How does that sound?"

"You're looking for Lajos," Ansgar purred.

Ritter stopped walking. "Is he playing with us?" he asked, as though nothing were out of the ordinary.

"He ripped my mountain apart!" The room filled with quick, deep sobs. "*My* mountain! *Mine!*"

"Darling," Ritter murmured. "There, there."

Adoni jumped as Ansgar darted across the room and threw herself onto Ritter's back. She wrapped her arms around his neck and wailed as she throttled him. "It's *mine!*"

"There, there, my angel."

"He *broke* it!"

"My neck…"

"And you *let* him!" She swung herself around his body and shoved him against the floor.

"Stop it now," he said, his tone firmer than before.

She sat on his chest and slapped his face. "You let him rip my mountain apart!" Another slap. And another.

"Ansgar, stop it," Ritter said. "Stop it this minute."

Slap, slap, slap. "I *hate him!*" *Slap, slap, slap.*

"Now, now," he said. "You can always mend your mountain."

Adoni screamed as Ansgar's head spun right around to face her. "What are *you* doing here?"

"Ansgar." He reached up and stroked the top of her head. "Ansgar, look at me, please." Ansgar's hairless brow furrowed as she squinted at Adoni. "Mommy? Please look at me."

"I don't *want you* here," Ansgar said.

"There, there, darling, she's just—"

"He's *my* dolly!" Ansgar raged, her voice regaining its childish timbre. "You only want to play with him because he's my favourite!"

Adoni stared at Ritter, hoping he would find the right turn of phrase to put an end to Ansgar's fury. She stood and turned her body sharply, matching her gait with the direction she faced. "He's *mine*," she growled in her adult voice. "My chosen messenger."

Ritter scrambled to his feet. "Ansgar, where's Steppe?"

Ansgar appeared to consider his question. "We can play *House*," she said.

"Please tell me where he is."

"He'll be the daddy," Ansgar continued. "Daddy went away."

"Is he all right?"

"I'll be the mommy." The word brought on another peal of giggles. She fixed her limitless glare on Adoni's face. "You can be..." The smile returned. "My *sister*."

"Tell me what you've done to him."

She tilted her head. "And *he* can be the baby."

"Ansgar, you..."

The spark of life went out of his eyes. His outrage melted away as his

CHARLENE CHALLENGER

expression slackened. He teetered back and forth, his jaw hanging loose, as though he were nothing but a puppet hanging from a string.

The being that stood before Adoni was no longer Ritter, no longer a man. It was an empty shell, a cipher, shaped like someone she used to love.

She started to scream. *"What did you do to him?"*

"He's *my* dolly," Ansgar said calmly. "Mine."

"Put him back the way he was!" Adoni's eyes quickly brimmed with tears. A sob sprang into her throat. "Put him back!" she begged. "Please put him back! We only came to ask you some questions!"

Ansgar smirked. "I don't *want* to answer your questions."

Adoni wrapped her arms around herself and fought to regain her poise. "All the colony leaders have been murdered—"

"*My* colonies."

"And my friend can't remember anything about the In-Between, and Sylvester's been banished—"

"*Banished?*" Ansgar lowered her chin. "Only *I* have the power to banish."

"Please bring Ritter back," Adoni whimpered.

Ansgar tilted her head at an obscene angle. "You want to *bargain* for it?" she said. Behind her, Ritter's body swayed left and right, as though caught in a gentle breeze. Adoni let her eyes fall on his vacant expression for just a moment, and then returned her gaze to his captor. The hairless child was gone—replaced by a grown woman, fully clothed, with long black hair and deep black eyes. Adoni could barely breathe.

Belinda.

Ansgar, in Belinda's form, bent and studied Adoni's face. "He's not who I wanted," she said, in Belinda's voice. "I wanted the other one. I got the *imposter.*"

Adoni shook her head. "I don't understand you."

"I wanted Istvan. But I got *him* instead."

Ansgar's edge cut beneath Belinda's dulcet timbres, yet Adoni could still hear the tribute song Ritter had written for her—the song he'd sung to her memory, that had so enchanted Adoni the first time she heard it—echoing somewhere in the ether. She blinked hard and sniffled.

"He's *busted*," Ansgar growled. She raked her fingers through Belinda's hair. "I don't like it when they're busted. *Liar.* He's always been a liar."

"I don't understand."

Ansgar lit Belinda's eyes with fury. "He's not Istvan, stupid! Why are you so stupid? He's busted, broken, damaged, wrecked, you understand that?"

"That doesn't make him a liar!"

"Oh yes it does! Oh yes! He didn't come back when I told him to. He tried to hide from me. Years and years. But I *found* him, so he had to do what I said." She showed off Belinda's brilliant teeth as she laughed. "I said, '*You* talk to Sylvester. *You* make him shut up.' I'm bored with Sylvester. He thinks too much."

"You put Steppe in charge of The Welcome to *punish* him?"

"You don't know him," Ansgar said, her mirth dying on Belinda's face. "You don't know him at all. He's *mean*. You know what? He's *mean*, and he *burns* things."

"What are you even talking about?"

"So *you* bargain. You want to see my dolly come back to life? You have to make a trade."

Adoni felt another onslaught of tears and sank to her knees. "I don't have anything to trade with."

Ansgar nodded. "Yes you do." She pointed Belinda's slender finger at Adoni's face. "I want one."

"One what?"

"One eye."

Adoni stared at her.

"I want one eye," Ansgar said. "I *want* one. You're stupid! Sylvester told me everything. You took one of his, so I want one of yours." She smiled Belinda's sweetest smile.

Adoni remembered the feeling of Theresa's knife slicing through her flesh, the warm spill of her blood dribbling down her back, the awful ache that seemed to soak her entire being. She feared ever feeling such pain again. Then, she looked at Ritter's lifeless, captive form. With all cognition gone from his face, from his eyes, he took on a sinister aspect, as though he would spring into malevolent action at any moment. If she had the choice to bring him back and failed—if he never came back, as his old, charming self, with all of his virtues and all of his faults—she would never forgive herself.

She rose, and took a deep breath. "Promise you'll bring him back if I give you my eye."

"I promise."

Adoni wiped her tears away with the backs of her hands. "Okay. Do it."

Ansgar reached out with Belinda's hand. Behind her, Ritter's eyes flooded with sparks, with recognition. His limbs regained their strength and control. He stumbled forward, but caught himself before he fell. He straightened his back and gasped, as though he'd been held under water and had only just breached the surface. Adoni smiled when he caught her gaze. Ritter's look, however, swung from gratitude to alarm. "Donny, what have you done?"

Ansgar spread Belinda's fingers. With one swift, merciless strike, she tore Adoni's left eye out of her head.

Adoni shrieked and reeled back, waiting for a searing pain to shoot through her. To her surprise, the only thing she felt was a slight burning where her eye had been only a moment before. She reached two trembling fingers up to her face and touched the now-empty socket. No blood: only a smooth swatch of skin, as though she'd never had a second eye at all. She looked around, at the fire, at Ansgar smiling Belinda's smile, at Ansgar closing Belinda's fist, and finally, at Ritter. She took a step forward, a step to the side. She'd lost much of her depth perception, but could still see well enough to avoid tripping.

"What have you done?" Ritter muttered again. He shrank back as

Ansgar turned around, revealing Belinda's face to him.

"We're playing a game," she said. "She knows how to play. She's my *sister*." She stepped up close to him and growled in his ear. "You want to be the baby again?"

His breath quickened. "No. Please, don't."

"You have to be good."

"I'll be good."

"Promise."

"I swear. Please."

Ansgar nodded Belinda's head. "Good." She strolled into the shadows again. "New game. *Questions*."

"Where's Steppe?" Ritter asked.

"With me."

"Is he all right?"

"You ask."

Adoni heard the same striking sound as before. A second fire ignited more than a hundred feet away from where she and Ritter stood. The flames lit up the edge of the room, enough to see a smooth stone wall, and the lone figure standing flat against it.

Adoni recognized Steppe's rigid frame and sprang forward. Ritter clapped a hand on her shoulder, stopping her mid-stride. "Slowly," he said, strolling in front of her. She matched his pace, though the muscles in her legs wanted nothing more than to break into a run. The closer they got, the clearer Steppe's expression became. His mouth was a tight and twisted line, lying across his face like a crack through concrete. His eyes had rolled up in his head. A lock of his hair faded from brown to silver as Adoni approached. She heard him breathing in starts and fits. His body quaked, but he couldn't step away from the wall.

Ritter cupped Steppe's face in his hands. "Can you hear me?" he asked gently. "Steppenwolf? Can you hear me?" Steppe made no reply. "Tell me you're all right," Ritter whispered. "Oh god... please... please..."

"You know he isn't!" Adoni snapped. She turned around and shouted,

"Let him go!" into the void.

Ritter dropped his arm, took hold of her hand, and addressed Ansgar again. "What happened to the colony leaders?"

Ansgar's voice drilled through the darkness. "You know what happened. *Splat!*"

Adoni refused to hold her tongue. "Whose fault was it?" she demanded, ignoring the warning look Ritter shot her.

"Pretty eye," Ansgar said. "Just like a jewel."

"*Whose fault was it?*"

"Wrong question," Ritter said.

"*His* fault," Ansgar said. "It's always his fault. He's stupid, stupid! All he had to do was obey."

"Who killed the colony leaders?" Ritter asked her.

"Who made them go *splat?*"

"Yes."

"Sylvester."

The name hung in the air like a noose on the gallows. Ritter closed his eyes. "Did you give him that power?"

"You know I did."

"Why did you give him that power?"

"A trade. The Welcome wants to get rid of me? Because they can, when one of their pipers can scream out death! They made a trade. I made it *fair*."

"How can you say that?" Adoni snarled. "You know it's not fair! Sylvester killed one of your pipers! Steppe hasn't killed anyone!"

The voice that answered was not Ansgar's. "*Yes he has.*"

A boy's voice: one Adoni didn't recognize, with no familiar tune beneath the tone. She heard footsteps, and the voice spoke again. "So I made it *fair*." Ansgar emerged from the shadows, wrapped in the boy's body. He was clothed in heavy pants, a linen shirt, a pair of suspenders—a strangely old fashioned outfit, though the fibres did not appear to be especially worn. Something about his pale face, his stoic posture, distinguished him from every other boy she'd come across in the In-Between.

He looked almost like Steppe, as he must have looked at fourteen years, except for the slightest difference in the shape of his large blue eyes.

A twin? she thought. *He had a twin?*

Ansgar walked the boy over to where Steppe stood paralysed against the wall. "Remember me?" she asked in his voice. Steppe's trembling lessened; his breathing evened out. His gaze returned from the back of his skull. Ansgar smiled the boy's smile. "Yes you do."

Steppe started to weep.

"Stop it!" Adoni screamed at her.

Ritter wrapped an arm around Adoni and held her close. "Steppe didn't kill his brother."

"Not his brother. His *father*." She dug the boy's finger into Steppe's cheek. "He's *mean*, isn't he? *Isn't he?*" She brought a nasty smirk to the boy's lips. "Found him later, much later, when he thought he'd forgotten everything. Like father, like son. Grabbed his neighbour's pistol and fired once—pew!—Right here." She traced a circle on Steppe's temple. "Nice, clean hole. Hot red blood. Bang! Splat!"

Silence.

"Is that true?" Adoni asked, without expecting a response. She stared at Steppe, and then looked up at Ritter.

Ansgar's words failed to shake him. He refused to look away from Steppe's grief-stricken face. "I don't care if it's true," he replied.

"But—"

"You promised to never make another changeling," he said to Ansgar. "Did you break your promise?"

"I'm a *good* girl," she said. "I don't break my promises. *They* make me break my promises. Those two. They always want me to cheat. Why should I keep a promise to them?"

"Did you break your promise to me? Did you make a changeling? A changeling that looks like a girl named Natalie?"

Ansgar smirked. "Want to know what's true, if I say yes?"

"What's true?"

"If I say yes, it means a real girl went *bang, splat!*" She laughed. "I know what happened. I know everything. Bang bang bang, like it's all fun and games. Look what happened when I blessed The Welcome, look at that! Dirty little monsters."

Adoni shot Ritter a look of sheer panic. "Paj said Natalie was here when the shooting happened. If that wasn't her on the street, then..."

"You want that?" Ansgar asked.

"No," he said. "Please, mommy, tell me you didn't."

Ansgar rolled the boy's eyes up in his head and let a piercing laugh ring through the silence. "Stupid! No I didn't! I made a *promise!*"

Adoni wanted to scream.

"So she returned to the city without her memories of the In-Between," Ritter said. "Do you know why?"

"Nope."

"Did you have anything to do with it?"

"I always do." She grabbed hold of Steppe's nose and wrenched it with the boy's slender fingers. "You found it, didn't you?"

"Found what?" Ritter asked.

"The *seal*, stupid! I gave it to Sylvester. I traded it for *you.*" She pointed at Adoni without turning the boy's head.

"What does your seal have to do with the girl?"

"You don't ever think, dolly!" she said. "My changelings had their house burned. Sylvester's gone, gone, gone. He did it; *he* did it. That's what he wants most. To *forget*. To forget *everything*." She poked the boy's finger into Steppe's chest. "You don't *ever* forget," she said to him. "Not *ever.*"

Adoni shook her head. The hateful accusations, Steppe's weeping, everything converging in the firelight, in that cold, foreboding place; she leaned against Ritter, let him take most of her weight. Ritter held her tighter. "I don't understand... I don't know what's going on..." She brushed her hair off of her forehead. Finally, as she lowered her hand from her brow, her fingers disappearing as they passed in front of her empty eye socket, she started to tremble.

"It's all right," Ritter whispered. "It's all right."

"What are we gonna do?"

"New game!" Ansgar said. "New game now. Something much more fun." She bent over backwards and into a handstand. "Let's play *Fight*." Steppe's tears halted abruptly as the agony returned to his face.

"Ansgar," Ritter murmured. "Please. You're hurting him."

"Let's play! Let's play *Fight*."

"Do you want to fight?"

"*Not yet*." Hand over hand, she walked the boy's body into the shadows. "I want to see a fight. A real fight, a big one!"

"Who do you want to see fight?"

"*Him*," came Ansgar's childish voice from the darkness. "And Sylvester."

Adoni gripped Ritter's jacket in her fists.

"Sometimes I have favourites," Ansgar said. "Someone has to be the villain. But I'm bored, bored, bored of them, both of them. They don't listen. All they want is all they want, not what I want. No more. *Fight*. That's the only way to settle them. Death in their voices. I want to hear it again. It spells them out, don't you see? Sing me a song, and I can keep a piece of you."

"*Questions* before *Fight*," Ritter said, his frown as deep as a pit. "We're not finished playing that one yet. What do you mean, sing you a song, and you can keep a piece of us?"

"You sing them up, and I keep a piece of them. You sing them in the mornings and in the evenings. Because I said so, stupid! And I take a part of them. Then they won't have to go away forever. They stay young. My *friends*. I have so many friends now."

"So they never go back whole?"

"Not completely. Never completely whole."

"Ah, so," Ritter said with a nod. "Morning songs. Evening songs. You listen to them, do you?"

"They sing them for me," Ansgar said. "When they come to visit. Report, then sing. I know them all. They stick to me like skin." Her voice dropped an octave and regained its adult lustre. "No more questions. *Fight*."

Ritter put his hand on the back of Adoni's head and stroked her curls. Reassured by his touch, she loosened her grip on his clothes. "Do you want us to bring Sylvester back?" he asked.

"You know that already!" she replied. "But if you go away again…"

Adoni felt a gust of chilly wind on the back of her neck. She whirled around, and lost her breath.

Ansgar had crept out of the darkness again, wearing the long white hair, the shrivelled skin and sunken, milky eyes of a being that was half woman, half desiccated corpse. Adoni recognized Belinda's robe hanging from Ansgar's bony shoulders.

"… *he* gets it."

"You have to trade for it," Ritter said. He stepped in front of Adoni. "Do you want a fight to the death?" Ansgar bobbed Belinda's emaciated head on her shrunken neck. "All right then, you have to trade for it."

Ansgar licked Belinda's lips and waited.

"First, you have to give my friend her eye back."

Adoni's stomach skipped. She hadn't realized Ansgar could return her eye. Ansgar walked Belinda's decrepit legs away from him, shrinking them as she went. She returned to her naked, child-like form, strolling across the floor as though she hadn't a care in the world. Her empty eyes found Ritter's in the firelight, and her leer returned. "Pretty eye. Like a jewel. But I can give it back. I have *lots* of eyes. *Lots* of jewels."

"One more trade," Ritter said. "Whoever wins earns his freedom. That means when Steppe wins, you let him go. And you let him go *immortal*."

"You don't know that!" she laughed. "Sylvester's tricky. He's very, very tricky, and he's fast, and he has no mercy."

"Do we have a trade?"

Ansgar frowned. "Too much. That's two things. That's not *fair*."

"I have something to trade in return," he said.

"What's your trade?"

"My life."

Adoni grabbed his collar and twisted it around her hand. *"What are you doing?"*

"You let the winner go, and I'll stay with you forever," Ritter said to Ansgar. "I'll be yours, yours alone. And I won't ever leave you again."

Adoni's heart began to pound again. "What are you doing?"

"Dolly!" Ansgar said with delight. "There, now. That's *fair.*" She fixed the nothingness of her gaze on Adoni's face. "You go get him for me," she said. "You go get Sylvester. You go get him and you bring him back to me, and then you can watch the *fight.*" She raised her arm and pointed at Steppe, who was still a captive against the wall. "Every minute you're gone, *ouchy ouch ouch!*" Then she sang out, *"You better hurry."*

Adoni shook her head as Ritter moved between her and Ansgar. "Listen to me..."

"You were planning this the whole time, weren't you?"

"It's the only way, Donny."

"You can't do this!" she said. "You can't trade your freedom like..."

"Listen to me. Go down to Paj," he said. "Get her to open the agate for you."

"You'll be trapped here forever!" Tears stung her remaining eye. "She'll never let you go!"

"Donny," he said firmly. "Don't argue with me, darling. You get her to open the agate, take Tyler home, and then you *run* to Reese's truck. Sylvester will try something soon, I'm sure of it. You've got to stop him, all right? You've got to stop him and try to reason with him."

"But what if he won't listen?"

"You have to make him listen."

"Give Steppe his immortality back," Adoni said to Ansgar. The demigoddess smirked and turned a cartwheel. "I don't know when I'll see Sylvester again!" she cried. Ansgar turned another cartwheel, and another, until she was out of the fire's warm glow. "Please!" Adoni begged her. "It could be days!"

Ansgar's voice slunk into her ears. "No."

"Donny, look at me," Ritter said. "Don't tell him what happened here, all right? Don't tell him Steppe is... Just tell him Ansgar wants him back in the In-Between, that's all. She wants to see him and Steppe at her fortress."

"You can't do this!" she said. "You'll never be free again!"

"Donny."

"I don't even know where to find him!"

Ritter turned to Steppe and pressed his forehead against the forehead of his imprisoned friend. "Steppe, if you can hear me... You've been following him. You have to tell us where Sylvester is." Steppe didn't respond. "Steppenwolf? Can you hear me?"

"Let him speak!" Adoni shouted to wherever Ansgar lurked in the darkness.

"Steppe, please, tell us where he is."

Steppe sucked in a sharp breath, his arms stiff and down by his side, his fingers splayed as though rigor mortis had sent in, his body twitching.

"Make it... stop... please... make it stop..."

Ritter cradled Steppe's head between his hands. "I will, I promise. I swear it. Tell us where Sylvester is."

Adoni heard a thin cry of absolute anguish pass his lips. "Lower... Osgoode... Station..."

Ritter turned and caught Adoni's eye. "One of the city's ghost stations. It's underneath Osgoode."

"I've never even heard of it!"

"You'll have to wait at the station and keep an eye out for him. He must know how to get in. Be careful. The station was never used, never even finished, and it's dark in there. Take a flashlight if you can. Or use that infernal phone of yours as a light. You'll be fine."

"But what if I can't...?"

He fixed his piercing gaze on her face.

She wiped her cheek with the hood of her cloak. "All right. Okay."

"That's my girl," he said.

She threw her arms around him. He gathered her in his embrace. She heard his heart thumping in his chest. "Everything will be all right," he murmured against her hair. "I promise you."

She kissed his cheek. "I'll come back as soon as I can."

He released her and smiled. "Go on now."

Adoni searched the blackness for the smallest crack of light to show her the way out of the room, but couldn't find one.

"Where's the door?" she asked, loud enough for Ansgar to hear her.

She felt a sudden, intense heat on her left cheek and jerked her head away. The demigoddess had freed a tongue of flame from the fire pit and sent it floating past her. She followed it across the room, through a tall and narrow doorway, then down a chilly stone corridor. She heard it flickering as it danced in the air, as it fed off the breeze. It led her to the enormous doors that shut the fortress off from the In-Between. On the other side, familiar voices: Paj and Tyler.

She ran to the doors, the flame following behind her, and found herself within ten feet of the threshold when they pushed themselves open of their own accord. Paj and Tyler stood on the other side.

Adoni ran out of the fortress and threw herself against Paj. "We have to go back!" she cried. "We have to go back *now*!"

Chapter
22

Paj gasped. "What happened to your eye?"

"She took it—"

"She *took it*? Where's Ritter?"

"He's still in there. He promised he'd stay—"

"Why?"

"Because Ansgar wants…" Adoni shook her head, trying to put their conversation in order, trying to find the right words. Her thoughts were a thousand fuses, all lit and sizzling toward charges that were waiting to explode. If she couldn't share Ansgar's true intentions with Sylvester once she found him, would it be unwise to share them with Paj? "She's got Steppe in there, and she's lifted his immortality, just like she did to Belinda. He's getting older by the minute."

"Oh god," Paj said. "Oh god, *no*…"

"She won't put his immortality back, and she won't let Ritter leave until I bring Sylvester back to her. We've got to go now." She marched over to Tyler. "Come on," she said, holding out her hand to him. "I'm gonna take you back to my place. You won't be able to come back next time, okay? Just knock on the door and mom'll let you in."

Tyler pointed at her. "It's gone!"

"I know."

"Did it hurt?"

"No. Did you hear what I said? You have to go home, okay?"

He nodded and took her hand. *Thank god*, she thought. *He must be itching to get home after that changeling snatched him up.* "Steppe said Sylvester's somewhere in Lower Osgoode Station," she said. "Once I drop Tyler off at my place, we'll have to stake it out, because I don't know how to get in. Unless you do, Paj." She looked up, and found Paj staring at her. "What?"

"I'll open the agate, but... I can't come with you."

Adoni gaped at her. "If you don't come with me, I won't be able to get back here."

"I know."

"If I don't come back with Sylvester, Steppe will die, and Ritter will be Ansgar's prisoner for the rest of his life."

"Maybe... maybe Steppe's death is necessary."

Don't cry, Adoni thought. *Don't cry, don't cry, don't cry.* "How can you say that?"

"He killed four pipers..."

"We're not talking about this again! He didn't kill them. It was Sylvester. Ansgar said it herself; she gave him the death scream because The Welcome abandoned her stupid code. He's the one who murdered them!"

"Well then... if Sylvester has the power to destroy with his voice, maybe he'll use it the second he gets back. Maybe he'll use it on the pipers who are left. I'm sorry... but I can't risk that."

"She's torturing him! You don't know the pain he's in right now! You're just gonna let him *suffer*?"

Paj tented her fingers under her chin. "This war can't go on forever," she said. "The changelings will keep attacking The Welcome. And what if they find the name tree in the forest? They'll want to make an example of that, too." She closed her eyes. "My sister's final resting place. And look at what Steppe did to this mountain. I felt his anger in my bones from where I was standing. He's not the man he used to be, Adoni. He can't hold it back any more. We should... we should let Ansgar take Steppe and let the In-Between be done with it."

Ansgar's words came back to her. *He's mean*, she'd said. *He burns things.* He'd threatened to hurt Sylvester that night at The Welcome. He'd threatened to hurt her if she tried to enter Ansgar's fortress.

And Ansgar said he killed his father...

"No, no, no..."

"Maybe it's for the best."

"You know the kind of man he is," Adoni said. "You know what he did to keep you all safe. It didn't matter in the end, but it was the best he could do. I can't let him die. You have to come with me. You have to let me back in."

Paj held her finger aloft and drew it down, opening the agate before her. "Go now," she said.

"You have to come with me."

"I'm sorry," she whispered.

Adoni stepped away from the agate. "I'm not going without you."

"Take Tyler home, okay?"

Every muscle in Adoni's body stiffened, as though she'd merged with the mountain and nothing could shake her free. The chasm lay just a few feet away from where Paj stood. She could shout her to the edge, terrify her into coming along. Or she could order her rock creatures, still fixed together and bridging the gap, to pummel her until she relented. She could force her. She could hurt her.

She could kill her.

But when she looked at Paj, she found the piper patiently gazing at her. She nodded. "I know this upsets you."

"You don't know *anything*! And you don't get to tell me what to do!"

"But this is for the best."

"You can't do this to them!"

Paj gave Adoni one last, mournful glance. She turned to go.

"Don't leave me!" Adoni bent over, cradling her stomach, her knees locking together, pain shooting through her calves. "Don't leave me here all alone!" She stared at the ground, fighting her every urge to sob. She felt Tyler's tiny hand patting her head and very nearly lost control. "You've never had an ugly thought ever, have you?" she said. "You've never had an ugly thought or done an ugly thing or ran away when you should've turned and fought. You're just lucky then, aren't you? Well some of us aren't so lucky. Steppe did everything he could, so it wouldn't come to this, and yeah, maybe he's angry, maybe he's always been angry, maybe now he's angry enough to kill, but he's still a good person, he's just... And maybe Ritter's a coward, but I am too sometimes, and if you think that makes it okay for you to turn your back, because they did the best they could, just like everybody else, then... then you deserve to be hated for that, forever."

She brought Tyler close to her, cradling him against her hip as silence blanketed the snowy peak. Beyond his shoulder, the ice that clung to the mountainside shimmered as the afternoon sun finally burned through the clouds. Even in that dreadful place, there was beauty to behold.

"I just want this to be over with," Paj said softly, on the verge of tears. "I miss my sister... I miss Aniuk..."

"You can't punish them because of what happened to Aniuk. It's not fair."

"I know... I know, and you're right..." She shook her head. "But you didn't have to live in fear for so many years, never knowing when he'd show his face again. We knew from the start he was dangerous, but Steppe kept letting him into the chalet. Sometimes I'd pass him on the way down the stairs and he'd have this look in his eye, this look of *hatred*. We all knew he'd snap, and we warned Steppe... we warned him... And look what happened. I regret it every day. I regret every day that he crossed her path instead of mine. All he wanted was a twin—either one of us, it didn't matter. I wish... every day, I wish it was me instead of her..."

They stood apart, each woman as solitary as an island, as a tower.

"You know this is all Ansgar's fault," Adoni muttered.

"I know."

"She gave Sylvester the seal, she gave him permission to mess with Steppe's head. She let him get away with everything."

"I know."

"She's a monster, Paj. She can change shape and change her voice. She

CHARLENE CHALLENGER

changed into Belinda, she changed into Steppe's brother… she stole Ritter's brain out of his head, and he was just standing there… no life in his eyes… She's psychotic. We can't let her get away with this."

Paj wiped her face with her sleeve. "I know."

"So you'll come with me? You'll let me back in?"

Paj nodded.

"You'll have to be there when Sylvester's with me," Adoni said.

Paj looked into her eyes. "If Steppe doesn't kill him, I'll do it myself."

The sound of her own heart pounding filled Adoni's ears. Could Paj tell what Ansgar had planned for them?

"Sylvester's hiding at a subway station?" Paj said.

"Lower Osgoode Station, that's what Steppe said. Do you know where it is?"

"I always thought it was an urban legend."

"Ritter said I have to go to Osgoode Station and stake it out. I'll keep an eye out for Sylvester and follow him."

"Be careful." She wove her fingers through her hair, pulling it close around her face. "Please be careful."

"I'll be careful, I promise."

"Don't let yourself be alone with him. Don't trust him."

"I won't."

"He's dangerous."

"I know."

"All right," Paj said. "We'll go back to The Welcome, then we'll go back to the city and take Tyler home. And then, I guess…"

Adoni kissed Paj's cheek. "Everything's gonna be okay," she said.

Paj didn't answer.

❖

They reached The Welcome when the winter sun was low in the sky and on its way to setting. Adoni tread carefully as she stepped through the trees toward the first row of empty cabins. She waited, listening for any changelings who may have struck to avenge their terrified mate. All was silent and still. Paj came up behind her, pulling the sled, Tyler tucked under the blankets, all of them shivering in the cold. They made their way to the clearing, where the wishing well stood. Paj approached the chalet and checked the lock on the door before putting her ear to the wood. Adoni untucked the blankets from beneath Tyler's chin and helped him up. "This is the part I hate the most," she said to Paj. "I still feel sick whenever I go through the agate."

"Me too," Paj said. "It feels like losing my way. The trick is to keep in mind that in a moment the world will set itself right again, and everything will look normal."

Adoni looked down at Tyler. "Hear that? Did you feel dizzy when we came through?" He shook his head.

"Everything's secure," Paj said as she stepped off the porch. "Looks like they didn't come back while we were gone."

Adoni held her head high. "Promise me you're not just gonna leave me behind when we get there."

"I promise."

"That's what Steppe did, the first time I went back. He told me the agate was everywhere, and I just had to know how to open it up. He didn't tell me only pipers can open it once they're on the other side. Well, pipers and Ritter. He didn't want me to come back because he thought I'd get hurt."

"Well, he was right." She reached out and gently stroked the skin where Adoni's left eye used to be.

"It didn't hurt when she took my eye," she said. "It just felt weird, like when you lick a battery. Only on my face."

"No one's around," Paj said, squinting through the fabric of the In-Between at the city beyond. "Are you ready?"

Adoni slipped the cloak off her shoulders and draped it over the sled.

Paj raised her arm, then drew it down again. The agate opened up before her. Adoni picked Tyler up and held him close. She reached for Paj's hand and gripped it hard, both palms already beginning to sweat. *Everything will right itself in a minute.* She drew in a breath. *And hold tight.*

The three of them stepped forward. The light swallowed them whole.

Adoni fought to keep her eye open, but the brightness, the wind, the dip and rush, were too much to take in at once. She felt as though she were summersaulting through the air. *An even neighbourhood... flat street... solid buildings...* she thought. But when they finally passed through the agate to the other side, the dizziness had seized her forehead, and nausea crept into her guts.

A glacial gust of wind came over them, which helped to settle her stomach. She glanced up and found herself standing in the alleyway beneath her bedroom window. The afternoon was overcast, with evening on its way. The garbage bins were overflowing, the sidewalks icy, the streets still filthy with January snow. Paj took hold of her wrist and urged her back against the wall. "I've sung children away from this neighbourhood. They may still live around here. I can't let anyone recognize me."

Adoni looked up at her apartment. The living room lights were off, as well as the lights in her bedroom. "I don't think Mom's home yet." She reached for her backpack out of habit, ready to fish her keys out of the front pocket. "Shit! I left my bag in Ritter's room!"

"I can go back for it," Paj said.

"No, it's all right." She looked at Tyler. "Do you know where the spare key is?" she asked him. He shook his head. "It's up the stairs, under the loose board near the plant in the corner, where the apartments are. You know the board with the stain on it?"

"Come with me," he said. "She'll be mad."

"I can't let our moms see me." She pointed to her missing eye. "They'll freak out. I'll sneak in with you and get you the key, okay? But you have to be quiet." He nodded. She put him down. "I'll be back in a minute," she said to Paj. Together, she and Tyler hustled out of the alley, and around to the front of the building.

The door leading to the apartments leaned on its stiff latch, much to her relief. The superintendent still hadn't greased it enough to keep it from sticking out, so the door was left unlocked. She pulled it open and nudged Tyler through, tiptoed up the next set of steps, then turned right, where a large potted plant stood in the corner, in front of a narrow window dressed in cobwebs. Whereas the fern in the foyer was nearly dead, this plant was lush and green. Someone had placed it there several years ago to hide a sticky stain that had formed on the wood. Most of the people who lived on Adoni's floor kept their spare keys in this corner; some were tucked into the dirt, some under the dish that caught the runoff when the plant was watered. The keys were nondescript enough to keep anyone else from recognizing which apartments they opened. She knelt down, pushed the plant aside, and lifted the board.

The moment she held the key in her fist, she heard one of the apartment doors open. She sucked in a quiet gasp when she heard her mother's voice behind her. "Tyler, come inside."

Adoni froze.

"Where's your mom?" Ida asked.

"She left yesterday."

"Where did she go?"

"I don't know."

"Come inside." The boy put his hand into Adoni's hair and squeezed a handful of her curls. "Come on now," Ida said. "I'll make you some dinner."

"Go inside," Adoni muttered to him.

He obeyed, scraping his boots against the floor as he shuffled into her apartment. Adoni stood up as Ida stepped into the hallway and slammed the door closed behind her. "What the hell do you think you're doing?"

Adoni didn't answer.

"Where the hell did you go with him?"

"His mom wasn't home—"

"You *look at me* when I'm talking to you!" Adoni turned, keeping her mother on her right and showing her an exhausted profile. "Why didn't you bring him inside?"

"He wanted to come with me."

"Where did you take him?"

"Just around."

"Just around *where*?"

"Just *around*. Just around the city."

She saw Ida shake her head out of the corner of her eye. "You ever stop to think what his mother would do if she came home and he wasn't there?"

Adoni ground her molars against each other. "She should think about that the next time she wants to take off and leave him alone."

"You don't have the right to judge anyone, you hear me?" Ida said. "You're so high and mighty, wait until *you* have kids!"

"She leaves him alone all the time!" Adoni said, staring down at her boots.

"That's none of your goddamn business!"

"Whatever."

"*Whatever.* What, you want a kid now, is that it?"

Adoni tucked her left cheek against her shoulder. *Just leave*, she thought. *She'll be mad, but she'll get over it.*

"You want a kid of your own, is that it? Huh? Look at me!"

"No."

"You wanna talk about what happened when you left the last time? You wanna talk about how I heard her husband beating on her at night, telling her she lost his kid? You wanna talk about how I heard her crying and crying and couldn't say shit to her? Huh? I couldn't tell her my kid ran off with her kid, and he was probably safe because the both of them'd call social services on me! You wanna know what's it like to wanna call the cops when your kid goes missing, but you can't because they'd arrest her for kidnapping if they found her? Huh? *Look at me!*"

"I didn't kidnap him!"

"Where were you?"

"We were just out, that's all." *Go on and leave. Nothing's stopping you.*

"You went to visit that woman, didn't you? You think I'm stupid?" Ida's voice grew higher in pitch, and Adoni could tell she was close to tears. She turned her head sharply to the left as her mother stomped into the hallway and stood in front of her. "She found you in the street, eh? What, did you give her some sob story, and she let you crash on her couch? Huh? What did you say to her? Huh? I should call the cops!"

"Reese didn't do anything, we didn't even see her today!"

"Does she give you drugs?"

"No!"

"Oh, she doesn't, eh? Why else do you hang around her? Does she give you smokes? Do you drink at her place?"

"No I don't!"

"I thought you were going to school. I thought you were smarter than that!"

You're running out of time! she thought. But Ida stood directly in front of her, effectively pinning her to the spot. She wouldn't be able to leave without her mother noticing her missing eye.

"You go out and get pregnant, and you watch what happens to you when you think your kid's in trouble!" She pointed at the apartment door. "Get your ass inside, I'm sick of this shit."

"No."

"What did you say to me?"

She'll cry, and she'll be angry, but she'll get over it. "I've gotta go."

"Where the hell do you think you're going now?"

"I'm going out."

"Oh, you're too much, aren't you? Too much! I don't know what your thing is with that kid, but it stops now, you understand me?"

"Fine."

"What did you say?"

"I said *fine!*"

"You've got a nasty attitude, Donny!" Ida shouted. "A nasty attitude!

Did you hear what I said?" She leaned in until her nose touched Adoni's temple and yelled, "Get inside, *now!*"

Adoni shrank against the wall and tried to slip around her. Ida drew back her hand and slapped her daughter hard across the face.

Adoni covered her missing eye, shoved past her mother, and dashed down the stairs. She heard Ida call to her before slamming the lobby door behind her. "Sure, go ahead and leave! Go ahead and leave, just like everybody else!"

She thundered down the steps and marched toward the sidewalk. "Come on," she called to Paj, without turning her head to see if she had heard her. "We have to go."

A flurry of footsteps crunched over the snow. Paj matched her pace and followed her up the street. "Is everything all right?" she asked.

"My mom just smacked me out again." She swiped the back of her hand over her damp cheek. "I don't have my bus pass. Do you have any change on you?"

"No. I'm so sorry."

"So we're walking." She kept her eye fixed on the top of the street and didn't slow down, though her thighs felt like they were burning.

Is she gonna start this again? she thought as she huffed her way toward the intersection. *Is she just gonna smack me out whenever she feels like it?* She hadn't smelled any alcohol on Ida's breath. This time, not only was her mother stone-cold sober, Adoni could tell she was more than just angry; she was hurt, and confused. But why hadn't Ida told her how she felt about her disappearance? Why hadn't Ida ever asked her about where she and Tyler had gone, what they did while they were away? Why hadn't she ever taken the time to understand how Adoni really felt about Theresa, and what their relationship was really like? And why didn't Ida already know that no one, not even Theresa, could ever take her place?

Yeah, right. And you would've told her too, if she asked.

Adoni turned the corner and headed east. If she had decided to tell her mother about the In-Between, she couldn't prove it was a real, tangible place, not even with Theresa's story to back her up. She could have talked as closely around the truth as she dared—*We were together the whole time, Theresa helped us out, we stayed at her place, she and her boyfriend took good care of us*—and Ida might have been satisfied, if Adoni's story came at the end of a very long night, when her mother was too tired to keep the details straight. But the questions never came up, and Adoni assumed Ida didn't really want to know the truth.

Especially if she thinks I kidnapped him, she thought as she passed Nelly's, the neighbourhood coffee shop, and caught a whiff of freshly toasted bread when someone opened the door to step out. *She's right; it would make her an accomplice, maybe.* Not that she knew anything about the legal system outside of what she saw on television. It seemed right; the police would undoubtedly ask Ida questions she couldn't answer, and she'd look guilty of *something*, at least. Adoni frowned. *Doesn't mean she gets to hit me. Doesn't mean...*

Her march slowed to a more decent pace. *What did she mean, just like everybody else?*

"Please," Paj wheezed, "just give me a minute to catch my breath..."

"I should've remembered my backpack," Adoni grumbled. "I don't have any money in my wallet, but I could at least get my bus pass."

"Maybe we can ask someone for change."

"Yeah, right. No one's gonna do that. Paj, I know I said no before, but—"

"I'll be back in two minutes."

"Promise?"

"Promise." She rushed off to find an empty corner or an alley to tuck into.

Adoni looked off in the direction of Paj's retreat. *What will you say to Sylvester when you see him?* she thought. *Is he gonna call you "ambassador" like he used to?* She puffed up her chest. *Jerk.*

Paj rounded the corner shortly thereafter, with the backpack on her shoulder. Adoni noticed a bus approaching. "Just in time," she said with a grateful sigh. She yanked the zipper open and fished out her wallet. "Find me at Osgoode Station, at the turnstiles. It'll take me about an hour to get there and maybe another hour to find him after that. I don't know how long it'll take to get him to come with me." She found the time on her cell phone. "My battery's low. If we don't hook up by seven o'clock, find Reese. She parks her truck in front of Nathan Phillips Square. It's purple, you can't miss it." She rushed toward the bus stop. "Don't leave me behind!"

"Be careful!" Paj called.

The bus stopped at the curb just as Adoni arrived. She hopped up the stairs, flashed her pass, and took a seat in the back. *Let's hope it doesn't short turn*, she thought.

Then: *How old will he be when I get back to him?*

She pulled her hood over her head and looked out the window.

Chapter
23

To Adoni's relief the bus made relatively good time, arriving at the closest subway station less than half an hour later. She kept her head down and trudged her way across the bus platform. *This would be the worst time to run into Natalie*, she thought as she eased her way through a fairly substantial crowd of people. She didn't know how Natalie would react if she saw Adoni was now missing an eye. Would Natalie miss it too, if she found out it was gone?

She hurried down a flight of steps that led to the trains, her thoughts now racing along this new chain. Natalie hadn't ever complimented her looks during their time together. Not that Adoni enjoyed receiving compliments; they always seemed to bring out the heat in her cheeks, and she never knew what to say after receiving one. It was one of the reasons why she liked Natalie—nothing she said ever seemed insincere. There were no comparisons to limpid pools or starlit skies. *The eyes are the windows to the soul.* She smirked. *Do I only have half a soul now?* She walked to the middle of the platform and shifted her weight from one foot to the other while she waited for the train to arrive.

Natalie was the catalyst for this entire journey, Adoni remembered; her missing past, the impetus that drove Ritter back into Ansgar's wicked arms. Now that Adoni had a moment to think, she put Ansgar's words and disjointed thoughts together. First, she accused Steppe of finding the seal she had given to Sylvester. Then she mocked Steppe for wanting to *forget*—perhaps his childhood, perhaps his failures, or his trespasses—

and told him he never would. Natalie had witnessed the shooting at The Welcome, had somehow been spared the fate of the other children, and had disappeared shortly afterward. Around the same time, Steppe had returned to The Welcome, saw what had happened, and fled.

He used the seal to make her lose her memory.

She stared at the train tracks. It was just the sort of thing he would do: make a choice for someone, without asking them what they wanted, or how they felt. He must have been aiming to spare Natalie from having to relive the shooting over and over again. Or maybe he was trying to make up for underestimating Sylvester's wrath, for losing Aniuk, for putting pipers and children alike at risk. *Why didn't you think of that before?* She quickly put the notion aside. It made sense, but how was she to know Steppe had started to tread so closely to the line that separated good intentions from selfishness?

Then there was Ansgar's revelation that Steppe had killed his father.

It was odd, to think of Steppe as someone's son. Odder still to think of him as someone's brother. Yet of course he was, just as every piper had parents, and perhaps siblings, by virtue of their having once been human. Ritter said Steppe's brother had been murdered, but that Steppe wasn't responsible. Did Steppe's innocence of one crime justify his guilt for the other? Or did it prove he was innocent of both?

Do you think he's guilty of murder?

That was the real question, and it begged an answer she still hadn't fully considered. *Can he kill someone? Sure he can. But would he?*

When she first met him he tried so hard to be diplomatic. Now it appeared he was through with bargaining—for anything, it seemed—and wasn't above hurling his dissenters through the air or demolishing the very ground they walked on.

But killing your father… that's a big deal. A really big deal. And Steppe was nothing if not precious when it came to acts of finality. He had had the opportunity to kill Sylvester on multiple occasions, and didn't, because of Ansgar's code. He had had the opportunity to seek revenge on Sylvester the very moment the changeling leader spilled Aniuk's ashes and set them swirling away on the wind. Instead, risking the condemnation of all the pipers of The Welcome, he'd let Sylvester go. She thought a creature of Sylvester's breed wasn't worthy of half of Steppe's magnanimity and respect.

What had Steppe's father done to deserve that fate?

The train thundered into the station. Adoni felt the wind on her face, on her empty eye socket, and shuddered. The train came to a stop; a friendly bell tone sounded as the doors opened. She kept her head bowed as she boarded and took a seat next to the door. A father sat facing her, his son by his side. From his lower vantage point, the child peered up at Adoni's face and stared at her missing eye. Still too young to speak, the child pointed a fruit-stained finger at her. She tugged at her hood and started gnawing off the dried bits of skin on her lips.

The train swept along, eventually pulling into Osgoode Station and screeching to a halt. She hurried onto the platform, but found herself at a loss for where to go once the doors closed and the train pulled away. The station was packed with people, not just travellers but maintenance staff, off-duty conductors, security personnel. Adoni marched up and down the length of the platform, searching for conspicuous doors or hidden corners.

She had been through Lower Bay during a Doors Open event a few years ago; she'd read up on Lower Queen on a popular Toronto website. But Paj was right: Lower Osgoode Station was only ever an urban legend. There were no photos, no records, no visitors—nothing that proved its existence. Did she have to step off the platform, slip down to the tracks, find a crack in the wall that opened onto some dank hovel? Was he already there, hiding in the dark, waiting for night to fall before venturing out to find Theresa? Adoni quickened her steps. She couldn't wait until dark; she'd already wasted too much time.

Her stomach growled. It had been hours since she'd eaten Paj's grainy potatoes. *You'd make the worst cop ever*, she thought. *You can't go a couple of hours without stuffing your face. Focus.* The moment the minutes amalgamated to a full hour, with no sign of her target, food was all she could think about.

You have time to get something small, she decided at last. *It's not like you're gonna down a whole turkey dinner.* With no cash in her wallet, not even small change, her choices were limited. The kiosks in the station didn't accept bank cards. *You're gonna have to use a machine.* There was a bank at street level, just steps from the station exit. *In and out, as quickly as you can.*

She took the escalator up and passed through the turnstiles. The crowds had thinned; still, a fair number of people flanked her as she climbed the steps up to the street. Winter darkness had descended, though it was still early. Adoni took a moment to orient herself and figure out where the bank machine was. Across the street, the Four Seasons Centre sent beams of golden light through its stunning glass walls and onto the heads and shoulders of the people passing by. The bank stood behind her. She dug her wallet out of her backpack.

A single figure stood out from the rest of the madding Queen Street crowd: straight back and shoulders, and a strangely elegant gait.

Go after him!

She zipped up her backpack and tossed it over her shoulder, then waited at the intersection for the light to turn green. She could see Sylvester strolling amongst the audience members through the glass-panelled walls. Adoni slipped as she scurried across to the other side. Her hood slipped back, fully exposing her face to everyone she passed. Most people seemed not to notice her unusual appearance. If they did, they quickly averted their gaze. She found more of the same reactions when she pulled open the Centre door and locked her sight on the back of Sylvester's head. *So I'm a freak* and *invisible. Awesome.*

She stayed at what she thought was a safe distance and watched him amble up to the bar. He wore grey trousers, a crisp white shirt, a finely tailored suit jacket. *He looks good for someone who's been living in a hole in the ground,* she surmised. He caught the bartender's attention and said a few words to him. The bartender poured him a drink from an amber-coloured bottle. Adoni recognized it as one of Ida's favourite choices of hard liquor. She frowned. He took a wallet out of his breast pocket and slipped the bartender a bill, then turned away without taking his change and leaned back, propping his elbows against the bar. Adoni watched him take a long swig of his drink, and noticed how smoothly his arm curved when it brought the glass to his lips. His movements weren't stilted or rehearsed. His entire body looked as though it were at ease with his surroundings. Though he still wore the hard expression of a scorned man, he appeared to be completely within his element.

She watched him finish his drink and order another. *He wants to go back*, she reminded herself. *He wants to finish what he started.* Still, she hesitated to expose herself. What if he'd changed his mind? What if he was more than happy to stalk Theresa through the city rather than face off against Steppe? The more she thought about it, the more it made sense to her. Though the sound of death vibrated in both their throats, Steppe's was a piper's voice, through and through, and he had other destructive sounds at his disposal. Maybe Sylvester preferred to pick on those more vulnerable than him; maybe this was his plan all along—to escape the In-Between and take his revenge on an unsuspecting population.

It doesn't seem like him, though. His attacks had all been targeted at the pipers, and ultimately, at Ritter. True, he had branded Adoni and threatened to go after each child at The Welcome, one at a time, until Steppe agreed to hand Ritter over. But that was just it—the attacks, the threats, were all to force The Welcome to give Ritter up. *So he wants to go back. And he won't hurt me until he does go back.*

After that, who knows?

She strolled into his peripheral vision, waiting for him to notice her. He sipped his drink and scanned the throng. She drew closer to him. There was the scar she'd left on his face when she last encountered him, pale as a morning star, jagged and angry. She remembered what caused her to shriek so violently that the orb burst in his skull: his hands were around her throat; he was going to strangle her.

She stood in front of him.

His eye found the missing socket on her face. He lowered his chin and, for a moment, looked as though he were about to tear through the crowd to pounce on her. He swallowed the rest of his drink and placed the empty glass on the bar. They stared at each other, neither one willing to make the first move.

How old will Steppe be when you get back? Get in there.

Adoni approached, stopping just a few feet before him.

Still leaning against the bar, he lifted his wrist and pointed at her. "You've been to Ansgar's fortress."

Here we go.

"She wants to see you."

"I think she might have been gentler with you than you were with me."

"You were trying to kill me!" The bartender peered over Sylvester's shoulder.

Sylvester leaned back and nodded at the array of liquor bottles on display behind him. "What can I get you?"

"I don't drink," Adoni muttered.

"Really. I thought you were old enough to drink by now."

"Even if I was, I wouldn't."

"Funny. You struck me as the type who would."

"What do you know?"

"Just making conversation."

"Ansgar wants to see you and Steppe at her fortress."

Sylvester smirked. "Has she finally had enough of us?" Adoni didn't answer. His one eye surveyed her from head to toe. "You're on edge. Why is that?"

"Because you're a psychopath."

"You're in a public place, surrounded by music lovers. I can't possibly do you any harm here."

"Doesn't change anything."

"So you find me repulsive."

"Pretty much."

He nodded. "I can understand that."

"Are you coming with me?"

"You have the power to open the agate?"

"Not me."

"So Ritter's with you." He ran the tip of his tongue along his bottom lip. *Watch it.* "No, he's not."

"Who are you with?"

"Does it matter who I'm with?"

"Yes. I'd like to know who I'll have to face before I return."

Adoni's mind began to race. Sylvester's hesitation made sense, especially if he thought it was Steppe who was standing by, waiting to open the agate to allow them passage. Sylvester had no guarantee that Steppe wouldn't obliterate him the moment he laid eyes on him. She couldn't think of a reason to keep Paj's presence a secret. But did he deserve fair warning that he was about to encounter the twin sister of the first piper he murdered?

He doesn't deserve any favours, she thought. *But he might run if he's surprised.*

Shit.

"Paj," she said.

Sylvester sighed. "You won't begrudge me another drink, then."

She fought to keep her impatience off her face.

He caught the bartender's attention and ordered a third drink. Adoni clenched her fingers into fists within her jacket pockets as she watched him take a leisurely swig. Ida was terrible when she drank the hard stuff, even though she couldn't match the pace Sylvester had set. Despite downing so much in so little time, the changeling seemed to be handling it well. "You're staring," he said as he lowered his glass.

"How's your liver doing?"

He chuckled. "It takes us longer to really feel the effects of alcohol. It's one of the perks." A patron sidled up next to him and ordered a drink of her own. Sylvester turned away from her. Adoni followed suit, keeping him completely in her sight. "Paj. I don't know her very well, but I'm surprised she remained at The Welcome, after the… unpleasantness." He stared at her until she almost couldn't bear to look at him.

"That's what you call it? *Unpleasantness?*"

"That's what I call it while there are others within earshot."

"Pretend we're alone."

"No, thank you." He took another swig. The new fluidity of his movements fascinated Adoni, though she hoped he couldn't tell. "If you don't mind, I'd like to get some things before I go," he said after what felt like a long while.

She squinted at him. "What do you need?"

"A coat. A pair of boots. My scarf. It's cold in the In-Between this time of year."

Don't let him out of your sight, or he'll try to run. "Where's your stuff?"

"Downstairs. You're welcome to join me if you like."

She frowned. *He can't run, or he'll never get back. Wait for him up here where it's safe.* "I'll meet you out front."

He came away from the bar and stood so close to her that she shrank back a step. "There's no reason on earth you should trust me," he said, "but I know you have questions, and I have answers. I know what might happen to me when I meet Steppe and Ansgar again. I have a few things to get off my chest. Unspoken things that deserve to be said. I can't do that here."

"You can meet me at Theresa's truck," she said. "Since you know where it is," she added, her lip curling.

"That's a bad idea. Besides, I don't think she'll be out tonight."

Adoni lowered her chin. "Why?" she growled.

"I haven't hurt her, if that's what you're thinking," he said. "Though not from lack of trying."

"Sicko!"

She heard the bartender chuckle and caught him grinning at her, a grin that disappeared when he noticed she, too, was missing an eye.

"Careful," Sylvester said. "You'll ruin my reputation."

"Get your stuff and meet me out front."

"Please, Ambassador. Do you think I don't know I'm about to face oblivion?" He downed what was left of his drink and put the empty glass back on the bar.

"If you think you're gonna *face oblivion*, why are you okay with coming with me?"

He smiled. "Because I've faced it before, and I'm still here."

She stepped away from the bar. "I'll be out front."

The smile fell from his lips. "Wait." She stopped. "We won't be too long. I want to invite you into my home this time, instead of dragging you in. I want someone else to see it."

"Why?"

"Because it's normal. I'd like to feel normal."

She felt the back of her neck flush with goose pimples. "Downstairs?"

"Yes."

"I thought you were hiding out at Lower Osgoode."

"We can get there from here."

"It's under the theatre?"

"Yes."

"I love how you're the Phantom of the Opera."

He smirked. "I'm not dead yet, Ambassador. This way."

Adoni followed him away from the bar, across the polished floor, and down a set of stairs to the lower level. He led her toward the corridor that bridged the centre with the subway station. A fluorescent green sign had been taped onto the door. Someone had written, "CLOSED. No Access to Osgoode Station" across the poster board in thick black marker. Sylvester retrieved a key from his breast pocket, which he used to flip back the bolt. "How do you have a key to this door?" she asked him.

"I nicked it from a staff member when he dozed off one night. They're quite adept at falling asleep at their posts. I had a copy made and slipped the original back on its ring before he woke." He pulled the door open. "You'll have to watch your step. The hallway's flooded."

Adoni followed him past the doorjamb and into the dimly-lit corridor, where several dirty puddles welcomed the soles of her boots. She inhaled the funk of mildew and wet newspaper. Her nose wrinkled. "They need to take a mop to this hallway."

"They do, when the wiring isn't on the fritz. Fortunately for me, they haven't been able to get it back up and running for months."

"I bet you've got something to do with that."

"I do. A pair of pliers and a rudimentary understanding of electrical work." He locked the door behind them. "This next stretch is a little unpleasant."

Adoni followed him as he made his way up the corridor, stepping as lightly as she could to avoid splashing filthy water up the backs of her legs. Sylvester crouched next to the wall, slipped his fingernails behind one of the tiles, and carefully took it away. He placed the tile on the floor and repeated the process for several minutes, stopping when he had fully revealed a hole in the concrete that was large enough for a person to crawl through. "I keep a flashlight here," he said, reaching into the hole. "The bulb is going. Be careful where you crawl. We'll be on our hands and knees for at least ten feet before we're able to stand up." He fished the flashlight out of the dark. "I'll go first." He switched the flashlight on. It gave off a feeble light that was nonetheless preferable to crawling through absolute pitch. Adoni waited for him to get far enough into the crawl space for her to ease herself into the dark.

The musty smell intensified. She slipped her mittens over her hands and shuffled forward on all fours. There was plenty of space above her head, but her shoulders and hips brushed against the jagged concrete walls. She pictured, briefly, morbidly, the tunnel caving in on her. She could still see the amber spill of the flashlight ahead, and took what little comfort she could from the glow. A train pulled into the station; Adoni felt the concrete shake beneath her palms and knees. A trail of dust fell across her cheek. Startled, she brushed it away with the back of her mitten and shivered. She heard a scratching sound, couldn't tell where it was coming from, and hoped it was only the scraping of Sylvester's knees ahead of her. *If I see a rat, I'm gonna scream.*

Sylvester reached the end of the crawl space and pulled himself through, taking the flashlight with him. Plunged in absolute darkness, Adoni's heart knocked against her chest. *He's gonna leave me here. He's gonna trap me in this hole.* Instead, she heard him flip a switch, and the space flooded with a brighter light. She picked up her pace and poked her head out when she reached the end of the tunnel. Sylvester stood in a cramped room, the floor of which was several feet below where she was crouched. The light came from a solitary bulb, ensconced in a wire cage, attached to an extension cord. Every corner was hidden by piles of debris—soggy plaster, rusty bolts, discarded rags, pairs of ripped, rubber gloves. The damp air carried an acridity that reminded Adoni of an underground parking lot after a rainstorm. The room narrowed into a passageway that ended with a sharp left turn. With no space to swing her legs around, Adoni waited for Sylvester to take hold of her arms and pull her the rest of the way through the tunnel. He stayed by her until she found her footing and straightened up, then started down the passageway. She followed him around the corner, to the top of a makeshift staircase. Another bulb hung overhead; Adoni was able to see all five sodden steps leading down to a second concrete floor. Sylvester turned left and headed down another gangway. "One moment," he said, disappearing behind a gloomy nook. One last flip of a switch, and a warm, pink radiance eased the shadows away. She waited for her vision to adjust to the light. "You're welcome to join me," he called out to her.

Adoni peered around the corner. Sylvester stood in an alcove that was almost as large as her bedroom. An inflatable mattress lay along the wall, neatly made with two large pillows and several fleecy blankets. The floor was covered with a shaggy carpet, one that Sylvester clearly hadn't tread upon while wearing his boots or shoes—the pale fibres that unfurled from the weave were free of footprints. Sylvester's clothes hung on a dressmaker's rack, each outfit securely zipped in a garment bag; his shoes, still in their boxes, sat on a shelf underneath. His winter boots stood off to the side. He had hung a mirror on the wall, and Adoni nearly laughed out loud when she noticed an open makeup kit, filled with his toiletries, sitting on top of a stylish end table. A wicker basket brimming with notebooks sat at the foot of Sylvester's bed.

The light came from a floor lamp that stood next to the clothes rack. The red shade gave a sophisticated aspect to what would otherwise have been an uncomfortable hovel.

"This is your place?" Adoni asked.

"Yes."

"It's not bad for a hole in the ground."

"I've done my best to make it liveable."

"You never thought of renting a place instead?" *Like anyone would rent a place to a guy with no employment background or ID*, she thought. *Hurry up!*

"I thought about it. I tried twice. The landlords spent two minutes with me before their backs went up." He slipped off his shoes and stood on the carpet.

"You think they could tell you're a changeling?"

"If not a changeling, some other alien creature. The same reaction I used to get when Ritter first brought me to this side: my very presence offended them. I was an affront to their comfort. My changeling brethren were the only ones who accepted me when I returned to the In-Between. I'd forgotten how my mannerisms affected humans. Being in their presence again was a rude re-awakening."

"You don't have them anymore," Adoni said.

"I do. And I don't mind them. But they're not as noticeable as they were while I dwelt in the In-Between."

"You move like a regular person, not..."

"... a puppet," he finished. "Isn't that right? I've heard how pipers describe changelings to each other. They say we move like puppets, look like puppets. Like dolls. They say we even smell synthetic. The only piper I've ever spent a decent amount of time with is Steppe. He never seemed to be bothered by my smell. My words, yes, but not my smell." Adoni noticed a bottle of men's cologne among Sylvester's other beauty products. "They say we don't have souls," he said gravely.

She gave him a cold, hard look. "Maybe they can't tell you've got them when you're attacking their homes and murdering them."

"Why? Because those of us with souls are only ever sweet natured and placid and always do what we're told? That a soul can't possibly dwell in the heart of someone capable of violence? I have a soul. I've felt it writhing for hundreds of years."

You're distracting him, she thought. *Stop talking.*

"But I do owe my banishment for my assimilation," he continued. "I've enjoyed being around humans these last few years, for the most part. I've watched how they eat, how they dress, how they carry themselves in the streets. I've listened to how they talk, and what they talk about. Humans are fascinating. The ones who live in this city in particular. No one gawks at me here. No one makes a fuss. Really, no one cares enough to do so."

"So why did you go back to the In-Between in the first place?" she blurted out.

He took off his jacket and hung it up on the rack. "There used to be so many of us, scattered all over the country. Sometimes we were lucky and found each other on this side. I encountered other changelings during my time on the farm. We'd all heard the rumours. Eventually the pipers would come back for us. All we had to do was wait. Some of us waited for years, but we kept our faith, and eventually every piper came for the changeling they left in a real child's place. They would appear in the night and open the agate and welcome the changeling back to the In-Between, where they would no longer age, where they'd no longer bleed. Sometimes the changeling was right where the piper had left them. Most of the time, they weren't."

"They just took off?"

He shrugged. "Or they didn't survive."

"Why would you leave if you knew you'd be rescued one day?"

"*Rescued.* Too little, too late. Why would I leave? I *didn't* leave. I stayed right where I was, and I waited for Ritter to come back for me. My eighteenth birthday. My nineteenth birthday. My twentieth birthday. I waited. While my human father drank himself into a stupor and thrashed me to within an inch of my life, I prayed my brother would remember me and come back to take me away. I stayed up at night listening for his arrival and could barely keep my eyes open while working the fields throughout the day. I was afraid of what life was like beyond the fence. I was afraid Ritter would come for me when I'd already gone, and I'd miss my chance to return to a world where I would never, ever, feel pain again. But he never came back." He paused. A moment later, he asked, "What do you think is worse? Coming face to face with the one who abandoned you, or being left entirely alone?"

Adoni didn't answer.

Sylvester went to the basket of notebooks. He retrieved one from the pile, along with a fountain pen, the cap of which had been thoroughly chewed. He sat back on his haunches, the notebook on his lap, his pen poised, and took a moment to write several lines down on the first blank page he found. When he was finished, he returned the notebook to the basket and began to dress for his return. He removed his shirt and pants as though there were no one else in the alcove but him. Adoni's face filled with heat as Sylvester, wearing only his shorts, turned his back to her and began rifling through his garment bags. She'd forgotten his back was covered in scars obtained during his years under the farmer's rule; among the many pink and silvery keloids were five gashes that ran from just below the nape of his neck to the curve of his lower back. *Those are from a rake, on a very cold night*, he had told her once. She stared at them until he covered himself with a sweater and a pair of thick cotton pants.

He leaned forward and crossed his arms, his fingers gathering up the sweater's sleeves. She heard him take a long, deep breath, and saw him lean his cheek against his shoulder and nuzzle the fabric.

"Ansgar came for me," he said. "She brought me back. She took me to The Welcome, to listen to the pipers sing. I hadn't heard piper voices until that moment. They only sing for real children, not for us. Never for us. When I finally heard them sing, it was so... beautiful. So, so beautiful.

I wanted to scream. They conjured every single child with such melodic grace that I wanted to break down the door. Why not us? Why didn't they sing so sweetly for us changelings, us *fools*? Why didn't they remember us?" He put on his boots, pulled a winter coat and scarf off of the rack. "Sometimes I'm afraid... I'll become so angry... that I won't remember what beauty is."

He lifted his arm and wiped his face with the back of his hand. When he finally turned to face her, his bottom lip was trembling.

"I'm ready now."

Chapter
24

Adoni followed Sylvester out of the alcove, through the passageways, the cramped tunnel, into the empty station hall. He crouched down next to the mound of tiles and set to work covering the hole in the wall. He had used a sticky blue substance on their backs to keep them firmly in place; when they were all fixed together again, the wall appeared only slightly damaged.

They returned to the locked door. Adoni peered through the window to see if the coast was clear. Sylvester took his cue from her nod and released the bolt. Together they stepped into the Centre. Adoni covered Sylvester as he secured the door behind them. They walked up the stairs, to the lobby, without calling significant attention to themselves. Sylvester's pace slowed until he fell into step behind her. The closer they got to the entrance, the more her heart knocked against her ribs. She passed through the doors, into the evening; the smell of women's perfume mixed with the cold air was a paltry comfort.

"I told Paj to meet me at the turnstiles," she said, pointing at the stoplights. He followed her across the street and down into the station. Adoni glanced at the time on the automated transfer machine. "Almost seven. She should be here soon. Unless she couldn't get bus fare." She leaned against the machine and scanned the faces of the commuters as they passed. Sylvester stood next to her, his hands in his pockets, his ankles crossed—an awkward schoolboy pose. Adoni cocked an eyebrow at him. "So you're older now than when I first met you?"

"A little."

"Aren't you like hundreds of years old? You don't just age like crazy when you cross over to this side?"

"The clock stops when we're in the In-Between," he said. "It starts when we're on this side, simple as that. Well... for most of us, anyway."

Adoni realized he was referring to Ritter. "One of your changelings ran off with my neighbour this morning. The thing climbed up into the trees and started swinging through them like he was in Cirque du Soleil."

Sylvester smiled. "Amazing, isn't it?"

"I asked Ritter if he could do that. He said no."

"He probably hasn't tried. You adopt certain skills when you've got all the time in the world on your hands. We like to keep strong. Our muscles don't ache in the In-Between."

Adoni searched his face to see how willing he might be to answer a question she'd been dying to ask. His blank expression seemed an open enough invitation. "I was at The Welcome last night, in Ritter's old room. Your changelings keep attacking the place." He didn't respond. "They were in his room and one of them wrote something on the floor. In blood. Like, changeling blood. It was black blood. A lot of it." *Don't tell him what Ritter said.* "If changelings heal so quickly in the In-Between, where did they get the blood from?"

"Beheading," he replied.

"Jeez," she muttered. "Why? What, does a changeling just volunteer for that?"

"They wouldn't do it against their brother's will."

"But would a changeling be all like, 'Sure, you can cut my head off, whatever!'?"

"No, they wouldn't *be all like* that," he said with a sneer. "They would come to a decision together. Just as you would. Just as anyone would."

"But why would they kill one of their own, just for that?"

"What did they write on the floor?"

"Just a word."

"What word?"

"I don't remember," she mumbled.

"Don't lie to me, Ambassador."

"Stop calling me that!" she said. "I'm not an ambassador! I'm not talking for anyone else but myself!"

He grinned sheepishly at her. "I don't remember your name."

"I ripped your eye out, and you don't remember my name?" He shook his head. She kissed her teeth. "It's Adoni."

"Adoni. That's fitting."

"Why? Wait, do you know what it means?"

"It has several meanings."

"You've *heard* it before?"

"Yes."

"No one's ever heard my name before!"

"Maybe you don't get out as much as you should."

"What does it mean?"

"Anointed one. My lord. My god."

"Really?" He nodded. "How do you even know that?"

"What did they write on the floor?"

She frowned. "Just one word."

"Which was?"

"*Brother.*"

"There's your answer, then. There are some words—some names—we think are worth dying for."

They stood quietly together until the transfer machine flashed 7:00. "We can't wait for her here anymore," she said. "I told her to meet me at Reese's truck if we didn't find each other by seven. We better go now. If Reese isn't there, Paj'll just be wandering around." She crossed the floor, to the stairs leading up to Queen Street.

The temperature had dropped to well below zero. Adoni kept her head down and marched east along the frozen sidewalk toward the Square, dodging the other pedestrians she passed along the way. She glanced back at Sylvester every so often, to make sure he was still following behind her.

To her surprise, when she caught sight of Paj, she wasn't wandering around at all, but standing right where she'd been told to stand, in front of Theresa's food truck. *I knew Reese'd be out here again!* she thought. *She's not afraid of anything.* She shuffled forward, steering clear of every icy patch she crossed, her eye fixed on Theresa's serving window. As they drew closer, Paj turned and noticed Sylvester's approach. Theresa leaned through her window and set a plastic bowl of piping-hot vittles down on the ledge, then followed the piper's gaze. Both of them stood motionless: Theresa wide-eyed, Paj glaring nuclear war.

Adoni caught up to them and turned to Theresa. "Are you okay?"

Theresa gasped. "What the hell happened to your face?"

Adoni waved the comment away. "Sylvester told me he tried…"

"Tried to burn my face off," Theresa finished with a growl.

At first Adoni thought she hadn't heard correctly, but Theresa's constant stare made her spin on her heel and confront him. "What did you try to do?" she barked at him.

"You heard her," Sylvester replied.

A terrible silence fell over them.

"You should be ashamed of yourself," she said at last.

"I'm many things, Adoni, but I am not now, nor have I ever been, ashamed of myself. And I never will be." He sniffed the air and noticed the bowl on the serving ledge. "Don't let me interrupt your meal."

From where she stood, Adoni could see the handle of a butcher knife under Theresa's palm.

"By all means, enjoy it," he said. "I don't mind waiting."

Theresa took the bowl off of the ledge and dumped its contents back into a pot on the stove. A moment later, she locked the serving window and turned the truck's power generator off. Adoni heard her rummaging around her kitchen, clattering pots and cutlery the way Ida did when she was angry and didn't want to speak without thinking first. She climbed out the back and secured the door behind her. She wore a thick winter coat with a high faux-fur collar, heavy boots, a scarf and mittens. "All right," she said. "Let's go."

Adoni stepped in front of her. "Wait. You need to know this first."

Theresa folded her arms. "Ansgar's... she's worse than you think. She's worse than Ritter ever said she was. Reese, she's *psychotic*. You won't know what she's gonna do next. She changes shape, she changes her mind whenever she feels like it, she's—"

"—just like my father," Theresa said. "I know how to take care of myself."

"No, you *don't understand*. She pulled me and Steppe into her fortress just by force, like she could make the air do whatever she wants. She took my eye out."

Theresa's arms unfolded slowly. "Jesus..."

"She took..." Adoni leaned forward, speaking her next words soft enough for just the two of them to hear. "She took Ritter's personality right out of him. For five minutes he was like... he wasn't there. He looked like a changeling, not like himself. I don't know what she did with his brain, but if she can do all that—"

"There's no way I'm staying here. I have to make sure you're safe. I have to make sure *Steppe's* safe."

"If he's already with Ansgar," Sylvester said, giving Theresa a sickening smirk, "then you know he isn't."

"I'm going to be there," Theresa said to Adoni.

Adoni shook her head. "I know, but I'm serious, Reese. You have to be careful. Ritter wasn't kidding when he called her a monster. She is a monster."

"I'll be careful."

Adoni caught the waver in Theresa's voice and gave her arm a squeeze. "Okay. Okay. Just..." She pointed at the concrete overpass that wound its way around the Square. "No one'll see us open the agate from there. Follow me."

The four of them made their way to the lowest, darkest corner beneath the overpass. Adoni walked with Theresa. Sylvester came after them.

The last to arrive was Paj.

They stood in a semi-circle, their backs to the street.

Before Paj opened her mouth to sing the agate open, she stepped up to Sylvester, reeled back, and spat in his face.

Sylvester slowly raised his arm and wiped his cheek with the back of his sleeve.

"You *murdered* my sister."

He stared at her, and didn't say a word.

"I wish Steppe had had the guts to tear you apart when he had the chance," she hissed.

Theresa murmured, "Give me your hand," into her ear.

Paj wove her fingers together with Theresa's. Adoni felt Theresa's other hand gently close around her wrist.

Adoni held her hand out to Sylvester.

And he took hold.

Paj sang her quiet melody. The agate rippled into view. They paced forward, Paj leading the way.

The familiar fuzz and whirl took hold of Adoni's senses as the agate surrounded her. She kept her eye open, breathed deeply, unabashedly squeezed Sylvester's hand. They came through the fog, through the noise. Adoni found herself standing in a stretch of forest beyond The Welcome's borders.

Theresa crouched in the snow, looking as though she were about to be sick. Adoni let go of Sylvester's hand and went to her. "Still bumpy, eh?"

"You know it." She straightened her back and rubbed her eyes. "Jeez, it's freezing," she said, pressing her mittens against her cheeks. "Where are we exactly?"

Paj looked around them. "I can't tell," she said, peering into the dark.

"This way," Sylvester said. He started off toward a cluster of trees. The rest of the party stayed where it was and watched him. He stopped and turned back to them. "I know the way," he said in earnest.

"What guarantee do we have that you won't use Ansgar's *gift* against us?" Paj asked.

"You don't have a guarantee," he replied. "But I'm not one to make a kill if it isn't necessary or strategic for me."

"Jeez, you're something else," Theresa said.

"You think I kill for no reason?"

"I *know* you do."

"Think what you want. You have no idea the kind of man I am."

"Why are we talking?" Adoni asked. "It's gonna take us a while to get to the fortress. We've got to leave now."

"What's your hurry?"

"I'm just—"

"Impatient," he said. "And twitchy."

"It's cold out here," she said, stealing a quick glance at Paj.

"'Tis the season."

"Are we gonna stand here all night debating stuff like intentions and strategy?"

He looked from one body to the next before his pale blue eye rested on her face. "The moment I set foot in Ansgar's fortress, I'll be at her mercy. Tonight might very well be the last night I ever see. The last time I smell this air, see these stars, walk this path. Whatever my fate, I'll face it at my own leisure. Don't try to rush me again. You still have an eye left." He turned. "It's this way."

They followed him.

Theresa caught up with Adoni and linked an arm through hers. "All right, kiddo," she said in a low voice. "He's a psychopath, but he's got a point. I wouldn't be beating down Ansgar's door if she called me to see her. Are we running against the clock?"

Adoni slowed her footsteps so that they fell behind the others. "Steppe and Ritter are in trouble," she mumbled.

"I figured as much. What kind of trouble?"

Adoni whispered to her. Theresa's grip on her arm grew tighter the more she revealed, until she finally had to reach over and ease Theresa's fingers open. With barely any moonlight falling across their path, she could only see Theresa's profile in silhouette. Adoni heard the woman's jaw crack. "How long has it been since you saw him last?"

"A couple of hours."

"So he might still…"

"Recognize us?"

"God… The older you get, sometimes…" Theresa cursed under her breath. "Steppe…"

Adoni put her arm around Theresa's shoulders. "Something else you should know."

"Christ… what is it?"

"Steppe's real name."

"God." She stopped walking. "So it's not Istvan. I thought as much when Ritter gave me that old article he found. I stared at it so long I thought I'd wear a hole through the paper."

"It's Lajos."

Theresa looked down at the ground. "*La-yosh*," she said softly. "You know, it suits him."

"I guess we can still call him Steppe," Adoni said. "But… if we have to say goodbye…"

"We say it right." Theresa nodded. "Got it."

"Are you all right?"

"No." She held her head up and resumed her walk.

They continued their trek north, and the night air soon filled with snowflakes—fluffy clusters of them that drifted gently to the ground. Adoni remembered Sylvester's wonder from all those years ago, the way he held his hand out to catch the flakes, the way his fingers welcomed them as though they were jewels floating through the sky. She caught a glimpse of him passing through the trees up ahead. She thought he might pause for a moment, as he had that first night of her stay at The Welcome, and marvel at their tranquil beauty. This night, however, he couldn't be bothered; his steps, while not quick or eager, nonetheless propelled him north, and he seemed not to notice the snowflakes at all.

CHARLENE CHALLENGER

Soon they came upon an open stretch of land that had felt the wrath of Adoni's voice. The way she had carved in pursuit of Tyler and the changeling was still relatively clear, save for an inconsequential layer of snow that had fallen since that afternoon. Sylvester crouched and scrutinized the track, his eye following its every deliberate zigzag. The expression he wore was inscrutable, and she hoped it meant he couldn't recognize the work as hers.

A rustling came from the trees behind them. Sylvester quickly stood and faced the noise. He drew in a breath; Adoni's ears popped, as they did when she'd been in Steppe's presence as he prepared to unleash the supremacy of his voice on the In-Between. The party caught sight of several thousand spindly wooden legs crawling between the trees, climbing up the trunks.

Theresa saw them next. "Holy shit!" She grabbed onto Adoni's shoulder and twisted up a fistful of her sleeve. "What the hell are those?"

Adoni grimaced as she pulled away. "They're just branches."

"Walking branches! Oh my god, they look like spiders!"

Sylvester squinted at the branch creatures. "What in the world…" He shook his head. "I've been gone too long. Ansgar's gotten bored." He started to laugh. "Funny, isn't it? She loves her abominations."

"Your words…" Paj muttered.

"Let me ask you something," he said, getting to his feet, directing his scowl right at her. "Did you ever leave a changeling in a real child's place?"

"No," she said. "Ansgar had stopped the practice by the time I became a piper."

"You never had to look a little one in the face and wish it good night? Never had to hear it wonder out loud where you were going when you turned your back and walked away?"

"No."

"You're lucky then, aren't you? You never had to endure the inconvenience of another creature counting on you for protection. You just followed the rules."

"Steppe never told us exactly what you said to him on your visits," Paj said, black eyes bright, even in the gloom. "But my word... sitting with you, day after day, listening to you go on like this, as if you're the only being alive who has ever faced hardships... *that*, is the only inconvenience I thank Ansgar I never had to endure."

"Yes, thank her," he said. "Don't ever forget to thank her."

"I *do*!" she shouted. "I can't imagine having to talk in circles for years. No matter what we say, no matter what amends we try to make, you'll never be satisfied! If words won't appease you, why do you keep asking for more?"

"What *amends*? What have you *done*, exactly, to make up for the evil you caused us?"

"There, you see? You've gone and changed it again! You used to say it was Ritter who was the cause of all your problems. Now it's all the rest of us too! You just spew hatred, more and more of it, whenever the spirit moves you!"

"Ritter is Ansgar's chosen messenger," Sylvester said, looking at her as though he wanted to tear her heart out of her chest. "He was the first in a long line of amoral pipers who ignored our plight. And Steppe tried to justify it, if you don't know that already, in every single meeting we had. He tried to say it was just the way things were back then, that the thinking was different, that it even made sense. I thought that humans couldn't possibly have lasted for as long as they have without one set of rules, one moral code. You would have known what you were doing was wrong. You *should have* known. Hatred is fluid. Sometimes the beast rages and sometimes it sleeps. It may be Ansgar's will to leave her *gift* for the throats of those least able to use it. Only she knows. She has her whims. We all have our whims. I won't deny mine." He smiled. "You've caught me on a bad day."

"Ritter may have been the first to leave a changeling behind," Theresa said, "but he was the one who put a stop to the whole practice. It tore him up to leave you behind after what Ansgar had done to you."

He stared at her. "What did you say?"

CHARLENE CHALLENGER

"I said it tore him up. He still blames himself. So he's too much of a coward to face you down—"

"Ritter's not a coward!" Adoni snapped at her.

"What did Ansgar do to me?" Sylvester asked.

"Made you sentient."

"Sentient?"

"Made you aware of what was going on, so you'd feel everything that happened to you right away, when you were too young to understand it. Ritter argued for all your sakes. And she listened to him. If anything, you owe him your respect for all the changelings that would have come after you that he managed to save!"

"Monstrous," Paj said, "creating a being that was designed to suffer right from the start."

"Are you saying… it was *cruel* of her to give me *knowledge*?"

"Knowledge enough so you could tell you'd been abandoned and that you were going to live the next few years of your life trapped with a monster, while the kid who replaced you grew up comfortable and safe?" Theresa nodded. "Yeah, that was cruel."

"To *know*? To *feel*? That isn't cruel, it's a *gift*." He stalked toward her. "Ansgar didn't let me wallow in ignorance while I endured the lash, mimicking until maybe the truth dawned on me later. She gave me the greatest gift of all: the ability to know and feel anger. *My anger*, the one thing that comforted me when I lay my head down at night! I don't know how any of you can dare… dare… to look me in the face and tell me that my sentience was anything other than a blessing!"

"She should have spared you—"

"You have *no* right!" he screamed. "None of you! *No right at all!*" He lunged at her.

Adoni let a snarl fly through the air, tripping him and sending him face first into the snow. "I've had it with you guys," she growled. "We're wasting time. We've got to get to the fortress before Ansgar kills Steppe and keeps Ritter prisoner forever!"

Sylvester turned his head around sharply, his mouth open, his eye wide with fury.

Adoni pointed at him and shouted, "*Fin aust!*"

Theresa shrieked as the branch creatures sprang into action. They leapt from the trees and flew past her, then surged across the frozen ground to where Sylvester had fallen. He got to his feet but staggered backwards and nearly toppled over again. The creatures surrounded him, swarmed up his legs, pinned his arms behind his back and wrapped themselves around his mouth. Adoni gave the command "*Vinat.*" They stopped their advance and held him fast. He struggled against their grips, his words muffled.

She ignored his glare and put her finger in his face. "Be nice," she said. "You've got an eye left too."

"You can *command them?*" Theresa asked.

She considered answering the question in front of Sylvester. *What harm can it do now?* "I can make things come to life and obey me."

"Holy *shit!*"

Adoni looked at Paj. "How do you say 'follow me?'"

"*Sefret,*" she replied. Paj looked at Sylvester and hid a smirk with the back of her hand.

"You think this is funny?" Adoni asked. "It's not funny. None of this is funny."

Paj's smile turned defiant. She shot Sylvester one last glance before turning her back on him.

Adoni's heart sank. She found the path she had screamed clear earlier that day. "Do any of you know where we are?"

"I do," Paj said. "I recognize the tracks. We're not far now."

"Good. *Sefret.*"

The creatures, their prisoner in tow, followed Adoni as she fell into step with Paj. She felt her jaw throb and concentrated on not clenching her teeth while she walked.

Adoni's fingers were numb with cold by the time they reached the foot of Ansgar's mountain, despite the mittens she wore. Her jacket wasn't warm enough to keep the sub-zero wind from blasting through the worn lining. She wished they had found their way to The Welcome, and to the sled, before they arrived at the opening of the rocky passageway that led to the fortress. *I could've used Aniuk's cloak*, she thought. *Guess it doesn't make a difference now.*

As they drew closer, she could see a tarn of firelight radiating out from the cliff sides that flanked the pathway up the mountain. She charged ahead and whipped around the corner. The way to the fortress was lit by changelings, standing next to each other, one after the other, each holding a torch. Adoni froze. They turned their heads and stared at her, standing straight, their faces blank, but their eyes wet and sorrowful. Not one of them made a move against her; there was no hissing, no swiping, no obvious urge to do her harm. She heard the footsteps of the others behind her and held her hand out to keep them at a distance. "Changelings."

"Is everything all right?" she heard Theresa ask.

"They're not moving. They're just looking at me." She backed away.

Paj stepped into the glow. The changelings remained motionless, their torches popping and flickering as they burned, their eyes now fixed on her rather than Adoni. "They know something," she said. "They must know why we're here."

The branch creatures continued to advance with Sylvester in their clutches. "*Vinat*," she ordered them. They halted. She heard the twist of their wooden limbs. Sylvester winced and grunted. "If they see him like this they'll attack," she whispered to Paj. "I'm gonna get the branches to let go of him."

"Well," Paj replied. "It was good while it lasted."

Adoni went to Sylvester and locked eyes with him. To her relief, the rage had softened to the dull hatred a prisoner has for his captors. For a moment, she felt almost unworthy to look him in the face. She'd taken his voice, his ability to move freely, and though he had once done the same to her, she was still ashamed.

Her next words were deliberate. "Your brothers and sisters are waiting on the path."

He gazed back at her.

"They've even got torches to light the way up," she said. "So I'm gonna let you go. But you have to promise me you'll stick with us, and you won't get them to attack. Maybe you can shout death, but you don't want to know what I can do in the In-Between now. Okay?" He nodded. "All right. You're going up first. And I'm watching you." She put a hand on the creatures that pinned his arms to his sides. "*Dau bruge.*"

They immediately let go, climbed down Sylvester's body, and crawled away from the mountainside. He rubbed the circulation back into his wrists, flexed his now-purple fingers. Adoni noticed he was trembling and quickly looked away.

Theresa whispered in her ear. "What if he bolts?"

Adoni shook her head. "He doesn't want to."

Sylvester started up the pathway, and the changelings stepped aside to let him pass. Adoni followed after him, watching his every limb, making sure he didn't try anything that warranted her uttering that final, devastating word: *shrictus.* The word that she couldn't get out of her head; not since she'd first heard it, not since she'd spoken it in the cellar last night. Not since she had seen what it could do.

But Sylvester didn't stray, didn't flinch, didn't command his changelings to turn against her or attack. The firelight fell over a head he held high and across squared shoulders. The changelings' eyes brimmed with tears as they looked upon their leader. Adoni couldn't tell if they wept with hatred for what he'd done to them; with pride that he was about to avenge them for the time and dignity they'd lost on the other side of the agate, or with sadness that it all had come to this.

Chapter
25

Adoni welcomed the light and heat from the torches on her face after scuttling through the forest under the cover of darkness. All around her, the mountain seemed to hum with anticipation, the ice and stone beneath her feet seemed to vibrate with her ascent. Her knuckles brushed against Theresa's, electrifying her every nerve. The crunch of her boots in the snow, the sound of her breath huffing, and not a single one of them saying a word: a grave score for what they were doing, for what they were about to do.

They arrived at the rock bridge just as a light snow began to fall. Sylvester stopped walking and scanned the chasm, peering between the flakes, squinting as he surveyed from left to right. Beyond the bridge, the doors to Ansgar's fortress were shut tight. He placed a foot on the rocks and leaned forward, then pulled back quickly. They remained silent and still. "I see Steppe has already arrived," he muttered. Adoni heard him draw in a breath that he held in his lungs for longer than she thought was natural. He was the first across the bridge, and his steps were slow and careful, though the path was wide enough for a misstep on either side. Adoni stayed several paces behind him. A cold, dank-smelling wind moaned on its way up from the bottom of the pit. Her mind went to the same dark place it had before, where she kept her most saturnine and terrified thoughts. Sylvester could turn around at any moment and push her off the bridge. Would she be able to order the rock beasts to catch her before she hit the chasm floor? She considered allowing him to reach the other side before starting after him, but he could just as easily shout her down then, too. Was his voice equal to Steppe's in every way? Could he split mountains? Or was death the only sound they shared, that bound them together?

What does death sound like?

He was halfway across the bridge when she started after him. She had been confident in her earlier crossings, her mind occupied by other thoughts. Now, all she had ahead of her were Sylvester and fifty feet of rock, ice, and snow; Paj and Theresa followed behind her. She felt her heart flutter against her ribs. Her pulse was strong enough to strike her eardrums until they rang like bells. She had to fight to keep herself from looking down.

At last she found herself safe and sound on the other side of the bridge, standing next to Sylvester, waiting for the others to join them. They walked as purposefully as she had, with their eyes cast down on the rocks that held their weight. Paj, being slightly more familiar with the bridge than Theresa, kept relatively calm as she crossed, her brow furrowed and her expression frozen. Theresa kept her arms out to the sides as though she were walking a tightrope and didn't dare to lift her eyes off the bridge.

Adoni thought Sylvester might say something to her while the final two in their party made their approach. He didn't admire the snowflakes, and he didn't speak.

She raised a clenched fist and rapped on the steel doors. Her knuckles made a pathetic excuse for a knock. She tried pushing them aside, thinking Ansgar would have left them unlocked for her return. They didn't budge. "Maybe she wants us to freeze to death," Theresa said as she stuffed her hands in her pockets and stamped her feet.

"We've got to get her attention somehow."

"How'd you do it before?"

"Steppe split the mountain apart, and she opened the doors and he just—"

"He split it apart?"

Adoni nodded. "He didn't want us to ask questions. He wanted us to go home." She watched the slim crack where the doors fit together, searching for a sliver of light or a passing shadow, some sign of life. "If we'd just gone home... I think I'm gonna be sick..."

Theresa wrapped her arms around her. "Don't," she said. "Okay?"

Adoni pressed her face against Theresa's neck and breathed deeply, hoping the air, combined with Theresa's smell, would calm her down. When she lifted her head and looked across the way, she saw that the changelings had all congregated on the other side of the bridge, with their torches still in hand.

This is all my fault, she thought. *If we'd just turned around... Ansgar wouldn't have dragged him in, Ritter wouldn't have followed me, I'd still have my eye... they'd be free...*

"Hey," Theresa said. "Look at me." She eased Adoni out of her embrace and held her at arm's length. "Don't—"

Adoni cut her off. "Just let me do this, okay? Let me feel it. Let me..." She turned to Sylvester. "I'm sorry. You have no idea how sorry I am."

Sylvester didn't look at her. "You have to kick it," he said. "One hard, swift kick." Without warning, he spun around and slammed the sole of his boot against the steel.

The doors opened. Sylvester stepped inside.

Adoni took one last look at the changelings, then followed him into the fortress.

Four bonfires raged in their places around the foyer, their flames slurping at the stale air. Sylvester strode to the pool in the centre of the room. He pulled off his mittens and crouched down for a drink. The sound of his lips sipping at the water reminded Adoni she hadn't had a drop since morning. She sat at the edge of the pool and took a drink of her own.

"Jeez," Theresa murmured. "Steppe never described what it looked like, but... this isn't what I pictured at all." Shadows cloaked the hallway that led to Ansgar's playroom. "Is that where they are?"

"Yeah," Adoni said. "They're waiting for us."

Sylvester stood up too quickly for Adoni's liking. She leapt back from the edge of the pool, ready for an attack. "Calm down," he muttered. "Your life means nothing to me. You're safe." He left her where she stood and started down the hallway. She held her breath and watched him fade to obscurity before taking a step in the same direction.

"You're going to follow him?" Theresa asked.

"I brought him here, didn't I?"

"I thought you said that was a bad idea."

"I'll be fine." She turned to Paj. "Ansgar might lift your immortality if she sees you," she said. "I don't know how to stop her." Paj patted her shoulder, a smile beneath her sorrowful eyes. Adoni offered her a sad smile of her own. "But you're coming anyway, right?"

"Yep," she replied.

"Thanks."

Adoni headed up the hallway, Paj by her side, not looking back to see if Theresa was behind her. She heard the rustle of Paj's skirts, then the clack of Theresa's boot heels striking the stone floor. Her ears embraced them, since her arms could not.

She inched her way through the dark and arrived at the door that separated Ansgar from the rest of the fortress. The smell of Sylvester's cologne lingered outside the room, oddly sweet compared to the odours of lichen, water, and rock that permeated Ansgar's domain. She pushed the door open and stepped inside.

The room appeared as it had the first time Adoni saw it—a mere corner in an otherwise expansive lair, a single fire burning in a pit in the floor, a wooden chair facing the flames. Sylvester stood next to the fire with his hands in his pockets. He stared at the blaze as though it were an old friend who had shattered his trust, his brow creased, his chin tucked in. There were no signs of Ansgar anywhere, no smell of her wafting in from beyond the glow, her voice no more than an unsettling memory in the back of Adoni's mind. She approached the fire pit and waited for Ansgar to notice her arrival. Paj and Theresa entered the room. "Where is she?" Theresa whispered.

"Are you here?" Adoni asked the darkness.

"She's here," Sylvester replied. "She's always here. Ansgar loves making an entrance. Isn't that right?" he said, his raised voice dissipating in the vastness above their heads. "You have to put your face on, don't you? Don't you?"

No response.

"Answer me!" he shouted. "Answer me, damn you. Show me that pretty little face of yours! Or don't you have the stomach to look at me now that you're sick of me?"

Silence.

He started to laugh. "So you'll play your game right until the end, will you? You'll hide, and I'll seek? Show yourself, goddamn it, or let me go!"

Silence, and then: laughter, deep in their ears. Theresa flinched and shook her head, trying to knock the sound free. "What the hell is that?"

"That's Ansgar," Adoni said softly. "But that's not her voice, it's..."

Oh god...

Ansgar walked Ritter's body out of the shadow, into the light.

"Ritter," Theresa said with a sigh of relief.

"Always the same," Ansgar said with Ritter's voice. "Do this! Do that! That's why no one likes you!"

Theresa shook her head and scowled at him. "Ritter?"

Adoni shot Theresa an unmistakable look of warning. It was all she could do to convey the peril they were in.

Ansgar brought a wicked glare to Ritter's eyes. "You like it?" she asked Sylvester, bringing Ritter's hand to his cheek and stroking the skin. "It's my very favourite."

"I know," Sylvester said with a bitter laugh. "I know too well."

"Jealous!" Ansgar pointed Ritter's finger at him. "You're a jealous little crow. You've always been jealous of him!"

"What do you want with me?"

"We're going to play a game."

"Oh?" He turned and glared at Adoni. "No one told me you wanted to play a game."

"No one has to tell you, stupid!" Ansgar said with a huff. "I want to play a game!" Adoni gasped as Ansgar leered at her with all of Ritter's teeth. "Winner goes free, he stays with me. Ha!" She clapped his hands. "A promise is a promise!"

"You're forgetting something," Adoni said.

"No, I'm not. That's what he said, that's what he said. He stays, my favourite. We'll have so much fun, just like forever ago."

Adoni pointed to her face. "My eye. You promised you'd give it back."

"Not now," Ansgar said in Ritter's smoothest voice. "Not now. After the *fight*. You're impatient! After the fight, that ends the promise. *After.*"

"I'll be able to see it better with two eyes," Adoni tried.

"You don't have to see it. It's for *me*."

"Is that what you've done?" Sylvester asked Adoni. "Traded your eye as a hostage in exchange for bringing me here?"

Ansgar laughed. It stretched the corners of Ritter's mouth and threw his head back. "You're the bad dolly," she said. "Well, someone has to be. Ritter's the good dolly. But you can't play unless you have the bad dolly too. You need the whole set."

"Where's Steppe?" Adoni asked.

"He's here, he's here. He's been here all this time. You've been gone for hours. Too slow!"

"You have to let him go now."

"No I don't! I can make it last forever." She drained the life out of Ritter's eyes until they were nothing more than cold, green shells. "A minute a day, seven minutes a week. Tick tock, tick tock, tick tock. That's what I can do."

"There won't be a fight if you don't let him go," Adoni said, softly, as though sharing a secret.

"Only when I say. It's only when I say. You!" She pointed at Paj and Theresa. "You weren't invited. Party crashers, party crashers. You only get to come in if I say." She squinted at Paj. "I know you. You wouldn't stay put. Seventeen Bay, that's where you were supposed to be." She wound Ritter's arm back and mimed throwing a ball across the room. "Strike one! And the other one, the one that looks like you…" she threw another imaginary ball. "Strike two!"

"You have to let Steppe go now," Adoni said. "What if he's too old to fight? You don't want him to be too old to fight, do you?"

"You," Ansgar muttered. The bright light of recognition returned to Ritter's eyes as they fell upon Theresa's face. "I know you. Why are you still here?" Theresa shrank back a step. Though she didn't make an attempt to run for it, the doors to the room slammed shut and sealed them all in. "You're his favourite! You're his little favourite that he found one night! I remember! He came begging, begging." She clasped Ritter's hands together. "Please, please, please let me keep her! I'll feed her and walk her every day! Oh, he *liked* you, so much. So I said he could keep you. You're my present to him. I was being *nice*."

"Where is he?" she asked, her voice trembling.

Ansgar ignored her. "But you," she continued, turning Ritter's glare on Sylvester. "No little girl for you. You wanted something else. And I gave it to you, didn't I?"

"Believe me, I earned it," Sylvester said.

"You don't remember anything! Crying, crying at me, 'It's not fair! It's not fair!' Now look what you made me do."

The second fire ignited on the other side of the room. Steppe stood against the wall, still frozen and wracked with pain, still Ansgar's prisoner. Adoni could barely make his features out in the distance, but she could tell, right from where she stood, that his hair had grown longer in her time away, and that almost all of the strands were silvery-white.

Theresa let out a shriek and ran toward him.

"Reese, be careful!" Adoni cried.

Ansgar's invisible hand swiped her feet out from under her. She tumbled to the floor, knocking her chin hard against the stone, and let out a grunt.

"No, no, no!" Ansgar said. "You stay back! It's me now, it's *my* turn. You had him long enough." Theresa sat back, both hands pressed against her chin, blood beading on her bottom lip. Ansgar's glee distorted Ritter's face as she chortled. "Bonk! Ouch!"

"Please, mother," Sylvester said. "May I see him? *Up close?*"

Ansgar leaned Ritter back and placed his hands behind his head. "Mmmmmmmmmmm... you may."

"Thank you." He crossed the room slowly. Adoni didn't bother to ask Ansgar's permission and followed a half step behind him, making sure to stay within his periphery, hoping he was still intimidated by her presence. He ignored her and stopped a few feet away from where Steppe stood. Adoni, too, came to a halt.

"Jesus, Steppe," she murmured when she got a good look at his face.

There were more creases in his forehead and around his mouth. The tone and texture of the skin beneath his jaw had softened, and his lips were thinner. His nose and ears were slightly larger, and his hair, while longer, was not as thick as it once was. He looked old enough to be someone's grandfather. But his beauty paled in comparison to his agony, which Adoni could see in his rolled-back eyes, in the sharp, stilted breaths he took, in the way he shuddered, in the short yelps that broke through the otherwise silent room.

"Well, well, well," Sylvester said. He nodded. "Misery becomes you. Who knew?"

"That's it!" Adoni said, turning back to Ansgar. "You let him go now or it won't be a fair fight. You know what happens when the fight isn't fair? It's over in a few seconds. You want that?"

Ansgar glared at her. "I want a big fight," she growled in Ritter's voice.

Adoni pressed her lips together tightly. She'd tread dangerously close to giving an order. "That means you have to let him go," she said. "Please." As the words left her lips she wondered: *Where's Ritter?* She scanned the room quickly, hoping to catch sight of the real man somewhere, perhaps up against the opposite wall, on the outskirts of the firelight, unable to move or to speak. The room was too vast, the shadows too thick, to tell if he was even there at all.

God... I hope he's okay...

Ansgar allowed an impish smirk to grow on Ritter's lips. "A *big* fight," she said. "Who loves me the most?"

Steppe gasped and dropped to his knees.

Ansgar turned away from him and strolled unhurriedly to where the firelight blurred into shadow. She began walking the edge of the glow, circling them all, biding her time. Theresa scrambled to her feet and dashed to Steppe's side. She stopped short and held up her hands as if she were afraid of being burned. "Steppe?"

He drew in several long, deep breaths. "Reese..."

She got down on her knees and cupped his face in both her hands. He reached up and wrapped his fingers carefully around her wrists, then raised his head to look at her. Theresa gazed into his eyes—still sharp, still clear and blue—and started to weep. "Oh god, are you all right?"

"You came back..." His fingers moved from her wrists, down her arms, over her shoulders. He put his hands on either side of her face.

"No lectures," she said, chuckling through her tears.

"No lectures."

"I still love you. See? See? *I still love you.*"

"Theresa... Reese..." He kissed her gently.

"Happy birthday!" Ansgar chortled.

"Are you okay?" Theresa asked him.

"A little weak... " He moved to rise, bracing himself against her body.

"He's been a bad boy," Ansgar called out. "Burning, stealing. *Killing.*"

Theresa coughed and swallowed. "Will it go away?" she asked.

Steppe clenched and flexed his fingers. "The dizziness fades, but..." He winced as he raised his arms. Adoni heard the undeniable crack of his joints in their sockets. He shook his head and let out a hiss as his long hair fell against his cheek.

Theresa wrapped her arms around him. "I shouldn't have let you go alone!"

Steppe held her close and leaned his cheek against the top of her head. Sylvester stepped into his line of sight. They stared at each other. Neither one of them spoke.

"Kissy, kissy, mwah, mwah!" Ansgar said. "Kiss the killer, go ahead. Taste smoke and ash and death. It tastes like *blood* too, doesn't it?"

"What's she talking about?" Theresa asked, her voice just above a whisper. "I don't understand."

Adoni shook her head. "It's not important."

"Oh yes it is!" Ansgar said. "It's him, it's his soul, and she's *kissing* it!" She waved Ritter's arm.

Adoni felt the wind go out of her lungs. She and Sylvester crumpled to the ground, where an unseen force threw them both aside.

Ansgar stuck Ritter's nose within an inch of Theresa's face. "He's so nice, isn't he? Always there for hugs and kisses. Because you're stupid, and you can't see what he is! A liar! A soldier! A war on legs!" She straightened Ritter's back and turned his attention to Steppe. "I wanted the other one. Not you."

"What is she saying? Steppe, what does she mean?"

"My name isn't Steppe," he replied. He looked down at her. "My name is Lajos."

"*And?*" Ansgar growled.

"You won't love me when you know what I've done."

Theresa's tears returned. "What have you done?"

"New game!" Ansgar cried out, clapping Ritter's hands. "He's too weak for fighting. I want a *big* fight." She leered at Adoni. "New game, so we're ready. It's called *Confession*. I'm the holy man, and you're the confessor." Her invisible hands shoved Theresa out of his arms and sent Steppe whirling back to the wooden chair. "Sit," she ordered.

He climbed into the chair.

Adoni picked herself up off the floor and raced to Theresa's side. "What's going on?" Theresa asked, shuddering, the tears rolling down her face and collecting around her flared nostrils. "What's she talking about?"

"You have to ask her the right questions," Adoni whispered to her. "Otherwise she gets confused and upset."

"But what does she mean by 'killer?' He didn't kill that boy, he only..." She brushed her thumb over Adoni's empty socket.

"She's not talking about the boy." She called out to Ansgar. "Can I be a holy man too?"

Ansgar put a finger to Ritter's lips and began to pace back and forth with exaggerated steps. "You have to ask *my* questions," she said at last. "Understand?"

"Only your questions." Adoni nodded. "Yeah, I got it."

"*I* go first."

"You go first."

"You're a parrot. Ha!" She jumped up and turned cartwheels until she stood in front of Steppe and the wooden chair. "Did you send that woman to me?"

"What woman?" he asked.

"That woman, that *woman* that came here. It was years ago. I remember her. Long hair. Black eyes. And *bossy*. She thought she could tell me what to do. I showed her. That *woman*! Don't be stupid!"

"Belinda?"

"*Belinda.*"

His voice went hoarse. "I didn't send her. I would never have told her to come here."

"Well she did! She did, and she was demanding. I don't *like* demanding. She thought she was so perfect, I could tell. She had a *bitch face*. Do you know that? They say it on the other side. 'Bitch face' they say, because some people do! That's funny!"

Adoni approached the chair. "May I ask a question now?"

"Only *my* questions."

"Only your questions." She stopped in front of Steppe. Shoulders sagging, he looked down at his wizened hands.

"Why did you make stupid-face forget herself?" Ansgar said.

"Why did you take Natalie's—" A savage force seized the back of her neck and squeezed so tightly she thought her spine would snap.

"Only *my* questions!" Ansgar snarled.

"Why did you make stupid-face forget herself?" The force released her. She grunted and rubbed her neck.

"I didn't want her to suffer," he said. "I didn't want her to feel what I've felt all these years. I wanted to save her."

"But you can't do that," Adoni said. "You can't just take something like that away from someone. It's—"

"My turn!" Ansgar said. "You had your turn, it's my turn now. Dolly, where did the other one go? The one I wanted? Not you, the one I *wanted*."

"He was…"

"Say it!"

"He was murdered."

"And whooooooooodunnit?"

"My father."

Ansgar sighed dramatically. "Too bad, so sad." She pointed at Adoni. "You go now. Ask him this. Ask him… Did you kill your father?"

"Did you kill your father?"

Steppe covered his face with his hands.

"Answer it!" Ansgar said. "Or *happy birthday*! Happy birthday!"

"I did," he whispered.

Adoni murmured, "*Shit.*"

"Does that surprise you?" Sylvester asked. Adoni turned. Sylvester had recovered and now stood a short distance away from her. "Are you surprised he can be vengeful?"

"No," she answered. "I'm not."

"He's had long enough to rest," he said to Ansgar. "Why don't you stop this game and let me do what I came here to do?"

Ansgar laughed. "Bad, bad, bad! That's it! Oh, I've missed playing with a full set! No, he has to tell the story first. He has to tell the whole story, no skipping. I want to hear a story." She bent Ritter over, arching his back, curling his body until his ankles flanked his face. "Go! He was drinking."

Steppe said, "He was drinking. He had enough in him to think I was…"

"A ghost," Ansgar finished. "Woooooooooooooooooo…"

"I found him alone. He had his neighbour's pistol with him."

"For protection!"

"For protection."

"And what did you do?"

"I…"

Adoni crouched in front of her. "Does he have to say it? You already know what happened."

"I want to hear the *whole* story." She swung Ritter's legs back and pushed his body off the floor. "I want to hear the *bang splat!*" She extended his finger and thumb as though they were the barrel and trigger of a gun. "Like this!"

"He picked up the gun and fired it, what more do you want him to say?"

"No I didn't," Steppe said. "It was worse. It was so much worse."

Sylvester bent low and hissed in his ear. "Spit it out, goddamn you."

"He recognized me. He started babbling, begging for my forgiveness. I'd never heard him beg, not for anything. He was always too proud to ask for help. To see him sitting there, snivelling… that killer… that *traitor*… I let him think I was a ghost. I told him I would never forgive him for what he'd done to me. I told him he was worthless, as a father, as a man, he was good for nothing, his life wasn't worth living at all." He raised his chin, looked straight ahead. "He asked me what I wanted. I told him: an eye for an eye. He put the pistol to his temple. He put his finger on the trigger. And I didn't stop him."

Ansgar put Ritter's nose in Steppe's face. "*Coward.*"

"Enough of this," Sylvester said. "He's answered your questions. You know the sort of man he is. Funny, isn't it? That something so ugly can be made of star dust."

"Funny," Ansgar muttered under Ritter's breath. "Yes. He's made of stars."

She glanced at Adoni, who felt a sharp pain stabbing her empty eye socket. Adoni pressed the back of her hand against her skin and sucked in her breath. All of a sudden her cheek felt wet, and as the throb began to dissipate, she lowered her hand and found her missing eye restored.

"No more questions," Ansgar growled. "*Fight.*"

There was a rush of wind and light. Adoni put a hand to her brow to protect her eyes. Three more fires sprang up in pits around the room, which, Adoni now could see, was indeed as enormous as she had thought: a thousand feet long, a thousand feet wide. She fixed her eyes on the smooth stone walls and scanned the room as quickly as she could for any sign of Ritter.

He's not here. Her mind raced. *Maybe he's hanging above us in the dark.* She tilted her chin up toward the still-obsidian space above their heads. Nothing. *Or maybe he's trapped under the floor. Maybe there's a trap door somewhere, like on a boat. Or she's made him invisible. Can she make him invisible?*

Ansgar kicked the chair Steppe sat on, knocking it out from under him. "That's my spot now." She took hold of it and dragged its legs along the floor a short distance, then set it upright and sat down upon it. Theresa dove to the floor and wrapped her arm around him. He let her take his weight as he got to his feet. Soon both his arms were around her in an unremitting embrace. Her lips found his, and they kissed, deeply, passionately, the way all lovers kiss at the end of time.

Ansgar brought a bemused expression to Ritter's face. She tilted his head and eyed their intimacy as though she hadn't seen anything like it before. Adoni shuddered at the sight of so young and green a look on the face of a man as old and experienced as Ritter. But when she got a glimpse of those bright eyes, staring simultaneously in wonder and disgust, her blood ran cold.

That glimmer. A thousand years. Recognition.

Shit. She's inside *him.*

Ansgar let the embrace linger a moment longer before forcing the two of them apart. Theresa stumbled backwards into Paj, who had rushed up to catch her before she fell. "They need space," Ansgar said. Another blast pinned Theresa and Paj to the furthest curve of wall in the room. "Stay," she shouted across the vastness. "And no singing, no voices, or *happy birthday*." She set Ritter's sights on Adoni's petrified face. "Your turn now. Say goodbye."

Adoni couldn't bring herself to budge from where she stood. Instead she stayed perfectly still, her eyes fixed on Steppe's chest. He smoothed his hair back from his face and approached her with a straight back. "This isn't fair," she muttered. He put his arms around her and gave her a solid hug, a hug she couldn't bring herself to reciprocate. Her arms remained at her sides. "It's not fair. It's not right."

"I might not live through this," he said. "If I don't…"

"She can take care of herself."

"Right." His arms tightened around her.

She squeezed her eyes shut and let him hold her. "I'm so sorry… I'm so sorry for this…"

"I'm not."

He pressed something into her palm, held it there until her fingers closed around it.

Adoni gasped as Ansgar's force tore her out of Steppe's embrace and hauled her to the edge of the fire pit at Ritter's feet. "You're my sister, so you get to watch with me," Ansgar said. She thrust Ritter's fingers into Adoni's hair and aggressively stroked her curls.

Adoni winced but didn't dare pull away. She crossed her legs and sat at the fire's edge, her back to the monster, her arms folded in front of her. Unable to move her head, she cast her eyes down and slowly opened her hand.

There it was: the seal that Sylvester had used to brand her and keep her silent.

She held it close to her body as a queasiness shook her guts.

Steppe and Sylvester approached the fire pit. Both men wore solemn expressions as they stood before Ansgar. They knew to present themselves to her as subjects, knew not to make a move until she had given them her explicit instructions. Ansgar giggled. "You go when I say *go*. Only when I say. I want a real fight, a big fight. Punches first! Punches and kicks! No voices, or *happy birthday*. No voices or bang, splat! You understand? And the winner gets to *scream*."

Adoni searched for her friends' bodies, for their faces, for some sort of reassurance that, while unable to move or intervene, they were safe. She found them quickly, as Sylvester and Steppe moved away from the fire pit and took their positions. Paj stood in the residual burn of the firelight, her mouth closed and her arms by her sides. Had Ansgar taken her voice? Her body seemed calm and still—Ansgar hadn't lifted her immortality—but Theresa's chest rose and fell with a panicky cadence, and Adoni could tell she was on the verge of hyperventilating, which she thought, for one brief instant, might be a blessing in disguise; passing out would be a kindness, especially if Steppe lost the battle.

Steppe and Sylvester stared each other down, chins lowered, their glares penetrating through to each other's hearts. Adoni felt nervous laughter percolating in the back of her throat. She started to shake. The stone floor was dead still beneath her, the air around her as thick as a shroud. The tongues of flame were the only things that moved, but they seemed choreographed according to Ansgar's will, and she found no solace in staring at them until her eyes began to itch.

Ansgar twirled Ritter's fingers around Adoni's curls and urged her head forward and back again, left and right. "Ready?" she asked in Ritter's voice. The word, heavy with solemnity, dragged up the hairs on the back of Adoni's neck. *Not yet*, she thought as her shoulders stiffened. *Not yet. What do I do?*

Ansgar shouted, "Go!"

Neither man moved.

Their fingers twitched, they lifted their heads. Neither one budged from his place.

"Go, go, go!" Ansgar snarled.

Sylvester took a solitary step back.

Ansgar dragged Ritter's fingernails across Adoni's scalp and seized her hair. Adoni squealed. Sylvester stumbled forward as though someone had pushed him from behind. Adoni recognized Ansgar's unseen force.

Steppe did not.

He drew back his arm, formed a fist, and punched Sylvester's face with such force, the changeling's cheekbone snapped.

Ansgar started to laugh. "See what I did? A fair fight, a fair one! No quick healing for my bad dolly. Feel everything! A nice fair fight!"

Sylvester recovered and lunged at Steppe. He seized the back of the piper's neck and punched him, but not before Steppe landed a second and third strike to Sylvester's other cheek. Though he was older now than he was when the day first started, his incredible strength remained. Steppe bent and threw himself at Sylvester, knocking him off of his feet and sending him straight to the floor. He landed hard on his back and let out a screech. Steppe threw himself on top of Sylvester's prostrate form, fisted the hair on the changeling's crown, jerked his head forward and up, and relentlessly, mercilessly, pounded his face, pounded his chin, pounded his eye until it was nearly swollen shut. Until the bones and cartilage in his hand cracked.

He hissed and shook out his fingers. Sylvester bucked his hips, throwing Steppe aside, and managed to slam his fist into the piper's cheek before pulling himself up off the floor. His hands were nothing compared to Steppe's, but with the piper momentarily stunned, he took full advantage of the use of his legs and viciously kicked the side of Steppe's head. Steppe cried out, the sound a hybrid of cackle and wail, and rolled himself across the floor, away from Sylvester's boots, cradling his wrist as he tumbled; he had broken his hand for sure.

Noticing this, a cruel smile grew on Sylvester's face. Steppe swung his legs back and rocked them forward; the motion brought the rest of him up into a crouch. He was about to straighten his legs and rise, but Sylvester reared back and landed a violent kick to his stomach. Steppe gasped and curled in on himself, and as he turned over, bracing himself on his elbows, Sylvester leapt onto his back and smashed his forehead into the floor.

Adoni shrieked. Ansgar yanked her head back until her black eyes met Ritter's brilliant green. "Stop squealing!" she snarled. "Squeal, squeal! It's exciting! Aren't you excited? It's a show, a show just for us! Don't be stupid!" Adoni grunted as Ansgar pushed her head forward again.

Sylvester grabbed Steppe's hair and repeated the blow. Steppe lifted an arm and swung it back, flipping himself over so that he lay on top of the changeling once more. But Sylvester was quick; he put a hand on the back of Steppe's head, wrapped an arm around his neck, and squeezed. Adoni heard Steppe's strangled voice beneath his laboured breath. Even if he chose to ignore Ansgar's warning by screaming out his rage, he was quickly losing the breath to do it. He tried to shake Sylvester off by rocking side to side, kicking his legs, swinging his arms. Sylvester doubled his efforts and hefted the arm around Steppe's neck higher, crushing his windpipe, cutting off even more of his air. Steppe's tongue lolled out of his mouth. He lifted his arm and reached back, and jabbed three stiffened fingers into Sylvester's already injured eye. Sylvester screeched. His grip loosened, and Steppe was able to slip out from under his arm.

Adoni fought to keep a wave of sobs from rising in her throat. Held fast beneath Ansgar's grip, she was powerless to resist when the demigoddess jerked her head to keep her eyesight aligned with the battle. She didn't dare use her own voice to put an end to the fight; she still had no idea of the extent of Ansgar's power and couldn't risk the monster's wrath if her own powers proved inadequate. Ansgar wouldn't hesitate to exact swift and vicious revenge; she could pluck out both of Adoni's eyes, or hurl her so violently against the walls her ribs would snap in half. There were no rocks or branches anywhere in that vast chamber that she could see and sing to life, only the fires roaring away in their respective pits. What would

Ansgar do to Paj and Theresa, if Adoni brought the flames before her to life and set them against their captor? Could she even command creatures made of flame? What were the piper words for *burn, attack*?

The heat from the fire before her nearly scorched her knees. She saw Steppe rise from the floor, saw Sylvester shake his head and bring himself up to his feet. She had to do something, or their second round would be even more ferocious, and could, quite possibly, be their last.

The seal.

She pushed it between two of her fingers, lowered her arm to her side, and held the brass end as close to the flames as she could manage.

When you see a chance to move, take it.

Ansgar chortled away. "Look. Ha ha! So serious. Punch, punch, kick, kick. Then *grrrrrr*! So angry." Steppe and Sylvester turned their livid faces to hers. "More, more, more. Make it bigger!"

Adoni made eye contact with Steppe. She gave the hand that held the seal the briefest glance before returning her gaze to his.

Sylvester pounced on him, throwing him off his balance. He stumbled and fell to the floor, but the changeling failed to stun him; he swept out his leg and knocked Sylvester's feet out from under him. Now the two of them were on the floor and at each other's throats, heaving and snarling, each man trying desperately to subdue his foe. Using his uninjured hand, Steppe pried one of Sylvester's thumbs back far enough that the changeling snorted and started to pull away. As Sylvester eased off from his attack, Steppe shoved him flat onto his stomach, yanked back his arm, and stomped down on the changeling's elbow, popping it out of its socket.

Sylvester shrieked. He pushed himself up and staggered to his feet, jerking his now-useless arm out of Steppe's grip before the piper could think of his next move. Sylvester whirled around and caught Steppe with an arm around his waist. He swung him until his back faced the flames, heaved him up just enough to keep him from bracing his stance, then slammed him down as close as he could to the fire. Steppe immediately tried to sit up to keep the top of his head from burning. Sylvester lifted his knee and threw his weight against Steppe's chest. Adoni caught a whiff of singed hair and was nearly sick. She could see Sylvester beyond the flames, and Steppe struggling to throw him off. Ansgar's laughter reverberated throughout the room. From the wall, where Adoni's friends were still pinned, came Theresa's terrified voice: "Steppe! Fight back! Fight back!"

"Time!" Ansgar yelled in Ritter's gleeful tenor.

The unseen force hit Sylvester's chest and threw him halfway across the chamber. Steppe rolled over and, holding himself up on his elbows, panted and wheezed to regain his breath.

Adoni heard Ansgar sniff hard. "Pew! Smelly burned hair. Yuck." She loosened her grip on Adoni's curls, but didn't let go. "Not like yours." She stuck Ritter's nose into Adoni's ear and whispered, "You smell nice."

Steppe was hauled back onto his knees. Ansgar's power straightened his back and held his arms down by his sides. "So much fun! I like this game. Snap, pop, snap, snap! Ouch! You fight mean and dirty, don't you dollies? Mean and dirty! Ha!" Sylvester shook his head and dragged himself up to his feet. "I get to choose the winner," Ansgar said. "I get to choose. And I choose... *hrrmmmmm*... Sylvester."

Adoni felt as though her heart had stopped. She heard a tiny cry come from across the room. Theresa uttered, "No. No."

Ansgar giggled. "Yes, yes. I like you, Sylvester. You're so serious. You're so serious, and you say funny things. *Brethren*. Ha! *Vengeance*. I like you, Sylvester. I like you much better than *him*. He's too old now anyway." She pulled Adoni along with her as she got to Ritter's feet. "Too old. Too grey. Too useless. And he doesn't love me anymore. I didn't want him anyway. I never did." Adoni grunted as Ritter's fingernails scratched her scalp raw. Ansgar brought Ritter's lips to her temple and gave her a wet, noisy kiss. "Want to know my favourite colour?" she asked. "Want to know?"

"I can guess," Adoni said, wincing.

"Because you're my sister?"

She gritted her teeth. "Yeah."

"So, guess."

"Red."

"You're smart," Ansgar cried. "So smart. Yes, red, red, red, like rubies, like fire, like blood. Lots of blood. Want to see lots of blood? Get ready."

Sylvester lowered his chin and stalked over to where Steppe knelt. "For all my changeling brothers and sisters," he growled. "You're the first. Good night."

At first, Adoni heard nothing but Theresa's emphatic cry and the flickering of the flames. But then came the chanting, like a hideous whisper, bleeding through the walls, sweeping across the floor, swirling around Adoni's ankles like an unctuous fog. Steppe's body began to shake. His face twisted into a mask of sheer anguish, his entire body palsied as the incantation took hold of him.

He let out the whimper of a terrified child.

A trail of blood trickled from his nose.

Adoni shrieked and lunged ahead. A lock of her hair came away from her scalp as she broke free from Ansgar's grasp. Sylvester remained where he was, his one swollen eye fixed on his prey, steadily chanting torture, misery, death. Adoni brandished the white-hot end of the seal and threw herself on top of him. Before Ansgar could set her ether force against her, Adoni smashed the seal against Sylvester's forehead, searing his creator's name into his skin.

Take it away, she implored whatever magic made the seal do its wielder's bidding. *Take it away from him. Take the sound of death away from him. Please... please... please...*

Sylvester screamed and threw Adoni aside. The seal flew out of her hand and landed on the cusp of the fire pit. She herself would have rolled into the flames if she hadn't reached out at the last moment and grabbed the changeling's ankle. He lifted his other leg and brought his heel down on top of her head. She let go and brought both her hands up to protect her face. Sylvester pressed his palms against his burned flesh and hissed through his teeth before a furious growl escaped his throat. Adoni lay on her side, her head throbbing, her vision skewed. She saw Steppe curled up near her feet, his eyes shut, his breaths long and husky.

"No..." Sylvester muttered.

She turned over and pushed herself up off the floor. Ansgar's name now emblazoned as a savage welt across his skin, Sylvester opened his mouth and tried to summon the death scream as he had before. The result was nothing more than a pathetic wheeze. His eye filled with tears. He glared at her.

Behind her, Ansgar growled, "Where did you get that?" Adoni didn't answer. "I can guess. I can guess." She walked Ritter over to where Steppe lay. "You found it. You *stole* it." Steppe looked up at her. She smiled Ritter's sweetest smile. "Sneaky. You're sneaky. You always were. Sneaking, burning. Okie dokie." She waved Ritter's hand and straightened Steppe's body as she hauled him up. "You win."

Steppe shook his head.

"You win, you win!" she said, pulling Ritter's smile into a malignant sneer. "I want to see black, all over."

"No," he said.

"You do it!" she shouted into his ear. "You do it *now*."

"I won't."

Sylvester curled his lip.

"Oh yes?" Ansgar hissed. "Oh yes? You *won't*? You want a happy birthday?"

"I won't do it."

Ansgar opened Ritter's mouth and sank his teeth into Steppe's cheek. The piper grimaced and held his ground. She bit down hard until she broke through his flesh. He refused to move.

She pulled Ritter's now-bloodied lips away and pressed his forehead against Steppe's temple. "You *will*."

"I won't."

"You *will*. Or *splat*."

Adoni screamed as Ansgar's invisible hands tore Paj and Theresa from the chamber walls and hoisted them up into the darkness above her head. Steppe stumbled back and looked up, his eyes frantically searching the gloom.

"Do you know how high this mountain is?" Ansgar asked him. Her voice was low, her words measured, showing her true age. "Very high. And the stone is very hard. And the fires will burn whatever isn't broken. I want to see blood splashed across this floor. *Do it*, or the blood will be theirs, not his."

Steppe dropped his chin and advanced on her.

"Think I don't know what you're thinking?" she growled. "You can't kill me. Want to know what happens?"

He stopped.

"Every piper turns to dust, every changeling too. Poof! And every child is lost forever. There's no way out of here. Not unless I say. No. No, no. I die... *they* die. So simple, even stupid you can understand."

He looked into Ritter's bright, cruel eyes. "Don't do this."

From above, a terrible scream.

Paj!

"No, stop!" he cried.

Paj's scream came to an abrupt halt. Something had caught her before she could hit the floor.

Steppe gazed up at where he thought they dangled in the pitch. A tear rolled down his cheek. "Adoni," he murmured. "Cover your ears."

Adoni threw her arms around Ritter's neck and shook his body as she screamed at Ansgar. "Don't make him do this. Please! Why can't you just leave them alone? Leave them alone." She shook harder. "*Leave them alone!*"

Ansgar's might punched her stomach. She doubled over, gasping for the breath she had lost. "Leave them alone," she croaked.

Ansgar murmured, "No."

Adoni put her hands over her ears.

Steppe and Sylvester locked eyes.

Sylvester stood up straight and held his head high. "I hope you *suffer* for this," he said.

Steppe nodded, and drew in a breath.

The atmosphere changed. Every sound in the room seemed to swallow itself whole. Then the chanting returned, and with it: every ounce of anguish and rage that had ever flowed through Steppe's veins. Sylvester's body went rigid. His limbs began to shake. He focused on his killer's face, channelled every fear and every indignation he had ever suffered, released it all in one final, horrific shriek.

His body was torn asunder. And Adoni screamed.

Steppe sank to his knees. There was a single moment of silence. Then he started to sob.

"There, there," Ansgar said. She brought Ritter's hand down gently on the back of his head. "There, there. Don't cry. It was fun while it lasted, wasn't it? Talk, talk, talk. Run for cover. Wonder what would happen next. There, there."

Steppe leaned forward, pressing his forehead against the cold stone floor, his fingertips touching the edge of all that remained of Sylvester: a pool of black blood.

"There, there." She turned her back on him. "Don't cry. It's your turn now."

Adoni heard cries of terror sound from above. Her friends came tumbling out of the darkness, arms and legs whirling as they hurtled toward the floor. She screeched and shut her eyes.

Ansgar cackled. "Stupid! They're fine."

Two strong arms clasped around her shoulders and lifted her off her feet. "I'm here," Paj said. "I've got you."

Ansgar tilted Ritter's head and continued to snigger away. "No more *splats*," she said. "Not unless you're a bad sister. I think you might be. You like to burn things, don't you? Burn skin?" She put Ritter's finger into Adoni's face. "Give it back to me."

"I don't have it," Adoni whimpered.

"Give it back!" Her power forced Adoni from Paj's embrace and shook her to and fro. "You're hiding it!"

"It's gone! I don't have it!" she yelled, willing her eyes to keep from glancing at where the seal lay poised on the edge of the fire pit.

Ansgar flung her to the floor. "Well. No lying," she said calmly. "No lying, or you get what's coming to you."

Beside her, Theresa started to wail. Adoni turned.

Theresa sat before the pool of blood, cradling an old man's thin, frail body in her arms.

Chapter
26

Steppe's face was hidden against Theresa's chest, but Adoni saw his wizened hands, his hairless pate, and a pair of bony, bulbous knees. His body had shrunk so much he seemed almost buried in his own clothes. Theresa stroked the back of his head, choked on her tears. Paj knelt down next to her and smoothed a hand over her back. Her touch couldn't keep Theresa from weeping.

Steppe turned his head and opened his eyes. The deep blue had drained out of them; the irises, now almost white, were nothing but dull orbs. They rolled in his head as they scanned the faces of the women looming over him. Every trace of the anger they used to hold was gone.

His gaze settled on Theresa. He smiled. "Hello," he said. A trickle of water could still be heard beneath his feeble voice.

She sucked back her tears and fought to quiet her sobs. "Steppe."

"Hello."

"Steppe!"

"Pretty. So pretty."

"Oh god…"

"Pretty lady." His hand shook as he raised it and tried to point a finger at her. "You."

"Tell me you recognize me."

"If I was… younger…" He winked at her, his smile widening.

"Steppe, tell me you know who I am!"

"Angel." He nodded gently.

"It's Reese, Steppe. I'm Reese. Theresa. Tell me you remember me. You found me behind St. Mary's. You found me with my mother's knife. You sang me to The Welcome. You fell in love with me." She sobbed. "I fell in love with you."

He started to hum, in a soft voice that cracked with age.

"Steppe! Tell me you remember!"

"... not since... I was a boy..."

"Steppe!"

"Father sang it to me." His brow furrowed. He closed his eyes.

"Steppe?" She stroked his cheek. "Don't go."

It took him a moment to find enough strength to open them again. "Steppe?"

"You'll be okay. I'll take you back with me." She nodded. "I'll take you back with me. I'll take care of you."

"Steppe?"

"I call you Steppe, remember?"

He smiled. "Hello. My name is Lajos."

Theresa swallowed a sob. "Hello. I'm Theresa."

Ansgar's voice slithered into Adoni's ear. "I didn't want *him*."

Adoni set her glare on Ritter's face.

"It can be the way it used to be," Ansgar continued, swinging Ritter's arms, walking his legs in a circle around them. "Me and dolly."

"You broke your promise," Adoni snarled. "You promised Ritter you'd let the winner go!"

"You *cheated*." She turned sharply. "You're a cheater. Sylvester was the winner. You made him the loser. That's not fair. You killed him. You're a *killer*."

"Steppe wouldn't kill Sylvester if the fight was unfair," Adoni said. "Didn't you see what happened? Steppe stopped fighting. He didn't want to do it. You *made* him do it. Just for a... a senseless *game*."

"Senseless? Who's got sense?" She pointed at Steppe. "Not *him*."

"You fucking *monster*!" She threw herself forward, hands ready to wring

Ansgar's changeling neck. The blow that threw her back again was the worst one yet; if Paj hadn't been standing in her way, her arms outstretched and ready to catch her, she would have collided with the chamber wall and cracked her skull.

"You're the monster," Ansgar said. "You don't *belong* here."

"Adoni," Paj said in her deepest, lowest voice. "The code. This is the way it's always been."

"Do something," she said, on the verge of tears.

"There's nothing I can do."

"He's gonna die," she cried. "He doesn't deserve to die."

Paj put her hands on Adoni's shoulders, a warning to keep her words in check.

"Hiss, hiss," Ansgar said, a smile on Ritter's lips. Invisible fingers seized Adoni's collar and pulled her through the air. They held her up off the floor, where she dangled a few inches from Ritter's face. "She thanks Ansgar for Her benevolence," Ansgar said. Adoni fell to the floor. "Now. Say goodbye."

Adoni scuttled over on her hands and knees to where Steppe lay in Theresa's arms, in the centre of a pool of blood that had spread across the floor and now drenched their clothes. Neither of them seemed to notice; they each were too transfixed by the other—Theresa gazing at him with eyes that knew they were looking their last, Steppe peering at her as though he had never seen her before. "Steppe," Theresa whispered. "Can you still sing?" He smiled, but otherwise didn't respond. "Your piper voice," she said. "Remember? All those sounds?" He found Adoni looking down at him and grew preoccupied by her presence, squinting at her with a faint hint of recognition that soon dissolved into the placid expression of any stranger.

"I can help him," she whispered to Theresa. Their eyes met. "I can bring him back to life."

"What do you mean?"

"Like the branches and the rocks."

Theresa stared at her.

Paj knelt down next to them and took one of Steppe's hands in hers. "He doesn't have much time left."

"I can bring him back to life," Adoni said again.

"You don't know what that'll do to him," she murmured. "Or how long it will last."

"Maybe he'll be immortal again. Maybe it'll last forever. It's better than dying. It's better than dying like *this*."

Paj grew solemn. Adoni searched her face, hoping to find an inkling of approval or encouragement. Theresa leaned forward and, in a hushed voice, said, "Ask him."

Adoni took Steppe's other hand and bent over him. "Hey. Can you hear me? Do you remember me?" She leaned back to allow him a better view of her. He stared up into the darkness, his eyes nowhere near her face. "Steppe, it's Adoni. You let me stay at The Welcome. Listen..." *What do I say? How do I say it?* "You're dying. Okay? Ansgar took your immortality, and you're gonna die really soon. Okay? But do you remember... remember when Sylvester burned me with the seal, and Theresa cut it off? Most of it off." She lowered her already-softened voice. "It means I can bring things to life. It means I can keep you from dying. I might even make you live forever. You'll have to stay this age, but... at least you won't be dead. Do you understand?" He shook his head. "You'll stay alive," she said. "You won't die. Because this is all my fault..." She started to cry. "And you warned me to go away, and I didn't listen and now... I can't take it back... and... I wasn't even supposed to be here in the first place..." Changeling blood soaked her pants. "I'm no good for war."

He shook his head again. Adoni couldn't tell if his old age had wrested control over his muscles and nerves, or if he didn't understand what she had offered him. "I can stop you from dying," she said, her tone desperate. "Just say yes or no, okay? Do you want to live? Yes or no, okay?"

"He doesn't understand," Paj murmured.

"Yes or no," Adoni said. She brought his hand to her cheek and nuzzled it. "Do you want to keep on living?"

Steppe's milky eyes found Theresa's. "Hello," he said. "My name is…"

"Lajos," Theresa said, nodding gently. "Do you know who I am?"

"Angel," he said, his voice barely above a whisper. "Come to take me away." He smiled and closed his eyes. "Ready now."

She stroked his hair. Aside from the crackle of the fires around them, the chamber was still. Adoni looked around. Ansgar was nowhere to be seen; she might have ascended to the top of the mountain and now looked down on them from behind its veil of pitch, or else she had shifted into a more ethereal form, one that couldn't be detected with a human gaze.

Adoni clenched her teeth together hard enough to set them aching. *She doesn't want to watch this*, she thought with a bitterness she could almost taste.

Steppe's breathing grew more and more shallow, his expression more and more serene. He opened his eyes and took one last glance at the face of the woman who held him close to her heart, and smiled. It was the happiest she had ever seen him look. Then he closed his eyes, and breathed his last, and gently passed away.

The silence gave way to Theresa's weeping. Paj put her arm around Theresa's shoulders and leaned her cheek against the top of her head. Her long black hair served as a mourning shroud, shielding Theresa's face from the incandescent orange flames. Theresa clasped Steppe's body ever tighter, until her arms began to shake and her fingers took on the aspect of an eagle's claws clutching their prey. She started to rock back and forth, setting the black lake rippling with the hem of her jacket. Her sobbing grew louder. Paj leaned forward and put a hand on her cheek. "You have to let him go," she said softly.

"No." Theresa rocked faster, harder; her body curving over Steppe's to protect him. Paj stroked her back.

"Give her a minute," Adoni said to Paj. "What does it matter now? Give her enough time to say goodbye."

Theresa's rocking slowed to a more delicate pace, her weeping gave way to hot, silent tears that streamed down her face and dripped off the end of her nose. No one wished to disturb her, and it was a long time before anyone spoke again. This time it was Paj, who put her hands on Theresa's arms and urged them apart as she murmured, "It's all right. He's gone. It's all right."

"Not yet."

"We can bring him with us. We can bring him to The Welcome and give him a proper—"

"Not yet!" Theresa cried.

Paj brought her hands back to Theresa's head, where she swept them both in a soothing arc over her hair. "It won't be like the others," she said. "We'll give him a marker. You can visit whenever you want."

"You can't put him in the ground. Not in the cold ground. He hates the cold." She sobbed. "He'll be lonely!"

Paj stretched her arm across Theresa's chest and held her fast. "No," she wailed. "No. No. *No. No! NO!*"

"Let him go."

"Not yet. *Not yet! Please!*"

The body slipped from her arms and settled against the floor. Theresa gave up the fight and let Paj bring her to her feet. She looked at Adoni. "You said you could bring him back. Bring him back. *Bring him back.*"

Adoni shook her head. "He said no."

"He didn't say no."

"I asked him, and he said he was ready to go."

"Bring him back!"

"For who? For you?"

"Yes!"

"I can't, Reese." She gulped and breathed in hard.

"Why? *Why?*" She turned and threw her arms around Paj. "*Why?*"

"He wouldn't want me to."

"It's all right," Paj said, holding Theresa tight. "It's all right."

"*Why?*" Theresa cried.

Adoni drew her fingers into fists that she squeezed with force enough to shatter rocks. She hauled herself up from the floor and yelled up into the darkness, "Where are you? Where are you, you COWARD?" The fires flickered wildly. The stone floor rumbled beneath their feet.

Ansgar's voice slunk into her ears. "*Don't call me names.*"

She slipped out from the shadows above and sank down to the floor, landing perfectly on both of Ritter's feet. "You got what you wanted," Adoni said. "A big fight and both of them are dead." She sneered. "Are you keeping Ritter too?"

She nodded his head.

"Then let him go so we can say goodbye."

"You don't get to say goodbye."

"Why not?"

"You're not going. You're not going anywhere. You get to be the bad dolly. I want a full set."

Adoni's eyes went wide.

"Ansgar," Paj said, "I'll stay in their places."

"I don't *want* you," Ansgar said. "I want *her*. I want a good dolly and a bad dolly. Ritter's the good dolly. He's my favourite. Stupid! I have to say it over and over, stupid. A good dolly and a bad dolly, that's how I play."

Adoni shouted, "Let go of him!"

"You do what I say! I don't have to say it over and over. You have to do what I say. You're my new puppet, my new dolly, and you have to do what I say."

"Let go of him!"

Ansgar brought a cold, hard stare to Ritter's eyes. "You don't know the way things work," she said, in the same levelled, adult tone she'd used to threaten Steppe. "The In-Between is *my* world. I'm its keeper. I bring children here, and I give them everything they could ever want. Most of them love me for that. You know who doesn't love me for that? Ungrateful *brats*. They whine and complain and talk back and fight. They want to leave my world and never come back. I give them a gift, and they say *no*. You know what I do, when someone says no to me? It's so easy. *I break her spirit*."

Steppe's body was dragged across the floor, through Sylvester's blood. Ansgar's force hurled it onto a fire. It started to burn.

Theresa screamed.

"No one says no to me," Ansgar growled.

"*Monster!*" Paj shrieked. She drew in her breath and released her most terrifying peals of laughter. Her voice flew through the chamber, caught the seams of their skirts and cloaks and started them flapping like flags in a hurricane. The fires thrashed the air around them, the flames lifting themselves higher, glowing brighter than they ever had before. Ansgar lost Ritter's footing as Paj pushed her back against the wall. Ansgar wasn't disoriented for long. She leapt forward, baring Ritter's teeth, held out his hand, and snapped his fingers.

A clap of thunder. Paj's body turned to a fine white dust that whirled away in the wind.

Something inside Adoni snapped, a part of her she had been too terrified to unleash.

Her rage.

There would be pain. There would be blood. But at that very moment, nothing mattered to her more than vengeance.

She dove for the fire where she knew the seal had fallen and saw it there in the pit, sticking out of the flames. Ansgar, gloating over Theresa's misery, didn't notice her reach down and scoop it out with one mitted hand. Adoni kept it fisted in her palm and pulled her other mitten off with her teeth. She jerked her jacket zipper open, grabbed her shirt collar and yanked it down, exposing her unmarked shoulder.

Make me as powerful as Ansgar, she thought, again and again and again. *Make me as powerful as Ansgar, so I can put an end to all of this*.

She sucked in her breath, gritted her teeth, and pressed the white-hot end of the seal against her skin.

Huffing against the pain, she kept her eyes locked on Theresa and her thoughts fixed on the one thing she needed to be in order to save her from Paj's fate. *Give me Ansgar's power. Give it to me.*

She held the seal against her flesh as long as she could, gritting her teeth, her anger shaking every muscle and bone in her body. When she couldn't stand it any longer, she ripped it away and shoved it into her pocket. Suddenly her head was spinning, her lungs couldn't get enough air. She doubled over, gasping, her fingers tented and bracing her against the floor. Every sound in the room fell silent.

Adoni screamed, "*LET GO!*"

She felt a searing pain stab both of her shoulders as the words left her lips and shot across the room, burning her throat as they flew, as though they were lances made of fire and lightning. As the scream reached its apex, the monster was thrown free from Ritter's body.

He collapsed into a heap on the floor, his eyes staring straight ahead, without a trace of a soul behind them.

"You wanna play a game?" Adoni sneered. "All right. Let's play a game." She reached out her arm and drew her fingers into a tight fist. She felt Ansgar's child-like neck in her clutch, though the monster lay several hundred feet away. Adoni turned on her heel and whipped her arm through the air toward the opposite wall. Ansgar's body flew across the room, and she landed with a shriek against the stone floor. "Isn't that fun?" Adoni yelled. "Are you having fun? I'm just getting started." She drew back her leg and kicked at air, her toes connecting with Ansgar's torso from across the room.

Ansgar flipped onto her stomach and shot forward on all fours with terrifying speed. The monster leapt to her feet and snarled in Adoni's face.

An overwhelming force swept Adoni off the floor and flung her into the darkness above. She hurtled through the air, head over heels, twisting and spinning, until she let out a scream and forced the atmosphere to hold her up. She hung there for a moment, waiting to see what Ansgar's next move would be. No doubt the monster wanted Adoni to reach the ceiling before letting her drop to her death. Adoni refused to give her the satisfaction; she braced herself, then forced the air beneath her to give way. Her stomach flipped over and over as she plummeted feet first toward the floor. Just as the stone came into view, Adoni brought herself down on one knee and landed perfectly.

Ansgar's empty eye sockets narrowed. Adoni drew in a breath and screamed, picturing a blade sharp enough to cut a demigoddess' skin. The force of the shriek sliced Ansgar's cheek open; though no blood poured from the wound, the monster squealed and threw Adoni back toward the fire pit.

Adoni quickly regained her footing. She felt the fire at her heels, but as her power grew stronger she could tell it was no longer her enemy. She grinned. "What's wrong? Don't like this game? Fine! *New game!*" She reached back and grabbed a fistful of flames, without pain, without fear, and hurled a fireball at Ansgar. The monster dodged it easily, but that didn't stop Adoni from whipping another and another, each time with greater force. Adoni's smile grew wider as Ansgar darted left and right to avoid the onslaught. The flames lit up the room as they soared through the air; they burst into sparks when they hit the stone floor and the walls.

She was about to throw another when Ansgar suddenly froze and glared at her. "That's *my* fire," the monster growled. "It's *mine.*"

Her body shifted—limbs extending, face growing longer, gaining in size and mass, her body growing pearly scales, a thousand pointed teeth springing from her jaws. Adoni gasped as Ansgar changed into a menacing, eyeless dragon.

"Donny!" Theresa shouted. Adoni glanced at her quickly. She'd gathered Ritter's prone form into her arms. He wasn't moving.

Adoni had no time to panic. Ansgar raised a massive claw and struck out at her, flinging her aside and driving her up against the furthest wall in the room. Disoriented, Adoni scrambled to her feet and swung her arms, hoping to fling the dragon aside as easily as she had before. Ansgar remained where she stood and leered at her. Adoni caught a glimpse into the black holes that gaped where the creature's eyes should have been and let out a piercing scream, hoping the force of her voice would knock the dragon's head aside. The creature didn't budge. Adoni shrank back against the wall, slipped around the dragon, and started to run.

She threw several more shrieks at Ansgar, each time thinking, *If I just scream louder, if I just use more breath*, but the dragon would not be swayed from its pursuit. It crawled forward, its mouth open wide enough for Adoni to smell the flames that burned away in its belly—demonic flames she was certain would harm her, despite her newfound power. Adoni spotted the wooden chair lying on its side and dashed over to it. She grabbed a leg and stomped on it, breaking it off with a mighty snap. Holding it in her fist, she squeezed hard and thought of iron strong enough to penetrate dragon scales. The wood crackled as it turned into a pointed stake in her clutch. She hurled it at Ansgar's, hoping to strike right between those terrible eyes. The dragon turned its head just in time; the stake pierced its shoulder, and while it remained lodged there as the dragon stalked forward, it did nothing to slow Ansgar down. Adoni kicked off another leg to turn to iron, threw the stake as hard and as fast as she could. She landed every blow, but Ansgar was not deterred; the dragon picked up speed, drew in an enormous breath and, just as Adoni leapt out of its way, unleashed a bolt of white fire.

I have to change shape, she thought as she landed and darted across the room. *I can't make a dent in her like this. What's more powerful than a dragon? Shit!*

"We've got to get out of here," Theresa said. She struggled to prop Ritter's limp body against her shoulder. "Donny!"

Adoni cringed and continued to run. *She's gonna draw attention to herself.* Her mind raced through every fantastic creature she could think of, but none of them struck her as being capable of defeating the most fearsome beast of all. She bolted over to the chamber doors, forced them open with a single wave of her arm, and dashed into the corridor. She heard the dragon's legs thundering behind her in pursuit; it let out a roar that drowned out Theresa's screams. *Ice dragon*, she thought, *or water dragon.*

Something equally strong, something that can put out fire. She looked down at her hands, barely able to make them out in the dark, and concentrated on raising her own set of scales.

She hissed as her skin began to bubble; she smelled her own burning flesh and was very nearly sick. When she reached the foyer, where the four fires burned bright enough to show her what she'd done to herself, her stomach turned—her hands looked as though they were badly sunburnt; blisters began to form on her knuckles. She thrust her hands into the pool. Relief lasted only a moment; the dragon's colossal frame soon filled the corridor. Adoni jumped away from the pool and faced her enemy down. She felt Ansgar's fire rumbling in the dragon's belly and knew another bolt of flame was imminent. *Knock her off her feet*, she thought. *Buy some time.* She dropped to her knees, put her hands on the stone floor, and sent her force through the mountain, shaking it to its very foundations.

The dragon stumbled and slid forward, striking its chin on the floor. Unable to regain its footing, it scratched and clawed its way around the pool and ended up in a heap against the fortress doors. Adoni was about to speed back to the chamber when she caught sight of Theresa in the corridor; a dazed and dumbfounded Ritter limped next to her. "I was screaming," he muttered. "I was screaming. You couldn't hear me. I was screaming for your lives…"

"Are you all right?" Theresa asked.

"I'm fine. I'm fine…"

"You know what happened?"

"Yes."

"Get back!" Adoni bellowed, shooting a glance at the dragon as it slowly righted itself. She rushed toward them and took hold of Theresa's wrist. "Come on!" She slung Ritter's free arm over her shoulder and urged him back toward the inner chamber.

"We've got to get down the mountain," Theresa said.

"We can't, Ansgar's blocking the way."

"You're not strong enough to finish her off. We need to run."

"We *can't* run! And I *am* strong enough, just not in this form."

Theresa and Ritter collapsed just inside the chamber. Adoni threw the doors shut and ran her hand along the space between, thinking *close, close, close*; they sealed themselves together. "She's gonna break through that in a minute," she said, turning back to her friends. "I'm gonna try turning into a dragon again. I tried it before but my hands started to burn. I've gotta figure out how to do it without—"

The dragon threw its weight against the sealed chamber doors.

"You can't..." Ritter croaked.

Theresa bundled him against her shoulder. Adoni glared at him. "I started to!"

"If you try to change shape, you'll end up a half-formed monster."

"I know what a dragon looks like. I watch *Game of Thrones*!"

"You don't know how a dragon's formed, what its bones are like, what its blood is like, where its fire comes from..."

"So what, you want me to turn into a chicken?"

"Your mind... you won't be able to recover... you'll go insane, the way Ansgar's gone insane..."

"I won't go insane. It's only this one time."

Ansgar roared and released another bellyful of fire. The chamber doors began to glow red.

"They're gonna melt!" Theresa shouted.

"Donny, trust me," Ritter said.

They scrambled to the other side of the chamber and huddled together. "What am I supposed to do?" Adoni asked. "I can't beat her in a human body!"

"You have to outsmart her. *Think.*"

Outsmart her. Adoni watched as the doors began to liquefy. The dragon stuck its snout through and bucked its head, splashing molten metal over the floor. Adoni's heart pounded in her chest. *I still feel human. Am I supposed to be immortal? I can't do this; I can't beat something so strong. I've got to change into something that can defeat her, like a demon or something. The* room seemed to darken around her. "I don't know what to do!" she yelled as the dragon's body broke through.

"Neither do I," Ritter said, his eyes fixed on the monster, on their doom.

She remembered what Ansgar was—a spoiled, selfish child, driven to madness by her own power. *Ritter's her favourite toy*, she thought. *So... what if I break her favourite toy?*

Adoni grabbed Ritter's collar and dragged him up to his feet. "You don't want to fight fair?" she shouted at Ansgar as the dragon leapt into the room. "Fight fair, or he gets it."

Ritter twisted in her grasp. "What the hell are you doing?" he snarled.

The dragon stopped and sneered at her. "You're a stupid girl," it growled, its deep voice shaking the room. "Think I don't know who you are? He came to see me for you, yes, just for you, so you could stay. You're *friends*. He was my friend first!"

"Fight in your real form, or I swear—"

"You love my dolly just as much as I do. You wouldn't *dare*."

Adoni stared into the black holes of the dragon's eyes and sneered back. "Sorry man," she whispered into Ritter's ear.

She pulled his arm away from his body, and using only a fraction of the strength she was capable of, snapped the upper bone in two.

Ritter screamed. He would have sunk to his knees, but Adoni kept his collar twisted in her fist. "He's not faking it," she said, dragging him up as he gasped for breath. "Fair fight, or I break the other one too."

Ansgar chuckled. "You think I can't fix him? I can fix him. I *made* him!" The dragon raised an arm, a claw, and swiped out at her chosen messenger. Ritter's hand flew to his newly restored arm, his breathing growing heavier still. Adoni let go of him. He dropped to the floor and curled up into a ball, his arm cradled in front of him. "You break him, I fix him," Ansgar snarled. "But no one will fix *you*. I break you, and you stay *broken*."

Adoni glared at her. "If I kill him, you can't fix him. He'll be gone forever."

The dragon dropped its chin. "You can't kill my dolly."

"I'll cut his head off. That's how you kill a changeling in the In-Between, right? Cut its head off, and it can't heal itself. Spill its blood everywhere." She knelt behind Ritter and grabbed a handful of his hair. "You think I won't? He's the whole reason we're here, isn't he? If you didn't have him, you'd leave me alone. I'm not a *full set*."

"You kill him, I make him again," Ansgar growled.

"You won't be able to make another like him," Adoni said. "You don't know how anymore."

Ansgar's belly rumbled.

"That's right," Adoni said. "You don't know how to make another changeling like him. You've spent the last thousand years playing your stupid games and ruining other peoples' lives, you don't remember how. Even if you tried, it wouldn't come out like Ritter. Think you're gonna get the same doll to indulge you? You're too selfish and spoiled to be able to *think* of a doll like that. Ritter's your chosen messenger. He's one of a kind. You can never make another like him ever again, and you *know* it."

The dragon glared at her, its black eyes narrowing into a menacing pair of slits, its hind legs coiled and ready to pounce. "I remember," it snarled. "I remember, I do…"

Adoni felt the fire raging in its belly, felt its destructive power through the stone floor.

She sucked a breath in through her teeth and dropped to one knee, one hand in Ritter's hair, an arm slung across his neck; she seized his shoulder with her other hand and tightened her grip on his scalp. She started to pull.

Ritter screamed.

"STOP!" the dragon roared. Adoni froze. In a single blink, the dragon disappeared—replaced by Ansgar in her childish form. "He's *mine!*" she cried, reaching for him with both arms outstretched, her fingers splayed.

"Fight fair," Adoni said. Slowly, she loosened her grip on his hair and his shoulder, but didn't let go.

"I can fight forever," Ansgar said. "I'm strong, stronger than you. Even stupid you knows that! Well, I don't want you anymore. You're a crummy broken one, you showed me, you proved it!"

"One last fight. You win, you get to keep him, and I'll leave you alone. I win... I get the In-Between."

Ansgar laughed. "The In-Between is *mine*. You think you're so great!" Another peal of giggles. "All right." Her mature voice returned. "A fight to the end. A fight to the *death*. No tricks. You stole my power, but *I'm* still *god*."

Adoni let Ritter go and stood. He stayed crumpled at her feet as she took a single step forward.

Ansgar lowered her chin. "You've got a big fat mouth. I bet you like to scream. You want to die the way Sylvester died? All right. That's *fine*."

She opened her unnatural mouth and released a shriek that knocked Ritter and Theresa aside. They cowered together and covered their ears. If Ansgar so much as turned her head an inch, they would be in her direct line of fire.

Adoni stood her ground and launched her own piercing cry. Every nerve in her body quivered, every muscle and every vein shook—both with Ansgar's assault and her own magnificent force. She saw Ritter swing his body around Theresa's, shielding her from Ansgar's terror as best he could. The sound that flew from Ansgar's lips was like nothing Adoni had ever heard before, an alien drone that seemed to come from the deepest depths of space. Adoni kept up her own incredible sound and tried to march forward, but Ansgar's voice seized hold of her feet and wouldn't let her budge.

The monster doubled its efforts, sending the terrible din like bolts against Adoni's body. Adoni struggled to keep her voice from faltering; each blow threatened to throw her off balance and expose her to the full extent of Ansgar's wrath. She succeeded in matching the monster's assault by slamming the same invisible force against Ansgar's juvenile frame. Ansgar wouldn't be tossed aside. Adoni's legs began to give out on her; she dropped to one knee, screaming for everything she was worth, the mountain around them quaking as the battle reached its zenith. She stared at the monster's ugly, malevolent little face. She felt the urge to cough and drew her arm across her chin; her sleeve came away bloody.

Adoni caught sight of movement from the corner of her eye, a blur in the darkening room. She could no longer see her friends and prayed they were able to crawl away. *They should run now*, she thought, her gaze focused squarely on Ansgar. *They can run for the fortress doors. They can get away. Where are they? They can get away...*

Ritter rushed to her side from out of the darkness and grasped her shoulder. There, just below his collarbone: Ansgar's name, newly welted into his skin.

Her heart stopped.

"I love you," he said. "Shout her down." He drew in a breath and opened his mouth.

Adoni gasped as he sent his piper voice careening down her throat.

His essence strengthened her every muscle, her every limb. She slung her arm around him and hauled him up, holding him against her as he shouted his last. A moment later his body went limp, and as Adoni pulled away from him, he fell to the floor.

Ansgar stopped as Ritter's body hit the stone. The mountain went eerily quiet.

The monster crept toward her chosen messenger.

Then Theresa gasped and let out a sob, and Adoni, shaking, burning, wove Ritter's voice with her own. She stepped over his body, drew on every ounce of strength she had left, and sent both their voices—all their voices—straight into her enemy's heart.

She heard earthquakes and typhoons and raging fires; she heard drums and engines and famine and war. She felt Ansgar's power pulsing in every part of her. She heard Belinda screaming for revenge.

Ansgar leapt forward, her body twisting back into the dragon's form. She turned to dust before she hit the ground.

All went silent.

Adoni turned and found Theresa cradling Ritter in her arms. Slipping on what was left of Ansgar, she dove to the floor. "Come on, man, come on!" Ritter's eyes remained shut. She begged in her own voice, in Ritter's voice, in their voices together.

"Is he all right?" Theresa sobbed.

She put her ear to his chest. "He's still breathing. Ritter! What the hell did you do to yourself? Wake up!" She shook his shoulders. He coughed, gasped, brought his terrified gaze to her face. Her chest heaved, and she half laughed, half cried, "Don't freak me out like that you lousy *fucker*!"

"I love you too, darling," he murmured. He reached for her, drew her close to his chest, held on to her, to dear life itself.

"You better be all right!"

"I can't hear her in my head," he whispered. "I can't feel her in my heart anymore."

Adoni held him tightly. "You turned on her," she said. "You turned on your maker. You said you couldn't ever do that."

"She wasn't the same being who created me," he said, pulling away and turning to Theresa. "Not anymore. I should have turned a long time ago. But I was weak, and a…" He put his hand over his heart.

Theresa embraced him. His chest heaved once, and he started to weep. "Steppe couldn't hear me," he sobbed. "I screamed every word, but he never heard them, not one, not one."

Adoni tried to think of something to say. *Of course he heard you,* or, *he didn't have to hear them, he knew what you wanted him to know.* But every response was a bigger lie, and every lie would eat away at him until there was nothing left but regret. "I'm sorry," she said.

"Tell me," he said. "No judgement, I just want to know. You broke my arm." He stretched it out and drew it back again. "Were you really going to kill me?"

Adoni's chest heaved. She collapsed into tears and wailed, "*I don't know.*"

They crouched together, with heavy hearts and heavy thoughts, until Theresa murmured, "I want to go home."

"We can't go home," Adoni said. "I killed her. You heard what she said.

Without her the agate doesn't open. The kids stay prisoners. All the pipers must be…"

"But you're Ansgar now," Theresa said. "Aren't you?"

Adoni squinted and held up her finger. She traced it through the air above their heads. Almost instantly, the agate bled into view. She bit her quivering bottom lip and shut her eyes tight.

Ritter put his head on her shoulder. "Thank you."

She looked down at him. "Want your voice back?"

"In a minute," he said.

"You used the seal."

He nodded. "To give you my voice without losing my head. Still a coward, I guess."

"You're not a coward."

He smiled. "Who am I to argue with a demigoddess?" He opened his mouth.

Adoni leaned over him. As his voice left her, she suddenly realized how heavy a thing it was to carry, in her chest, in her heart; the weight of a thousand years of life, entwined with her own young soul.

Ritter closed his eyes and murmured, "Well… how about that?"

"Huh?"

He sang a few notes, in a voice as unremarkable as a pebble on the ground. "It's not there."

"What do you mean, it's not there?" Adoni asked. "I gave it back to you."

"It didn't work."

"I just gave it back. I don't have it." She caught Theresa's eye. "Did you take it?"

"No," Theresa said. "No way."

He raised his eyes and peered into the darkness above. "It's gone."

"It's *gone*?" She shook her head. "It can't be gone. Where's the seal? Maybe you just have to brand yourself again to get it back."

"No," he said softly. "No. I don't want it back."

"Don't talk bullshit!"

"I'm serious. It's for the best. I never wanted to be a piper in the first place."

"What about all those years you spent collecting sounds and instruments? What about those other voices? What about *Belinda's* voice?"

"Maybe I'll hear it on the wind sometime."

"Ritter." She levelled her gaze with his. "If you don't have your voice, you won't be able to open the agate when we get back to the other side. What wind's gonna carry her voice back to you if you leave?"

"So much the better. I was never worthy enough to keep it anyway. It tore my dearest friend and me apart. The next time I leave this place, I don't ever want to return."

Adoni searched his face. "But you've been a piper your whole life. You were the first one. You might even be the last one, who knows? I mean... are you sure?"

"I feel... so much lighter..." He smiled. "Yes. I'm sure."

Adoni and Theresa exchanged a single look that seemed to say everything at once.

They sat another moment in silence before finally getting to their feet; then they walked through the corridor to the foyer, passed over Ansgar's threshold, and breathed in the crisp night air.

Clusters of snowflakes drifted to the ground, covering every step with a blanket of winter magic, including the stones Adoni had sung up into the bridge. On the other side of the chasm, the changelings stood with their torches in their hands, watching and waiting for Sylvester's return. With Ritter and Theresa following behind, she crossed the bridge and stopped in front of them.

"He's not coming back," she said.

Theresa lifted the blackened, bloody hem of her jacket for all their eyes to see. They stared at her. Adoni thought they might attack as they had in the past. She remembered Ansgar's chilling words—*I break her spirit*—and wondered if Sylvester's death meant they no longer cared to fight.

Ritter stepped up next to Adoni. "I'm sorry for my part in what happened to you all," he said. "I'm your brother, and I betrayed you to save myself. I did you such tremendous evil. I did it willingly, and I can never undo it."

The changelings didn't stir.

"Ansgar's seal keeps you silent," Adoni said. "But she's dead now. You should be able to speak again."

The changelings looked at each other. One of them—a young woman, who appeared to be Adoni's age—put a finger to her palm and made a motion of writing. Adoni squinted and shook her head. Ritter held out his arm. She took his hand in hers, put her finger to his skin and began to trace a pattern. When she was done, she folded his fingers over his palm, turned, and started down the mountain. The others followed her one by one, until Adoni, Theresa, and Ritter stood there, alone, in the cold.

"What was that?" she asked him. "What did she do?"

"She wrote me a message," he replied.

"What did she write?"

"There's nothing left to say."

❖

They returned to The Welcome, and found themselves standing at the wishing well, gazing up at the darkened chalet. "This place will fall to ruin in time," Ritter said. "Paj took good care of it while she was mistress here."

"Where do you think their voices went?" Adoni asked.

"Just what I said before. I like to think they float along on summer breezes and give us goosebumps when they pass. I told Steppe that very thing one night. He laughed at me. He had such a marvellous laugh."

"What happens now?"

He looked up at the chalet. "I thought about waiting right here until The Welcome falls to the ground, but I don't have the patience."

"So we're going home?"

He held his hand out to her. "Lead the way."

"But…"

"But what?"

"I can make this whole thing a better place. I can make it, like…"

He squinted. "A *utopia*?"

"Don't look at me like that," she said. "I'm not like Ansgar. I study sociology! I can make the In-Between into what it was meant to be. It can be… It can be a safe place for pipers and for kids. I can set it up like… I don't know, like someplace in Sweden…"

Ritter laughed. "When have you been to Sweden?"

"I've got the power to change it! What are pipers supposed to do if they're not singing kids away? Maybe if they sang them here, and like… I can set up a school, and the pipers can take care of them…" Theresa and Ritter frowned. "So what, just leave them where they are? I've wanted to get back here for years, so I can save them."

"Maybe they have to save themselves," Theresa said.

"How can you even say that? They're just kids."

"You don't think they're able to?"

"I don't know. But there's this whole place around them, and I can't just waste it."

"Adoni, look at me," Ritter said. Her jaw went tight as she met his gaze. "If you do this, if you stay behind and try to rule… you'll never see me again."

She choked on a sob. "What?"

"I know what Ansgar's power did to her, and I know what it will do to you."

"I'm *not* like Ansgar!"

"You'll go mad trying to make a perfect world for yourself and for the souls who still live here. If you want to stay and try your luck, fine. But I won't stick around to watch you destroy yourself."

"Why are you so afraid of me?" she asked, her voice trembling, her throat aching.

"I'm afraid of Ansgar's power in any form. It's a vindictive, malignant power, and it kills."

"Reese isn't afraid of me, are you?"

Theresa shook her head. "It's not about being afraid, Donny. This place isn't for us anymore."

"So what happens if I stay and fix it? Will I ever see you again?"

"Come on—"

"No, you answer me!"

She shrugged. "This place changes you. I don't think you'll be the same sweet person I know and love if you stay," she said. "So no, you won't see me again either."

Adoni turned away from them and kicked at the icy ground. "This is so unfair. I can't just leave when everything's still such a mess! If I don't do something, no one will!"

"Donny," Ritter said. "There's nothing about Ansgar's power that can make this world a better place. Please. Come home."

Her head and heart aching, she took one last look around her, at the shabby wood, the broken well, the half-destroyed pillars standing up against the night sky. In her heart, the fires danced, and the air smelled of cedar and spices. Who would tell the pipers that they no longer had to abide by Ansgar's code?

"How do you say 'come here?'" she asked.

"What are you planning now?"

"Just tell me."

"*Me vyotek.*"

She mouthed the words until she felt comfortable chanting them louder, and soon the air filled with the sound of her voice. She spotted her branchlings crawling between the trees, creeping over the ice and snow.

They stopped at her feet. She summoned the demigoddess within her, and spoke to them in a crisp, clear voice. "Tell every piper in the In-Between that Ansgar's code is broken. Tell them Ansgar's dead, and that they're free."

Ritter frowned. "And just how do you think they'll be able to—"

"*Tell every piper in the In-Between that Ansgar's code is broken.*" Adoni's words echoed throughout the clearing as the twigs and branches vibrated with her message. "*Tell them Ansgar's dead, and that they're free.*"

"And thank you," she said to them. "Thanks for listening to me."

They turned around and started on their way.

She stepped up close to Ritter and leaned against his chest. "Promise you'll stay with me," she said.

Ritter put his arms around her and kissed the top of her head. "You have my solemn word."

"Fine. Let's go."

"Are you all right?"

"I'm tired. And I wish..." She shook her head. "You know what I wish."

She held up her hand, traced a line from the top of her head to the snow-covered ground. The agate opened up before her, rippling blue and orange and gold. She took Theresa's arm in one hand and Ritter's in the other, then moved though the light, through space and time, until she brought them safely to the other side.

Chapter 27

Despite the hour, Adoni's neighbourhood still hummed with life. A siren wailed in the near distance, a bus rattled by. Two drunken men stood across the street. One had his back turned while he urinated on the roots of an unkempt bush. The other faced them head on. Adoni locked eyes with him and froze. "Jesus Christ!" he shouted. He slapped his friend's shoulder. "Did you see that?"

"Asshole!"

"Those guys just… *popped*, man. They just *popped*."

"I'm taking a leak."

"Look." He slapped his friend again.

"Ow, stop it, man."

"Look at 'em!"

Adoni rushed into the alleyway beneath her window, followed by Theresa and Ritter. They tucked themselves as far back as they could and waited for the less belligerent of the two to insist they move on. Theresa stood behind Adoni and put her hands on her shoulders. "We didn't come out here the last time," she said. "I remember. We came out on a street nearby."

"She must have nailed the landing this time," Ritter said.

"Paj told me to keep my eyes open," Adoni said. "She said it keeps you from getting sick."

"Keeps you focused, too. Well done, Donny girl."

He took a few shaky steps toward the mouth of the alley, stopped, and put the back of his hand against his forehead. Adoni came up behind him and put her hand on his back. "What's wrong?"

He chuckled. "So that's what it feels like to age."

"Age?" Theresa moved to his side.

"What do you mean, 'age?'" Adoni asked. "You're aging? Are you okay?"

"I'm fine," he said. "Just fine. I just... didn't expect to, that's all."

"You're not immortal anymore?" She looked into his pale face. He shook his head. "But why not? What happened? Did Ansgar take it away from you?"

"No..."

"Then what..." Her eyes went wide. "Your voice. You must have lost your immortality when you lost your voice."

He nodded. "That must be it."

"But that means you'll age every minute you're on this side, and..." Her stomach flipped. "And you can't ever get back."

He sighed. "So it would seem."

"Goddamn it!" She swung out her arm and knocked a heap of crusty snow off of a trashcan. "I shouldn't have let you leave it behind. I should have made you take it back!"

"I didn't want it back."

"Maybe... If you ever meet a piper again, maybe they can open the agate for you and you can, like—"

"Take a few weeks off the aging process from time to time?" He smirked. "It's the In-Between, not a spa."

"You knew this would happen, didn't you?"

"I didn't. But I meant what I said. I don't want to go back."

"Maybe I can open it," Adoni said. She took a step toward the back of the alley.

Ritter put out his hand and touched her arm, stopping her. "Don't you dare."

"But that means you'll die one day." She shrugged. "You've been alive for almost a thousand years. I mean..."

Doesn't that scare you?

"Donny. If living a mortal life is the side effect of my freedom, then I'll live it."

Theresa pressed against his side and put her head on his shoulder. He opened his arm and gathered her close to him. "Don't cry," he said as she choked back tears. "I'm not dead yet."

"But you gave it all up," she whimpered.

"Darling, I'll take life over regret any day of the week." He kissed her temple. "And twice on Sunday."

Adoni felt her pocket vibrate. "My phone," she said, drawing it out and holding it up. "I'm surprised the battery lasted this long." She unlocked it.

A text message from her mother: *I'm sorry. Pls come home.*

The screen went black.

"I better go," she said. "My mom's worried."

"Go on up then," Ritter said, opening his arms, pulling her into his embrace. She leaned her head against his chest and listened to his heart beat. No sound could have comforted her more.

"Hey," she said.

"Yes, darling?"

"Are you sure you're okay? I mean, you… for a minute anyway…"

He paused. "I was afraid of the darkness. I was so afraid of the darkness, of the void. I've lived so long; there isn't much that scares me. *Nothing*, Donny… nothing *scares* me. It always has. But nothing is nothing compared to watching my loved ones die."

"One thing before you go."

"I'm all ears."

"Reese told me you're not supposed to hear a piper's song unless it's meant for you."

"That's right."

"But that night when I followed you, you weren't singing for me. You were singing for Tyler. How come I heard it too?"

"Was I singing for him?" She pulled away and looked up at him. He smiled. "I don't think I was. I think I just wanted someone to hear me. I'm so glad that someone was you."

She hugged him again.

He kissed the top of her head. "All right now. It's late. If my lady Reese would be so kind as to allow me to escort her to her home, I'd be much obliged."

"Wow, can you ever spread it on thick," Theresa said with a sad chuckle. He eased her out from under his arm and held it out to her, a picture of perfect gallantry. "Oh, *fine*." She took hold of him. "Make sure you spread your coat on the ground if we pass a puddle."

"I've never done such a thing and I never will. This is a designer coat, I'll have you know."

"Whatever." She leaned down and kissed Adoni's forehead. "Be good, okay? Come by my truck tomorrow."

"You're still going to work?"

Theresa nodded. "I've got to make the rent. I'm still behind."

"Don't you want to... like, take a day? Just to..." She shrugged.

"I can't."

Ritter lay his lips against Theresa's temple. "Reese. Darling. Please. Take a day."

She squeezed her eyes shut and brought a hand to her mouth. "I can't... or I'll..."

"... think about him." He lay a hand on her cheek. "That's the idea."

"I know. I know." She leaned against him. "I don't know if I'll be able to sleep tonight."

"Shall I sit with you?"

"Yeah. Yeah. I'd really... Thank you."

"It's my pleasure." He smiled at Adoni. "Will you be all right?"

"I'll be fine. Sounds like mom wants to talk. If she's awake, anyway."

"Call me if you need anything," Theresa said.

"I will." She met Ritter's gaze. "Call me when you get back. You know what that means? It means get a phone."

He rolled his eyes. "You won't rest until you've dragged me kicking and screaming into this century, will you? All right, I'll get a phone. And I'll call you every night to find out what you're wearing the next day, so we can match outfits."

"Jackass."

He winked at her. "All right, Reese, shall we go?"

Reese nodded. "I'll make you some tea."

"I'd like that."

They left the alley and said their goodbyes in front of Adoni's building. Arm in arm, Ritter and Theresa made their way to the sidewalk and headed up the street. Adoni watched their silhouettes fade to nothing, then turned and walked up the steps to the building's front door.

It was when she slipped her backpack off her shoulders to retrieve her keys that she noticed her pants were still covered in Sylvester's blood. The realization stayed her hand; she stood in the foyer, listening to the buzzing of an overhead light on its last legs, unable to move until she made peace with what had happened to him, to Steppe, and to Paj. The longer she stood there, the more she recognized how long it would take to comprehend what had befallen them all. *Go inside*, she thought. *You know mom's awake.*

She passed through the foyer and soon found herself standing in front of her apartment door. She put her ear to the wood.

No music. No voices.

She opened the door.

Ida was sitting on the couch with a mug of tea in her hand. She turned her head and caught sight of Adoni. Her puffy eyes filled with tears. She turned away again, and pointed at her lap.

Adoni put her backpack down on the floor, slipped off her wet boots and jacket. She heard Ida sniffle, and swallowed hard. Ida pulled a tissue out of a box on the coffee table and gently blew her nose.

Adoni walked around the couch and sat down on the coffee table. Tyler's head lay in Ida's lap. The boy was fast asleep. "His mom's not home yet?" Ida shook her head. "Are you gonna call social services on her?"

"Yeah," Ida replied.

"You don't want to though."

"Nope. But she can't just take off anymore. Maybe they'll help her out."

"You don't sound sure about that."

Ida shrugged. "Who knows what'll happen? Sometimes it works and sometimes it doesn't. Let's just hope it works this time." She wiped her nose. "What happened to your pants?"

Adoni hesitated, then said, "I went to play paintball."

Ida chuckled. "Sounds like I don't want to know where you really were."

"You said you wouldn't hit me again."

"You were giving me attitude."

"Yeah, because you don't trust me."

Ida shook her head. "What was I supposed to think, eh? The last time you left with him you were gone for days. It doesn't look right. You know if you're in trouble you can talk to me, but you don't. So what am I supposed to think?"

"You're supposed to trust me."

"You *earn* trust. And sorry, baby, I love you, but I don't trust you for shit."

"Why not?"

"Because you keep things from me, why else?"

"You keep things from me all the time."

"I'm your mom, I don't have to tell you squat."

Adoni kissed her teeth. "That's bullshit."

"No, that's parenting."

"Right. So if I ask you a question you're not gonna answer it?"

"Depends on what it is."

"You know your friend Kofi?"

Ida looked away. "Get him out of your head."

"Why?"

"Because he's not coming back."

"Why not?"

"Because I messed up. Like I always do. I messed it all up, so it's over." She leaned her elbow against the armrest, pressed her knuckles to her lips.

"Mom?"

"Yeah, baby."

"Is Kofi my dad?"

Ida closed her eyes and nodded.

"What happened?" Adoni asked.

Her mother shrugged. "Sometimes you meet someone when you're one way, and then one day you wake up, and they tell you they don't like you the way you are."

"So he's an asshole."

"No, he's not an asshole. He was right. Man, you don't know what I was like when I was younger and still drinking. I was a piece of work. I really was a piece of work. But I got sober, and we had you. First thing I did when I stopped nursing was go out and buy a six-pack to celebrate. First thing he did was pack his bags and leave." She blew her nose again. "They tell you in group that you have to make amends to the people you hurt when you were drinking, so I looked him up on Facebook and asked him if he wanted to meet up. I didn't think he'd get back to me, but he did. So he came over, that day you saw him, and we had a nice talk. Talked about all the stuff we used to do when we were together, all the good times we had, you know. Told him how sorry I was. He said he forgives me. Then I was stupid, and you know what I did? I asked him if he was into going out sometime, like we used to do." She shook her head. "He's not interested. He's moved on. That's the way things are. I don't even blame him for it. It just is what it is."

"So he's not coming back? He can't even be your friend?"

"I can't be his," she said. "I know it too. I'm too embarrassed."

"Why should you be embarrassed?"

"It's too hard to explain. It's just… to look at him and know things won't ever be the same… that's too hard for me. You know what I mean?"

CHARLENE CHALLENGER

Adoni nodded. "Yeah. I've got someone like that too."

"Oh yeah? What's his name?"

"Natalie."

"Like, a friend of yours?"

"My girlfriend. Well... she was never really my girlfriend... not for real..." Ida didn't speak. "She was just some girl I... I was, like, fourteen."

"I was fourteen too," Ida said. "My first boyfriend was a kid called Andy. He was so ginger. I've never seen anyone more ginger than him."

"She used to have purple hair," Adoni said.

"So she was... a plum. Nice. Nice." She patted the empty space beside her. Adoni sat down on the couch and curled up under Ida's arm. "I love you, baby," Ida said. "Always remember. No matter what, I'll always love you."

"Love you too, mom."

They were quiet for a time.

"Mom?"

"Yeah, baby?"

"I'll tell you all about it someday, okay? About where I went that time I ran away. I promise."

"Oh, you better tell me."

"It's just weird. The whole thing was just... I don't even know..."

"Maybe wait until your vocabulary gets bigger before trying, eh? That school better hook you up. I want to hear you give a speech when you're valedictorian."

Adoni snorted. "Yeah, right."

"Or at least when you open that city you're gonna build."

"Maybe then," Adoni said.

Ida kissed Adoni's cheek. "Maybe then."

Epilogue

Adoni was sitting near the window in The Spill, watching raindrops bounce up from the pavement. First year was over, and she had managed to pass with fairly decent marks. She could have chosen anywhere in the city to sit with a cup of hot chocolate and stare at the rain, but she kept returning to The Spill in the hopes that she would see Natalie again.

"I haven't seen her," she confessed to Reese the day before. "Whenever I go in, her co-workers say it's not her shift."

"Have you asked for her schedule?"

"They said they can't give it to me. I keep going on random days. I wonder if she hides in the back until I'm gone."

Theresa handed her a bowl of stroganoff and leaned her back against the serving window ledge. "She might turn up, you never know."

"I want to tell her what happened," Adoni said. "About her memory, I mean. I don't know if I can tell her the rest."

"I wonder how the pipers reacted when the branches told them Ansgar was dead."

"I bet they were thrilled. Freaked out, but thrilled."

"I don't know. The way I understand it, some pipers were quite content to be where they were."

"Yeah, because they could get anything they wanted from their cupboards and their hope chests. Ansgar's seal is useless to them now. I bet it's only a matter of time before everyone crosses back to this side for good."

"What a waste," Theresa said. "What a waste of time. What a waste of life."

Adoni sighed. Neither one of them had mentioned what had happened on their last night in the In-Between. There had been looks and heavy silences; Theresa had stopped what she was doing and burst into tears in front of Adoni on more than one occasion. The right words to talk about what they had seen and heard hadn't yet come to their minds. They talked around the subject instead, straying close to the wound but never opening it up again.

"I got a postcard from Ritter," Theresa said at last.

"Oh yeah? Where is he now?"

"He's in... wait..." She rifled through her apron pocket and pulled it out. "Valletta, Malta."

"Where's that?"

"In the Mediterranean somewhere."

Adoni chuckled. "Next thing that guy needs is an email address."

"I know, right? I keep telling him, but he keeps complaining about it. He says they're too impersonal."

"He's such an old man. I bet he thinks if we take his picture the camera will steal his soul. What did he say?"

"Let me read it to you." She cleared her throat. "Here we go: *Dearest Reese.*" She snorted. "*I'm here on the lovely island of Malta. The weather's nice, though I'm told it's rainier now than in the summertime. I've had my fill of the local cuisine and visited some of the most beautiful churches I've ever laid my eyes on. I don't know why it's taken me this long to visit, but given what I know of my own whims, it must be because I took the world's beauty for granted, again. Do you think I'll ever grow out of that?*

"*I'll be home in a few weeks and can't wait to see you. All my love, Ritter.*

"*PS: Tell Adoni I love her too. It'll soften the blow when I ask her to show me how to check my voicemail again.*"

"I showed him *three times*," Adoni said. "He's got the attention span of a fly. How do you live for a thousand years and not know how to check your voicemail?"

"It's sweet though, isn't it?"

"Sweet my ass. What happens if you leave him a really important message and I'm not around to show him how to get it?"

"He loves you," Theresa replied, batting her eyelashes.

"Yeah, I know. I know."

Adoni watched the sky turn an angry shade of dark. The rain fell harder, hitting the street and splashing up again, not as individual drops but a fine spray. Pedestrians ran by with newspapers or shopping bags over their heads, their mouths open, laughing breathlessly as the weather soaked their clothes. Then, as quickly as it had descended, the darkness gave way to a delicate shade of pale, and the driving rain became a steady patter, and the promise of spring.

She smiled. It had been a long time since she let herself get caught in the rain. She finished her drink, gathered her things, and headed out into the shining afternoon.

THE END

CHARLENE CHALLENGER

Acknowledgements

Thank you...

... to Jim Nason, Heather J. Wood, and all the folks at Tightrope Books, for jumping through the agate with me one more time.

... to Jessie Hale, editor extraordinaire, whose sense of story and style has made me a much better writer than Googling "show don't tell" ever could.

... to Nathaniel Whitfield, for a beta read to end all beta reads, and to Jayne Whitfield, whose enthusiasm for the first book kept me motivated while writing the second.

... to my writing group Dudes, who are always awesome: David Blackwood, Patrick Fleming, and Simon McNeil.

... to my family, the Baldacchinos and the Challengers, who are very dear, and very patient.

... for encouragement and support while I was writing this book—Beverly Bambury, Khadija Coxon, Alyx Dellamonica, Istvan Dugalin, Alys Latimer, Michael Matheson, Karim Morgan, Tara (Wifey) Reed, Kelly Robson, Andrew Wilmot, and Rikki (Trixie) Zucker.

... for being the greatest, the super wonderful-est, my sunshine, my rainbow connection: Russell Challenger.

About the Author

PHOTO: Christine Baldacchino

Charlene Challenger is a graduate of the Ryerson Theatre School. Her first book, *The Voices in Between*, was shortlisted for an Aurora Award and longlisted for a Sunburst Award. She lives in Toronto with her husband and their adorable dog, Omi.